JOHN GOODE

STEP 1
Meet boy.

Be sure he is your soulmate.

STEP 2
Fall in love with boy.

Open up to him.

STEP 3
Move in with boy.

This requires money.

STEP 4
Marry boy.

This requires *more* money.

STEP 5
Enjoy perfect life.

WHEN I GROW UP

A TALES FROM FOSTER HIGH STORY

WHEN I GROW UP

By John Goode

After graduation, Kyle Stilleno and Brad Graymark move to California to pursue their dreams. But high school sweethearts are called that for a reason, and their love rarely stands up to the test of time. As money, school, sex, and jealousy test their relationship to the breaking point, Kyle and Brad fight to hold on to the love that brought them together

But when a frantic phone call sends them back to Texas, they discover love and understanding might not be enough this time.

This is dedicated to all of my Lost Boys—you know who you are. Those of us who choose never to grow up. Older, maybe, but never up.

Kyle

YOU KNOW what, grown-ups? Fuck you. No, don't give me that look. I'm talking to you. Yes, *you*, the grown-up with the kids and the job and the bills, the person who pretends you know what is going on. Fuck you.

We spend our entire lives thinking that when we get older, we're going to know what's going on and how to handle it. You give us this illusion that you know what you're doing, so of course in time we'll figure it out too. It's a generational lie, and I don't care if your parents did it to you 'cause I'm talking to you right now. And I know my mom wasn't mother of the year, but you know, she used the same damn line on me every time.

How dare you? How dare you lie to us like that and give us hope that someday the world will make sense! What possible reason do you have for perpetuating a lie as big as this one? I thought the whole Santa thing was mean. The Easter Bunny, not so much—it's a giant rabbit, please. But the thought of a magical fat guy sneaking into our house and leaving us stuff is more believable than what you tell us. Why not just say it out loud?

You have no idea what you're doing either.

Life sucks, and no matter how old a person is, it never makes sense. There's no instruction manual. Living on your own and paying your own bills isn't going to give you secret knowledge. If you had just admitted you were adult fuck-ups when people like me were kids, then we might be ready for all the crap when we graduated. We'd know there is no magical bullet for our ignorance, just more questions and a lot of improvising.

Do you get a power trip from making us believe you have answers when you don't? Is acting all-knowing a survival technique? If you'd told us you were clueless, did you believe we might panic and run around like we were on fire?

1

I think we could have figured it out together. If you'd told us, "There are no answers and we're all just making it up," I really think we kids would have said, "Let's make it up together."

But no, you go on about how things will make sense when you're older and one day you'll understand. Well, here I am, waiting. And it makes no fucking sense. Instead I'm sitting in an airport typing so hard on my laptop I'm pretty sure they're going to call security on me. There are no answers at the bottom of that cereal box, just another useless piece of plastic designed to distract us from the abysmal pain that is life.

So tell me, grown-ups, tell me what I should do.

Leave him? Stay? Let her die in a hospital thousands of miles away? Tell me, give me a fucking answer.

Tell me which decision I make is going to be the right one.

Nothing? Not a single word? What a shock! Imagine my surprise! You don't know what to do any more than I do. I need to talk about this. I need to settle my thoughts and figure out the next best move. My flight doesn't leave for two hours. So I'm going to figure this out on my own, since you don't have a freakin' clue.

I wanna say me sitting here alone started when he joined that idiotic softball league, but I know better; it started well before then.

When we moved into our new place, that first day, I should have said something, but I didn't.

And now here I am.

She is really going to die.

No, not there yet.

Eight months ago, Brad and I moved into our new place. And things started falling apart.

PART ONE:
SEX, CHINESE FOOD, AND DOCTOR WHO

Name three things you want more of the second you're finished with them.

Kyle

WE PULLED up in front of the Chinese restaurant, and I was instantly whelmed.

Not overwhelmed, not underwhelmed, just... whelmed. I mean, I knew the apartment we had rented was over a restaurant, but in person the building looked so... small? A short, narrow flight of stairs off to the side of the building led to our place... well, to what would be our place once we parked and snagged the keys. My stomach rolled in nervous anticipation. I was about to get the keys to my first apartment.

"This is so badass," Brad exclaimed from the driver's side.

I looked over and saw the wonder on his face as he leaned forward and tried to see the upper floor of the building through the Mustang's windshield. And just like that, my nervousness was gone. He glanced at me and gave me a grin that reminded me of the first day we met in the hallway. That careless *nothing can touch you while you're with me* smile was so much bullshit, but he had a way of making you want to believe it. "This is it," he said, sounding just like a little kid staring at a mountain of Christmas presents all labeled to him.

I smiled back and grabbed his hand. "This is it."

He started to slide over to kiss me when the guy behind us leaned on his horn and reminded us we were still in the street.

"Park now, kiss later," Brad said and pulled into the alleyway off to the side of the restaurant.

An older Chinese lady—oh crap, that's racist. Oriental? Um, Asian? Wow, this makes me sound bad. Look, I don't know the difference between Chinese, Japanese, or even Korean people, so I'm not even going to try here. Someone who looked a lot like Mulan's mom came out from the kitchen door. Is that racist too? Shit, this is what I get for being raised in the middle of Foster, Texas. Every word I have for another race is just racist, from a movie, or worse, both. Screw it: an older woman of Asian descent stepped out of the kitchen door, waving her hands at us, shouting that we couldn't park where we were.

4

I got out of the car, and her shouting stopped instantly. "Kyle?" I nodded, and a smile broke out across her face. I could tell smiling was her face's default expression. "Richard! Come out, Kyle is here."

"You must be Mrs. Phan?" I asked, though we had Skyped a month before when I found out she was renting out the apartment.

She walked over and hugged me. "Lisa, you must call me Lisa," she said, half hugging me and half feeling me up, but not in a weird way. Well, it was weird, but not sexual. "You're too skinny!" she decided, taking a step back. "We're going to change that quick."

Brad got out, and she glanced at him, then back to me. In a low voice, she said, "You got a looker in that one."

I felt myself blush.

Her husband came out, a stained white apron on, and gave us both a smile that looked like it came from his wife. "Kyle!" he said excitedly. "Braf!"

Mrs. Phan leaned toward me. "Ignore him; he still has a horrible accent. You'd swear we just walked off the boat."

"My Engresh is fine!" he snapped at her.

"English," she said, spinning and facing him. "En-glish! And the boy's name is Brad, not Braf." She rolled her eyes and looked back at us, her smile brightening her face again. "Welcome!"

Brad opened his mouth to say something, but Mrs. Phan decided to give him a pat-down hug like she had me. "See? This one not all skin and bones," she admonished me. "I bet he knows how to eat."

Brad whispered at me, "Did she just—"

"Oh yeah," I answered, cutting him off.

"So how was your trip?" she asked, smiling and, just possibly, looking for interesting details about our drive.

"Shut up, old woman," Mr. Phan snapped, swatting at her. "They want to see place and rest up, not stand in alley and talk to gossip."

She exploded into a stream of…. Chinese? Vietnamese? Sigh. I am so going to hell. She started yelling at him in a language of unknown origin. He fired back just as fast in the same language. I wondered if the stream of sounds was what American talk radio sounded like to foreigners.

Brad chuckled, and I took a deep breath, realizing just a little more that we were living our lives. We weren't kids anymore.

"The trip was great, and we'd love to see the place," I half shouted into their discussion.

Mrs. Phan stopped in what I assumed was midword, and her smile was back. "Let me get the keys."

She shooed Mr. Phan into the kitchen ahead of her, and the door slammed behind them.

Which was when we burst into laughter.

"Dude, those are our landlords?" Brad asked me after we caught our breath.

"Looks like it." I paused and a weird feeling passed through me. It wasn't déjà vu, but it was close. I wasn't remembering something that had happened; I was realizing I was going to remember this particular moment forever. The whole scene locked into my mind: the smell of the food from the kitchen, the sounds of traffic from the street, the way the light hit Brad's face just right and he was all I could see and hear and touch.

Perfect: the moment was perfect. Leaning into him, I kissed him as hard as I could, pushing him up against the car door to keep him where I wanted him. He wrapped his arms around me and kissed me back, hungry at first and then more gently. And though I was caught up in the emotion of the kiss, part of my mind whispered something that made my heart glow.

This was the first moment of our lives together.

"You see?" I heard Mrs. Phan say behind us. "That is true love. Not a new vacuum and a card. Romance!" I could hear her smack her husband's arm as I pulled away from Brad.

"You boys ready to see place?" Mr. Phan asked, not sounding all that pleased.

"Lead on," Brad answered, grabbing my hand as we climbed the steps. Mrs. Phan opened the door, and I took a step to walk in and almost made it through the doorway. Brad stopped me when he scooped me off my feet so I ended up in his arms like a little kid or a—you know what? I don't want to finish that thought. I glared at him, but his grin didn't waver. "I'm walking you over the door... er... thingy."

I wanted to be upset, but I couldn't. I just smiled and felt my heart swell in my chest. "That's for marriage, dummy."

"Then I'll pick you up again, won't I?" He maneuvered us through the doorway, and we both took our first look at our new place.

Our apartment was actually one huge room with a couple of half walls to give the illusion of different spaces. A fridge and small stove next to a sink was the kitchen area. A small partition off to the right looked like it could be a bedroom. The rest of the space, which wasn't much, would be our living/sleeping room. There were two windows, one that looked out to the building across the alley, and another that was smaller than my head but had a bright beam of sunlight coming through it, illuminating the dust in the air disturbed by our entrance.

The carpet was threadbare, and the walls looked like they had been recently painted to cover the cracks that congregated near the ceiling. There was no furniture nor any dishes, getting a bed big enough for both of us through that door seemed problematic, and the only way we were going to get a decent shower was if one of us stood over the other with a bucket of hot water. The only sounds were the steady drip from the sink and the muted noise from the people downstairs in the restaurant, which I had a feeling would be there every time it was open for business.

All in all, our apartment was a dump.

But it was our dump, and I couldn't help but love it.

"This is incredible," Brad said, still not putting me down.

"We made it," I added, and he looked over at me.

We kissed until Mrs. Phan coughed a couple of times and then walked past us into the room. "No parties, no drugs, and no excuses," she announced, her previously pleasant demeanor gone. "You have paid for the year, but we haven't spent the money and will refund it if we have to kick you out. You thinking of getting pets?" We shook our heads. "Good, too much trouble." She took one last look around and then handed me the keys. "You boys want food, come down to the back—we always have extra—and we have a washing machine you can use on Sundays or else you pay for somewhere else."

She stopped and looked at us, and her face lit up as she smiled. "You boys good together. I have a good feeling about this." She shooed Mr. Phan out and closed the door behind her.

"You gonna put me down?" I asked.

He just gave me an evil grin.

"You really want to have sex on the floor?"

Biting his bottom lip, he nodded.

"Just on the floor? No blanket or anything?" Another nod.

I tried to keep the smile off my face but failed pretty spectacularly. "Pick a room."

We decided on the living room first.

Brad

SO WE drove for like fifteen hours out of Arizona and made it into Berkeley sometime after three. Now, I had driven in Houston, Dallas, and Austin, but nothing had prepared me for this place. There was, like, a street fair going on, but there were no signs for it, just people on the sidewalk selling things to other people walking by. The streets were narrow, but it didn't seem all that cramped, like the people who were driving understood the limitations of the road and were willing to deal with them. Yeah, I know I'm projecting here, but the farther west we got, the more… hippie-like the people got.

Man, I'm starting to sound like my dad.

The people all had longer hair; they wore ponchos and stuff. I mean, they were all dressed like they were all going to Burning Man, but none of them were under thirty. Okay, not everyone was like that, but there were enough to make me weird out some. But I kept it to myself because this was where I was going to live for the next few years and I needed to get used to the place….

Slowly.

After we had christened the house—twice—we grabbed our stuff from the car and brought it up. That consisted of clothes and our laptops, which left a whole lot of apartment to fill. The Phans had Wi-Fi, so Kyle could get his laptop up and running and find us a place to buy a bed. I texted my mom and told her we had arrived safely and were unpacking as we spoke. She said she was so excited for me and missed me a lot.

I looked over at Kyle sitting cross-legged in our empty living room, laptop balanced on his upper legs. And I just paused. The afternoon light coming through the window cast a shadow across him, and I was stunned all over again that this guy had ever decided to shack up with me. He was so perfect, so together… I held my phone out and took a pic of him deep in study.

I posted it to Facebook and called it "New Life: Day One."

There was no way I would ever love anyone as much as I loved him in that moment.

"What?" he asked, looking up from his work.

I closed Facebook and put the phone back into my pocket. "My mom says hi."

"Crap!" he exclaimed and pulled his phone out. "Text mine and tell her we made it before she sends out the Marines." He slid his phone across the floor to me; I unlocked it and sent a quick text to his mom.

"What did she say?" he asked, not looking up from his laptop.

"She said we should have had sex in the bathroom and made it a stand-up triple."

He whipped his head around to glare at me, and I burst out laughing. "She said to call her when you had a chance." I handed him back his phone with his mom's text open to prove it. "You, Mr. Stilleno, are too easy."

He closed his laptop. "And you, Mr. Graymark, are sleeping on the floor tonight."

"We both are if we don't hurry," I said, helping him up.

"There's a futon place down the street. It's probably the best we can do right now because I can't imagine getting a real bed through that—"

I kissed him before he got himself worked up about furniture moving.

"Two rocks and your arms are good enough for me. A futon will be perfect," I said softly.

"We need to get moving," he said. But he wasn't moving, just leaning into me.

"I know," I said, feeling my body react to his.

"Stand-up triple, huh?" he asked, bumping his hips into mine.

"Your mom is a smart lady."

"Come on and stop talking about my mom," he ordered, pulling me into the bathroom.

We both let out a laugh when he began to strip my clothes off me again.

Kyle

SEE WHAT I mean?

What, you didn't see it? Oh come on! Really? Okay, look at it again. Here we are, new place, new life with a ton of stuff to get done, and what does he want to do? Have sex. Does he want to do the work that needs to get done? Does he want to do the chores we both know have to be done? No, he wants to roll around on the floor and have sex. And even though I liked it and went along with it, I should have known. I should have known this was going to be like two people trying to carry a heavy couch when one of them had no desire to lift his end, leaving the other to manage the whole thing.

And yeah, I understand taking a couple of minutes to celebrate, but it was the start.

Don't look at me that way. Of course I was into it at the time—have you seen Brad? But I shouldn't have allowed myself to be swayed, and he shouldn't have been swaying. Sigh. You don't believe me, fine. Let's move on.

Brad

WE SPENT the weekend getting the apartment up and running and making sure the futon worked.

A lot.

I tried to stay out of Kyle's way because he was wound up pretty tight. The fact he had about a month before classes started didn't mean a thing to him. He acted like it was tomorrow and he hadn't studied at all. Once we bought everything we were going to need in the way of pots and pans, we went looking for furniture and ended up at the only place we could afford to furnish a whole place with.

10

IKEA.

They had all this stuff out on display, and most of it looked so cool that we bought a bunch of things. A couch that was a futon as well, a couple of chairs, an entertainment center—we were in gay heaven, just grabbing everything that looked like it would go together. We got home and started to unpack the stuff. Yeah, we knew it was all do-it-yourself, but I had watched people use tools before. I wasn't so useless that I couldn't put together a damn entertainment center! I mean, come *on*, how hard could it be?

If I ever get my hands on those Swedish-chef-sounding motherfuckers, I'm going to make them assemble their own spleens without instructions.

First off, there were, like, seven hundred parts for what basically looked like some wood and paint in the store. Two, the instructions, if I can call them that, had no language on them. No, I am not having a stroke; they had no fucking words on them. They were just pictures of parts that looked nothing like what we had, going together with other parts that we also didn't have, and a couple of really happy people who had an entertainment center. We did not look like those people, because all we had was some wood.

Of course, Kyle, never to be outdone, went online to see if the actual instructions were missing. Nope, those were them. Then he went on some sites trying to see if other people had put some together. They had. Of course, they didn't say how they did it; they just posted pics of their beautiful entertainment center with them standing next to it. Smiling.

Swedish chef assholes.

So of course then it came down to *we can't be this stupid and this can't be this hard so let's just sit down and work it out.* After the second hour, I was ready to swear off TV altogether or maybe just watch it on my phone, 'cause this shit was pissing me off. The worst part was that this was *just* the entertainment center. I couldn't even fathom putting the couch together; that had moving parts. After a while I was exhausted, and Kyle looked like he was going to cry, so I told him to go to bed and I would figure it out. He wanted to argue with me, but he was too tired to vocalize it, so he slouched off to the corner we'd put our futon in and collapsed onto the mattress. When I was sure he was asleep, I did what any full-grown male twenty-first century high school graduate does when he needs to learn a new skill instantly.

I went to YouTube.

I slipped on my earbuds and watched a guy, who cussed as much as I did, put together the monstrosity called an entertainment unit. When I lost track, I paused the video to catch up. I have no idea how people back in the day learned how to build log cabins and shit without YouTube. Not only does it seem like it would be way harder, but there was also no Sylvester the Talking Cat to make me laugh during breaks.

I spent an hour putting the beast together. That broke down to twenty minutes of actual work, thirty minutes of pausing the fucking video to watch the guy do it again, and ten minutes of burying my head in a pillow and screaming at the top of my lungs that I was going to kill the first Swedish person I met. But an hour later, the pieces of wood and screws had come together to make a thing that was kind of like the thing we saw in the store but a little lopsided, and there were three screws and a bolt left over, but fuck it. It stood up and was in one piece.

I threw the extra crap away.

Feeling like a real man, I shucked off my pants and changed into some shorts, grabbed a Pepsi from the fridge, and found a video about the couch. There was no way I was letting a bunch of evil Swedish guys get me.

By the time the sun was coming up, we had an entertainment center, a couch, and a chair-like thing that was more a collection of cushions and a frame than anything else. Still, it was better than the damn floor, so screw it. I put together the end table and placed the stylish yet oddly modern lamp we had bought on it. I convinced myself I'd sat down on the couch, not just fallen backward and hoped the couch was there. My eyelids kept trying to shut, but I kept them open long enough to realize I had made us furniture.

I closed my eyes for a second, and sleep took over.

Kyle

WHEN I woke up, I could hear Brad snoring in the other room.

Well, not an actual other room, in the… you get it.

I got up and saw that he had put everything else together somehow. He was passed out on the couch, and the entertainment center was upright, though I wasn't sure if it was ready to support an actual TV yet, and I thought those cushions might be the chair. He looked so peaceful lying there, mouth open, drooling out of one side. I looked around and found his phone on the floor. I aimed it at his face and snapped a pic of him in all his glory and then made it his wallpaper.

After putting the phone down, I grabbed a blanket off the bed and curled up next to him on the couch. He moved a little in his sleep and his arm went around me automatically, pulling me close like he always did. I loved that motion; even in sleep he held me, like it was what he was there for.

The morning sun was coming over the building across the alley, so some light made it into the place, and for a moment the world was still. I still couldn't believe I was there. No, that's not true. I could believe I was there; I couldn't believe we were.

I was living with my green-eyed boy. We'd made it out of Foster intact. It was so much more than anything I had ever dreamed of when I was growing up that my mind was still struggling to accept it. Brad had always been this perfect guy to me in junior high and high school, but now he was my boyfriend, my lover, my partner.

This was *our* place.

I turned over to face him and kissed him lightly on the cheek. He didn't stir, so I did it again, and again, and again. His eye twitched and I saw the side of his mouth crook up in a grin. "Best. Alarm. Clock. Ever," he said, not opening his eyes.

"I love you," I said, the feeling too much to contain a second longer.

He opened his eyes and looked into mine, and I felt my heart skip a beat. He began to open his mouth and I held my breath as I waited for him to say he loved me back.

"I know."

"Oh no you didn't," I said in mock outrage. "You did not just Solo me!"

He began to laugh as I started to tickle him. He cried out for mercy as I hit every single one of his vulnerable spots. Months of dating had tipped me off to where he had no defenses, so he knew how much trouble he was in. To stop me he wrapped his arms around me, and we went tumbling to the floor. He lay on top of me, and I could tell he was as aroused as I was.

"You know…," he said with a sly tone in his voice, "…the couch is a virgin."

"Not for long," I said, pulling his T-shirt off over his head.

Yeah, come back after lunch, we might be busy.

Brad

I NEED to build furniture more often.

Kyle

THE WEEKS leading up to school were the worst.

I had nothing to do and all the time in the world to do it. I had already mapped out my route to class—the Phans lived less than five minutes from the campus, which meant walking every day, instead of trying to drive and find a parking place, was an option. That, coupled with the fact Brad's car might have been his real boyfriend all along and I had been something on the side this whole time, made me very happy I could walk.

The funny thing was, we really didn't need his car for much.

Everything we could need was within walking distance, a fact the other people who lived around us seemed to take pride in. A grocery store was, like, two blocks away, and once we bought a couple of reusable shopping bags, it was kind of fun to walk there and back with our food haul. Brad, of course, wanted to drive everywhere, which was just silly considering how expensive gas was. I don't even want to go into how much it had cost to get us to California; suffice it to say that without Robbie's help, we would have been living in a cardboard box instead of an apartment.

My thought was to walk as much as possible because gas cost money, and gas in California cost triple that.

Brad's thought was, what was the point of having a badass car if you couldn't drive it?

That was just one of the many things that began to bug me in that month before class started. Brad seemed obsessed with finding us some kind of entertainment for the evening. We hadn't bought a TV yet—we were planning to, but it was kind of low on the priority scale, so we did without. So to Brad that meant finding something else for us to do.

We hadn't broached the subject of a gym membership, something I was pretty sure he was going to want, so he was finding free ways to keep in shape.

Running was the first thing he decided on.

"Come on," he urged, unaware that the distracting pair of shorts and tank top made him look like he was getting ready to shoot an infomercial for a Soloflex or something. "After a few miles the endorphins kick in and you'll love it!"

I had on a worn pair of sweatpants and a T-shirt and looked like I was nine. "I hate running," I reminded him as I tied my shoes.

"You hated running in school," he corrected me. "It's different when you do it on your own."

"No it's not. Still one foot in front of the other, sweating, tripping, panting… that all still happens."

His smile dropped for a second. "You really don't want to go with me?"

I sighed and stood up. "I'm dressed, aren't I? Just don't think I'm going to like it."

His face lit up as he smiled. "Awesome! This will change your life."

If you're curious, it did not change my life.

Running reminded me that I was nowhere near as healthy as Brad was. A fact I tried to ignore, since all it did was remind me that he could get a dozen guys better-looking than me in a heartbeat. Trailing after him, watching the perfect ass bounce farther and farther away, was not helping me adjust to the fact we were so different. Seeing people do a double take as he jogged by was not making me feel more confident that he wouldn't wake up and realize I was just a normal guy. And the way I had to stop after, like, twenty minutes to catch my breath was only pointing out to him that I was not the guy he thought I was.

"You okay?" he asked after going another half a block before realizing I wasn't behind him, turning around, and jogging back to where I was sagging against a streetlight.

I tried to answer, but I had no air to speak. The fact he stood there and jogged in place while he waited for me to recover made me madder than it should have. I wasn't mad at him; I was mad at me, at life for making me so soft. Brad hadn't done anything wrong but been born with perfect genes. I nodded since there was no way I was going to form words.

"If you stop moving, your body cools off," he said, trying to sound helpful and failing badly. "Once you stop it's harder to start again."

"I didn't"—huge gulp of air—"want to"—another gulp—"start in the first"—last word—"place!"

Since I was trying not to throw up, I didn't see the hurt look on his face, but I knew it was there nonetheless.

"You might end up liking it," he said, finally stopping.

"Do I look like I'm liking it?" I managed, now more embarrassed than tired. I wasn't athletic; everyone knew that. Round up every single person I ever met and ask them to describe me and I can guarantee *athletic* will not make one list. Ever. "I'm going to go back to the apartment. Just finish your run," I said, turning back in the direction we'd come.

"I'll go with you," he said, taking a step toward me.

"Brad," I replied, trying to keep my voice as calm as possible. "Please go run. I'll see you when you get home."

He said nothing for a few seconds, which made me feel like I had kicked a puppy. "Did I make you mad?"

"No," I admitted. "Honestly. I'm just mad, okay?"

"At me?"

Sigh.

"No, just... we can talk about this later," I announced. My legs started to cramp up as I walked back toward our place. I didn't look over my shoulder at him, because I knew I had just been a complete asshole and he had done nothing to provoke it. But I couldn't turn off the way I felt that quickly. I needed to be away from Brad so he didn't get hit by my stray drama.

It was everything I'd felt about myself in high school only worse because I was living Real Life, which meant feeling inferior and weak should not be common experiences. I never could run fast or throw a ball to save my life or any of that crap, and I was fine with that. I stayed away from the gym, and they stayed away from my books.

It seemed like a fair trade.

But I couldn't be Brad's workout partner or jogging buddy or whatever. And even if I could have done it, it wouldn't have mattered, 'cause I didn't want to any more than he wanted to be my study partner in calculus. He wanted to do this so we could have some form of entertainment, but this was not entertaining. Well, not to me; maybe to the guy with the cell phone who put "Geek loses shit on street" up on YouTube.

I got home, threw off my clothes, rinsed myself off, and then headed to my laptop. Three clicks later a TV was being sent to our place via the magic of the almighty Amazon. When Brad got back, he had that healthy glow about him that turned me on as much as it made me sick because I would never have it. He opened his mouth to apologize, and I just pointed to the bathroom.

"Shower first, talk after."

He sulked off to the shower, head down, sighing.

I waited two minutes before joining him and apologizing for my freak-out.

The TV arrived the next day, and things got better.

Brad

THE WEEKS leading up to Kyle going to school were like magic.

We'd wake up with nowhere to go and all day to get there. We'd spend the morning waking each other up and then take a shower and wake each other up again. Then we'd go find breakfast, occasionally, but most times lunch at the Phans', who served us huge portions of their food and never charged. Then I would try to find something for us to do during the afternoon to see if I could keep Kyle in a good mood.

I tried to take him running, but that didn't work, so we bought a TV. I hooked up my PS3 and got him to try *God of War*, which he was okay with; *Call of Duty*, which he hated; and then DC Online, which finally sold him. He ended up rolling up a Green Lantern, and we started spending our afternoons fighting Lex Luthor and The Joker. We'd take turns playing, one of us pushing buttons while the other called out tactics.

It was, like, four kinds of awesome.

Once it got dark, we'd either cook something or go out and wander around our neighborhood to see what was happening. We ended up becoming addicted to Blondie's Pizza, which sold these huge slices of the best pizza we'd ever eaten. I ended up extending my daily run to burn off the slices we'd chow down on every night before coming home and putting each other to bed.

It was everything I thought being a grown-up would be like.

I knew once school started, I was going to need to get a job. Not that we needed the money, but there was no reason for me to sit home and do nothing all day waiting like a golden retriever for Kyle to get home. I had no idea what I was qualified for, but I wasn't worried. So far things had been working out awesome, and I had faith that trend would continue.

The week before his first classes, Kyle said he was going to close the DC account because he wasn't going to have time to play once the semester started.

"You don't know that," I said, pausing the game. "We could find some time, like on the weekends."

He shook his head and continued looking at something on his laptop. "Weekends are going to be even worse. I bet they're the only time I'm going to have to catch up on reading or sleeping." He glanced up at me. "It's just a game, Brad; it's okay."

But it wasn't just a game. It was something we could do together.

Those last few days, I was desperate to find something we could do that didn't involve school, because I knew what was going to happen. He was going to start classes and be doing stuff that I had no idea how to help with. I mean, I barely got through high school; college stuff was going to be hieroglyphics to me. He was going to go off and do his college thing, and I was going to be the fucking dog waiting for him to get home no matter what.

The more I pushed, the worse it got, until the weekend he finally blew up.

I had gone out and bought a couple of board games I thought he'd like. Axis & Allies, which looked like Risk for smart people; some Settlers game I saw online; and Cards Against Humanity, which I didn't understand at all. When I pulled them out and asked him to pick one, he just stared at me like I was insane.

"You bought all these?"

I nodded.

"Brad, why?" His voice got a little louder. "I told you I'm not going to have time to play games once school starts—*any* games." He glanced over the games. "Settlers and Cards are to be played with a group, not just two people anyways," he sighed. "Did you keep the receipt, at least?"

"You don't even want to try them?" Now I was pretty sure I was whining.

"No." His voice made it pretty clear that he was done talking. "We need to start thinking of important things now. We're not going to be able to spend all day wasting our time forever."

"Wasting…?" I asked, crushed. "You think we're just wasting time?"

"Until school starts, yeah." He put the games back in the bag. "Why, what did you think it was?"

I didn't say a word; I just grabbed the bag and walked out.

That was right before I met Colt.

Kyle

NOW YOU had to see it there, right?

I mean, who blows, like, eighty bucks on board games? It was insane, and he pouted all weekend like I had kicked him or something. Less than forty-eight hours before I started college, and he was upset because I didn't want to play stupid games. I should have said something then, sat down and tried to get him to understand that we didn't have time to be dumb kids anymore. I needed to do everything perfectly because there were no second chances for me. If my grades sucked, I was out.

But instead I said nothing, and he ended up meeting that fucktard Colt.

Brad

I FELT more like his parent than his boyfriend the first day of school.

We had already walked the path to and back from the campus a couple of times to familiarize him with where everything was. The Phans' place was less than ten minutes' walking distance, which was perfect for Kyle. He'd bought himself a new laptop, and I had gotten him a satchel that could carry the couple of books he needed each day. He had two classes a day plus labs, which sounded like a dick move. I mean, seriously? Not only do you have to come to this class, but then come back and do *more* stuff for the same class later.

Kyle didn't seem to mind.

"Got your phone and charger?" I asked him as he checked his satchel for the millionth time. He loved that thing, but he'd never admit it. I'd found it on Etsy, and it'd cost me a couple hundred bucks, but that was okay 'cause I'd sold a bunch of my baseball cards on eBay to pay for it and given it to him as a graduation gift. It was worn leather and just screamed Kyle—new, old, smart, sexy. Jesus, I got misty watching him get ready for school.

I had officially become my mom.

He nodded at my question and then asked, "You going to be all right? You want to meet up there for lunch?"

"Nah," I said, trying to play as casual as I could. "I need to run, clean up around here, and then find a job doing something."

He put the satchel down and moved over to me. "You know there's no hurry," he lied.

"I know," I lied back. "But I need to do something."

"There are tons of junior colleges around here…," he offered for the millionth time.

"Dude," I said, giving him a grin. "I just got out of lockup. No way am I letting them drag me back alive."

He chuckled, but I could tell he didn't think it was funny. "Okay, just saying. We have enough money to get you some classes, easy."

"Go to school, young man," I ordered, pointing at the door, trying to deflect the coming argument.

He kept staring at me for a couple of seconds before shaking his head and grabbing his satchel. "I'll see you after class." He kissed me on the cheek. "Have fun getting sweaty and stuff."

I pulled him into a hug. "I'd rather get sweaty with you."

He gave me a real kiss, and we silently decided to drop the subject altogether.

Avoiding fights had been happening more and more, and suddenly I understood how my mom and dad got into the stalemate they called a marriage. Landmines seemed to have popped up all around the apartment, and we were both discovering them. I didn't want to go back to school no matter what; he didn't want to try anything I liked doing; he hated the fact I was obsessive about the way I kept my clothes; and I was tired of watching documentaries on Netflix.

But we said nothing, because what was there to gain by having a fight?

I wasn't going to school, I didn't expect him to keep his clothes in the same shape I kept mine, he didn't want to work out, and I became addicted to *Candy Crush* on my phone while he watched his snorefests on the only TV we owned.

Problems solved.

For now.

Anyway, he walked out, and I could feel my world shifting under me as everything changed again. The apartment was stupid quiet with him gone; I had never noticed before it was bigger than it looked. I poured myself another bowl of cereal and watched *Supernatural* on TNT for another hour or so.

I rinsed my bowl and stood in the middle of the room, wondering what to do next.

Kyle

SO, TECHNICALLY, I had time before declaring a major, which was good because I didn't know what I wanted to do.

Part of me figured business as a sure thing; another part looked at medical. However, when I walked into civics, the choice was made for me.

Civics was a required entry-level course, which meant the lecture hall was filled with freshmen and the occasional sophomore. The room was huge, an amphitheater setup where the seats went up and up, all focused on the small stage where the teacher... taught. A huge screen projected what was on the professor's laptop, so no matter where in the room I sat,

I'd have no trouble following lectures. The quote that greeted us when we straggled in was "'For good ideas and true innovation, you need human interaction, conflict, argument, debate.' Margaret Heffernan."

I found a seat near the back and set up my laptop before I pulled out my books. There were two books listed as advanced reading for the course, and neither seemed to make any sense to me. One was *Dude, Where's my Country?* by Michael Moore, and the other, by Glenn Beck, was *Arguing with Idiots*. Honestly, you couldn't have found two books that were more completely opposed to each other if you tried. The syllabus had no textbook, no study guide; all I saw was that I should buy those two books and bring an open mind.

All I wanted was a simple class with answers that were right or wrong.

The place filled up pretty quickly, and when the bell rang, an older gentleman who looked like he was the last of the great hippies walked out onto the stage and smiled at us. "Welcome to Fundamentals of American Civics, or just civics to its friends." He paused for a laugh, but all he got were fifty pairs of eyes blinking silently at him.

"There are a lot of ways to pass this class," he continued. "There are only a few to fail it. One, don't show up. This is not a test-based class; it's participation do-or-die, which means you have to be here and at least pretend to participate. The second is by calling me anything but Professor Madison. I am not 'dude,' 'hey,' 'teacher,' 'sir,' 'old guy,' or even 'bro.' You get one pass, and after that I will fail you." There were a couple of chuckles. "I am not kidding. I went to a lot of trouble to get the title Professor, and I expect you to use it. If you ever go as far as doctorate, you'll understand why. The third way you can fail this class is by not being able to defend your point of view. There is no right or wrong answer in this class; there are strong and weak arguments. 'Just because,' 'that's the way I feel,' 'it's my opinion,' and even 'because everyone else says so' are not reasons for you to believe something. They are excuses. We will be talking about a lot of topics, and there are no time-outs. You will either defend your point of view, or your point of view and opinion will be ignored. Today there is too much emphasis on rewarding people for managing to arrive somewhere on time and just participating. This classroom is not one of those places. You will fight for your grade, most of the time against each other."

A lot of people glanced uncomfortably at other people glancing uncomfortably back at them. I'm pretty sure I wasn't alone when I thought I had had no idea what I'd signed on for in Civics 101. This sounded more like a death match.

"There is only one A in this class, period. It will be given to the student who attends every class, participates in every class, and is able to defend his or her position in the strongest way…. There may be a lot of B's, but I promise you I will award only one A. If you want it, fight for it."

Suddenly, I wanted it, badly.

"Did anyone read the books I assigned?"

One black guy down in front and I raised our hands. Everyone else glared at us like we had screwed them over.

Crap! Now I'm freaking out again! Is "black" right or just something we say in Texas? African American? Colored? Why is it whenever I think about these things, I feel like I'm one white hood away from being a Klan member? The other guy was not white; that good enough? Jeez, I suck at this.

"Well, I see two people who are going to be ready for the first day participation grade. The rest of you? Better luck next time." Quiet groans escaped some of the people around me. They were accompanied by definite glares. Look at me—my first day and I was making friends.

"And you are?" Professor Madison asked the guy closest to him.

"Teddy Bergman." The guy stood up before he replied, his voice easily projecting to the rear of the room. He was cute in a nerdish sort of way. I mean to say that he was trying to look like a nerd rather than being one. He had the glasses, the bow tie, the skinny jeans. He was, in fact, one sonic screwdriver away from being a Time Lord.

Teddy looked like a living example of what Robbie had been talking about back in Foster when he said I was rocking the nerd chic, except that had been the way I dressed. I had not been making a statement.

Teddy here was making a statement.

"Very good, Mr. Bergman. And you?" he asked me. I opened my mouth and he added, "Stand up. If you have something to say, say it with authority."

"Um, Kyle Stilleno, Professor." I wanted to sit down, but Teddy was still standing, which meant this torture was just starting.

"Very well, then. Since you two have read our two books, you are the only ones here ready to answer some questions based on what you've read. Mr. Bergman, why did I choose those two particular books?"

He cleared his throat and gave a little smile like he was preparing to belt out a song from *Oliver!* instead of answer a question. "The two books show the vast array of opinions held in America today, each book covering one end of the political spectrum."

"And those are?" the professor asked.

"Conservative and liberal," he answered, with another smile. What did he want, a freaking bone?

"Do you agree, Mr. Stilleno?" the professor asked me.

I was going to just say yes since that was the textbook answer to the question, but something stopped me. This guy wasn't a textbook professor. We didn't need to read the books to know what Teddy had just said; the blurbs on the back could have told us that. He was looking for a deeper answer, an answer that had more meat rather than a regurgitation of facts.

"No, sir, I don't."

The professor raised an eyebrow. "Well then, why did I pick those two books?"

"Because they show the absurdities that each side of an argument can harbor while claiming the other side is insane."

No one said a word, and Madison looked at me thoughtfully, possibly mulling over my answer. "Which book sounded more correct to you?"

"Neither. They were both pretty out there," I answered honestly. "I mean, each one had some good ideas, but once the authors went deeper into their topic it was obvious they had an agenda that had little to do with being fair and balanced."

"Why would either book want to be fair and balanced?" the professor asked.

That stopped me cold.

"Mr. Bergman, would you like to amend your answer in lieu of Mr. Stilleno's observation?"

Teddy shot me a glance, clearly trying to regroup. "I think you chose the books because their authors' opinions are at the farthest ends of the political spectrum. Neither one is right; at the same time, neither of them could be called wrong."

The professor looked back at me.

"No, they are both wrong, just in different ways."

Teddy turned back and looked at me. "You can't say they are right or wrong, you can just say if you agree or not."

"No," I said slowly. "I can pretty definitively say that neither of those books is right about much. All the authors are doing is telling their side of the problem to the people who agree with them."

"How do you expect the choir to sing if you don't preach to them?" Teddy asked me, playing the crowd as a few of them chuckled.

"Well, to run with your analogy, we'd all have to agree on the same piece of music to sing before there is any preaching, singing, or taking a bow. Those books don't agree on anything, not the problem, the cause, or the solution. If we were to say that either one had any validity, then we'd spend the entire time arguing about what part was right or not instead of actually doing anything."

The professor looked back to Teddy, and I could see from here Teddy wasn't happy at all.

"But both points of view are valid," he argued.

I shook my head. "I disagree; they are opinions, but that doesn't make them valid. Opinions are just that: opinions. Everyone has one, and most of them are wrong."

Neither of us was waiting for the professor anymore. "And people aren't allowed to have opinions?" he asked me.

"Sure, you can have an opinion on whatever you want, but it doesn't make it right, valid, or even interesting. It means it's just something you think. What value does that have?"

"To the person who has it?"

"To anyone *but* them," I answered back. "If we make all opinions worth something, then nothing matters anymore. The truth and facts have to mean more than just a point of view."

The professor looked back at Teddy, who was struggling to find something to come back with. "I don't agree" was all he could muster.

"Where are you from Mr. Stilleno?" the professor asked.

"Foster, Texas," I said, realizing with some surprise that I had a little pride in my voice when I said it.

Teddy scoffed. "Oh, well, that makes sense, then." He tried to make his words sound like he was just thinking out loud, but he still projected well enough for everyone to hear. "In Texas opinions might not count, but here in California, where we care about everyone, they matter."

I saw the professor open his mouth, but I cut him off at the pass. "So how long did you live in Texas?" I asked him. Teddy pointed at himself and I nodded. "Yeah, exactly how much time did you live in Texas?"

"I haven't." He had the same amount of pride in that statement that I had in my own.

"So, then, your vast experience living in Texas has proved to you that Texans don't consider others' opinions. Even better, once someone lives in California, his or her opinions about things like places they've never been are considered to be valid. That's an impressive ability."

"Your state's history speaks for itself," he said, playing up the drama. "You can't tell me that you'd defend it as an open-minded, forward-thinking place that welcomes change."

Now I was pissed.

"We're wandering off topic, but I'm willing to follow your train of thought. Well, let's see: in small-town Foster, Texas, I came out as gay, my boyfriend played varsity baseball and led the team to our divisional championship, the school started a gay-straight alliance, and when the administration tried to ban us from going to our prom, both schools in town boycotted their proms and threw one for just us. All that took place in a small Texas town—you know, where we don't value other opinions." His mouth opened in shock, and I could feel more than a few people staring at me. "So next time you want to hang an ironclad conservative tag on an entire state, realize 'there are more things in heaven and earth, Horatio, than are dreamt of in your philosophy.'"

I paused, and I heard a few people around me clap.

"And Mr. Stilleno has earned our first A," the professor said, clapping himself. "He had you when he turned that whole choir metaphor around," he added to Teddy. "But be happy with a B. You tried."

I sat down as he looked out at the class. "As for the rest of you, enjoy your Cs, except for you back there texting and your friend next to you sleeping. You two have earned the first Fs. This is how it goes, people. Show up, participate, and be ready to defend your point of view." He clicked something and the slide changed.

"Now, let's start going over when participation in the system moved from a point of pride to an annoyance."

After class, people started to file out of the room, and the professor asked me to wait. Teddy walked by, giving me the weirdest look. He didn't say a word, just looked at me and shook his head. Once the room was empty, Dr. Madison asked, "You have a major yet?" I shook my head. "Then let me be the first in a long line of people who will offer you an opinion on the matter."

I waited, dying to know what he would say.

"When you defended your contention that opinions are simply that, no more and no less, and that they should be tested against current reality, you showed a basic grasp of something that law professors spend years attempting to teach their students. If you have even a passing interest in the law or politics, do us all a favor: go pre-law."

"Thank you, Professor," I said honestly. Pre-law? Me?

"No, Mr. Stilleno, thank you for coming to class prepared. You and Mr. Bergman made my point so much better than any lecture would have."

He didn't say anything else, so I grabbed my stuff and left, feeling really good about my first class. I was going to love college.

Brad

So I sat around the house, played two games of *COD*, jerked off, and then decided I was going to go run and get it over with.

I tossed on some shorts and grabbed my iPhone and headed downstairs. I stretched out on the sidewalk and slipped my earbuds in place. Josh had made me a workout playlist last year when we were training for State, and I had to admit, he had some awesome taste in music. Like always, the first few steps were hell, but after about half a mile my mind moved into automatic and I just began to run. The music, the city, everything faded away as I fell into that groove most runners know and went with it. I didn't think about where I was going or how far I was going to go. I just ran and let my body go where it wanted to.

I ended up in front of a gym called Flex.

It was a gay gym, or the owners really liked rainbows, if the giant decal in the front window was any sign. There were silhouettes of bodybuilders on the door, and I could see a pretty big workout area past the window. I sighed and got ready to keep running, since there was no way I could afford a place like this until I had a job and was bringing in a paycheck. Just as I was about to take off, a guy opened the door and waved at me to get my attention.

Pulling my earbuds out, I paused and looked at him.

"Tell me you're looking for a job."

And just like that, I was employed.

Turns out I was right. Flex was a gay gym, and the owner was looking for personal trainers to help the customers. When I tried to explain to Todd, the manager, that I wasn't a personal trainer, he just laughed. "Gurl, please, these 'mos don't care. Just wear a tight shirt and those track shorts and trust me, they'll do whatever you say."

That didn't sound right. "But what about a license and that stuff?"

He sighed at me and batted his eyelashes, which were much darker than the blond tips of his thinning hair. "Okay, fine, how about I send you to a quick course, and then you can say you're a personal trainer. Deal?"

"How much is the course?" I asked.

"A blow job?" he asked and then laughed way too loud. "Just kidding, it's on me, kid. Trust me, you're going to pay for yourself, I can feel it." He paused and got serious all of a sudden. "You don't have a problem with gay guys, right? 'Cause I can't have no homophobic douche in here making waves. These guys are going to flirt, and I don't expect you to flirt back, but you sure aren't gonna be mean."

"I have no problem with gay guys," I answered honestly, deciding not to say a word about my sexuality to him.

He had me fill out an application and then asked for my ID and stuff, which of course I didn't have. Running and sweating, remember?

"Don't sweat it, green eyes, just bring it tomorrow with said tight shirt and little shorts and we'll get you into the system."

"How much does it pay?" I asked, confused at how fast this was happening.

"Let's start at sixteen an hour plus any tips you get. For every client you sign up for lessons, you get a ten-buck bonus, and we'll see where it goes from there, okay?"

"Sixteen dollars? An hour?" I exclaimed, shocked.

"Okay, fine. Nineteen, but tell no one. The other employees will kill me." He gave me a sly smile. "You're a shrewd negotiator, Brad. I like that."

I was expecting maybe eight, nine bucks tops. Double that? This was insane.

"So ID, social security card, and tight clothes, got it?" I nodded. "Awesome. Also, it goes without saying that you and your girlfriend can use the gym whenever. That comes with the job."

"Can I work out now?" I asked, shocked that I had killed two birds with one stone so easily.

"Honey, looking like that, you can do whatever you want." He batted his eyelashes again, and I wondered how many people he used this routine on.

"You have a towel? I don't want to sweat all over the machines," I asked, feeling like I was pushing my luck.

He grabbed a towel with the gym logo on it and tossed it to me. "Keep it. I bet I can sell it when you're done for more than it's worth." He saw the look on my face and laughed again. "Kidding! I joke a lot."

That was no joke, and we both knew it.

It was around noon, so the only other person working out was an old guy, older than my dad; he looked like he was more watching the TV above the leg press than actually working out. I went at it like a kid in a candy store. It had been so long since I had really worked out, I had lost some strength, but not enough to matter. I worked up a sweat and got that joyous feeling of my muscles aching from exertion, and that's something you can only get after a great workout. I worked out for about an hour and a half, and by the time I was done, five guys had gathered around me. All of them were just watching me lift.

"Did you guys need to work out here?" I asked, taking my earbuds out.

"Nope," one of them said, a huge shark grin on his face. "You keep doing what you're doing."

Oh dear God.

"Do the gloves help?" one of the other guys asked. I had found a discarded pair of lifting gloves in a box and slipped them on before I had started on my chest.

"Well, the bar can cut your palms up pretty bad," I said, slipping one off and showing him the calluses on my hand from all the lifting I had done.

He traced a finger over them and seemed impressed. "So why wear the gloves?"

I put it back on. "That's with gloves. Can you imagine what they'd be like without?"

He nodded, finally getting it.

"You're interrupting him," Shark Guy said to his friend.

"Oh, give it a rest already," he snapped back. "If you want porn, go download some. Leave the poor boy alone." He looked back to me. "Ignore them; we don't get many guys your age in here this early."

"It's okay," I said, even though it wasn't. "I'm Brad."

"Frank," he said, shaking my hand. "Can you show me how to do that… with much less weight, of course."

We both laughed and I nodded. "Use that bench," I said, pointing to the one next to mine. "I'll show you form before we add any weight."

That was how I spent the rest of my afternoon, showing Frank how to lift properly and ignoring the leering from Shark Guy and his friends. In fact I had lost track of time until my phone rang. I looked down and saw Kyle's name. "Crap," I said, taking a few steps away from the bench.

"Hey," I said into the phone. "You home already?"

"Yeah," he said, sounding happy. "Where are you?"

I laughed. "I could tell you, but you'd never believe it. I'll be home in a few."

He said nothing for a few seconds and then asked, "Is that music in the background?"

Of course Todd had house music blaring over the speakers, trying to infuse some kind of energy into the gym, though it was wasted on these guys. "Kind of." I laughed again. "See you in a few," I repeated and hung up.

"Hey, I need to bounce," I told Frank, "but I'm going to start tomorrow if you want some more pointers."

"I think you have your first customer," he replied, shaking my hand again.

"Awesome!" I broke out into a smile. "See you tomorrow."

I headed out and saw Shark Guy and Todd over at the counter. "He looks just as good leaving as coming," Shark Guy said, loud enough for me to hear.

"How do you know? You haven't seen him come yet."

"See you tomorrow, Todd," I said, waving at him and ignoring the comments.

"Remember?" he called back.

"I know," I said at the door. "Tight."

Kyle

SO MY boyfriend could go out for a run and end up getting a job.

He was so excited about it that I didn't even bring up the class. I mean, why ruin his news with the fact I stood up in class and didn't pass out? We ended up going out for dinner to celebrate, and the night ended with him showing me the body that got him the job.

I have to admit, it was worth a couple of bucks.

The next morning we were both getting ready, and I could tell he was excited about his first day. He was excited and hanging to the left, if we were being blunt. "Um, you are going to bring something to wear *over* your underwear, right?"

He shot me a confused look. "What? These're running shorts, not underwear."

"True," I said, trying not to get mad. "Underwear actually covers more than what you're wearing."

A sly grin slid across his face. "You didn't complain before."

"You weren't going to go get ogled in a gay gym either."

31

"I am not going to get ogled," he said firmly. And then paused. "Wait, is ogled touching?" I shook my head. "Oh yeah, then I might get that, then."

"Brad!" I began to protest.

"Kyle, come on," he said, taking a few steps toward me. "What do you care if a bunch of guys look at me? You think people don't look at you?" I tried to lower my head, but he stopped me. "Hey, don't! You are hot. *We* are hot. Let them look. We both know we're the only ones who get to touch."

He kissed me, and I kissed him back, confused about how upset I was. "But I don't want—"

He kissed me again.

"I don't care if people look at me. Let them. I work my ass off to stay in shape. You trust me not to do anything, right?" I nodded. "Well then, what's so upsetting?"

"Other people shouldn't stare at you—you're mine," I said in one breath.

He raised an eyebrow at me. "I'm yours?"

"You know what I mean." I tried to backpedal.

"No, I don't," he said, way too calmly for my taste. "So am I supposed to walk around in a sheet like muslin chicks and wait patiently for you to get home?"

"One, it's Muslim, two, I didn't say that, and three… it just pisses me off that guys are going to be scoping you out."

He smiled and pulled me into a hug, which I tried to struggle against but didn't try all that hard. "You can't stop people from enjoying all this." He gestured down his body with one hand and then laughed when he saw my look. "But instead of getting mad at the fact they're looking, why don't you get off on that you're the only one who gets to touch it? The only one I want to touch it. In fact, the only guy who will ever touch it, if I get my way."

I heard the joking tone, but I could see the earnestness in his eyes. "You want me to not take the job, I will. But you want me to dress down so people won't look at me? You're crazy and you know it. So if you're going to veto the job, do it now and I'll call Todd and tell him no thanks."

There was a time when I was the logical one and he was the one who said stupid things.

"Fine." I sighed. "But they better not touch one hair—"

He laughed and kissed me passionately. "Got it, warn them that there's a jealous Pikachu at home and he will bite."

"I'm a Pikachu now?"

He grabbed a tuft of my bangs and pulled on them. "It's the blond hair and huge eyes. You're an adorable Pokémon."

"And one that will shock the fuck out of anyone who touches you," I added.

"And that too," he agreed, kissing me again.

I'm not kidding when I say I almost threw him back on the couch and mounted him right there just to mark my territory, but, thankfully, thousands of years of evolution took hold and I gave him a hickey instead.

Same effect, less time.

"You are a shit," he complained, rubbing his neck.

"I am *your* shit," I corrected him and grabbed my satchel. "Have fun explaining that at work."

I saw him run to the mirror as I walked out. I wish I felt a little bad about what I'd done, but come on. You would have done the same.

Brad

MOTHERFUCKER.

I swear, if he didn't have such a talented mouth… you know what? I withdraw that previous statement on the grounds it will get me killed.

Short of wearing a turtleneck sweater, there was no way I was going to be able to cover up the hickey. I knew Kyle could be jealous, but this was a whole new level for him. It was because he didn't think he was cute and so was automatically threatened by anyone he thought was better-looking than him. He did it with Josh, and he obviously thought the guys at the gym were in that category. Jennifer had given me one of these possession hickeys junior year when she saw Maggie Hayes talking to me between classes, but damn, Kyle's was going to last.

Nothing to do but own it.

I grabbed my iPhone, slipped my earbuds in, and took off jogging toward Flex. I got more than the normal number of stares as I made my way across the street, no doubt owing to the fact that my clothes looked like they'd been shrunk in the wash. Now, I'm not as blessed as Kyle is in the downstairs department, but I'm not small, so the shorts were showing more than they were concealing, and I'm pretty sure more than a few people took an extra second to have a look.

Which wasn't as upsetting as I thought it would be.

I was never shy about my body—I mean, I took showers with thirty guys next to me. If you were weird about your body, a locker room was not the place to figure that out. I never thought of myself as perfect-looking or anything, but I worked hard on my body and was proud of it, so showing it off wasn't something I freaked out about.

But this was something else.

I was eighteen, in great shape, and not ugly, and people were responding to that. Not treating me like a cute boy or an attractive teenager—they were reacting to me as a sexy guy, and that was a turn-on in itself. Foster was way too small for people to look at each other like that. In Foster, ogling would have been like having feelings for a relative, maybe a distant cousin but related nonetheless. In California, people didn't know me and I didn't know them, so everything was something new.

They thought I was sexy and I liked it.

Not "liked it" in, like, I wanted them to hit on me or anything—liked it in that it was proof I was good-looking. I know what you're thinking: wasn't having Kyle find you attractive enough? Well, yes and no. Him being as turned on by me as I was by him was awesome, but my reaction to it was muted, because he kind of had to. Like your mom saying you looked handsome or whatever, you know? What was she going to say to you? "Wow, my kid is fugly." She had to be nice to you the same way Kyle was nice to me. Not that I doubted the truth of his feelings; I'm just saying it wasn't all that objective.

Strangers, on the other hand, didn't owe me a thing. They weren't my parents or my boyfriend; they didn't even know my name. All they saw was the way I looked and they liked it, and that meant something to me. Not sure why, but it did, and I was going to enjoy it while I could.

All these thoughts rolled around in my head as I jogged to the front door of the gym. It was closed, but I could see Todd inside, setting up the register. I knocked on the window and he came over and unlocked the door for me. He looked me up and down. "Well, well, this is too nice a job to rush."

I tried to walk in, but he stopped me. "Hold up, let me take a good look." His eyes consumed me like I was a hot plate of food, and then he added, "Turn around." He must have seen the way my jaw clenched because he quickly held his hands up. "I'm kidding! I kid, remember?"

"Can I get inside?" I asked, pissed.

"After you," he said, letting me go by. I could feel his stare aimed straight at my ass.

I took back everything I had just thought about liking people finding me sexy.

"So what do I need to do?" I asked, hoping I could get his stare above my waist.

"Well, check the gym and locker rooms for anything that needs to be picked up. Straighten up anything that looks out of place, and then turn the TVs on MSNBC with the sound off. The queens around here will try to get you to change it to Bravo or some shit; tell them the remote is broken and you can't." He handed me the remote. "So can I ask, you Jewish?"

I looked at him and began to ask why when I saw he was looking at my dick.

"Inquiring minds want to know."

I ignored him and began turning the TVs on.

Kyle

WHEN I got to class, Teddy was waiting outside. I prayed he wasn't waiting for me.

"Hey," he said, nodding at me.

Crap.

"Hey," I answered, not sure if it would be rude to just walk right past him into class.

"So about yesterday…," he began.

I waited.

"That was nothing personal or anything," he added when he figured I wasn't going to say anything.

"I didn't think it was," I replied, though we both knew it kind of was.

"You're from Foster, Texas. I read about you online."

That gave me pause. "You what?"

"I wanted to know more about the things you said, and I found a couple of newspaper articles about you and the school. A couple of people who went to school with you had written blogs too." He sounded embarrassed, but I wasn't paying attention to that. I was trying to get my mind around that people in Foster knew what a blog was.

"Anyway, where you grew up is clearly the exception, and I apologize."

"It isn't the exception," I corrected him. "Foster can be just as bad as anywhere else." I thought about Riley and Robbie and added, "In fact, it was worse than a lot of places."

"But they accepted you guys," he argued. "You have to know that is atypical."

"They accepted us after we stood up and refused to go away. You look and you see a place that's different, and I look and see a place that has changed. There's a big difference between the two."

He looked like he was getting upset again. "And what do you think the difference is?"

I shifted my backpack and tried not to sigh. "Because your statement that all of Texas is intolerant and fucked-up precluded the fact that there might be good parts in Texas. Ever. Your assumption stops you from realizing that every place has its own set of rules and ideas. Responding to stereotypes just makes you ignorant."

"I didn't say it was intolerant and fucked-up," he shot back.

"No, you said, 'Your state's history speaks for itself. You can't tell me that you'd defend it as an open-minded place.' Asking me to defend it as an open-minded place is the same as calling it a closed-minded place or intolerant. The fucked-up part was implied by the look on your face when you said it. Look, you want to know where you went wrong in there yesterday?"

He arched an eyebrow, daring me to correct him.

"You did the same thing that you were accusing people from Texas of doing. You judged a whole group of people based on the actions of a few assholes. Should I judge you on the actions of other black people?

I mean, if I was the intolerant Texas redneck you seem to think all of us are, then I should have been scared that you're going to mug or shoot me. Instead I reacted to you based on *your* words and actions, not stereotypes."

"And the Shakespeare quote?" he asked.

"I'm a *Star Trek* fan; when in doubt, quote the Bard."

"Classic or *TNG*?" he asked quickly.

"Neither, to be honest; I was more a *Deep Space Nine* guy."

He looked at me like I had spit on him. "You can't be serious."

"Have you seen all of *Deep Space Nine*?"

He shook his head. "No, but what I saw I didn't like."

"Well, maybe you shouldn't judge things based on a small sample size," I said, sidling past him. "That's really the only way we learn anything new."

I got inside and sat down.

Professor Madison's class was weird because it was the only class I had that met on three consecutive days. That was nice because I was done for the week by Wednesday, but less nice because he intended to cover a lot in those three days. I pulled out my laptop and set my stuff up before Teddy sat down next to me.

"I was trying to apologize," he said, pulling a MacBook Air out of his bag. "You make that kind of hard."

I looked over at him and took a deep breath. "I don't like it when people make judgments based on false or misleading information, even if I agree with their opinion. I know Texas is generally a closed-minded, conservative state, but I know that firsthand. Which means I also know firsthand that there are some incredible people who live there and defy every single stereotype that's hurled at the state. And I'm willing to bet the same can be said for California and your belief that everyone here cares about other peoples' opinion. You want to go outside and take a poll and see how many self-centered assholes we find?"

He began to laugh and held his hands up in surrender. "Okay, okay. I give. I was wrong, completely, and you caught me. Can we try again?"

I smiled. "We can do that."

"I'm Teddy," he said, holding his hand out.

"Kyle." I shook it.

"You free this weekend?"

I paused. "Free for what?"

He cocked his head. "Coffee? A movie?"

"Um, like a date?" I asked, unsure of the terminology.

He nodded.

"I'm sorry, I can't," I said as nicely as I could.

"Oh," he replied curtly. "Not into black guys?"

My head spun over to look at him. "What? No, I have a boyfriend."
I could see the look of disbelief in his face. "Are you serious? You think
I would make a boyfriend up to avoid going out with you?"

"You wouldn't be the first white boy who has," he said, pretending
to study his laptop.

I pulled my phone out and showed him a picture of Brad. "This is
my boyfriend; we've dated for almost a year. He moved out from Texas
with me, and we live together."

He glanced over at the picture of Brad, looked away for a second,
and then looked back quickly once his mind processed the image. "*That*
is your boyfriend?" I nodded. "Show me another picture." I slid the
picture aside and showed him a picture of us at the prom by the lake.
Brad's arm was around me, and we both had smiles as wide as our faces.
"Does he go here?"

I locked the phone. "Nope, he just got a job at a gym."

"Ah," he said, going back to his laptop. "That makes sense, then."

"What does?" I was starting to get pissed.

"You like pretty boys; I get it. Most guys are superficial like that."

My mouth opened and closed a few times as I tried to process what
he had just said without screaming. "Superficial? So just because Brad is
cute, that means I only like him for his looks?"

Teddy looked back at me, and I could see the satisfaction in his
eyes that he had gotten to me. "Well, let's see. He doesn't go to college;
he works minimum wage at a gym, which means you're probably paying
for most of everything with your scholarship. He can't be all that bright
if he isn't even trying to go to junior college, and you seem too smart to
be true. So tell me, Kyle from Foster, Texas, what exactly do you guys
have in common? You guys discuss current events and politics or just
have a lot of sex? He read the books you read? Like the movies you

like?" I said nothing. "Right. Which means he has a perfect body and a cute face. You tell me why you're going out with him, then."

"I love him," I said, as pissed as I had ever been with a stranger, and that included Mr. Raymond. "You know, you might think you're Sherlock Holmes over there, but you don't know a thing about me and him."

"I don't?" he said with that same fake air of concern. "Then tell me where I got it wrong, Kyle."

"That boy stood by me when no one else would," I said, realizing my hands were balled into fists. "He came out to the entire school because he didn't want me to stand there alone and get bullied. He had nothing to gain and everything to lose: his friends, his spot on the baseball team, everything. I *begged* him not to do it and he still did. He has never once wavered in his faith that we should be together. Even when I got scared and tried to push him away, he was still there for me. So before you open your fucking mouth about shit you don't know about, maybe you should learn the rest of the story."

"Methinks thou protest too much," he said with a grin. "I like *Next Gen* myself."

"The quote is 'The lady doth protest too much, methinks,' so if you want to pull from Shakespeare, get it right, and you can think anything you want if it makes you feel better. But that whole race bullshit? It's you deflecting from the fact that guys probably didn't reject you 'cause you're black; they probably said no 'cause you're a smug asshole."

I grabbed my stuff and moved to another seat before I said more.

Brad

So THE morning was busier than I thought it would be.

A small group of guys, all my dad's age, came in and got a workout in before lunch. Most were in okay shape—well, great shape for their age—and all of them flirted hard-core with me. One guy was staring pretty hard at my dick as I stood over him and spotted him on his bench press, so I eased up on how much I was holding. His arms instantly began to shake, and I could see him struggle to get it back up to the bar.

"Helps to concentrate on the weights," I advised, pulling it off him. He glared at me, but he could no more accuse me of dropping the bar than I could of him staring at my junk. There was a line of guys waiting for me to help them work out. By noon I had helped four guys train, and when I took my lunch break, Todd handed me a fifty.

"Gurl, lunch is on me. I have never had so many queens sign up for lessons that they will never use. I was right about you."

I was going to say that I could do the same thing with more clothes on, but I had fifty bucks in my hand, so I shut up. I walked out to grab some food as another guy my age walked in the other door. He was shorter than me but had a great build on him. It was a perfect gym body, one of those physiques guys spent hour after hour on in the gym, making sure every cut was deep and perfect. It's funny because I'm sure the guy was in great shape, but his muscles didn't serve any real purpose. I mean, my arms were big from throwing a ball a thousand times a day; I lifted to get as much power behind my throw as I could get. This guy had huge biceps because it made guys look at him.

I nodded at him as I walked out; I heard him hit his head on the door and curse as I looked around to find somewhere to eat.

"Hey," he said, moving toward me. "You work out here?"

He had short-cropped brown hair with spiky bangs that were gelled upward with something that had to be weatherproof, it looked so stiff. He had bright blue eyes that looked fake, they were so vivid. I instantly thought of contacts.

"Um, I work there, but I'm on break. I'll be back in an hour," I said, seeing a Subway down the street.

"Okay," he called after me. "I'll be waiting in there."

I didn't even look behind me and waved over my shoulder as I crossed the street toward the food. I spent the next hour devouring two footlongs and downing a huge Coke Zero before heading back for the rest of my shift. When I walked in, I saw Frank talking to Todd at the front counter.

"Hey, Brad," Frank said, waving at me.

"Frank!" I said, smiling. "You're back."

"He's back and he's your next client," Todd said cheerfully.

"Awesome," I said, finishing my Coke. "Lemme wash up and we'll start. Any idea what you want to work on?"

"Um, what do you suggest?"

"Well, you did some chest yesterday, so let's focus on legs and abs," I said, tossing my cup away.

Which was when the guy who had talked to me when I was leaving came over. "Hey again," he said with a smile.

"'Sup," I said before heading to the bathroom to wash my hands.

Eager Guy followed me. "So you're, like, a trainer?" he asked as I washed my hands.

I nodded. "Just started."

"I'm Colt," he said, holding his hand out even though mine were still under the water. He saw and pulled his back. "Oh, sorry 'bout that."

I dried my hands. "It's cool. I'm Brad."

"I was doing some squats; mind helping me out?"

I shook my head as I walked past him. "Sorry, man, I have a client."

"The old guy? You're going to help him instead of me?"

I looked back at Colt. "Well, that guy paid for me to help him and it is, like, my job. So I kinda have to."

"So I have to pay to talk to you?" He sounded upset.

"No, we're talking right now. But I have a paying client waiting for me, so, I'll talk to you later," I said, walking back to the gym floor.

"You aren't going to need gloves for legs, Frank," I said, smiling, trying to ignore the weirdness that was Colt for the moment.

I started Frank out on an elliptical to get his heart pumping; the whole time Colt worked out over at the squat machine and glared at us. Next, I moved Frank over to a leg press and set him up with a little weight.

"You seemed to have pissed Colt off," Frank said between sets.

"Not sure how," I said, not even looking toward wherever Colt was.

"You didn't fall all over yourself trying to get to him," Frank explained. "It's why he comes here—for the attention."

My brow furrowed in confusion. "Attention? For what?"

Frank chuckled. "Same attention you got yesterday. Young, hot guy working out gets a lot of looks from guys my age."

"He comes here to get that?" I asked, shocked.

Frank nodded. "Some guys get off on it. They like to be chased."

I was never going to understand how being gay worked.

"Okay, another set. You don't want your body to cool off too much or you lose the burn," I said, clearing my thoughts of Colt and his drama.

"I appreciate you not blowing me off," Frank said as we moved to another machine.

"Huh?" I asked, confused.

"The last trainer Todd hired would give us a list of things to do and then spend most of the session flirting with Colt. I guess Todd knew better, hiring a straight guy this time."

"I'm not straight," my mouth said before I could stop it.

Frank paused and looked at me like I had grown a third eye. After a few seconds, he said in a low voice, "Do yourself a favor. Tell no one in here that, or you'll spend all your time fending off guys trying to get with you. They can be relentless."

"I have a boyfriend," I said in the same low voice. "So it doesn't matter anyway."

Frank shook his head. "Must be a hell of a boyfriend for you not to even give Colt a glance." He gave me a look. "He's a lucky guy."

Smiling, I said, "I'm the lucky one, and you're stalling. Give me four sets of eight."

Kyle

THE CLASS blurred by as I sat there and stewed about Teddy.

I mean, come on; I was literally in a relationship. Who just assumed someone would be lying when they said no to a date instead of accepting the fact they might be telling the truth? I paused, because before Brad, that would have been my exact thought process if I had asked someone out and gotten turned down. Of course, I would have never asked anyone out, since we all know I was the Hunchback of Foster High most of my life, but if something had fallen on my head and I woke up not knowing who I was and maybe started speaking with a French accent, my first thought at rejection might have been that they were lying to protect my feelings.

Every particle of my being wanted to glance over at Teddy to see if he was staring at me, but I resisted. Instead I pulled up Facebook on my laptop and decided to repay the stalking. Teddy Bergman grew up in San Rafael, which according to my Google search was a pretty affluent place. He went to a private school and won the Junior National Academic Championship when he was thirteen. According to his profile he had two moms, both white, and was head of the tolerance club at his high school.

There was a picture of him and some other kids meeting President Obama, another of him with Condoleezza Rice at some kind of award thing. There were a ton of postings about this contest or that event... but none with friends. In fact, out of the 317 friends he had on Facebook, most looked like they were because of various games he played. The only actual posts he had were by his moms.

That was sad.

By the end of class, I felt sorry for the guy. I mean, I was a complete shut-in before Brad, but at least I made friends. Maybe I was wrong; maybe his friends didn't get on Facebook. Maybe he had a ton of friends and they just used different social media.

When the bell rang, I grabbed my stuff and was not shocked to see him waiting out in the hall.

"That was uncalled for," he said without preamble. "I had no right to say any of that, and I apologize."

I smiled. "A friend of mine used to say we all get one crazy. Consider that yours."

He smiled back. "So how about I try this again? I am Teddy; you are Kyle and in a relationship. I am gay also but would like to pursue a friendship with you if that is okay."

Laughter slipped out of my mouth. "Okay, Teddy the gay robot. I am Kyle and would love to be friends."

"If I'm a robot, I am Data rocking an emotion chip," he corrected, shaking my hand.

"If that's you with emotion, you need to see if that chip is under warranty, because it seems a little weak."

His face got serious until he saw me laugh, and then he smiled back. "So what you got now?"

43

"An hour and then history."

"You wanna hang out in the quad until then?" he asked, sounding a little too eager.

I ignored the tone and nodded. "Sounds like a plan."

We bought a couple of drinks and found a place on the grass. "So how did you meet the supermodel?" he asked after a few minutes.

"Please don't let him hear you say that," I replied, smiling. "I would never hear the end of it. To answer your question, he asked me to help him with his history grades."

"Kinky," Teddy said, taking a drink. "I've seen that porno."

I coughed a little. "It wasn't like that; we just happened to connect."

"Connect above or below the belt?"

The smile slid off my face. "For your information, we didn't have sex until we were dating for almost three months."

He looked at me in disbelief. "You had that guy after you, and you waited three months before jumping his bones? You're braver than I thought."

"Nice quote, but for someone who claims everyone else is shallow, you sure do seem to fixate on people's looks."

Teddy shrugged. "And people who are starving fixate on what other people get to eat. It's the nature of the world."

It took me half a second to decipher his words. "So you think you aren't attractive, so you're obsessed about the way other people look? How does that work?"

"Easy, I'm not attractive," he said with all the finality of an SAT question.

Teddy is a gay black man. He would be considered:
A. Ugly
B. Fugly
C. Hideous
D. What does it matter? He's black.

"Why do you think that?" I asked, finishing my Pepsi.

"Years of observational data," he said, sounding more sad than bitter. "If you think being gay is bad, try being a minority in a minority and see how much fun it is. The only people who even give me a second's notice are the size queens who want to believe all black men have big dicks." He glanced over at me. "Do not ask."

I held my hands up in surrender. "I wasn't going to ask a thing."

"I run like a girl—no, that's not true, I know a ton of girls who run better than I do. I run like the spaz I am, sports bore the shit out of me, and being smart doesn't seem to be the milkshake that will bring the boys to my yard."

I chuckled at that, and he looked over and tried to look pissed but couldn't hold it. We both laughed for a few seconds and I asked, "Well, have you tried dressing less like Urkel?"

He pulled up a clump of grass and tossed it at me. "I'll have you know this is a carefully crafted ensemble that is worn less for attention and more for identification. I would hate for someone to think I am a normal person and not the raging geek I actually am."

"It's a defense mechanism that makes sure people won't find you attractive so at least you can blame your clothes rather than yourself." He stopped in his tracks. "I know. I had a hoodie back in high school that was bulletproof as well."

"And what happened?" Teddy asked.

I smiled and thought of Robbie and the box of clothes he'd dropped off at my doorstep and the hours and hours of arguing over how to dress properly. It had been like a gay version of *My Fair Lady* with Olivia Newton-John supplying the music.

"I had a friend pull me out from under my rock and show me there were better ways of presenting myself. You know, there's nothing stopping you from reinventing yourself. This *is* college."

"So what am I supposed to use this time for? Experiment with women?" He saw I wasn't going to allow him to deflect, and he sighed. "And what if, Mr. Foster Texas, I reinvent myself and people still aren't attracted to me?"

"There are two answers to that," I said, thinking it over. "The first, and the serious one, is that this isn't about making other people like you—it's about you learning to like you."

He motioned with his hands. "And the other, less Dear Abby one?"

"If you don't like it, then simply regenerate again."

He shook his head. "You did not just try to nerd me."

"I did and it worked."

He nodded. "It did at that. So where do we start?"

"Honestly? With the bow tie."

"Bow ties are cool!" he exclaimed, shocked.

"Maybe on Matt Smith, and maybe on special occasions, but for just another day at class, it's a little Darren Criss trying too hard."

"Ugh," he said, pulling the tie off. "You had to invoke the dreaded G word."

"In all fairness I didn't say the show that will not be named, just implied it."

"Bad enough," he said, stuffing it in his pocket. "What else?"

"How married to those nut huggers are you?"

"I'm really going to hate this, aren't I?"

I smiled and nodded. "Oh yeah."

Brad

IT WAS close to four by the time I was done for the day. The gym had cycled from the older guys who were there during school hours to younger guys in the afternoon. Some were getting off work and seemed to be rushing to get a workout in before five. Colt was still over in a corner talking some guy up; he had ignored me the rest of the day, which was fine with me.

"So we good?" I asked Todd as I tossed my towel into a bin.

"Better than good. We, my dear, are perfect. Those hags ate you up and are going to be drooling for more."

I didn't say anything, but I must have made a face.

"Look, sweetie, you have a body to die for, a face that most would kill for, and a dick that people would cut others for. Those skills have three professions that need them: personal trainer, bartender, and stripper. You seem to have way too much of an attitude to strip, you're too young to bartend, so that leaves this. Now you can get a shit-ton of cash for being pretty and letting old fags stare at you, or you can resist on principal and live bagging groceries. During which, by the way, people will still be staring at your ass, but you'll make less money. You're attractive and young. Get over it and enjoy the moment." He flung an imaginary lock of hair out of his face. "Trust me, I wish I had when I was your age."

"It's just...," I began to say.

He opened the register and pulled out two twenties and handed them to me. "Will this help?"

"It's not the money," I stammered.

He put another twenty on top. "It might not be about the money, but look at it this way. You can take your girlfriend out to dinner and fuck all the gay cooties out of your system."

I was about to tell him I was gay when Colt walked up to the counter. "So you finally off the clock?" he asked me.

"Yeah, just finished," I said, grabbing the bills and stuffing them into my gym bag.

"So look," he said slowly. "I know I came off like a jerk earlier. It's just I assumed you were gay and... well, that was stupid of me." I glanced over at him. "Look at you. No way you'd be gay. Anyway, I was wondering if you need a workout partner. I'm trying to get to the next level, and it's hard because most of the guys in here are just tourists and not here to really work out."

I resisted the urge to say he was, in fact, a tourist himself and instead just nodded. "Yeah, I understand."

"When do you plan on working out, like, for yourself?" he asked.

"I was planning on coming in before my shift."

Todd perked up. "Well then, that kills two birds with one cock." He slid a set of keys over to me. "You can come, open up, work out, get sweaty, and have the place open by nine, and I can stay home and get my beauty sleep."

Colt glanced over at Todd. "You could go into a coma and it wouldn't help you."

"I hope you get raped by wild dogs, you little shit."

Colt just gave him a grin. "Still better than having to do you and your friends."

"So I can come in early and just work out?" I asked, ignoring their insults.

"As long as the place is ready to go at nine, you can sleep here for all I care." Todd paused and leaned across the counter. "But if you're going to sleep here, let me know and I'll hook up some cameras."

"So if I meet you here around seven, we can work out?" Colt asked like I was offering free ice cream.

"I'll actually get here around six so I can get my cardio and abs out of the way at the same time."

"Watch out, Colt," Todd said snidely. "This one is going to out-jock you."

"I can be here at six," he said like it was an auction.

"Yeah, sure, I guess," I said, not certain what just happened.

"Perfect," Todd said, clapping his hands. "I get to go out tonight and party."

"See you at six, man," Colt said, smiling and walking away.

I didn't remember agreeing to anything.

Kyle

So I agreed to meet Teddy after class on Wednesday. We were going to go out shopping for a new image for him. I was pretty blown away; not only had I made a new friend, but I was going to be the one showing him how not to be a nerd, which was all new to me. I texted Robbie, who just sent, like, four texts of *Bwahahahahahaha* back at me until I told him to go fuck off. He sent me a fifth text saying he would call me later; he was in the middle of something.

I want to point out, whatever that something was, it hadn't stopped the first four texts of *Bwahahahahahaha*. I couldn't say my friends didn't have priorities.

When I got home, Brad was there, shirtless, on the couch. He was still in his stripper shorts, talking excitedly on the phone. He waved at me as I put my stuff away. Whatever he was describing, he was excited as he said it came out of nowhere and he was pretty sure it was a promotion. I changed my shirt as he finished his call; he looked over at me and said, "My mom says hi."

"Hi, Mrs. Graymark," I yelled back.

Brad listened for a second and then blushed a little. "Mom," he said in a low voice. "I am not going to tell him that."

"Tell me what?" I said eagerly, grabbing at his phone.

He pivoted away, but he was shirtless and vulnerable, which meant, by our own Geneva Conventions, tickle warfare was fair game. He yelped and tried to jump off the couch to escape, but I grabbed the edge of his shorts and held on. There was a ripping sound as the seam tore and... um... and the rest of Brad fell out. "*Kyle!*" he screamed, trying to cover himself and to keep talking on the phone at the same time.

I died. I mean literally ceased to draw breath I was laughing so hard.

"Mom, I'll call you back," he said quickly. "Nothing. Tell Dad I love him."

He hit End before she could ask another question.

"I cannot believe you ripped my shorts!" he complained, just before he realized that standing naked in front of me was nothing new. Instead he tore the rest of it off. I watched, enjoying the show.

"What did your mom say to tell me?" I asked, grinning.

"It wasn't worth ruining my shorts over," he pouted.

"Well, from the way those shorts gripped your junk, they were from, what? From tenth grade, easily? So they were due to be retired."

"I got those junior year, and they fit fine all day, for your information."

I opened my mouth to say something when the door opened quickly and Mrs. Phan took a half step. "Is everything okay? We heard a scream and—"

And she realized Brad had turned around in shock.

"Oh," she said, not averting her eyes at all from Brad's naked body. "Well, I see things here are... healthy. I am sorry." And she backed out of the room, eyes still plastered to Brad's body.

I fell off the couch, now crying from laughter.

"Oh my God! I just got eye-fucked by our landlady," Brad said, sounding like he was going to be sick.

"Least we know if things get tough, you can always just trade sex for rent," I said through gasping laughs.

"One of us has too many clothes on," he said, dropping on me, pinning my arms to the carpet.

49

"The door's unlocked," I said, feeling his body press against mine.

"Well, let's start working on that free month of rent."

There was something completely liberating about having sex in the living room in the middle of the afternoon with the front door unlocked. No parents to come rushing in, no distractions, just him and me and our ever-present need for each other. No matter how often we had sex—and so far it had been at least twice a day, once in the morning before our shower and again after the lights went out to make sure we drifted off—there was always a hunger for more. In fact, Saturday night we fucked for, like, two hours. I almost passed out for an hour or so, and when I got up to go to the bathroom and saw him sleeping nude… I wanted him again.

Thankfully when I woke him up, he wanted it too.

Even now, tired, hungry, and badly wanting to rinse off the day's sweat, all I could think of was hearing him moan in ecstasy with me. Since we were our only sexual partners, we hadn't been using condoms, which was kind of a good thing because I'm pretty sure by now we would have gone through at least a box, if not more. We had become aware of what each other enjoyed early on, but these last few days, without the distraction of getting caught or interrupted, we had really explored those depths, and I knew exactly how to make him go crazy.

I knew when he was close from the way he panted my name, the way his legs would tighten around my waist, the look on his face as he clenched his eyes shut and bit his bottom lip to keep from screaming. Watching him explode was almost as pleasurable as getting him there, and no matter how far away I might have been before he climaxed, I always followed within seconds.

Today was different, though.

He was way into it, most likely a reflection of his good news, whatever it might be. He was also still pumped up from his day at the gym, and the way the setting sun shone on his sweaty muscles made him look like a freaking god. He had me sitting on the floor, my back against the couch as he faced me, pretty much doing all the work while I watched him grunt. Once he found the perfect angle, I heard him call out to God and throw his head back in delirious pleasure. I could see the freckles on his shoulders from summer after summer under the hot Texas sun and wanted badly to taste them. The only sound was the slapping of our flesh and the jingle of his necklace as it slid from pec to pec when he moved up and down.

Normally I wouldn't go into such detail, but I have a purpose.

In the middle of all this, I was struck by how incredibly beautiful he was, and it was surprising. I mean, I knew Brad was hot, sure, but for the past year the things inside were so powerful to me that I had honestly stopped looking at the outside. But Teddy's words had gotten under my skin, so I looked at him and realized Teddy was dead wrong, because if I focused on exactly how stunning he was, I could have spent all my time wondering how long it would take for him to dump me. I reached up and grabbed his face and pulled him closer and kissed him. How this... perfect person had chosen me to be with I would never know, but I did know I wasn't going to waste a second with him.

Because there was no way this was going to last.

Kyle

OH, STOP it.

Let me guess, typical Kyle, always thinking the worst, right? Well, a couple of things. One, I'm in this airport alone, aren't I? Two, what happened? He ended up meeting more of his own kind, and what did he do? I know I'm not there yet, but goddammit... I hate being right.

Brad

SO ONE second I was on the phone with my mom, telling her that I got a job and I was almost the opening manager, and the next I was naked on the floor with Kyle.

I wish there was a way I could show you what he looks like when he forgets who he thinks he's supposed to be and just goes with it. The way his eyes become piercing and full of passion, the way he doesn't slump his shoulders forward because he thinks being tall just makes him stand out. The firmness in his hands as he grips my waist and pulls me down to him… I mean, it's like he's a whole other person.

To me he's the guy I'm head over heels in love with.

I'm just saying, if you think you know Kyle, you don't know shit until you see him fuck. I just wish he could be this guy all the time: confident, aggressive, taking charge and not afraid to hurt someone. He spent so much time being afraid of being noticed that his first instinct is to just shrink down and be quiet… except when we're having sex. Only then does he give himself permission to take the kid gloves off and go for it.

And it drives me crazy.

I mean, sure, I act it up a bit because I know he loves watching me react, and that's cool 'cause I love the way he watches me squirm, but frankly the boy is amazing in bed, and I don't think he knows it.

When we were finished, we both needed a shower, which of course led to a little rubbing and some more kissing, which might have led to another round if I hadn't said, "So I got keys to the gym."

And he gave me a weird look.

"On your first day?"

"Well, kinda my second." I replied quickly.

"They gave you keys to unlock the place by yourself on the second day?" He pulled away from me a little.

"Um, yeah. Why?"

"You don't think that's weird?" he asked, the water rolling down our bodies in no way making him look any less pissed.

"No, why should it?"

"Because he doesn't know you from Adam. What if you're a criminal or a crackhead and just take everything? Why would he trust you so quickly?"

Crackhead?

"Maybe he can tell I'm trustworthy," I said a little defensively.

He scoffed and turned the water off. "Right."

"What's that mean?" I asked as he got out of the shower.

"Nothing," he said from under the towel.

I grabbed one and began to dry off. "Nothing my ass. You have something to say, come out with it, Stilleno."

He paused and looked back at me. "He gave you keys because he could look into your soul and tell you were a good person. Not because you were wearing shorts so tight he could tell if you were cut or not."

"Oh, I forgot," I called after him as he walked out of the bathroom. "Because God forbid Brad get anything based on merit. Anything I get has to be 'cause of my looks, right? You know, I was in a great mood before you got home."

"Well, I'm sorry to point out the old gay guy who saw you on the street and hired you might be trying to get into your pants. Or shorts. Or whatever you wear tomorrow to show off your body."

"We're back to this?" I asked him. "You want to leave another hickey? Maybe you could spell out your initials so they know who I belong to." I pulled on my jeans, not even bothering to look for underwear.

"If I got a job where they told me to wear something tight and revealing, you'd lose your mind."

"If you got a job, I'd have set off fireworks to celebrate. You know why? 'Cause I'd be happy for you instead of so jealous that I'd make sure to spoil the moment for you." I tossed a shirt on and slipped into my sneakers. "I was really happy, Kyle, and you ruined that."

"Where are you going?" he asked as I walked toward the door.

"Out. To celebrate in peace." I slammed the door.

No idea where I was going, but I wasn't staying there.

Kyle

SO LET me guess. I should have run after him? I should have thrown myself down at his feet and begged him to forgive me? Because that's what guys like me do to keep guys like him, right? You know as well as I do that there is no earthly reason for someone to give a guy they literally met off the street keys to their place.

And before you bring up Tyler, Foster is a small town and he literally knew exactly where Brad lived, so that doesn't count.

See, this is the same problem, just dressed up as a different thing. Brad has always been desperate for people to like him, even if he didn't give a rat's ass about them. It was like the only validation he could get about himself was from other people. So to him it wasn't creepy or inappropriate for some old gay guy to give him that much attention; it was a good thing and meant Brad was desirable.

And don't even get me started about Colt.

When I explain what comes next, it's going to look like I chased Brad away and into Colt's arms, but I assure you… that was where this was ending up anyway.

Kyle

A VOICE in the back of my head screamed that I should go after him.

A louder voice asked, why doesn't he just turn around?

I can't deny that I wanted to rush after him, but I wasn't wrong and he knew it. Who the hell just sees someone on the street and offers them a job? I mean, Brad isn't fucking Lana Turner. The guy wanted into Brad's pants. Hell, I can't imagine the line to get into Brad's pants wasn't legendary. And how long would it be before the millionth muscle guy hit on Brad and he finally realized he could be with another hot guy?

I slumped back onto the couch and thought about calling Brad and telling him to come home. When the phone lit up telling me Robbie was calling, I almost threw the thing across the room. Instead I took a deep breath and answered. "Hey."

There was maybe a second's pause and he asked, "What's wrong?"

"Why does something have to be wrong?" I asked, hating that he could know there was a problem from one syllable.

"You want to go three rounds about why I'm asking what's wrong, or you want to just come out and tell me?"

Sighing, I began to explain the whole gym thing to him.

"Oh," he said when I got to the end.

"Oh?" I asked. "Just oh?"

WHEN I GROW UP

"Well, I don't know if you're in a place to hear what comes after the oh."

"How am I wrong?" I asked, anger creeping into my voice. "You know the guy who owns the gym is just cruising him."

"Yeah, but that's not what you're upset about," he countered.

"Yes it is."

"No it's not."

He sounded so fucking sure, I got madder.

"Well then, oh wise one, tell me why I'm actually upset."

"Okay, oh whining brat of little patience. You're upset 'cause you're threatened by the fact other people are finding your guy attractive. You're imagining him at a gym with strangers hitting on him, and you can't do a thing about it."

I said nothing in response.

"See, in Foster you were safe. There were no other gay guys except Tyler, and God knows he doesn't like his chicken still in the egg. Now you're out in the big, bad world and you think Brad is going to realize he's dating an overbearing control freak who thinks too much and has come to the highly *intelligent* decision that Brad is going to leave him."

My eyes were actually stinging from his words.

"Now here's the good news. Moose isn't that stupid; he knows you're an overbearing control freak, and against all odds he loves you for it. This has so little to do with Brad and so much to do with you, and I should know because I did the same thing."

"You did?" I asked, wiping my eyes.

"Fuck yeah," he said, laughing. "When we got to Foster, I spent the first few weeks there just waiting to be dumped by Riley."

"Why?"

"Why?" he scoffed. "Look, you might not be aware of it, but the guys that come from Foster are ridiculously hot. No, not all of them, but when people like me stand next to people like Tyler, people like me tend to get forgotten, and I got paranoid about it."

"What did you do?" I was shocked to hear a new story from Robbie.

"Riley got fed up and called me on it. He told me that if he wanted to date Tyler or someone like him, then he would have, but he didn't. He

55

fell in love with me and I needed to accept that fact, because it wasn't other guys who were going to cause us to break up. It was going to be my issues."

That sounded exactly like what was going on with me.

"But I'm right about the gym," I pointed out weakly.

"Look, Pinocchio, you have a choice. You can be happy, or you can be right, but in this case you can't be both. So what if the guys at the gym drool over Brad? You've seen him naked, they haven't. You're going to have to trust that he loves you as much as you love him and let the rest of the drama go."

"Easier said than done," I muttered.

"Easier said with a couple of glasses of wine." He didn't say much for a few seconds, and then I could hear him sigh. "Look, Kyle, being with someone isn't about being right all the time. It isn't talking about every single little thing the other person does that bugs you, and it isn't about keeping score. Brad does things that bug you. You do things that bug Brad. What you need to ask yourself is if you love him enough to put up with that aggravation. If you have to think about the answer to that, then you're in a relationship with the wrong guy."

"What if he leaves me?" I asked, my voice cracking.

"Do you think Brad would ever leave you?"

The million voices in my head all screamed different things, but my heart said no.

"Then get off the phone with me and go get your man back," Robbie ordered. "You cannot leave a boy that hot and that clueless to wander around a big city for long. Someone will come by and offer him candy or something, and then you're fucked."

I smiled, and I could feel the storm clouds fade from my mind. "Are you okay?"

"*Go!*" he screamed through the phone and hung up.

I threw my shoes on and ran for the front door.

When I opened it, he was standing there looking miserable.

"I don't want to—"

"I'm an idiot," I said, pulling him inside. "I'm sorry." I kissed him. "I'm sorry." I kissed him and slammed the door. "I'm sorry."

His arms moved around me. "I'll quit the job if you want me to."

God, did I want him to quit that job.

"I'm crazy," I said. "And you knew that when you decided to leave town with me. So please, ignore most of what comes out of my mouth as just that. Crazy."

"I don't want to do something that's going to upset you." His eyes were so wide, he looked terrified.

"You won't," I said, kissing him. "I trust you."

I should have told him to quit the fucking job.

Brad

AFTER A bout of crying, some dinner, and another round of sex, we finally went to bed.

I lay there staring up at the ceiling as Kyle drifted off to sleep. What was happening to us? One second we were perfect, and the next, it was like we were two cats thrown into a pillowcase. I was still hurt by the fact he didn't think I could earn the responsibility to open the gym, but I let it go because there was no point to arguing anymore. I used to know how to make him happy; now I wasn't even sure how to make it through the day with him.

For the first time since I'd kissed him, I wondered if I had made a mistake falling in love with Kyle.

Kyle

WHEN I woke up, Brad was gone.

There was a flash of panic as my first thought was he had finally left me. Not even a month, and I had succeeded in driving him away. That had to be a world record somewhere. As I got up, my mind kicked into gear and I remembered he was opening the gym today.

And my panic morphed into guilt just like that.

Robbie was right. I was a possessive asshole, and I needed to either trust Brad or just break up with him. Punishing him for imagined slights was unfair to everyone. I took a quick shower and threw on some clothes before heading out. I stopped by a deli and grabbed two bagels and headed over to where he'd said the gym was. I couldn't erase my mistake from yesterday, but I could at least try to make it better.

It was a little bit of a walk, and I was frustrated by the fact Brad jogged there and back every day like it was nothing. It was easy to find the gym since it was adorned with a huge rainbow decal and silhouettes of muscle men on every window. If it wasn't a gay gym, then it was a gym that was dealing with its sexual identity in a big, bad way. I crossed the street and caught a glimpse of Brad in the window….

Talking to a fucking model.

This guy made Josh Walker with his perfect skin and no body fat look like a burn victim. He had a chest you could park an aircraft carrier on and his arms looked like he was a He-Man figure come to life. He and Brad were laughing like they were old friends, and I felt my stomach plummet. Every single fear I had ever dreamed up manifested into reality right in front of me. This was the guy Brad should have ended up with; this was the mate the world at large would assume he would gravitate toward. They were both sweaty, looking like they had just finished having crazy monkey sex and were now doing a few reps on the bench press to keep up appearances.

I resisted the urge to barge in there and yell, "Aha!" because I had nothing to aha except my own paranoid delusions. But watching him stand there, shooting the shit with another of his kind….

Just reminded me of everything I wasn't.

I tossed the bagels in the trash and walked home before I was late for class.

Brad

SO COLT was there bright and early at six o'clock, waiting like a puppy that had been left outside overnight. A puppy that was pumped with steroids and had been waxed smooth, wearing a tank top that barely counted as a shirt, but a puppy nonetheless. I had opted for a pair of basketball shorts that weren't as tight as the ones Kyle had torn but were comfortable enough for me to move around in for the day.

"What happened to the sausage factory?" Colt asked as I unlocked the door. I looked over at him in confusion and he added. "It was what we were calling your shorts yesterday. Dude, no joke. You have a great cock."

I sighed and pushed the door open. I had been there less than a minute and my junk had already been brought up. It was going to be one of those days. Colt followed as I turned on all the lights and switched the TVs on. I made sure the door was locked again and the sign said Closed facing out. I wanted to work out in peace—well, as much peace as I could with Colt there.

"So I'm going to run for about forty minutes and then start on my chest," I said, not waiting to see if he was going to agree or not. "Not sure what you're going to work on, but the gym is yours."

"I'll run," he said, putting his gym bag down. "I drank too much last night. Might be good to burn the alcohol out of my system."

I shrugged and slipped my earbuds in as I turned on one of the treadmills. I saw out of the corner of my eye Colt taking the one next to me; he seemed to be watching what I was entering carefully. "You always do that steep an incline?" he asked when I was done.

"Yep," I said, turning on my music. "Helps build my calves."

He paused and looked at my legs for a second. "They are nice."

Sighing, I stopped the treadmill and turned off my music. "Okay, look, man. You said you wanted to really work out. Not make cracks about my dick and my legs. If this is just some lame attempt to chat me up, you're wasting your time."

His eyes went wide and he stared at me for a long second.

"No! I was serious, man," he said, recovering quickly. "I mean, yeah, you're gorgeous, but I work as a bartender and the better I look, the better my tips. Also I want to try stripping at some point, so I really need something to get me to the next level. Looking at you, you're already there, so this isn't me trying to come on to you. Promise."

I wanted to say more, but honestly, this was just left over from last night's fight with Kyle, so I dropped it. Instead I nodded and turned the treadmill back on. We jogged in silence for a few minutes, our bodies adjusting to the pace.

"Bad night last night?" he asked once we got into a groove.

"Kinda," I said, not wanting to say anything but badly needing to talk to someone about it.

"Girl problems?" he asked, and I said nothing. "Boy problems." I gave him a sideways look, and his mouth fell open. "I knew it...," he began to say but then vanished from view. I heard a loud crash as he tripped, hit the treadmill face-first, and went flying off the machine.

"Holy shit!" I cried, turning my machine off to help him up. "Are you okay?"

"I knew it," Colt said, shaking his head slowly. "I knew you were at least bi."

"Dude, didn't that hurt?" I helped him to his feet.

"Yeah, but fuck that. You're what? Bi?"

"Gay," I said and saw the smile start to come to his face. "But in a relationship," I blurted out quickly.

"Holy shit," he said, looking me up and down again. "You're gay? Damn, I thought I was the only one."

"Only gay guy?" I asked, confused.

"Only gay jock," he amended.

"You have to play a sport to be a jock, man," I pointed out. "Not just a gym bunny."

"I play softball!" he protested.

"You do?" I asked, my interest piqued.

"Yeah, there's a gay league here. You play?"

"I was offered a full ride to A&M and turned it down," I said with more than a little pride.

"Oh snap, why?"

"Because they wanted me to hide being gay. So I told them to fuck off." I got up on the treadmill and began running again.

"If it's that important, then why not tell Todd?"

I paused and looked back at him, realizing I didn't have an answer.

"It's cool, man. I tend bar at a gay club up in Walnut Creek, and I tell most of the guys I'm straight. They tip like a mofo trying to get into my pants, so I get where you're coming from. These old fags will do anything for a chance at a straight-looking guy like you."

"I just don't want to explain to every single person I meet I have a boyfriend and that I'm not interested. Easier for them to think I'm straight and leave me alone."

"You mean Todd."

"I mean a lot of people. You included," I pointed out.

"Fair enough," he said, nodding. "You're taken. I get it."

"Good." I began to jog again.

We said nothing for the next forty minutes as we worked up a sweat.

When I got off my machine, he stumbled off his too. He was breathing hard and his face was red as a beet. "Dude, don't you do cardio?"

"Not"—he gasped—"for forty"—another gasp—"minutes uphill"—hands on his knees as he tried to take a deep breath—"after drinking."

"Well that's how you get to the next level," I told him as I headed out toward the weights. He followed, gulping down an entire bottle of water. Which, if he wasn't careful, he was going to hurl during his first set.

I put a towel down on one of the press benches and grabbed a couple of forty-five-pound plates. Colt leaned against one of the machines and tried to catch his breath. "So let me see him," he asked me after a few minutes. I glanced over at him, and he added, "Your guy. Let me see a pic."

I unlocked my phone and pulled up my photos, most of which were of Kyle.

"Oh," he said scrolling through the pics. "He's cute. Kinda small and skinny, though, isn't he?"

"What's wrong with skinny?" I asked, my voice almost dropping to a growl.

"Nothing," he said, closing my phone. "Just not who I'd expect you to be with, that's all."

My common sense told me to drop the subject and not engage, but honestly. In all the time you've known me, have I ever used my common sense?

"And who am I supposed to be with?"

Colt shrugged and tossed the empty water bottle away. "Someone more like you, I guess. Beefier, jockish. I mean, he's cute in a skater way and all, but he doesn't look like he works out."

"He doesn't. What does that matter?"

"He into baseball?" I shook my head. "Any sports?" Another shake. "He ever date girls?"

"Why do you assume I dated girls?"

He laughed and sat down on another bench. "Because guys like us spend most of high school hiding the fact we like guys because people will freak. Did anyone know about you guys dating, or was it on the DL?"

"We came out the middle of senior year." Something about all Colt's questions bugged me.

"Wow, really? Like as in to the whole school?" I nodded. "Dude, was that your idea?"

"Yeah, it was," I said, thinking it over a second. "He was getting bullied, and I liked him, so I told everyone I was into guys too so they'd lay off him."

He stared at me for a few seconds and then shook his head, grinning. "So you aren't just built like a superhero, but you are one as well?"

I was a superhero? No, that was Kyle. I was....

What was I?

"Anyway, I'm glad you guys are happy." He didn't sound happy, but what was the point in me bringing it up? Something was hinky, and I couldn't figure it out.

"When did you come out?" I asked him as I lay back on the bench.

"I guess I haven't yet. I mean, my parents don't know, but they live in Wyoming, so they'll never understand. I don't talk to any of my old friends anymore. When I moved out here, I just reinvented myself and said fuck it."

"So you're a bartender now?"

He nodded. "Yeah, stupid good tips and great hours. Hey, you know, they're looking for a barback; you grab ice and boxes for us, and we give you a cut of the tips. Also, not a bad place to meet some hotties."

"Dude, I just said I was seeing someone."

"Yeah, but you're young, man. Don't want to limit your options."

"You ready to work out or what?" I asked him, and I knew I sounded done with all the questions.

"Sure," he said, getting up. "What you putting up?"

"I'm just doing some warm-ups, then I'll put some real weight on," I explained as I lifted the bar off the rack.

Colt stood over me, watching me intently as I did some warm-up reps. "You have an amazing chest, dude." I paused and stared at him, making no attempt to hide the fact that I was more than done with his attitude. He added quickly, "Not hitting on you, I swear. That was jealousy."

I chuckled and finished my reps.

"So is this guy your first boyfriend?" Colt asked as he lay down on the bench.

"Yeah," I said a little defensively.

"Hey, no judgment," he added quickly. "Probably better than the way I did it."

"Did what?"

"Come out. Be gay. Be a grown-up." He saw the confusion in my eyes. "Sex, dude. When I realized I could have sex with whoever I wanted, I probably did it wrong."

He lifted the bar up and I asked, "What did you do?"

"You ever heard of a scavenger hunt?" I nodded. "Well, instead of finding random things, I just fucked random guys. You're tall? Check. You're short? Check. You're tan? Check."

I started laughing, and he put the bar back up.

"I mean it, man. I slept with more men than are named in the Bible. Old and New Testament."

I was busting out laughing.

"See, I'm going to like you," he said, laughing with me. "You think that was my line instead of me quoting a movie."

"What movie?" I asked.

"No movie. I'm just that fucking funny," he said smugly, which just made me laugh even more.

"So anyway, man, you want to know what it's like to sleep with a certain type of guy, I have hard data on it. Some of them even twice."

"I've never heard someone so proud to be a slut before," I said, wiping my eyes.

He shrugged. "Who cares? I'm twenty-two, hot, built like a Mack truck, hung like a mule, and don't care who knows it. Why should I give a fuck what other people think?"

"You ever have a boyfriend?"

His face soured a little. "Tried; it never took with me. 'Sides, the type of guys I like never want to date."

"What type of guys?"

He looked me dead in my eyes. "Like you."

And just like that, I stopped laughing. And I realized what the hinky feeling was. It was my mind knowing that Colt wasn't going to give up until I flattened him.

"We should get to the reps," I said, ignoring the uncomfortable silence.

"Sure," he said, lying back down.

Kyle

WHEN I got to school, I went full-on Vulcan.

To those who are geek impaired, let me explain. Vulcans are an alien race from *Star Trek*, and though they possess the same range of emotions the rest of us do, they have spent countless centuries mastering the art of not letting emotions affect their judgment. It is a society built on logic and science and spending a lot of time ignoring whatever might be bothering you deep down.

I was a Vulcan from way back.

My mom would get drunk and scream at me? Vulcan that shit and refuse to shed one tear over it. Some asshole my mom was sleeping with came in to discipline me? Vulcanized as I just stared at the far wall and tried to ignore what was happening to me. Watch people all around me having a real life while I stood there like a homeless person watching through a restaurant window while people feasted? Vulcan a persona that was nearly invisible when compared to the screaming masses of teenagers around me. Warning, though—not guaranteed to work against green-eyed boys.

So I was miserable, pretty sure I had just seen the guy Brad was going to break up with me for, and I had absolutely no idea what to do. I was a Vulcan, which meant I had to lock that crap down and move on with my day. I'd have time later to fall apart; now was not that time. Please God, don't let now be that time.

Teddy was waiting outside of Professor Madison's room.

"Dude, you're going to be late," he warned, opening the door for me.

"There's still five minutes before the bell rings," I said, moving past him.

"Um, yeah," he said, following me down the steps. "But you're usually here earlier to set up your laptop and stuff."

I found a seat and started pulling my stuff out. "Since the first five minutes of class is wasted on taking roll and passing up our homework, I have more than enough time."

He sat down next to me and stared. "What's wrong?"

I looked at him, making sure my expression was as blank as a new canvas. "Nothing is wrong."

His voice dropped to a whisper. "Did you and your guy get into it? 'Cause you look upset."

"I don't look anything," I replied, hoping he would drop it.

"Yeah, 'cause hiding outrage and pain is a skill only you have mastered. Come on, man, you can talk to me."

"Nothing is wrong," I said again, my tone flat and apathetic.

He stared for a few seconds and then sighed. "Okay, I'll back off. But if you need to talk, I'm right here."

He began unpacking his stuff in silence. It was obvious he was a little put off by my attitude. Who was I going to talk to? If I called Robbie, he'd say I was stupid and that all I'd seen was Brad talking with another guy. I could try to call Jennifer, but what was she going to do from Texas? Teddy was the closest thing I had to a friend, and if I didn't start trusting him, he might not even be that.

"So Brad got a job at a gym," I said after a few minutes. He looked over at me and nodded. "And... I went by to surprise him...."

"And you saw him what? Making out or talking to a hot-ass guy," Teddy answered for me.

"Talking. How did you know?" I asked, shocked.

"Because that's what perfect people do—they find other perfect people. It's like some weird form of social magnetism. Not that you aren't stupid cute. I'm just saying anyone who looks like your guy could get anyone he wants. Lemme guess, Foster is a tiny town and there were no other gay people?"

I nodded.

"Well, now he's in a bigger pond. There are more guys to choose from, and working at a gym? A lot of in-shape, hot guys to choose from. I'm not saying your guy will cheat on you, but every time I've heard this story, it ends badly for people like us."

"You don't think I'm being paranoid?"

He chuckled. "It's not paranoia if the thing you're afraid of happens all the time. You think people who are afraid of heights are paranoid? Fuck no, they're afraid of falling to their deaths. Do I think a gay guy is paranoid to worry about his fine-ass boyfriend cheating on him? Again, no, because it happens more than it doesn't."

"Well, you cheered me right up there," I said bitterly.

"Wasn't trying to cheer you up, just trying to keep it real. You need to look out for yourself, man. You don't have time to worry about this shit. This is freshman year. If you stumble now, you may never find your stride again. You want my advice? Throw yourself into school and let your love life work itself out. If he's the guy you say he is, then he won't cheat on you. If he's like every other guy in existence, then at least you know and can move on with your life. But stopping and worrying about it? That's a formula for failure."

There was a binary logic to what he was saying. Either Brad would dump me or he wouldn't, and worrying about it wouldn't change that outcome. All worrying would do was take me away from my studies and my goal of making a life for myself. It was the most logical advice anyone had ever given me.

"Thanks," I said, genuinely touched. "I needed to hear that."

He smiled. "No problem. Remember I'm here if you need someone, man."

I took a deep breath and put Brad on the back burner. This was the rest of my life, and I wasn't missing any more of it.

Kyle

SO CAN you guess how the next month went?

Yeah, about that good.

Brad

SO AS the days went on, my life became better and worse at the same time. It was weird—I wasn't used to having things I liked so separated—but that seemed to be the way Kyle wanted it. I went to a month and a half of classes and ended up getting my personal trainer license, something I was pretty proud of, to be honest. Kyle seemed happy about it, but like everything else lately, it seemed distant.

I joined Colt's softball team and found a whole new level of love for the game.

These guys weren't playing for a school or a scholarship; they were playing because they wanted to, and that was awesome. Colt's team was called the Oakland Gays, which was funny in its own way, and I became their second baseman. Kyle didn't come to the games because of school, but he always listened when I got home and explained how the game went. There were some decent players on the other teams, but honestly no one that was on my level. That was a fact I tried to keep from going to my head, but I had to admit, I liked being the best guy in the league.

Kyle spent more and more time at school, studying, researching, basically being Kyle, which left me with a lot of spare time. Working at the gym and playing softball helped, but I missed him pretty awful. It was during that time that we stopped having sex. Well, we stopped doing anything intimate, if I'm being honest. He was always tired or asleep by the time I got home. On the weekends I tried to get him to go do stuff, but he always seemed to be bored or just distracted, which made me even sadder.

I wasn't going to say anything to him, though, because I knew what school meant to him, and just because I was lonely wasn't a reason to upset his schedule.

It didn't stop me from complaining to Jennifer, though.

"So where is he now?"

I shifted on the couch as I scrolled through Netflix looking for something to watch. "Library," I answered, trying not to sound like a little bitch.

"It's like, what? Ten over there? Who stays at a library this late?"

"Have you met Kyle?" I said, turning on Ken Burns' baseball series. "He's there every day this late."

"But it's Friday," she said, like that was supposed to mean something to Kyle.

"Tell me about it. I ordered pizza and everything, and he texted me he was going to eat there."

She was silent for a couple of seconds, which was Jennifer for "Here comes some truth you won't like."

"Brad, you need to talk to him."

"Nope," I said instantly. "This is his dream. I'm not going to screw it up."

"What about your dreams?" she asked. "What about your life?"

"I wanted to be with him," I said, trying not to feel like I had wished for the wrong thing. "This is my dream."

"Sitting home alone on a Friday night talking to your ex-girlfriend? Dude, you need better dreams."

I was about to disagree with her when my phone beeped. I looked down hoping it was Kyle, but instead it was Colt. "Hold on a sec," I said, clicking over to the other line. "What's up, man?"

I could hear the muted sound of a club behind him. "Brad!" he screamed, making it pretty clear he was drunk. "Where are you?"

"I'm at home," I said, wondering if I'd ever called anyone when I was like that.

"Come out!" he whined. "It's insane tonight! You don't want to miss this."

"I'm waiting for Kyle to get home," I said, hoping I didn't sound like a housewife from a bad sitcom.

"Bring him!" he screamed. "It'll be fun."

"I'll ask him when he gets in," I assured him.

"Call me back!" he screamed yet again.

"Okay, man, I will." I went back to Jennifer. "Sorry."

"Kyle?" she asked.

"I wish. Just a guy on my softball team."

"Calling you on a Friday night? Hmm...."

"Hey, Veronica Mars," I snapped. "He knows I'm dating someone seriously. He was asking *both* of us to go out." It was kind of a lie, but she didn't need to know that.

"Just saying, guys calling you on a Friday night is not platonic."

"Where's Josh?" I asked, trying to change the subject.

"He and Tony Wright went fishing this weekend."

"Fishing or Brokeback fishing?"

"Fuck you." She laughed.

"Just saying, Josh is *way* too comfortable with his sexuality."

"Josh is fine with his sexuality, trust me. I've already dated a gay guy, and I know the difference now."

"That sounds a lot like you're saying Josh is better in bed than me."

"I am, but you can always use the excuse I wasn't your type, and stop trying to change the subject. You need to talk to Kyle."

Sighing, I shook my head. "Okay, this was a mistake. I'm gonna go, Jennifer."

"It wasn't a mistake and you know I'm right."

"Bye."

"Talk to...."

—click—

I turned Netflix back on and waited for Kyle to get home.

And tried not to think about how much fun it sounded like Colt was having.

Kyle

I GOT in around 10:30 and found him lying on the couch watching TV.

"Hey, you," he said, not even looking up.

"Hey," I said, putting my bag up. "What's up?"

"A lot of nothing." He sounded bored as hell. "You wanna come lay down with me?"

"I need to change," I said, deflecting the question. I'd felt so cut off from him lately I couldn't even bring myself to fool around with him. If I kissed him, all I could think about was how many kisses were left? Was he kissing that other guy? Did he want to kiss him? I trusted Brad with my life, but lately not with my heart.

"You tired?" he asked as I threw on a new shirt.

"Not really," I said, hoping that wasn't a lead-in to, "Let's go to bed."

"Really?" he asked, sitting up. "You wanna do something?"

"Like?" I asked cautiously.

"Anything," he said, standing. "We could… go out, maybe see if there are any midnight movies playing? Um… anything."

"Do you have a particular anything in mind?" I asked.

"Um…. Colt asked if we wanted to come down to the club he works at."

And the other shoe dropped.

"Colt? The guy on your softball team?" He nodded. "The guy you work out with?" Another nod. "The guy you spend all your time with asked *us* to go out, or you?"

He looked honestly shocked by my tone of voice. "What's that mean?"

"It means what it means, Brad. Did he ask us or ask you?"

"He asked us," he said, getting angry. "And whose fault is it I spend all my time with him?"

I felt a wave of shame pass through me but shook it off as I asked again, "Asked us or you?"

"What does it matter?" he raged. "What are you implying?"

"I didn't imply anything," I half lied. "I just stated a few facts and asked a question. You're the one who's getting mad."

The look on his face was one I had never seen before. It was half hurt, half anger; I wondered if this was the first time I had ever seen him truly angry. "You know I've tried. I have kept my mouth shut, found other things to do, all because this was what you wanted. But you come in here and accuse me of what? Cheating? Wanting to cheat? I'm confused, Kyle. What exactly are you accusing me of?"

Now I was pissed. "So this is my fault?" I demanded. "It's my fault you're spending all your time with some musclebound model?"

"He's not a model."

"Right, the perfectly tousled blond hair and insanely toned body are for serving drinks."

Brad paused and his eyes narrowed. "How do you know what he looks like?"

"I don't," I said way too quickly.

"Seriously?" he practically screamed. "You can find time to come spy on me, but you can't actually stop and say hello or something." He looked like he was going to say something more but then just shook his head. "Fuck this." He pulled on his shoes. "You know what, Kyle? I have no idea what the fuck is wrong with you, but right now, I don't care." He stood up and picked up his keys off the table. "I told you that day by the lake that I was here until you told me to leave and I meant it. I still mean it. But if you want me to leave, be a fucking man and just tell me to leave. Because this shutting me out thing, it's just mean."

"Where are you going?" I asked as he headed toward the door.

"Why do you care?" he asked and slammed it after him.

He was coming back; he always came back. He would walk around the block or whatever, cool off, and then come back, and we could really talk about this.

Five minutes passed.

He was coming back. I knew it.

Ten minutes.

He always came back.

Fifteen, and I opened the door and looked down in the alley.

His car was gone.

He wasn't coming back this time.

Brad

I CALLED Colt and got the name of the club where he worked. I followed Google's directions until I reached the Foothills in Walnut Creek. A lone road led upward, and I could see lights flashing from somewhere on the top of the hill. I drove up, not sure what to expect. A parking guy stopped me and gestured for me to roll down my window.

"Parking's ten bucks and…." He paused and actually looked at me. "You know this is a gay club?" I nodded. "Okay, then. There are some spots in the back."

"Ten?" I asked, moving for my wallet.

"Sweetie, trust me. You aren't going to pay for a thing tonight." He grinned and waved me in. I rolled up my windows and found a spot in the back. The lot was lousy with cars; the club had to be packed. I was about to get out when I took a glance at myself in the mirror. I looked like shit; my clothes were destroyed like I had slept in them, mostly because about an hour ago I had been. I didn't have any product in my hair, and I looked miserable.

I needed something to improve all that.

Popping the trunk, I got out and started digging through the box of stuff I hadn't unpacked yet. All my sports stuff, trophies, uniforms— everything was in that box. I'd kept putting off bringing it upstairs because there was no real room in the apartment for it, and I wasn't sure if Kyle wanted me to put it up. I grabbed my Foster High cap and found my letterman jacket folded up at the bottom. I slipped it on and felt a thrill go through me.

This was how I used to dress to go out on Fridays before I met Kyle. I pulled my boxer briefs up a little so the waist was showing over the top of my jeans, made sure the cap was on just right so you could see my eyes under the bill. Jennifer used to call it my jock camouflage.

I called it my suit of armor.

A small line straggled along the front of the club, and I waited to get in. When I got as far as the doorman, he paused and looked me up and down. I made sure not to smile. "You have got to be kidding," he said rolling his eyes. "Do you know what kind of club this is?" I nodded. "And you want me to let you in why? So you can drag one of my friends in the back and beat the shit out of him? Bitch, please."

"I'm meeting a friend here," I tried to assure him.

"Does your friend know what kind of club this is?"

"His name is Colt; he works here."

And just like that, the attitude vanished. "Oh, you're one of Colt's boys. Goddamn, I wish I knew where he finds you all." He gestured to the door. "Well, go on, before they start coming out here to cruise you."

"Cover?"

He just laughed and waved me through.

This could be fun.

The music was deafening, but it was upbeat and frantic and I could feel my heart start to beat faster just hearing it. The people around me took a couple of steps back, some in shock, a couple in fear, most with lewd smiles on their faces. I doubt anyone dressed like me had walked in here before; everyone had on tight shirts, if they were wearing them at all, leather pants or shorts, and a lot of body glitter.

A space cleared around me as I walked through the place, half looking for Colt, half just taking it in. I wasn't a fan, but I can't deny that the attention was making me feel good. These weren't old guys like at the gym. They were young—well, older than me, but younger than thirty. Most were in good shape; the ones who weren't were skinny as hell and looked like they needed a sandwich in a bad way. No one was dressed normal, no one was acting normal, they were all... so....

Gay.

Yeah, yeah, get off my back, I know what I am, but I'm not this. Not that this was bad. It just wasn't me at all. I was starting to think coming here was a mistake when someone grabbed my arm and pulled me around. My other hand curled into a fist, a reflex from being weirded out, not a sign of attack.

"Whoa, slugger," Colt said, drawing back. "I come in peace."

He was shirtless, of course, but it was his pants—or lack of pants—that stood out to me. He was wearing these leather—I mean to say, they were made out of leather, but... oh, fuck it. He looked like he was wearing a pair of leather diapers, the shorts were so small. They... it... they, I guess, showed off his body, which was nice and all, but it was just so over-the-top that it lost all sensuality for me. I liked the way Kyle's shirts were too baggy and when you lifted them you found the flat stomach underneath, or the way his pants hid the fact he was....

Oh, while we're at it, Colt was lying about being hung like a mule, unless that mule was maybe an infant. Because if Kyle was wearing those shorts, there would be more hanging out than in. I don't say that to be mean; I'm just saying. If you're going to brag about having a big dick, either have one or don't wear leather diapers in public.

In fact, don't ever wear leather diapers in public. Ever. Like ever, ever.

"I was looking for you," I shouted over the music. He broke out into a grin, and I knew he had taken that the wrong way. "Because this place is freaking me out and I was about to leave."

His smile lessened.

"What's wrong with this place? It's epic!"

"Yeah, if epic included a bunch of people trying way too hard to look pretty," I shot back.

"Well, some of us weren't born looking like you, so we have to try harder." He was still smiling, but I could hear a slight change in his voice when he shouted. Or it could have been I was going deaf from the pounding bass and he sounded exactly normal. "The jacket makes you look way butch, man."

"I didn't know what to wear," I admitted.

"That's easy," he said, pulling the jacket off me. "Nothing!"

I let him take the jacket off because it was hot as hell wearing it, but when he reached for my shirt, I grabbed his hands. "No."

"Brad, that shirt looks like ass! You have a body people would pay money to eat off of, and you're too hot to be shy. Take the shirt off and see how the other half lives."

I didn't move my hands, but as I looked around, I could see more people were shirtless than weren't, and the ones that weren't looked… well, kinda gross. If I didn't take my shirt off, would they assume I had nothing under it? And why should I care? I mean, no one here knew me anyway.

"Fine, but the first guy who touches me gets a broken finger." I pulled the shirt off, and there was a small cheer from the people around me. I looked around and saw there were maybe ten to fifteen people watching me tuck my shirt into my back pocket and openly admiring what they saw.

"See? You didn't explode, and no one is grabbing at you," Colt said, nudging me. "I'll put your coat behind the bar and we'll have some fun. You like lollipops?"

Who the hell asks that?

"Um, sure, who doesn't?" I answered.

"Awesome, be right back."

I was about to tell him not to leave me, but he was gone in the crowd.

Glancing around, I nodded and smiled to the people who were still staring, wondering why I had agreed to this. I should have been freaked out, but instead it was oddly comforting. I couldn't figure it out for a second, and then I realized the looks I was getting reminded me of the looks I got in Foster. Either on the baseball field or even just out, that look people gave you when they liked what they saw. I hadn't had that admiration in a while, certainly not from Kyle.

It felt good.

I was about to go find Colt when he appeared out of nowhere with two shots in his hand. "Here. Drink," he said, putting the shot glass to my lips.

It burned as it went down, and I felt myself choke a little as the warmness filled my chest. "What was that?" I gasped.

"Patrón," he said, laughing. "Same as this one," and he did it again. This time I actually managed to swallow the drink instead of trying to breathe it and the warmness expanded. I suddenly wished I had eaten before leaving the house. His laughing got louder. "There we go. Let's see if we can get that gigantic stick out of your ass." He pulled me to the dance floor. "Or better yet, get a gigantic stick up your ass."

For some reason that was funnier than hell and I burst out laughing, which was proof enough.

I was buzzed.

Kyle

WHEN IT was clear Brad wasn't coming back, I sat down on the couch, stunned.

He always came back, always. I mean, sure, maybe I shouldn't keep pushing him away, but still… he didn't come back. I felt numb—no, that's not true. If I was numb, it wouldn't have hurt like that. It was like being immersed in freezing water. There's a feeling of pain, but your body is so overwhelmed that it doesn't really connect to your brain. That was what this was like; my heart was just too stunned to acknowledge it was in pain.

For now.

How did we come to this? In my mind I traced the steps back and found I was way too close to the problem to be objective about it. I knew Brad needed a life too, but did he have to do it at a fucking gay gym? And I knew he needed friends, but couldn't he find a normal-looking guy? Wow, saying it like that, the problem really sounded like it wasn't him at all, but me.

I needed to talk to someone but had no idea who.

It was past midnight in Texas, which didn't actually rule Jennifer out, but it made calling her this late problematic. It was even later in New York, which meant calling Robbie was out too. Was I so messed up that I was actually considering calling my mommy and crying?

Screw that.

I opened my laptop and checked Facebook. Maybe someone was still up and I could send them a message. Jennifer's last post was a selfie of her on the couch in PJs with some ice cream in her hand and the caption: "While the boy is away, I get to spend time with my first love. Ice cream." That was hours ago, which sucked. Robbie's last post was three hours ago, and all it said was, "Men suck. That is all."

Seemed like a shitty night all around.

I was about to cry when Facebook made a beep at me. I looked down and saw that Teddy had messaged me.

Teddy B: Hey you on?

Kyle Stilleno: Yep.

I so didn't want to tell him about this, but what choice did I have? I literally had no other friends in the world. Man, I thought life was supposed to get *better* once you got out of high school.

Teddy B: What you and your man doing?

I swear it was like he knew something was up.

Kyle: He went out with a friend.

Long pause.

Teddy B: Without you?

My eyes began to sting as I typed back.

Kyle: Yep.

Several seconds passed, and it didn't say he was typing anything. I waited because I had nowhere else to go. This was my life, alone in my apartment wondering where my boyfriend was. No, scratch that, wondering if I still had a boyfriend. Finally, another message popped up.

Teddy B: Want to talk?

If I called him, then I lost all high ground when it came to defending Brad from him. In fact, by telling him what happened, it would justify everything he already thought about pretty people. I tried not to think about how much I was starting to agree with him.

I sent my number and closed the laptop, taking a deep breath.

I picked up on the first ring, and he didn't even wait for a hello.

"So what happened?"

"He wanted to go out to a club where his workout partner works and I didn't." It was enough of the truth without getting into the ugly details.

"Workout partner? Let me guess, perfect body? Ripped, cute as hell, and gay, right?"

"They play softball together," I said miserably.

He barked an ugly laugh. "Sounds like he has more in common with the meathead than you."

There was a small spark of anger, and my impulse was to argue the point. To defend Brad. But just as quickly as it appeared, it was drowned by the overwhelming sorrow filling up my heart. Instead all I said was, "Yeah, probably."

Neither of us said anything for a while. I was trying to find the strength to say something, and I'm sure he was looking for something sympathetic that might make me feel better.

"Well, he's an asshole," he finally stated.

"He's not an asshole," I said weakly.

"Yes he is, and it isn't his fault. Look, Kyle, people like that are used to people falling over themselves for them. They live on the attention. It isn't anything you did. It's just his nature."

"Brad isn't like that," I said, not even believing it myself.

"Really? So he didn't spend most of high school being popular because of his looks and his ability to play... whatever sport he played?"

"Baseball," I mumbled.

"So he wasn't considered a god because of baseball? Really?"

I had no answer.

"I'm not trying to be a dick, man. I'm just saying. He's reverting to type."

"I'm going to go," I said, the pain finally starting to sink in.

"I'm going to be up all night if you need to talk."

"Okay," I said with no emotion in my voice at all.

I think he said something else, but I had already hung up the phone and begun to cry.

Brad

WHEN I woke up....

Wait a minute, when did I fall asleep?

I sat up quickly and regretted that and every action I had taken since I was seven years old as my head exploded with pain. I had been hungover before—shit, I've played nine innings with a hangover—but this... this was different. I fell back onto the... couch? I was on a couch? Where the fuck was I?

Pushing past the pain the sunlight was bringing me, I looked around and realized I had no idea where I was. It was a guy's place, from the 'Niners flag pinned up on one wall and the flatscreen that had an Xbox and PS4 hooked up to it. There were empty beer cans on the coffee table and scattered clothes on the floor. They weren't mine, so that was a good sign. I had a ratty blanket over me, and I looked underneath, and yep.

I was naked.

Fuck! I hated waking up naked with no idea where I was. It hadn't happened to me before, but I could tell no matter how many times it might happen, I was never going to be a fan. I rolled the blanket around my waist and got up, almost falling in the process because my body still seemed to think I was drunk. I stumbled past a small dining room table with more beer cans and two empty days-old pizza boxes on it on my way to the kitchen and fumbled open the fridge, hoping that, wherever I was, they had water.

Instead I found two containers of mustard, more beer, and an almost empty gallon of milk. Nothing else. It looked like my parent's fridge when they went on vacation and left me at the house for two weeks. By the end of those two weeks, I think I was actually eating ketchup out of the bottle.

"Fuck it," I mumbled to myself and grabbed a beer. I needed something to get the taste of dead raccoon out of my mouth.

Now that I was up and mobile, I looked around again for my stuff. My wallet, car keys, and cell phone were on the coffee table between the beer cans, but still no clothes. I unlocked my phone and saw it was almost noon on Saturday. I had five missed calls and two voicemails from Kyle.

The first one was a standard, "Hey, it's me. You didn't come home last night. Just let me know you're alive, okay?" and nothing else. He didn't sound mad or upset; he was just checking on me. The next one was much worse.

"Okay, stop playing games, Brad. You want to not talk to me, fine, but at least let me know you're alive, for fuck's sake. You owe me at least that."

I dialed him back, no idea what I was going to say.

"Are you okay?" he said in lieu of hello.

"Yeah," I answered, relieved as hell to hear his voice.

"Good." And he hung up.

Fuck.

I called him back but got his voicemail this time.

"Come on, Kyle. I was passed out, not ignoring you. Call me back."

"Oh hey, you're up," a voice said from behind me. I spun around and saw a black guy in his midtwenties standing in the hallway wearing a pair of A&F sweats and nothing else. "Everything okay?"

"Don't take this the wrong way, but who the fuck are you?" I asked, my anger from Kyle, being naked, everything starting to bubble over.

"Oh, one of those nights," he said, smiling. "Hold on."

He walked back down the hallway and banged on one of the doors. "Colton, wake up. Your friend is awake and pissed."

"Colt's here?" I asked, more to myself than to the stranger.

"Yeah, I'm Bruce, his roommate. We met last night?"

I shook my head.

"We talked for, like, an hour?"

Another shake.

"I stripped you naked?"

"You did what?" I growled.

"You puked all over yourself and passed out," he said quickly. "I had to strip you and throw the clothes in the washer. You didn't want me to let you sleep in your own vomit, did you?"

I'm going to be honest, it was a toss-up.

"Where are my clothes?" I asked as calmly as possible.

The calmness seemed to affect him more than me getting pissed. "Okay, let me go get them, okay?" He kicked Colt's door again as he walked by. "Colt, if your friend kicks my ass, I am killing you."

I sat down, trying to remember anything from last night. There was me going onto the dance floor, there was a flash of drinking again, and then nothing. Come on, man, I was way too young for memory loss after a night of drinking. I heard a door open and saw Colt stumble out of his room in just a pair of white Calvin Klein briefs. If I hadn't been fighting the urge to kill him with my bare hands, I would have said he looked pretty good in them.

"Why are you awake?" he asked, walking into the living room.

"Because it's almost noon and my boyfriend is furious at me because I didn't come home," I growled back. Shouting would have hurt, and growling was way more effective. At least when it came to the roommate, whatever his name was.

"You were wasted, man. I should have let you drive drunk?" he said, plopping down into an oversized leather chair.

"You could have not gotten me so fucked-up I couldn't drive," I suggested.

He dismissed me with a hand wave. "Dude, you had a blast last night. You needed it."

"I wouldn't know because I can't remember a fucking thing."

Now I was getting pissed.

He shrugged. "It happens, man. First time doing GHB?"

I froze.

"What?" I asked.

He looked up at me, confused. "Was that the first time you did lollipops?"

I crossed the distance between us in a second and raised my fist. "You gave me drugs last night?"

He shrank back into the chair. "Dude, it was a little bit. You needed to relax. I asked you if you liked lollipops!"

"I didn't know that meant fucking drugs."

"Oh" was all he said.

My fist was quivering as I fought the urge to hit him.

Which was when Bruce walked in with my clothes. "Um, am I interrupting something?"

I turned away from Colt and grabbed my clothes and headed to the bathroom. I could not believe this was fucking happening to me. There were no socks or underwear, but I didn't care. I slipped on my jeans and a shirt and walked out looking for my shoes.

"You know, dude, a lot of people would thank me for a night like last night."

I found one under the coffee table and kept looking for the other.

"That shit isn't cheap!" he added.

I turned back toward him. "You can bill me."

"Here," Bruce said from behind me. He was holding my shoe out to me, ready to drop it in case I swung at him.

"Thank you," I said, taking it and putting it on.

"Yeah, run home to your boyfriend like a little bitch," Colt called after me. "Let him know who has all the power in the relationship. Don't stand up for yourself or anything, man, just go be his doormat."

His words stung, but I ignored them as I walked out of the apartment. My car was parked out front; I thanked whatever god had arranged that and got in. I paused, because I still had no idea where I was. Thankfully Google told me the way home, but it couldn't tell me the answer I really craved.

If I even lived there anymore.

Kyle

I DIDN'T even remember falling asleep the night before.

One second I was crying on the couch, and the next it was morning and Brad still wasn't home. So of course, being me, I panicked. I grabbed my phone and desperately pulled up his number and then stopped. This was his whole game, right? Me in a panic, dying to take him back. That was what last night was all about, and frankly, I was done with it. I splashed some water on my face, took a deep breath, and then called him.

Of course I got voicemail.

That was the next step of this game. I leave a frantic voicemail, he comes back like a knight swooping in the front door, and all is forgiven. Nope, not going to play your game, sir. I left a calm and pleasant message that in no way conveyed the blind panic I was feeling inside. Were we broken up? Did I want to break up? Was this the end?

I poured a bowl of cereal and waited. The ball was in his court now. Let's see him return that swing. I pretended to watch TV, but instead I was counting the seconds that passed without him calling. I waited an hour.

Okay I waited, like, forty-seven minutes, but that's close enough to an hour.

The next voicemail was less than calm.

When I hung up, I waited another ten minutes and then started crying again. This was how it ended, us not talking to each other?

My phone rang and I scrambled to answer before I saw it was Teddy calling.

"So what happened?" he asked, sounding concerned.

"He didn't come home," I said, the reality finally settling in.

"Oh" was all he said.

Oh? Oh? I was so fucking sick of ohs.

"I left a voicemail, but he hasn't called back."

"Please tell me you didn't leave a whining-ass Taylor Swift 'please come home' message."

"I don't know what that would sound like, but no, I yelled more than I whined."

My answer seemed to placate him. "So what are you going to do if he calls?"

"When he calls," I corrected him.

"If, when. What are you going to do?" he asked again.

My silence answered for me. I had no idea.

"If he calls, just ask him if he's okay, and when he says yeah, hang up," Teddy advised.

"What?"

"When he calls, just ask him if he's okay, and when he says yes, hang up on him."

I looked at the phone for a second to make sure it was working properly. "Why would I do that?"

"Because your message is going to sound like you missed him and want to apologize. You gotta take the power back."

"What power?" Now I was completely backward.

"The power in the relationship, man!" He made it sound like he was talking about something as simple as boiling water and I still wasn't getting it. "You need to lay down the law with him, tell him how's it's going to be."

"So this is my law?"

"*The* law. Look, you need to make it clear to him what's acceptable and what isn't. If not, he's going to walk all over you. Again. And you're going to be miserable all the time."

I shook my head even though he couldn't see me. "It isn't like that between us."

"Well, maybe that's the problem. Take control of the situation, Kyle."

The other line beeped. I looked down and saw it was Brad. "It's him," I told Teddy.

"Just ask if he's okay and then hang up," he pleaded with me.

"Hold on," I said and put him on hold and went to the other line.

I clicked over. Brad's voice was frantic and pleading. "Please Kyle, don't hang up, I know I screwed up and I want to make it better and I know I worried you last night but please... don't hang up."

Yeah, right. He just said, "Hey."

"Hey," like nothing had happened. "Hey," like he was just calling one of his buds to see what was up. "Hey," like I didn't just ditch you and go to a gay club and stay out all night. Just "hey." That "hey" made my mind up for me.

"Are you okay?"

He paused for a moment and then said, "Yeah."

"Good." And I hung up.

I dropped the phone. My hands were shaking, my heart was racing… I'd said four words, but I felt like I'd just run a marathon.

My phone beeped to remind me that Teddy was still holding. When I picked up the phone, I saw Brad call back. I sent it to voicemail and picked up with Teddy.

"Well?" he asked me.

"I asked if he was okay and hung up," I said, not feeling the least bit satisfied.

"Good," he said, sounding like he had won something.

"He's calling back right now."

"Don't answer!" he shouted. "Make him come back if he wants to talk. He knows he fucked up—make him pay."

I didn't want to make him pay. I didn't want to do anything. I wanted to go back in time to when we were happy and this was easy. What the hell happened to us? Was this real life? Was this growing up? No wonder guys read comics and play video games at thirty; who the fuck wants to grow up?

"What are you going to say when he gets there?" Teddy asked, and I realized I had zoned out and completely forgotten I was on the phone.

"I don't know," I said honestly.

"Okay, look, you got him on the ropes. Now you need to follow it up with—"

My phone beeped, telling me I had a voicemail, and I'm going to be honest, Teddy was starting to bug me.

"I need to go," I said, cutting him off. "I'll see you at school Monday."

"Kyle!" he called out. "Don't let him push you—"

I hung up with him and looked at my phone.

Brad: Voicemail & Missed Call

My finger hovered over it, not sure if I wanted to hear it or not.

Brad

PART OF me wanted to blow through every red light and race home.

The other part wanted the trip to take forever.

84

I still had no idea what I was going to say to Kyle, but I knew it was time to talk. When had this whole thing gone off the rails so badly? Why was love so fucking hard? I pulled into the alley, turned off my car, and took a few seconds to collect my thoughts. What I was about to say was for everything, and I couldn't go in there half-cocked.

As I walked up the steps, I wondered if I should knock or just go in. Knocking would make it seem like I was unsure if I even lived there anymore, and walking in looked like I was assuming I did. See, this was the shit that made me freak out! When just knocking on the door took a few minutes to figure out, you knew the relationship was in bad, bad trouble....

I walked in. Since my stuff was still there, technically I still lived there.

He was sitting on the couch, the couch I had built for him. That day seemed like it was years ago instead of a couple of months. I went over and moved the chair across from him and sat down. "I wasn't ignoring your call last night."

"I know," he said in a tiny voice completely unlike Kyle.

"I ended up...," and I paused, because if I told him I'd ended up doing drugs last night by accident, he would lose his shit completely. It would just confirm that I was a complete fuckup and there would be no coming back from that.

"...getting fucked-up last night and I passed out. I didn't even hear my phone ring," I finished.

"Okay," he said, still not looking up.

"It's the truth," I said, trying to get through to him.

"I'm sure it is," he replied after a few seconds.

"We need to talk," I said, not sure what was going on anymore.

"Are you breaking up with me?" he asked, finally looking up at me.

"What? No."

"Why not?" he asked.

"Because I love you," I said unhesitatingly.

"You love me?" he asked. I nodded. "You can still say that?"

"I will always be able to say that," I said without reservation.

He sighed and shook his head. "I'll give you two weeks to find a place, and then I want you out," he said, getting up from the couch.

"Kyle? Don't do this!" I moved toward him.

He turned around, and I saw the burning fury in his eyes. "Do not touch me."

I froze, unsure what was really happening. "You're that mad at me for staying out all night? Really?"

"Check your Facebook and then start looking for a place to live. I don't care where you go, but you're not staying here."

"What did I do?" I was crying now.

He just walked into the bathroom and slammed the door.

I opened up his laptop and saw he was still logged in to Facebook. It was open on my page, and what was there chilled me to the bone. It was a post by Colt.

It said, "You forgot these," and under it was a picture of my boxer briefs.

My world collapsed as I realized Kyle had just broken up with me.

Kyle

SO YOU see? I told you it got messed up.

He tried to tell me it wasn't what it looked like, but honestly, what was he going to say? "Yeah, I fucked him, but that shouldn't count against me?" The weird part was I didn't even want to fight about it anymore. Brad and I were over, and I just wanted to move on to the next part. Brad wasn't ready for that. He kept trying again and again to explain himself and to convince me it wasn't what I thought.

Honestly, I didn't care if it was what I thought or not. The fact that we were at a place where he ended up leaving his underwear at a stranger's house was enough for me.

Normally that would have been enough. For normal people I'm sure that was enough crap for life to dish out, but I'm not normal, and my crap quota is much higher than that. If all that happened was he cheated on me and we broke up, I wouldn't be here in an airport waiting for a flight wondering what I was going to do.

Nope, of course things got much worse.

Brad

SO THIS was how my life ended, one act of fuckery at a time.

I begged him, I pleaded, I did everything in my power to get Kyle to understand that nothing happened that night with Colt. He wasn't interested in hearing my story. He said it didn't matter if nothing had happened or not, that my underwear got removed at a stranger's place and then posted on Facebook was enough for him to tap out.

I couldn't blame him all that much.

I walked around that weekend in shock. He wanted me to move out, but I had nowhere to go but home, and there was no way I was going back to Foster to sleep in my parents' house. It would be a black hole I would never escape from. I'd rather live in my car before admitting defeat, so I checked the paper for apartments and realized I had no chance at all of staying out here.

That Sunday I slept on the couch, and it was the most miserable experience of my life. I tried not to think how this couch used to be such a source of pride for me. Now it was literally the worst place in the world.

Monday, I went to work wondering what I was going to do. When I saw Colt waiting at the front door, I jumped out of my car and clocked him hard. I wasn't surprised to see him go down like a lead weight. I can't imagine he got into many fights. He fell to the sidewalk, and I started screaming at him.

"What the fuck were you thinking, asshole? Why would you put that shit up on Facebook?"

"I'm sorry!" he called back.

"You broke me and Kyle up, you fucking dick," I screamed, wanting very badly to kick him a couple of times.

"I didn't mean it! It was a joke."

"You see anyone laughing?"

I looked around and saw we had an audience. "If you want to come in, wait until we're open," I said, unlocking the gym. "But leave me the fuck alone." I slammed the door and locked it behind me.

That didn't make me feel any better at all; if anything, I was just more depressed.

Colt was knocking on the front door, screaming, "Come on, Brad, I'm sorry! Let me try to make it up to you."

I pulled the blinds back and glared at him. "Go away, Colt."

"I'll talk to Kyle for you! I'll tell him nothing happened."

"What makes you think you talking to him will have any better effect than I did?"

He paused. "I'll tell him nothing happened."

Now I paused.

"You mean you'd tell him the truth."

He cocked his head. "I don't think that would help. You're better off if I tell him nothing happened."

I unlocked the door and pulled him inside. "Nothing happened."

"You really don't remember?" he asked and I felt my stomach lurch.

"Remember what?"

"You and Bruce? Really?" He looked shocked.

My head swam, and I felt the floor tilt beneath me at the thought of cheating on Kyle.

"Dude, you were fucked-up—it doesn't count."

I'm sure the look on my face made it clear I didn't share his opinion. "You're saying I kissed Bruce?"

He chuckled. "Dude, from what I heard in my room, you did a lot more than that."

And just like that, I realized the truth. Guys like me didn't deserve guys like Kyle. We were incapable of being the people they deserved, and sooner or later the real us slipped out. Maybe it was being fucked-up, maybe it was being lonely and out of town, but sooner or later, no matter how hard we tried, who we really were appeared.

And just like that, it was over.

I stopped trying to convince Kyle we should get back together after a week or so. Instead I began to look around seriously for a place to stay. I asked Todd, who of course offered me a place in his bed, but then said ·

88

he was joking when I glared at him. I was tempted to put a notice up asking if anyone needed a roommate, but I wasn't sure anyone in the gym would take it seriously.

Finally Colt came up to me after a session and asked in a low voice, "Dude, you still hate me?"

I didn't hate him; I hated me. He just happened to remind me of who I was going to become in a few years.

"I think I'm going to have to move back to Texas," I admitted, the first time I'd said it out loud.

"What? No way, man! You can't go backward."

I agreed with him, but what could I do? I wasn't going to ask Kyle for any of the money Robbie had given us, because that was for *us*, like, together. I couldn't afford to stay here, and I wasn't ready to sell my ass just to have a place to live. Better I went home, got laughed at by everyone who'd just known I was going to fuck things up, and got it over with.

"You can crash on my couch, man," he offered when it was obvious I wasn't going to say anything else.

"Yeah, right," I scoffed.

"No, really." He pounced on the idea. "I got you into this, so let me fix it, man. You can crash on the couch until you can get back on your feet. No funny business, unless you want to go at it with Bruce again because you're single...."

"Shut up," I said, not even wanting to think about that night.

"Just think about it. I'm completely serious. Bro to bro, let me help you."

I didn't say anything, just got my stuff and went back... went back to Kyle's place.

When I got there, he was in a panic.

He was throwing stuff into a duffel bag, and the place looked like a small tornado had hit it. "What's up?" I asked.

"Fuck, I forgot about you," he said, pausing.

That made me feel all tingly inside.

"I have to go back home," he said, tossing a couple of shirts into the bag.

"What? Why?" I asked, knowing this had to be serious if he was talking about setting foot back in Foster.

"Doesn't matter," he said, cutting off any chance I had of finding out. "I don't know when I'm going to be back. I'll call you when I do."

I nodded, wishing I could help.

"When I call to tell you I'm coming back?" He looked at me, and I nodded. "Don't be here when I get home."

He could have punched me in the gut and it would have taken the air from me easier.

"Kyle, what's going on?" I asked, hating this so much.

"Handle your own shit," he barked at me. "I can handle this. Leave the keys with Mrs. Phan when you go." He tossed his toothbrush and his laptop into the bag and looked around.

"Can I give you a ride to the airport, at least?"

He shook his head. "I called a cab."

"Please let me help you." I was on the verge of crying again.

"You want to help?" he asked. "Find somewhere else to live."

A car honked twice outside, and he slipped his bag over his shoulder.

He paused, and we looked at each other for a second. "Well, goodbye, Brad."

I wanted to reach out and hug him, beg him not to do this… but he stuck out his hand like he wanted to shake. I held mine out in shock and he shook it.

"Have a great life."

The car honked again and he ran out the door.

I didn't even care anymore. I just broke down and sobbed at how badly I had fucked things up.

Kyle

SO THERE you have it.

This is why I'm sitting in an airport wondering if I made a huge mistake. I've never gone through anything like this before, so I don't know if what's going through my mind is normal or not. I mean, you normally go back over every second you were together with the person who hurt you and wonder if you missed a clue somewhere, right? Like suddenly

I'm *CSI: Heartbreak*, going over everything he ever said, looking for any indication that I could have stopped this before it shattered my heart into a million pieces.

Worse—yes, it gets worse—is that next week I have my midterms, and I'm going to miss them because I'll be in Foster figuring out....

Nope, not going there yet.

So you tell me: should I have forgiven him? Should I have looked past all that and just said no harm, no foul? That's not even true, because there was a lot of harm, and I feel like I've been fouled. Now I'll admit I don't know what you do in sports when you're fouled, but it better involve a lot of Adele and ice cream, because I've never felt so depressed in my life.

This wasn't my fault, so why do I feel like I fucked up?

Yeah, Teddy tried to get me to stay, reminding me that most of the grade in the class was based on actually showing up and if I wasn't there it would be an F, no questions asked. Which meant I would have to ace the rest of the semester just to keep my grades at the minimum level to keep my scholarship. So one day I had a great boyfriend, a scholarship, and a life, and now I was looking at losing it all because of one stupid twist of fate that I should have seen coming.

We all should have seen it coming.

Why is this happening to me?

Yeah, I think I just broke my keyboard.

That's my flight they're calling, so I guess I'm done here.

No boyfriend, no school, and my mom might be dying because she had a car accident and she hasn't woken up yet.

Aren't you glad you know the whole story now?

PART TWO:
BOOMERANGS, KARMA, AND THE PAST

Name three things that will come back to you no matter how fast you run.

Tyler

"I FUCKING hate this town!" I screamed as I kicked one of the plastic chairs in the waiting room. It went flying across the small space, bouncing once before settling to the floor.

"Tyler," Matt admonished me. "We're in a hospital; you can't throw a fit in here."

He was right, kicking chairs in the ICU waiting room was not the proper thing to do, but I was too pissed to care. "He kicked me out!" I raged. "Me! Where the hell does he get off kicking anyone out of anywhere?"

"Calm down," Matt said in a tone that told me he was done feeding my childish outburst. "You want to get tossed out of the hospital altogether? Keep on kicking and screaming. You want to try to fix things, grow up."

He was right, of course, but it did nothing to make me feel better.

"How am I going to fix things?" I asked him. "How can this be fixed?"

He opened his mouth to answer and then thought about it. "I don't know," he finally admitted. "But I do know that what you're doing? It's the wrong way to go."

I sighed and sat down on one of the other chairs. "Where the hell is everyone?"

Matt sat down next to me and took my hand. "Look, babe, you did everything you could. That guy is an asshole and we need to wait for people to show up. Kyle hasn't even left California yet, so you need to relax and calm down."

Tears stung my eyes as I looked up at him. "She's going to die."

He pulled me into a hug. "You don't know that yet."

But I did.

If you know me, then you know my past, and my past tells me the people I love die. And when they die, I just sit there and watch, unable or unwilling to help because I am Tyler Parker, a worthless human being.

93

Then it was my friend Riley; now it's my best friend, Linda. I enjoyed the hug the best I could, but I knew it wasn't going to change the truth. She was going to die.

"Don't look now, but I think the cavalry has arrived," he whispered in my ear.

I turned around and saw Robbie walking into the ICU, a worried look on his face when he saw Matt and me. His hair was short, very short, like he'd shaved his head and was recovering from it short, but that wasn't what got my attention.

It was the hot blond guy following him.

"Is everything okay?" he asked once inside. "It took forever to rent a car, and the drive from Dallas is insane, but we got here as fast as we could. How is she?"

I looked away from the model to Robbie. "Who's this?"

The guy stuck his hand out. "I'm Sebastian, his boyfriend."

Both Matt and I said at the same time, "Of course you are."

Robbie rolled his eyes. "Are you serious? Isn't someone dying or something?"

"I'm Tyler," I said, shaking his hand. "And this is my boyfriend, Matt."

"Pleased," Matt said with a smile.

"Wow, you're big," Sebastian said to Matt.

"Okay, honey, we said hello," Robbie announced, stepping between him and us. "What's going on?"

"She's still unconscious and has that thing breathing for her right now," I explained, trying not to put feelings to the words. "There's some kind of surgery thing they can do to relieve pressure on something, but they can't do it without someone saying they can do it."

Robbie understood instantly. "You mean Kyle."

I made a face and answered, "Well… not exactly."

"Wait," he said, looking around. "Why are you even out here? Why aren't you in there with her?"

"Here we go," Matt said under his breath. To Sebastian he suggested, "Hey, why don't we go grab some coffee and stuff and let these guys catch up?"

Sebastian looked confused, but Robbie nodded once and the two of them walked out.

"Okay, so why aren't you in there?" he asked again.

"That's a long story," I said, sitting down and patting the chair next to me. "I should start at the beginning."

"Tyler, what the hell is going on?" he asked, sitting down warily.

"See, it all started with that letter...."

Tyler

I HATE to admit it, but it was weird being back in an AA meeting.

After I blew my knee out and had to come home, there was a length of time where I went off the rails. I got pulled over a few times for drunk driving, but the old sheriff always let me off with a warning because of who I was. When Sheriff Rogers took office, the first night he pulled me over, he arrested me and threw me in lockup. I didn't know it at the time, but his wife had been killed by a drunk driver, and he was forced to raise his daughter alone because of idiots like me. He didn't take kindly to my situation at all.

Which landed me in court, which landed me in AA.

That was a long time ago, and I had convinced myself that I didn't need AA to get by. Sure, I drank back then, but it wasn't an all-the-time thing, and it wasn't until I was sloppy drunk, either. But I went, did my time, and never went back. I honestly didn't think I ever would go back.

But here I am.

I've known Linda Stilleno since high school. I'd known of her since we were both in grade school, but it wasn't until high school that we became friends. I was so deep in the closet that if I sneezed too hard, hangers would come flying out of my mouth, and she seemed to have known it forever. At first I hated that. I had spent a lifetime—well, sixteen years—cultivating a James Bond-like cover about my sexuality. Since I was a jock, there were more than a few girls who were always asking me out, and being a jock, it was completely feasible for me to be a douchebag guy and play the field.

That worked for a while until Linda "Goldfinger" Stilleno figured me out.

I denied it. I tried to lie about it. I ignored her. Then I pleaded with her and begged her not to say a word. In the end she became my best friend and the first person to accept me as I was.

Which explained why I was in an AA meeting on a Saturday afternoon.

The Granada High gym was this group's meeting spot. Being there brought back a whole mess of memories I thought I'd repressed about being a teenager. The place even smelled the same, which was tripping me out because it seemed impossible I'd even remember that. Well over a decade had passed since I'd sat in the bleachers counting the seconds before school got out, but at times it felt like it was yesterday. Other times it felt like it had been someone else.

Before the meeting started, Linda had elbowed me and nodded to the far wall. I saw a row of glass cases with jerseys inside. Mine was the third one over: PARKER 42.

"See? You're still a celebrity," she whispered with a wry smile.

"Yeah, right. You know how many kids look up there and ask, 'Who the fuck is Parker?' Trust me, no one remembers those days."

That sounded a lot more bitter than I had intended, but it was too late to take it back.

"Thank you for coming," she said after a respectable pause. "Gayle couldn't get out of the lunch shift, and I hate coming here alone."

"You do know that these people aren't judging you, right? They're in the same boat you are."

She rolled her eyes. "Please, half of these people are the fucks who wrote me off in high school as the loser party girl, then forgot me completely when I became the pregnant girl."

That was true. When Linda ended up pregnant after dropping out of high school, no TV show followed her around celebrating her decision to keep the baby and hold on to her pride. Instead there was a town full of hostile people who couldn't wait to condemn her as the town slut. I remember her parents almost moving back to Foster because they didn't think she could raise a kid by herself, but she'd refused their help. In fact, she'd refused almost everyone's help.

"Yeah, but those people didn't give birth to Kyle, so you know they're jealous as fuck," I whispered back, making her smile.

"Kyle isn't here anymore, so they've gone back to shunning me. I'm glad someone is here." She squeezed my hand, and I suddenly felt like shit for not wanting to be there. She needed someone, and there were very few someones left in her life. Her parents had passed away a few years ago, and the only real friends she had made were party friends, which were as dependable as gypsies when it came to support. You had some weed and drink? They were all there. Decided to go sober? Crickets and tumbleweeds.

"I'm always here for you," I said, squeezing her hand back. "And if things get bad, I can always ask Matt to introduce you to his old friend Sophia."

Linda pulled her hand free of mine and slapped my shoulder. "Fuck that bitch—every time he tells a story about her, I want to hop a plane to California and smack her in the mouth."

Truer words were never spoken. Matt's former friend was a despicable person, and he relished telling us horror stories of hanging out with her to pass the time. I had only met her once, and let me tell you, I think he was being nice when he spoke about the things she'd done to him.

"So, you hear from Kyle?" I asked her as the last of the stragglers shuffled into the gym.

She shook her head. "I left a message, but he's so busy getting moved in he hasn't called back yet. You know how it is."

I did know how it was, and it wasn't in any way right.

Kyle and Linda had gone through some pretty rough times over the years. She hadn't been the most responsible of parents, and he wasn't known for his forgiving ways. It wasn't until Kyle had come out and the whole town came crashing down on him that she'd decided to clean her act up and come to her son's aid. But in the end, it was too little, too late, and I'm pretty sure Kyle ran out of town as fast as he could and wasn't planning on coming back.

But it didn't mean he couldn't call his mother.

Father Mulligan took the podium, and everyone quieted down as I pulled out my cell phone.

Tyler: You better tell your man to call his mom.

I tried to look like I was paying attention to what Mulligan was saying while I waited for Brad to answer.

Brad: Have you ever tried to make Kyle do anything? Not going to happen unless he wants to.

I smiled at that. From what I knew of Kyle, he seemed like the stubborn type.

Tyler: Bribe him. He needs to call his mom.

Brad: Are you telling me to offer sex to my boyfriend to get him to call his mom?

I stifled a laugh as I responded.

Tyler: I didn't say a word about sex, but I see where your mind is.

Brad: So how much sex are you and Matt not having?

That got a small bark of laughter from me that was like a gunshot in the quiet gym. I looked up and realized I was now the center of attention. "Hi, I'm Tyler and I'm putting my phone away now."

Father Mulligan smiled at me. "Hi, Tyler, and thank you."

Linda whispered next to me, "Busted."

Yep, just like it used to be in high school.

The meeting lasted for a little over an hour. An hour of my life I was never going to get back, but then again, you did things like this for friends. As the group broke up, I looked over to Linda and asked, "Is it bad I have impure thoughts about Father Mulligan?"

She laughed. "No, but it would be bad if I told Matt about them."

"Please," I said as we got into my car. "We have a list. Before this they were just celebrities, but I think I could add a priest and still be within my rights."

"You have a list?"

I nodded. "Yeah, a list of people that if we met and were offered sex, we could sleep with and it not mean anything." She stared at me like I was insane. "Straight people don't do that?"

"We pretend we do, but it isn't real."

"Oh. Well, I'm just saying if I meet Chris Hemsworth and he wants to show me his hammer, I'm not saying no."

"You are so bad," she commented as we drove out of the parking lot.

"Have you seen *Thor*? That man could get anyone in his bed."

We laughed and talked as we pulled up to her house. A normal Saturday all around, right? Except for the guy leaning on his car in front of her apartment.

"Who is that?" I asked as I turned off the engine. He was well-dressed, but the car was a rental, which meant he wasn't from around here. Why a stranger would be waiting in her parking lot didn't make any sense.

Linda didn't say a word as she got out and walked toward him.

"Linda Stilleno?" he asked.

She nodded.

"I have something here about Kyle," he said, opening his briefcase.

"What's wrong?" she asked, the dread in her voice like nails on a chalkboard.

He handed her a letter, and the moment she took it, he said, "You've been served."

She stared at the letter as the guy got into his car and drove off.

"What the hell is that?" I asked.

She stuffed the letter into her purse so fast I thought there was going to be a sonic boom. "Nothing. Thanks for coming, Tyler. You're the best."

"Really?" I asked. "You're really not going to tell me what that is?"

She kissed me on the cheek and walked toward her apartment. "Say hi to Matt for me." And she walked inside.

"What the fuck?" I asked no one, standing in the parking lot alone and clueless.

Matt

WE GRABBED a cup of brown water the hospital called coffee and took a seat in the back of the cafeteria. It was pretty much empty, which was good, because I really didn't want an audience for what I was about to do next.

"So you and Robbie, huh?" I asked once we were settled.

99

Sebastian nodded. "Yeah, so far, so good," he said, giving me a brilliant smile that I'm sure had melted more than a few hearts in its time.

"Great," I replied. "So what are your intentions with Robbie?"

He was in midsip, so he looked at me with his cup still raised, I suppose checking to see if I was making a joke. He saw I was not making a joke.

"Um," he stalled. "Good ones?"

I gave him a smile back, but I'm pretty sure it wasn't as dazzling as his was. "Yeah, not a great answer. Wanna try again?"

"You're joking, right?" he finally asked.

"I am not joking. What are your intentions with Robbie?"

He put his coffee down. "You do know I already went through this with his mom, sister, and uncle, right?"

"Awesome." I beamed. "So what are your intentions?"

He cocked his head in confusion. "I'm sorry, I wasn't under the impression you and Robbie were close."

I nodded. "We're not. So, your intentions?"

He chuckled, but I could tell it was nervousness over the uncomfortable situation. "Look, dude, I have no idea where this is coming from, but...."

"You know about Riley?" I interrupted him.

His chuckle died, and I saw his eyes grow cold. "Yeah, I do. I also know what your boyfriend did."

Nodding, I pushed on. "Great, then you know what kind of life Robbie has gone through. I don't know if you realize how close he came to breaking from all that. He keeps his cards pretty close to his chest, so it's easy to mistake his sarcasm as a personality trait, and not the defense mechanism it is. So I want to make sure he doesn't go through anything like that again."

I let him digest that as I took a sip of my own coffee.

"So let me ask again. What are your intentions?"

"Bro, I don't know where this is coming from, but I assure you I am not going to hurt Robbie."

"Well, bro"—my voice got harsh—"I ask because I know who you are."

His face got a little pale as he looked at me intently, trying to place me somewhere in his past.

"I know exactly who you are because I've met you a dozen times in my life." He seemed to sigh in relief as he caught my meaning. "You're a good-looking guy, great shape, charming as hell, and you think that means something. See, I know different."

He said nothing, but I could see him trying to stare a hole through me as I talked.

"I know that all of that, your looks, your body, all of it, is going to just fall apart someday. Piece by piece it will fade and vanish, leaving what's underneath left, and I'm asking you, what's underneath all that pretty? Because Robbie deserves a lot more than just looks."

He said nothing for almost a minute, just staring at me. Finally he blinked and asked, "Are we done? Or you have anything you want to add?"

"I said what I needed," I answered, shocked he wasn't going to say anything back.

"Great. Thanks for the coffee," he said, getting up and walking out.

Well, that was useless.

Tyler

"SO WHAT was in the envelope?" Robbie asked me impatiently.

"I'm getting there," I assured him.

"Well, get there faster," he ordered.

"Okay, okay! I didn't hear from her for a couple of days, which is odd for us. So I went by her work to see what was up and take her out to lunch...."

Tyler

THE BEST Buy had been built on the outskirts of town because the city council didn't want it staining the pristine presentation of downtown. What that meant was that old people didn't like change, and since they were still in power, what they wanted became law. Instead of making a shopping center in the middle of town, where small businesses like mine could benefit, it was built in the middle of Bumfuck, Foster, which made people do all their shopping once they were there. Going anywhere else was just too much of a hassle.

Linda said Best Buy was a soul-crushing place to work because the managers were hired by corporate and weren't from Foster. That meant they didn't understand anything about the people they were hiring to work for them. In a small town like Foster, people had a variety of responsibilities that Best Buy did not recognize as valid.

Did your family own a ranch and needed you at certain times to help out with it? Too bad; Best Buy didn't care. Did you have a child who had to be picked up from school by three? Too bad—your shift was until four; get someone else to do it. I asked her how she'd handled working there so long, and she just looked at me like I was stupid and answered, "Because Kyle needs to eat."

After that I just shut up and let it go.

I didn't see her on register, which was where she normally worked before lunch. Instead her friend Sharon was there. She waved at me as I walked in.

"Hey, you," I said, giving her one of my midrange smiles, the one that seemed to make women blush. Don't glare at me. I may know nothing about being gay, but I understand that girls find me attractive. I can't do a thing about that, but I can use it to my advantage. "Where's your partner in crime?"

She cocked her head for a moment as she tried to figure out who I meant.

"Linda," I reminded her. "Is Linda around?"

"Oh." She shook her head. "She called in today. I'm covering her shift."

That was odd.

"Where did she go?"

Sharon shrugged as she shooed me away from the counter for the customer behind me. "Welcome to Best Buy. Did you find everything you were looking for?"

"Why did she call in?" I asked her, ignoring the customer.

Sharon rang the lady's items up. "Don't know, she just said she had to take off for the day and could I cover for her."

"Just like that?"

"Is that all?" Sharon asked.

"I guess so," I answered, worried.

"She was talking to me," the woman huffed as she pulled money out of her purse.

"Thanks, Sharon," I called back as I ran out of the store. Something was wrong. I just knew it.

I got to my car and called her on my cell phone.

"Hey," Linda answered, obviously driving.

"Where are you?" I asked, sounding way more like my dad than I intended. "I just came by your work to see if you wanted to go to lunch."

"Oh, I took the day off," she said in a tone I knew well. She was trying to make it sound way more casual than it was.

"Where are you? I'll meet you for lunch."

"I'm not in town," she answered like she took off out of town all the time.

"Linda," I said, again in my dad's voice. "Where are you?"

"I'm crossing over into Oklahoma now. I'll be back in town by Friday, Ty; just chill."

"What the fuck are you doing in Oklahoma?" I almost yelled. "Is this about that letter?"

"I gotta go," she answered, completely avoiding my question. "I'll call you when I'm back." Then she hung up on me.

She hung up on me.

What the fuck was going on?

Robbie

IF THIS fuck doesn't hurry up, I'm going to slap the taste right out of his mouth.

And that has nothing to do with my previous issues with Tyler. These are all new ones stemming from the fact that he thinks he's fucking Charles Dickens all of a sudden, telling me it was the best of times and it was the worst of times.

Oh, screw off with that look. I've read a book or two.

I'm half listening to him, half wondering how much force it would take to kill him if I punched him in the throat, when Sebastian comes in looking like he's all kinds of pissed off. Tyler pauses and looks over at him, but I can tell Seb is having none of the Foster experience.

"I'm going to go back to the motel," he tells me in a tone that translates his words as: "I don't want to end up murdering someone in this town and spending the rest of my life at the mercy of the Texas legal system." I know this because I spoke in that same tone for years after Riley died.

"What's up?" I ask, wondering if it had been the best of moves to bring him along. I mean, we're barely figuring out what we're doing, and my mom, Nicole, and James make figuring hard enough. I'm not sure what I thought I was doing bringing him here.

No, that's not true. I'm testing him, of course, something I thought I was done doing.

"I'm just tired," he claims, which is bullshit because I've had extended carnal relations with him, so I know exactly how much stamina he has.

Oh, shut up. If you were sleeping with someone that pretty, you'd brag too.

To Tyler I say, "I'll be right back," and I walk Sebastian out of the waiting area. "Okay, what's wrong?"

"I know these guys are, like, your friends and all, but I'm not a fan."

How could he already have a problem with Matt and Tyler? I mean, Tyler has been in here with me the whole time, which only leaves....

Moose.

"What did he say?" I ask, gritting my teeth in anger.

"I'm not going to go running to Mommy when someone is mean to me on the playground." He pauses for a second. "You know I don't really think of you like my mom, right? I'm just saying that because I don't want to sound like a little bitch."

"What did Matt say to you?"

"Nothing." Now he sounded like he was twelve. "I just don't want to say something stupid and piss your friends off, so I'm going to go back to the room and wait for you."

WHEN I GROW UP

"Matt? You can say whatever you want to Matt, and if he gets mad, let him." Seb looks at me to see if I'm joking. "I mean it. He's a self-righteous asshole who thinks he walks on water or something. You can say whatever you want." Another disbelieving look. "I mean it."

"It won't be nice."

"Good."

"I mean it."

"Are you going to compare him to your mother?"

He thinks about it for a second and shrugs. "I might. She is kinda a bitch."

God bless pretty people.

"Don't hold back on my account," I tell him. "If he wants to tussle, go all Lucy Liu on his ass." He gives me a confused look and I sigh. "Okay, put *Charlie's Angels* on the list of movies you have to see and go get him."

He thinks about it for a moment and then smiles. "Okay. How's it going in there?"

"If Jessica Fletcher doesn't get to the point quickly, I'm going to suffocate him."

"Who's Jessica—" he begins to ask.

"Just go!" I say before he can make me feel any older.

Taking a deep breath, I turn and walk back into the waiting room.

I level a look at Tyler and say, "Just get to the point where she's dying, okay?"

Tyler

THAT WEEKEND I drove by her apartment and saw her car in the parking lot. Of course she hadn't called me, which worried me more than it pissed me off. I knocked on the door for almost five minutes before she answered.

She looked like hell.

If she had slept, it didn't show on her face. Her clothes were wrinkled, and it was obvious from the red eyes she'd been crying. She wasn't surprised to see me, nor was she pleased.

"Tyler, not now," she said in a weak voice. "I can't do this right now."

"Do what? Explain why you're acting crazy all of a sudden?"

She snuffled a little and looked up at me with a sad smile. "We both know it isn't all of a sudden."

"Linda, what is wrong?" I asked, kneeling, trying to catch her eye.

"I screwed up," she finally admitted. "I screwed up before, and now he's going to have to pay for it."

"Who?" I asked, confused.

"Kyle," she said, looking up, tears falling from her eyes. "Kyle is going to have to pay and there's nothing I can do about it."

That made no sense to me at all.

"Kyle is fine in California. What did you do so wrong that it's going to come back on…?"

"Billy and I never got divorced."

And suddenly what she was trying to say made perfect sense.

Of course, the way you're staring at me makes it pretty clear that it makes no sense to you, so let me explain.

In our senior year of high school, a new kid enrolled at Granada. He was the punk son of one of the ranch hands out on the Mathisons' place and thought he was too good to be in Foster. He was butt ugly to me, but to Linda he was the very thing she couldn't resist: a bad boy. They got together in a *Sid and Nancy* kind of way that only spelled doom for them both. She began smoking pot with him and the other loser stoners at our school. Weed led to more, and more led to her dropping out so they could be "together." I begged her not to do it, but she was in love and assured me that behind closed doors, he wasn't like I thought.

When she wound up pregnant, it turned out he was exactly like I thought, behind any door.

She moved back to Foster and had Kyle, and Billy ran for the hills so fast he might have caused a sonic boom. By that time her parents had given up on her and moved out of state; they offered to move back, but she refused. She thought she could raise Kyle by herself, and that meant by herself. I, of course, being me, had other things in my life, like me, my ego, and my issues, so by the time the dust settled, we were both back in Foster, and she had a kid, and I had a busted knee.

And we rarely talked about that time in our lives at all.

I wasn't that shocked to find she and Billy had been married. What stunned me was that it had been a legal ceremony, and not just them saying vows while "November Rain" by G&R played in the background.

"So you guys really got married?" I asked dazedly.

"We were in Reno, and he wanted to prove he was in love with me, and not the other chick I had caught him with."

"Wait," I said, rearing back. "You not just married that sleazeball, but you married him *after* you caught him with another woman?"

"It was a fucked-up time, okay?" she snapped. "I didn't want to come crawling back to Foster or to my parents admitting I made a mistake. Everyone had warned me not to go with him, and I didn't listen. At that point I was just betting more money on a bad horse." She took a sobbing breath. "Tyler, I don't need to be judged right now."

"Okay, okay, okay," I said quickly. "No judging. This is a no-judging zone." She cracked a small smile, and I relaxed. "So what does this have to do with Kyle?"

"Somehow he heard of Kyle going to college, which of course made him think there was money to be had. And somehow he found out about the money." I looked at her, confused. "The money Robbie gave the boys."

Now it was starting to make sense.

"But he can't sue for it or anything, right?" I asked, not sure how that went.

"I don't think so. The summons was him threatening to divorce me and try to get some of the money, so I went to Oklahoma and told him that I was as broke as he was and that the money was Kyle's and not mine."

"Uh-oh," I said, understanding.

She nodded. "Now he's going to just attack and pressure Kyle endlessly for money. And you know Kyle—he always wants to do the right thing. What am I supposed to say? 'Your father is a complete and utter waste of flesh. Ignore everything I said about giving people chances and tell him to fuck off'?"

"It's a start," I offered.

"You know he won't," she said, and I knew it to be true. "I'm going to have to go back up there again and threaten him to leave Kyle alone."

"With what?"

She shrugged. "I haven't gotten there yet, but maybe if I give him something, he'll leave Kyle alone." She began to cry again. "I just don't want Kyle to have to deal with Billy. That shouldn't be on him."

"You know he can handle this, right?" I said gently. "Kyle is a big boy."

"Tyler, it's bad enough that he lived his whole life knowing his father abandoned him. He shouldn't have to deal with the fact that it might have been the best outcome for his life."

"Billy won't stop."

"I have to try."

And she did.

And now she's dying for it.

Robbie

"How?" I finally blurted out. "Did he beat her up? Were they driving and he told her his name wasn't Michael Vaughn, and then they got hit by a semi? Why is she dying?"

He just told me a story that makes the *Odyssey* look like a dime-store paperback, and now he's grasping for words.

"I guess she drove up there and tried to talk to him, and on her way back she fell asleep at the wheel."

My hand went to my mouth, and I felt my heart freeze for a moment.

"She went off the road into a ditch and...." He paused as he started to tear up again.

"She was in a car accident," I said gently. "I got it."

He shook his head and tried to compose himself. "It's worse than that."

"Worse?" I asked, confused. "What's worse than crashing a car?"

He took a deep breath and said, "She hit her head pretty hard when she crashed. They've done all they could for now, but there's a chance there might be some swelling building up in the back of her head...."

I felt my mouth go dry as a panic attack threatened. I forced myself to keep breathing and listen to him as he continued.

"The situation isn't life-threatening right now, but they're saying by the time it does get that bad, there might be brain damage."

"Why don't they just operate, then?" I asked, my voice sounding so far away.

He sighed and dropped his head. "Billy."

"Billy what?" I gripped the chair as I struggled to stay upright.

I wasn't going to make it.

I'd gotten too caught up in the story, too involved with Linda's problems, and now they were mine in a way. And as with most of my problems, my mind was handling it the way it normally did.

By shutting down.

The haze that was way too familiar dropped down over me, and I knew it was just a matter of time before I hit the ground like a dame who talked too much in a thirties gangster movie.

Quiet, you. I have insomnia and TCM—deal with it.

Instead of sliding off the chair and onto the floor, I found someone in front of me speaking gently and reassuringly.

"—okay. You're in a safe place and nothing is going to happen."

As my pulse slowed and vision returned, I saw Seb kneeling in front of me, one hand on each of my shoulders as he tried to talk me down.

"You're in a hospital. The safest place in the world. It's okay."

The haze didn't go away, but it receded a little as I nodded silently.

"You can't see when someone is having a panic attack?" he asked Tyler.

"Um... no?"

"You want to lie down or something?" Sebastian asked me.

"No," I said, a little surprised I could talk. "I'm good." It was a lie, but what was I going to say? No, my dear boy, I'm a heartbeat away from being institutionalized, where I will be endlessly pissed that there aren't white padded rooms and straightjackets because it will mean that all TV, including *Buffy*, lied to me, and I couldn't take that kind of news.

Sebastian started to stand, but I stopped him.

"Thank you," I mouthed and gave him a weak smile.

He tossed a salute with a grin that would have made teenage girls everywhere squee if it was on the CW. "All part of the service."

He gave Tyler a death stare as he strode to the other side of the room and pulled out his cell phone.

"I'm sorry," Tyler said in a way that told me he was about to apologize for everything he had ever done to me.

"It happens," I replied, trying not to make a thing about it. "Just give me a second to recharge."

He nodded, sitting there looking like a little kid waiting for permission to talk.

Taking a deep breath, I asked, "Okay, where were we?"

"Billy won't let them operate on her."

Now I was pissed. "What? How? Why?" Great, I was three *W*s away from being a reporter.

"He showed up, and they're still married. He won't let them operate."

"They're *what* now?" I said, unsure I was hearing this right.

"He's saying it is against their personal beliefs and he isn't going to allow them to operate, and no one here can tell the hospital different."

"What in the fuck? Who cares? Why don't they just go in and do it?"

Tyler looked at me with those sad hound dog eyes. "Because they know if they do, Billy will sue the living shit out of them."

"But they haven't been married in forever!"

"The law doesn't care."

I was about to throw a fit when the waiting room door opened and Sheriff Taylor walked in. At first I thought he was there to check on Linda, but when I saw his partner at the door, I knew different.

"Tyler," he said in a low voice. "I'm gonna need you to step out here."

"You have got to be kidding me," I said, standing up.

He didn't look like he was liking this any better than Tyler was. "The hospital said there was someone kicking chairs in the waiting room, and they called us to escort him out."

"I'll be good," Tyler said in a voice that was breaking my heart. "Please don't make me leave, Sheriff."

Taylor sighed, and I knew it wasn't going to be good news. "They're asking you to leave, son, and there's nothing I can do about that. Why don't you go home, take a shower and rest up, and then come back when there's a shift change. They're saying to take you out now; that doesn't mean you can't come back in later."

"Why don't you arrest that scum bucket who's in there killing Linda?" I demanded. Even as I asked, I knew it wasn't his fault, but I was so fucking tired of this shit. Why does the world have to be *this* stupid? There are gay people who've lived together for fifty years who aren't allowed in the hospital rooms of their partners because they aren't really married, but this redneck fuck can hold Linda hostage?

"If I could throw Billy Stilleno out of here, I would," he said, leveling me a stare. "But I have to enforce all the laws, not just the ones I agree with." He looked over at Tyler. "Grab your coat, son. Let's head out."

Matt came barging into the waiting room, and he didn't look any happier than I was. "Oh, come on!"

"Matt," Taylor warned him. "They didn't ask me to take you out of here, but you throw a fit and I'm gonna have to. Now shut up, help your man grab his things, and take him home before this becomes a real problem instead of just me walking you out."

Matt looked over at me, and I nodded. "Go. I'll stay and call you if anything happens."

Mouthing the words "Thank you," he got Tyler to his feet and led him out with the sheriff. Once they were gone, Sebastian came over, not sure what was going on. "Did they get arrested?"

I had already taken my phone out and called Kyle's number. "No, they're taking them home because the hospital complained."

"Do we have to leave?"

"They can try, but they better bring more than two cops to do it." The call went to voicemail, and I almost screamed into the phone. "Your ass better be in the air, because you need to be here about four hours ago!" I hung up.

"So what do we do now?" Seb asked, uncertainly.

"We sit and wait and hope she doesn't die."

He sat down next to me. "Who doesn't die?"

111

Oh God, I was going to have to tell him the story.

"Okay, remember how I told you about Kyle?"

I owed Tyler an apology; there was no quick way to tell this story after all.

Matt

HE SAT in the passenger seat and said nothing.

I'm not going to lie and say Tyler was the easiest person to love. He was moody and withdrawn at times, and he had a streak of self-loathing that was only matched by his own ego. It was like he drew pride from looking the way he did and then punished himself for liking it. He was a good man, not a great one, not a bad one, just good. He had done horrible things in his life, but he had learned from them and honestly tried to change.

And then things like this happened.

After that freakjob had shot up the school and held Kyle captive in the library, Tyler had looked like he was ready to run in there and take that kid apart all by himself. Later, when we were at home, I asked him why. I mean, I knew he liked those kids something fierce, but why was it *his* responsibility to save them? He looked at me, and what he said ran chills down my spine.

"Because I can't let someone else I love die and do nothing. I just can't."

He wasn't saying he couldn't stand by and let it happen. He meant if someone else died, he couldn't take it. I'd almost asked him what that meant, but I dropped it, because when was the subject going to come up again?

If you aren't paying attention, I might not be the sharpest tool in the shed.

"You hungry?" I asked him, knowing he was but he wouldn't eat.

He shook his head, still staring out the passenger-side window.

"Mind if I stop at Starr's and get myself something?"

I wasn't that hungry, but I was hoping if he saw me eat, he'd eat.

The only response I got was a shrug.

112

Good enough for me.

I pulled into the parking lot and pushed the call signal to order. Starr's is one of those old-time drive-ins where the staff brings you your food on roller skates. It was pretty much everything Sonic tried to be, but with heart. My parents had come here on dates, and as I looked over the menu, I wondered how many people in Foster owed their lives to this place.

I ordered a ton of food, knowing Tyler ate like a machine when he was depressed. Lucky for him he liked working out, because that boy spent a lot of time depressed. It was weird because it wasn't like he was clinically depressed; it was just how he was. He was a sad person, and I wished I could make him happier sometimes, but I took solace in the fact that by just being here I was making it better.

"She's going to die," he said as we waited for our food.

"Come on," I said. "We don't know anything yet. Kyle will be here in a few hours, and the hospital is going to have a hard time refusing her only child. This will get taken care of."

"No it won't. She's going to die because she's friends with me. That's how it always goes."

This was a spiral I'd heard before, and I knew if it continued, he was going to just go nuts. So I decided to roll the dice.

"Well, actually, only one of your friends has died. That's a low sampling to be using the word 'always.'"

He slowly looked over at me, and I could see the disbelief on his face.

"It's true. Only Riley has died, unless you're saying Riley was your only friend besides Linda, and in that case it still isn't an 'always,' it's a 'so far.'"

"You think this is something to joke about?" he asked, his voice no longer melancholy but ramping up to pissed.

"I think this is a horrible turn of events, but it has nothing to do with you or your friendships."

"I could have driven her up there," he said, getting louder. "I could have gone myself and kicked the shit out of Billy and got this over with. Instead I did nothing, and now look at her."

I nodded like I was agreeing. "So then if she gets better, you'll be moving in with her?" He looked at me, confused. "To make sure she doesn't ever drive to work or cross the street alone. Because a pretty significant percentage of accidents happen in the shower, which is going to get weird, but then I suppose you could sit on the toilet and wait."

"Stop making jokes," he growled.

"Why? If you can make this worse than it actually is, I can make jokes."

"She could be dying!" he snapped. His hands were balled into fists.

"I thought she *was* dying. Make up your mind, Tyler: she is either already dead and it's all your fault, or she could be dying, which means anything could happen. But it can't be both."

"I don't want her to die!" he screamed, his face turning red with frustration and rage. And like that, his anger and grief crested and he began sobbing. "I don't want her to die, Matt."

I leaned over and pulled him into an embrace. "Then stop blaming yourself and start praying for the best."

He nodded into my chest as he just let it all out.

But I knew this was only round one.

Sebastian

MAN, AND I thought Jersey was a lot of drama.

Yeah, that's not fair and probably not appropriate, but when I get nervous, I make jokes. It's a defense mechanism that comes from a lifetime of trying to be what everyone in the world wants you to be. I'm not going to go into detail—I don't know you all that well—but frankly, no one has had a great childhood, and if they say they did, they're lying.

So anyway, I joke. Badly, for sure, but when I'm in an uncomfortable place, it's what I do. And let me tell you, I couldn't think of a more uncomfortable place than Foster, Texas, at the moment. The kicker is that the town hides it well. When we drove in, all I could think of was

Norman Rockwell paintings and Jimmy Stewart movies. How in the world could this town be as bad as Robbie described it?

And then it slipped for a second, and I saw just a glimpse of the monster underneath.

Not the whole thing, just enough to wonder if I'd imagined it, and if I was stupid, I'd shake my head and go, "nah." I've seen more than enough horror movies to know the jackass who goes "nah" gets killed in the most gruesome way, and you laugh and scream at him because he should have known better.

I fucking know better.

One, that "I'm her husband" shit wouldn't fly in a real town. The doctors would just go and do the fucking operation and let the chips fall where they may. Only in a place like this would trained medical professionals pause because some trailer-park trash gave them the stink eye. Two, who the fuck holds a person's medical treatment hostage? I can't even imagine what kind of fucking knuckle dragger thinks that's okay, and I've met some real slimeballs in my day. And three, being read by a guy who looks like he was kicked out of *Smallville* for being too muscular. I understand protective friends, but dude, at least wait until we've spoken more than three words before you come swinging at me like I'm a child molester or something. And don't even get me started on that Tyler guy. See, if that Matt asshole thinks he knows who I am, then I know exactly who Tyler is.

Because I *was* him up until last year.

I was one of those genetically gifted guys who had almost no body fat and lean muscle mass. It's called an ectomorphic body type: low fat storage, high calorie use. It basically means I start out as normal and get a lot better with a little work. I'm not completely bragging—I mean, I am a little bit, but not as much as you think. But if you think of someone famous who has a great body, I can assure you they're an ectomorph.

So what that means is I was stuck-up in high school.

I mean, I was cute, in shape, played football—I had it all going on. Girls flirted, guys looked, and I knew it. So much so that when a couple of friends asked me to head out to the Left Coast, all I could think about was how famous I was going to be. Good-looking guys were all over TV.

I could do that; who couldn't? I was sure that within a month, I'd be on Dawson's whatever or 9021addwhatevernumberyouwant and be living the high life.

And then I saw what actual beauty looks like.

I don't tell this story much, but it helps to explain why I know what kind of person Tyler is. See, my friends, who were also high school jocks who were now college jocks, and I decided to go bum around Hollywood and see how the other half lived. There were four of us, and we were built, young, and cute. We had nothing to fear. So we went to this place that was stupid popular and my bud Crash—no, that's not his real name—started hitting on the girl at the door to get us seats while the rest of us waited to be noticed.

Crash didn't get us a table, but he did get us to the bar, which was just as good in my opinion. So we downed some overpriced beer and leaned on the wood, waiting for someone to come up to us and say we were as stunning as we thought. About an hour into this, the beer added up and I went to go take a piss. I drained the lizard and, because my mom taught me well, went to wash my hands, and someone walked out of one of the stalls. Okay, not just any someone—a real someone.

Jensen Ackles came out and washed his hands next to me.

Now at the time he was just on a soap opera, so I had no idea who he was, but I was stunned by the way he looked just standing there. He glanced over at me, nodded, and flashed me a grin that made me think I'd never learned to smile correctly. But it was more than his looks. Don't get me wrong. He was so bangible it hurt. But he had something more than that. He had this aura, this presence, that was electric, even though he couldn't have been more than a year older than me. It was a thing I had never experienced before.

He finished and then moved toward me and paused.

"I need a towel," he said, still smiling.

And that was when I realized I'd been staring at him, most likely with my fucking mouth open.

"Oh yeah. Sorry. I mean… here," I said, turning around and trying to tear a paper towel off for him.

Which was when I almost tore the machine off the wall because it was one long cloth towel that was looped up inside.

"Fuck," I said as I realized the damn thing was about to fall off.

"You know, I'm good," he said, the smile never wavering, but his body language said he was freaked. "Thanks."

He rushed out of the bathroom, leaving me there with a broken hand towel and a broken ego.

Of course, by the time I got back to the guys, I had shaken it off. Silently convinced myself I had imagined everything, and whatever whoever the fuck that was had, I had the same and more. Deep down, I knew. I knew at that very moment that stardom wasn't going to work. I went out on auditions and tried my hardest to make people see how great I was, but in the end I was working tables, reading about the young, fresh-faced new guy who was signed as a series regular on *Dark Angel*.

When I got "discovered" for modeling, I thought maybe for a second I'd been wrong, that I did have it.

But I realized that the guy I modeled for had probably hired me because he wanted to sleep with me. I didn't even care when I stopped working and just became his boyfriend. Well… I did care, but I didn't argue, because I knew I was out of my league. Of course, when I walked in on him with not just one but two younger, better-looking guys than myself, I did what I should have done the instant I walked out of that bathroom.

I went back to a small pond to enjoy my big fish status again.

Of course, that isn't how it worked out: I met Robbie and things changed. For the better, to be sure, but you see, I knew Tyler well. He was a big fish here in Hicktown, USA, and I'm sure he'd gone off somewhere thinking he was hot shit and it hadn't worked out for him. So he'd come running back here where he could be the hometown hero with the heart of gold. A pretty boy who could do no wrong, living where the world revolved around him. He was definitely into that. So much so that, instead of stepping up when Riley was killed, he drove off and abandoned Robbie because his status was more important than doing the right thing.

You know, I hadn't really realized how much that guy pissed me off until I met him. I mean, I always made the joke to Robbie that I would have kicked that guy's ass for him, but now… I just might. He was so busy telling his horrible, dramatic story, where I'm sure he was the main victim and not the woman dying in the hospital room, that he couldn't even see Robbie slowly starting to pass out from a panic attack.

So I did what any good boyfriend would do. I called Robbie's mom and told her that he'd had an episode, but he was doing okay for now.

Why does this make me a good boyfriend? I'm glad you asked. Because it means his mom is going to call him and demand to know how he is, giving me time to sneak into the ICU and try to pull a *Crash* on the head nurse. See, I know Robbie well enough to know that his panic comes from two things—lack of control and fear of the unknown. Lack of control because there's nothing he can do for this lady, and fear of the unknown because he doesn't know how bad she is or what's going on in here.

Now, many a guy has called out "God" during sex, but this does not give me the ability to heal the sick.

Oh, come on, that was funny.

But I can charm a middle-aged nurse who's working a twelve-hour shift into giving me some information on my poor, injured friend who I just found out about and rushed to Foster to see.

"You're a friend of Linda?" asked the lady, who I assumed did a killer summer stock version of Nurse Ratched in her spare time.

I gave her an *awww shucks* grin and nodded. "I am; is she okay?"

Instead of answering, she just stared at me like I was a new life form or something.

"I mean, I know she was in a car accident, but I don't know how bad it was."

More silence.

"And I was just curious how she was doing."

"Friends from where?"

Yeah, I hadn't really researched the role of long-lost friend well enough to, you know, actually think of where I might know her from. So I winged it.

"I was her son's… coach?" Dammit, didn't mean for that to be a question.

"Kyle doesn't play sports" was her response.

Fuck.

"I meant, like, academic coach."

Her eyes narrowed. "So you're telling me that you were, what? Some kind of tutor?"

In improv, the worst thing you can do is say no. Any suggestion has to be run with; the correct response is "Yes, and...."

"Yes, and I kept in touch after he went to college."

"Her son. Kyle. Needed a tutor?"

She asked that like I had suggested cricket was superior to baseball.

"Well... not needed, but you know how teens are. It can be a challenge to get them to study."

Her expression got even darker, and I had a feeling my improv wasn't working.

"You do know that Kyle got a full ride to UC Berkeley based solely on his grades, right?"

I nodded. "Of course. We were very proud of him."

"And that for the most part was widely considered one of the smartest boys in town."

I did not know that.

"Well, yes, but...."

"And that he absolutely adored going to school and studying?"

Who was this lady? President of the Kyle fan club? Jeez, just marry him already!

"So you're not going to tell me how she's doing?"

"You're lucky I'm not calling security."

And with that I turned tail and went back to the waiting room.

It was official. I hated Foster, Texas.

Robbie

I MUST have fallen asleep, because when I woke up a girl who looked a lot like Jennifer but with shorter hair was standing in front of me.

"Don't you worry that some girl is going to come in and throw a bucket of water on you?"

"Don't you worry that with a haircut that butch, people will think you're Mandy Moore?"

Her face broke out in a smile. "Fuck you very much."

I got up and opened my arms to the first person in Foster who had actually tried to be my friend. "Rapunzel, what happened to all your beautiful hair?" I asked once the hugging was out of the way.

"Oh, you know, I cut it off and sold it for a watch chain for Josh, but turns out he sold his watch for a comb, so we were both screwed."

"You know, you keep spouting sass off like that, people might think you've read a book or something."

She cocked her head. "Mandy Moore doesn't read?"

"God, I hate you," I said with no emotion whatsoever.

"Right back at you, Mary."

There was the sound of either a grizzly bear reciting poetry or a Harley Davidson badly in need of a tune-up next to us. We looked over and Seb was halfway on one of the waiting room chairs, snoring his ass off and drooling a little, not that I really looked.

"You brought a bodyguard with you?" she asked.

Pulling out my phone, I snapped a quick blackmail pic. That should be good to make him do the dishes or do the laundry when we got back home. "That's one way of referring to him," I said, trying not to smile.

"Oh my God, Robbie got his groove on!" she almost yelled, waking Sebastian up.

"Kelly Clarkson!" he shouted, falling out of his chair.

Jennifer glanced over at me with a silent question of what that meant. I just shrugged. "Honey, wake up," I said pleasantly as he pulled himself off the floor.

"I mean... I'm good," he said, brushing himself off and looking around, confused. "Is someone sick?" he asked, realizing we were in a hospital.

"Texas," I hissed, slapping his arm real quick.

"Right." He shook his head, trying to wake all the way up. Then he noticed Jennifer. "Um, hi?"

"Jennifer, this is Sebastian. Sebastian, this is Jennifer." They shook hands and I added, "She's the only person I might have saved if the town was overrun by dead people or Republicans." I paused. "Wait. I think it has been. Never mind." I looked at her. "You're on your own."

"Ignore him," she advised Sebastian. "Everyone with a brain does."

"And yet you don't." I pretended to ponder. "Another point proving you're Mandy Moore."

"She's Mandy Moore?" Seb asked.

"Better than Kelly Clarkson," she mumbled and laughed.

I forced myself not to react other than to ask, "What are you doing here?"

She sat and patted the chair next to her. "My dad said you were here when he had to throw Tyler out, so I ran over to keep you company."

I sat down next to her. "So where is your moose?" I asked, looking around. "I mean, I thought everyone had a moose attached to their hip in this town."

"Josh is at A&M, hopefully studying and not partying like I'm pretty sure he is. I drove straight home when my dad told me what had happened with Ms. Stilleno. I knew this was going to be a thing."

"A thing is an understatement," I said, feeling the ancient hatred I'd held for this town for so long begin to rekindle. "Only here could a redneck hold a woman hostage in ICU."

"I'm sure there are stupid people everywhere. I mean, where do you come from?"

I flipped her off and felt the telltale signs of a nicotine fit coming on. "Come downstairs with me. I need to have a smoke, and all he'll do is lecture me about how bad it is."

As if on cue Sebastian said, not even looking up from his phone, "It's bad for you, and it gives you horrible breath, which minimizes my desire to kiss you."

"You see?" I said, walking out with her. "I'll be back," I called to him.

"With horrible breath," he shouted before the waiting room door closed.

"I like him," she said as soon as the door shut. "How long?"

"Don't start," I said, pushing the elevator button. "You know how they say not to tell people about a pregnancy before the first trimester because… you know?" She nodded. "With gay men it's like that with relationships. We try not to talk about it until a year passes or we buy a pet. So how is your lifelong dream to become Jill going?"

"I assume you're using some archaic pop culture reference I'm too young to know, so I will say my lifelong dream to be Batgirl is going fine. I'm third in my class, which is more impressive than it sounds since I'm one of only four girls in it. The book stuff sucks, but the physical stuff is so much fun I can't believe I skipped gym all those times."

"And Josh?" I asked as we walked outside and I lit up.

"He's good," she said, shaking her head when I offered her one. "He's sitting out this year, which is called a redshirt year." I looked at her, confused, and she said, "Don't ask, I think it might be a *Star Trek* thing. But it's so he can get comfortable with the team and all that, so he has *a lot* of spare time on his hands."

"Uh-oh," I said.

"Yeah. I've gotten no less than four videos from him in the past month. Only one was he actually wearing clothes." I almost choked. "I wish I could say that it didn't turn me on, but I can't. He has a pretty ridiculous body."

"I can't believe I'm standing here listening to you tell me about your boyfriend's sex tapes."

"Well, one, it isn't a tape unless you're a Kardashian, and two, a lot of couples do it now. You're telling me if that hunk of a man was away for a while and sent you a video of him showing off, you wouldn't watch?"

"Shut up," I said quickly, trying not to imagine it. Well, at least until I was alone…

"Exactly."

I was going to say something else when a cab pulled up to the hospital and Kyle got out. He threw some money at the driver and began to sprint inside.

"Hey, Bueller!" I screamed, getting his attention.

He looked over at me, dropped his bag, ran to me, and gave me a hug.

"Tell me she's all right," he said, gripping me so hard I think he might have broken a rib.

I patted his head and said, "She's okay for now. It's going to be okay."

Of course, I had no faith in those words, but I knew hearing them from time to time helped. He finally climbed off me and looked over at Jennifer. "I like your hair," he said and hugged her.

"Thanks," she said, hugging him back. "Where's Brad?"

He pulled away. "I don't know and I don't care." He glanced at me. "So, ICU?"

I nodded.

"Great." He turned around and grabbed his bag and went inside.

"Fuck" was all Jennifer said.

"Here we go again." I sighed, following him inside.

Kyle

I KNEW I was in Texas the second I stepped off the plane.

Don't ask me how, because the Dallas airport looked just like the Oakland one I'd just flown out of, but I could tell. Maybe it was the fact that the people weren't moving as fast as they were in California. Everyone here was just… moseying. That was it, moseying along. Like there was nowhere special they had to be, and even if they did, it wouldn't matter because the state was, like, fifteen times too big for its own good.

Or maybe it was me.

Maybe it was the way I felt dragged down the second my foot touched Texas soil again. Like gravity was increased a thousandfold, and this time there would be no escaping. I tried to banish those thoughts as I attempted to rent a car, which wasn't going to be easy. One of the better things I could say about Robbie's gift was that it allowed me to get one of those credit cards that's linked to an account. Not a bank card, but an actual credit card where the limit was, like, an amount of money you put aside, in case you tried to skip town without paying. I mean, it wasn't much, but it did give me positive credit.

Which then opened the floodgate and released the credit kraken.

There were a ton of companies that just threw their credit cards at me because I was a college student, which of course meant I was stupid and broke. So the plus side was that I had everything I needed to rent a car. The minus, of course, was the lady looked at me like I was twelve asking if I could touch the stove or some shit. Finally she came back and said I would need to have an insured driver sign for me before she'd rent me a car. Of course, I wasn't an insured driver because Brad was the one with the car, and I didn't drive it. I told her that, and she smiled and shrugged.

This repeated at the next three car places before I realized it wasn't happening. I would be stuck in Dallas forever if these people had their way.

So I took a cab to the bus station, grabbed a Greyhound, and said fuck it. Three hours later I was in Foster, sore, cranky, and just plain pissed off at the world. Another cab to the hospital and voilà, I was there. I almost ran past Robbie and Jennifer, whose first question was, of course, about Brad.

This was going to be trying.

I got upstairs to the ICU, where there was this hot-ass guy messing around with his phone in the waiting room. He glanced up at me and nodded. I nodded back and walked into the actual ICU. I recognized the nurse behind the desk, but her name escaped me. She was one of the hundreds of adults I had seen my whole life and never bothered to acknowledge growing up. Now I felt like shit because I'm sure she had a name, a family, a whole life, and all she was to me was random adult #4.

Didn't matter, though; she knew me.

"Kyle," she said like we were old friends. "You made it."

"Um, I did," I answered, not sure how to react to her. "Where's my mom?"

"There are some things you should be told," she warned, coming around the desk. "It's complicated—"

"It's not that complicated," I said, cutting her off. "My mom is here. Which bay?" I began looking around, and there was only one alcove that had the curtains drawn and door closed. The other rooms were empty, so it was easy to tell from here. "Never mind, I got it."

"Kyle, wait—" she called after me, but I had no time for this. I needed to see with my own eyes that my mom was all right. Well, not all right, but at least still breathing.

124

I opened the door and the room was dark, so I flipped the light switch on. There were two chairs in the room; each had a stranger in it watching TV. One looked my age, maybe a little older, military-short hair and a pretty decent build on him. The other guy was as old as my mom and looked like he was a friend of hers back in her party days. He had a faded Jim Morrison shirt on and a nasty-ass beard that looked like he was trying to impress someone.

I wasn't impressed.

"Who the hell are you guys?" I asked, trying not to look over at the unconscious form of my mother in the bed. I wanted to do that alone, not in front of two assholes squatting in my mom's room.

The older guy squinted at me and asked, "Kyle?"

Great. *Everyone* knows who I am today.

"Yeah, and you are?"

He got up, and I was struck by how skinny he was. Like beanpole skinny and tall. His jeans looked like they were worn in about a thousand miles ago, and his belt buckle let me know that he wanted to ride free or die. Yeah, this guy was a friend of my mom.

"You don't recognize me?" he asked, catching me off guard, because had we met before?

"Should I?"

"Show some respect," the kid said to me. Well, not kid, but he sure wasn't an adult.

I glared at him, and the guy snapped a quick, "Troy. Shut up."

Troy looked away from me, but I could tell he was pissed.

"I'm Billy," he said, like the name would have meaning.

"And I'm Kyle. Why are you in my mom's room?"

Nurse NoName came running in. "Oh dear" was all she could manage.

"Calm down, little dude," Billy said to me, instantly pissing me off.

"I'll calm down when someone tells me why you two are in my mom's fucking room." I was losing it.

"Now I know your mom wouldn't let you get away with that kind of language," Billy admonished me.

And I'd had enough.

"Yeah, well, she can't really say anything about it right now, can she? So tell me what you're doing in here, or get the fuck out."

"Dude," he said, shaking his head. "It's me. Billy. She never told you about me?"

I turned around and looked at the nurse. "Please call security."

She paused. "It's not that simple."

"Why not?" I almost screamed. "I'm her son, and these guys are strangers."

"I'm not a stranger," I heard Billy say from behind me. I spun around and faced him. "I'm your dad."

Please fasten your seat belts; the pilot has informed us there is some turbulence ahead.

Jennifer

BY THE time we got back to the ICU, there was yelling.

I took off toward the unit and called back to Robbie, "Call 911 and tell them we need my dad here now."

When I got in there, Kyle was backing away from a rock that seemed to be carved into the shape of a boy. He had a crew cut with laced-up military boots and looked like he was about to go to town on Kyle.

If Kyle was scared, he didn't show it at all.

Nurse Redmon was trying to keep the peace, but that ship had sailed a few minutes ago. Thank God there was no one else in there but Kyle's mom, or it could have hurt someone. Beefy guy took another step toward Kyle and raised his fist as if to swing.

Which was when I kicked beefy guy's knee to the left.

Not hard enough to snap it, though I wanted to—just enough to get his attention for a second and make him stop moving. He went down to a crouching position and glared up at me and snarled. Oddly I was completely calm in the moment. "Stay down," I ordered in a voice that I wanted to sound like my dad but probably just sounded like a teenage girl being butch.

126

He started to stand up anyway, and I pulled the baton that was tucked in the back of my belt and flicked my wrist. It extended and locked into place with a satisfying snap that made Beefy pause.

"Stay. Down," I said again.

I know it looks all Batgirl, but one of the first things they teach us is to keep a weapon that people can't see on you. Some guys had ankle holsters, some carried butterfly knives. Me, I went with the Jennifer Lopez *Out of Sight* baton. Flat black handle with a stainless-steel rod, it wasn't only dangerous, but it looked completely badass too.

Without ever looking away from Beefy, I asked Kyle, "You okay?"

He didn't say anything for a second, which I assumed was him nodding because he said, "Oh, you can't see me. Yeah, I'm fine."

Seconds later security came rushing in, and by "security" I mean two middle-aged rent-a-cops who had never run so fast in their lives. They were huffing and puffing as they tried to take in the scene.

"Guys," I said to them, still not blinking from Beefy, "my dad is about to come storming in here. Can one of you go downstairs and let him know what the situation is before he comes shooting up the place?"

I heard someone run off, and Beefy sighed and sat down on the floor. "Need a girl to do your fighting?"

"Fuck you, man, I—" Kyle began to protest.

A loud "*Hey*" from me froze them both. "I didn't say it was talking time. We're all going to wait here quietly for the police to arrive."

"And I can tell them you attacked me out of nowhere," Beefy half whined.

"Yeah, trust me, He-Man, I'm in more than enough trouble all by myself. Your little tattletale threat doesn't even register right now."

He seemed confused, but I wasn't in the mood to turn any more letters around for him. Instead I glanced over at Kyle and asked again, "You okay?"

His mouth opened to answer when an old guy looked out from the ICU bay. At first I thought he was a homeless guy from the way he looked—hair long and unwashed, wrinkled T-shirt, that hungry look in his eyes that living on the street too long gives people. But he started to talk and I knew he wasn't homeless.

He was a drug addict.

127

How did I know that from just him talking? Because he opened his mouth and I saw his teeth. Or what was left of them. There's having bad dental hygiene, and there's what was going on in his mouth. How had a crackhead gotten into that room?

"Dude, man, let's all calm down," he said, sounding like the world's oldest hippie. "You guys shouldn't fight; you're brothers."

I thought he meant "brothers" like we were all brothers of the earth or some shit. I tried to be as open-minded as the next person, but that granola-eating stuff really irritated me sometimes. But that illusion was shattered when Kyle shouted back at him.

"He's not my brother. You're not my father, and get out of that fucking room."

He's not what and what now?

Before anyone could react, the ICU doors burst open and my dad, his deputy, and one of the security guards came rushing in. I'm not sure who he thought he was going to see, but I would bet it wasn't me holding a baton on someone.

"Jennifer Caroline Rogers," he said in the exact tone of voice he'd used when he found Brad sneaking out of my room one night. "Put down that weapon right now."

Sighing, I collapsed it and began to slide it back into my belt.

"No," he said, holding out his hand.

"I'm going to need that back," I said, slapping it into his palm.

"Then we're going to have two talks. One, about carrying weapons and two, what the word 'need' means."

I scowled at him but moved aside because I wasn't the issue there.

He must have agreed because he stepped around me and looked down at Beefy and over at Crackhead. "You know, Billy, when I heard you were back in town, I imagined that it wouldn't come to this."

My dad knew this guy?

Billy was about to answer, but Beefy decided to squawk instead. "That asshole came in and tried to kick us out." He was pointing at Kyle.

"Well, 'that asshole' happens to be the only one of you I'm sure should be in that room, so let's not start pointing fingers, shall we?" He looked over at Billy. "If he wants you out of the room, Billy, you know you can't stay."

"I'm her husband, man."

"You are not," Kyle raged. "You've been gone my whole life! You can't just come in here and fucking say that."

The kid on the floor started screaming, and Kyle screamed back and it got stupid for a few seconds, and then an older guy in a suit came in, flanked by two security guards.

"Sheriff, this is a hospital. I can hear these two three floors away. Do something."

I had to give my dad credit. Instead of sighing or giving the guy a dirty look, he just turned to the three yelling idiots. "Okay, people. Mr. Childs wants quiet, so the next person who screams gets kicked out. The next person who raises his voice gets kicked out. The next person who speaks above a normal tone gets kicked out." He glanced over at Billy. "So please, yell."

Instead Billy looked down at Beefy and said, "Shut up, Troy. Now."

Troy scowled but said nothing.

"He can't be in there," Kyle said, turning to Mr. Childs. "He shouldn't be here."

"I understand your concern, young man, and we can have a conversation about that in my office. Not in the middle of the ICU." He looked over at the guards. "Show them the way," he said, and then to my dad, "Can I have a word, Sheriff?"

The guards escorted Kyle, Billy, and Troy out while my dad talked to Childs. Nurse Redmon came over to me. "You looked very brave in there, Jennifer."

I smiled. "Thanks, but I'm pretty sure he's ready to shoot me."

She chuckled. "That's just called being a dad. You did good."

The two of them finished and Childs walked out of the room. My dad said something to Deputy Kelly, who nodded and walked out too. "Here we go," I muttered to the nurse as my dad walked up to me.

"You have any idea the kind of people you're dealing with here?" he asked me.

"The dad is on crack," I said, not blinking. "The son acts like he's on steroids, but he might just be an asshole."

I saw the corners of his mouth flicker like he wanted to smile but stopped himself. "So you know Billy does drugs and still decided to pull a weapon on them. What if he had a gun?"

I didn't even pause to think about it. "Then he'd be pointing it at me instead of Kyle."

We locked eyes for a moment, and after a few seconds he sighed and shook his head. "You're either going to be a great cop or get shot the first week because you think you're Wonder Woman."

I began to argue with him and then looked down and saw he was handing me my baton back.

"Do not ever be in a room alone with Billy or his son. Got it?"

I nodded and slipped the baton back into my belt.

"Call me again if anything comes up. And it will."

I nodded again, and he reached over and gave me a hug. "And try not to beat anyone up while I'm gone."

I hugged him back. "I can't promise anything."

Finally he laughed and walked out of the ICU.

A couple of seconds later, Sebastian's head poked in. "Anyone dead?"

"You can't be in here," Nurse Redmon declared, walking over toward him.

I heard a startled "eep" and the door closed.

I walked out, knowing Robbie was going to want to know everything in detail.

Kyle

NO ONE spoke as we followed the guard upstairs.

Troy was seething as a Muzak version of "Gloria" played softly in the background. No matter how menacing he got, there was no way I was going to feel intimidated while Laura Branigan told me all about her flaky friend. I almost smiled, but of course Billy ruined it.

"I remember this song," he said like we were all good friends. "Your mom used to love it."

"She used to love a lot of lame things," I said, my bad mood returning. "Doesn't mean they warrant mentioning."

That shut him up pretty well.

We were shown into a nice office on the top floor. From there we could look out over Foster and realize how tiny and insignificant it really was in the world.

"Stay here and don't do anything," the guard warned us.

"Anything?" Troy asked. "Like, no breathing? No blinking? Can we sit? Is there sitting, or are we just standing the whole time?"

I smiled despite myself because it was the same thing that came to my mind.

"You know what I mean," the guard fired back and slammed the door behind him.

We sat down, and I stared out the window, trying not to think of my mother downstairs.

"So we going to get to this or what?" Billy asked me.

I ignored him and kept staring.

"Okay, little man, we can do it that way too."

It took every ounce of will not to scream. "Don't call me 'little man'!"

Mr. Childs walked in and sat down behind his desk. "Okay, I want to get this settled so what happened downstairs doesn't happen again." He looked at all of us. "Who wants to start?"

I didn't even wait to see if Billy was going to talk. "He has nothing to do with our family, and I want him out of my mother's hospital room."

Childs looked at Billy.

"She's my wife, and I have the marriage license to prove it."

He reached into his pocket and pulled out a folded-up piece of paper that looked, well, older than me, to be honest. Childs read it over and then glanced at me. "You're claiming this isn't real?"

"I'm claiming it doesn't matter because this guy has never been in our lives. Not once. I'm nineteen years old, and this is the first time I've laid eyes on the man, so he has no right to be in her room. Period."

"That's not what the law says, little man."

I was really close to slugging him.

"Do you have proof they ever got divorced, Kyle?" Mr. Childs asked me.

"What proof? You want nineteen years of no birthday cards as proof? You want nineteen years of no Christmas as proof? He doesn't exist in our life."

"That may be, but this is a legal marriage license, which puts me in a bind."

Was this for real?

"A bind? What kind of bind? Hobo the Homeless Guy comes bouncing into town and says he's married to my mom and that means something?"

"This piece of paper means something," Childs said, showing me the license.

"So I have no rights here?" I asked, as the feeling of falling down a rather large rabbit hole began to engulf me.

"You have rights, and you can even contest him being here, but it has to be in front of a judge, and that can't happen until Monday. So for right now, I can't tell him to leave."

"You could," I countered.

"He could, but I would sue him for denying me access to my wife," Billy said, the "hey little dude" tone of voice completely gone now.

"*She's not your wife!*" I screamed at him, completely losing it.

Both security guards came rushing in from the other side of the door, but Childs waved them off. "Mr. Stilleno, if you keep having outbursts like that, I'm going to ask *you* to leave."

"Why are you doing this?" I asked Billy, panting. "What possible motive can you have for being here?"

Billy glanced over at Childs. "Can I talk to my son alone for a few minutes?"

"I'm not your son," I growled.

"If I can have your word no fighting," the older man asked us.

"It won't take long," Billy assured him.

Childs got up and, when Troy didn't, Billy said, "You too, boy. Go wait outside."

"Dad!" he whined.

"Go. Now," he snapped back.

Troy sighed and stomped out with everyone else, leaving me and Billy far above Foster.

"So what is this about? Some lame attempt for you to reconnect with me or some crap? Because I have no interest in...."

"How much did you get?" Billy asked, ignoring my words completely.

"What?"

"How much money did that queer give you?" His voice was like steel now.

"What are you talking about?"

He got up, and he didn't look lanky and homeless anymore. He looked tall and menacing. "That queer downstairs gave you some money before you went off to college. How much did he give you?"

"I'm not telling you that," I said, confused and offended at the same time.

"You will," he said, giving me a half-toothless smile. "Your mom has something in the back of her head swelling up. They asked me if I would consent to allow surgery, but I said no. They said by the time it became life-threatening, that she would have suffered brain damage. So you will tell me how much it was, or we can wait and watch your mom turn into a vegetable." He shrugged. "All the same to me."

I've never imagined that simple words could hurt so badly, but they did. It felt like I'd been slugged in the stomach and was gasping for air as I stared at him. I'd only read about people like this in comic books. Lex Luthor and Joker crap that seemed so evil normal people could never do it. Who risks people's lives just for money? Who could do that and sleep at night?

Billy apparently could.

"So wanna try again, little man? How much did he give you?"

"Why?" was the only word I was able to squeeze out.

"Because there are some guys who I owe money to, and they aren't particular on how they get paid back. So I need to know how much money you got to help dear old dad out."

"You're crazy," I said, taking a step back from him.

"And your mom is dying. Want to say anything else irrelevant?"

I stood there, not even sure how to answer that. You'd see about shit like this on Facebook, a story so fucking horrible that you thought someone made it up just to get you to click it. But this... thing was in front of me, smiling with his yellow-stained teeth, waiting for an answer.

"Nothing?" he said, shrugging. "I got time. Your mom, not so much. You'll come around." He walked over to the door and opened it, and instantly stoner Billy was back. "Thanks, man, I just needed some mano a mano time with my son."

I saw Troy bristle at that, but he didn't say anything—instead he just glared at me.

"So did you two come to an agreement?" Mr. Childs asked.

Billy answered before I could. "I think we're going to stay with the course we have been. Let's wait and see."

"Give her the operation," I blurted out.

"Oh my," Mr. Childs said. "As I said, if you want to dispute this it's going to take a judge, and since it's Saturday, that means at least until Monday."

"She needs it now." I was almost crying.

Childs refused to look me in the eye. "I'm sorry, Mr. Stilleno, but there are rules."

I was going to scream at the top of my lungs and the problem was, if I started I was pretty sure I wasn't going to stop. So instead I just brushed past Billy and Troy, unsure where I was going but knowing I couldn't stay there.

Pretty much the story of my life.

Robbie

JENNIFER EXPLAINED all the fuss to us. Sebastian practically spat as he said, "That fucking bastard."

"So Tyler was right. That crackhead is holding her hostage," I said, trying to work it out in my mind by talking out loud. "And he might just pull it off since we're in the middle of fucking nowhere."

No one said anything for a long while. Finally Jennifer said, "What I want to know is, where's Brad?"

"What does that matter?" Sebastian asked her.

I answered instead. "Because if Brad isn't here, it means he's dead or they broke up, which means Kyle isn't at his best, and right now Kyle needs to be at his perfect."

"I'll call Brad," Jennifer said, walking out of the waiting room.

Once she was gone, Sebastian asked me, "We're really going to waste time trying to figure out if two guys are broken up or not? Shouldn't we be doing something to help whatever her name is?"

I tried to keep the annoyance out of my voice as I explained. "Her name is Linda, and trust me, this isn't wasting time."

Sebastian opened his mouth to argue and then closed it. He took a deep breath and sat down on one of the chairs. Looking up at me, he asked, "Okay, explain it to me."

I sat down next to him and tried to compose my thoughts. "Kyle is amazing, but at the end of the day, he's a nineteen-year-old kid and prone to nineteen-year-old drama. Brad on the surface looks like nothing special, but his devotion to Kyle is something out of a fairy tale. He keeps Kyle centered, and Kyle keeps Brad motivated. I'm convinced that together they could do anything; apart, they're just two teenagers with their heads up their asses."

He didn't say anything for almost a minute, which was killing me, because I had the feeling we were nearing a fight, but I wasn't sure why.

"So what do you think Brad here will do?" he finally asked.

"He'll put Kyle's head in the game, and trust me, once that kid is pointed in a direction, everyone else needs to get out of the way."

He opened his mouth to say something, but Jennifer walked back in. "Goddammit. Yeah, they broke up, and Brad is moving out."

"To where?" I asked, shocked.

"He said a friend's house, so if you were thinking he was coming back here, you'd be wrong." She sounded all kinds of pissed off.

"Did he say what happened?"

She sat down. "Yeah, but it didn't make much sense. Something about Kyle getting distant and him going out for a night, and then Kyle telling him he had to leave." She shook her head. "Something happened, because Brad sounds like he just gave up, and you know Brad never gives up on Kyle."

I nodded, my mind spinning as I tried to figure out what to do next.

The waiting room door burst open and Kyle came in, looking like he was going to scream or cry. "I hate that fucking man."

I got up and moved him to my chair. "Stop yelling. Tyler got kicked out of here last night for that shit. You wanna be next?"

He shot me a look. "What does it matter? I can't do a fucking thing anyway."

"Calm down," I said in my mom's voice.

His face turned red as he screamed, "She's going to die!"

The door to the ICU swung open and a nurse was there, glaring at us. "What is going on out here?"

Before anyone could answer her, Billy walked in and Kyle got up, looking like he was going to swing at him.

Sebastian moved quickly, pushing me out of the way and grabbing Kyle's arms before he could throw a punch.

"Why are you doing this to us?" Kyle screamed at the man.

"Seb, get him out of here," I ordered as Kyle's half brother moved in like he wanted a fight.

When the kid tried to follow Kyle and Sebastian out, Jennifer said in a threatening voice, "Troy, one more step and we're going to tussle again."

He turned around to glare at her, but she just stood there and smiled.

"Man, we don't need violence," Billy said, looking confused. "Troy, knock it off and get in there." He glanced at me. "Kids, man. What are you going to do?"

"Not hold their mother's well-being hostage?" I shot back.

The dopey look on his face faded for half a second, and I could see the malice he was trying to hide. He said nothing and followed his son into the ICU. The nurse shook her head and closed the door behind them.

When it was just Jennifer and me, I said, "Kyle is going to end up getting arrested or killed before this weekend is up."

"I asked Brad to come here, but he said Kyle wasn't going to want to see him." She sighed. "I know that tone in his voice. He's blaming himself for something and he won't budge."

"God, those two." I felt like kicking chairs myself.

She nodded. "I swear, if Linda's life wasn't on the line, I'd get on a plane and go drag him here myself."

I froze. "That's a good idea."

"What?" she asked, confused.

"Going and getting Brad," I answered quickly.

"Right now?" she asked.

"None of us can control Kyle when he's like this. Sooner or later he's going to take a swing at that walking pile of shit that's his father. Brad can keep him centered, calm at least."

"What if Brad's right? What if Kyle doesn't want him here?"

I shot back with, "Since when does Kyle have a clue about what he wants?"

She just stared at me for a long while and then said, "This is crazy, Robbie."

"Crazy or not, it has to be done," I said, trying to push past her reluctance.

"But why? What can bringing Brad here possibly—"

And I lost it.

"Because I can't do anything else," I almost screeched. "I can't make Linda wake up, I can't magically go back in time and be a judge, and I can't go and do surgery myself. I can't do a damn thing except go and drag a teenage boy back so he can make Kyle feel better."

She said nothing as Sebastian walked back in.

"Okay, that kid is about to explode. I got him down in the cafeteria, but he's one bad decision away from getting arrested."

Jennifer sighed. "Okay, fine. I'll go get Brad."

I pulled out my wallet and took out one of my credit cards. "Look, there are like a million miles on that, and there is more than enough of a credit line to cover anything you'll need. Just get Brad here."

"She's doing what now?" Sebastian asked, confused.

"She's going to California to drag Brad back here to calm Kyle down."

His face was deadly serious, a first for him. "Alone?"

Jennifer sounded annoyed. "Um, I'm eighteen. It's not like I need a note pinned to my shirt to fly."

He looked over at her. "Ever been to California?" She shook her head. "Know how to get around? Know where Brad is even living?"

"I can get an address?" she asked, unsure now.

"Look," Sebastian said, looking back at me. "You really think it's that important to get Brad back here?" I nodded, not even pausing to think about it. "I'll go get him."

"Brad doesn't know you," Jennifer pointed out. "He'll just think you're the best-looking kidnapper in the world."

"Fine," he said, changing tactics. "She and I." He paused and looked at her. "Thank you for that, by the way." He looked back to me. "She and I will go and get him and bring him back here."

"Fine, just go get him," I said, trying not to get more annoyed.

Seb looked at Jennifer. "Okay, get the address of where he is, and I'll book the flight."

They both turned as Matt's voice came from behind them.

"You're doing what?"

Oh fuck.

"Matt," I said, trying to intercept the moose. "When did you get here?"

"He's going to California to get Brad?" he asked, ignoring my question.

"Actually, I am going with her," Sebastian clarified, pointing at Jennifer.

"You don't know Brad," Matt pointed out.

"I know California," Seb countered.

"So do I," Matt said. "I lived in the city for years."

"Well, bully for you, sir," Sebastian said in a fake English accent. "Too bad you're not going."

"The hell I'm not."

"Matt," I said, trying to regain control of this train wreck, "Jennifer and Sebastian are going. I'm paying for them and just them."

Matt turned and looked at me. "You think I don't have money? I can buy my own ticket."

Oh, for the love of Liza.

"Then buy a ticket. Charter a whole fucking plane for your wide ass. I don't care." I looked over at Sebastian. "Book the flight and go."

Sebastian and Matt pulled their phones out at the same time and started dialing.

"And this is why I drink," I said to myself as I sat down and longed for a Xanax.

Brad

SUDDENLY I was glad I'd never unpacked all my sports crap from the trunk of my car. It saved me the trouble of packing it back up again when I got all my stuff out of the apartment. I wasn't sure where I was going, but Kyle had made it pretty clear he didn't want me there.

Seeing that all my worldly goods fit in my car was embarrassing. The entire sum total of my life in three boxes and some clothes. That was who I was, and even then, the clothes were worth more than me. Thankfully I still had the keys to the gym, so I went in and grabbed a shower in the middle of the night and caught a quick nap in the locker room. I could ask Todd for an advance on my check and hope he didn't ask me to blow him or something in return.

Was this how guys got into porn?

My phone alarm woke me up around five, which gave me time to change and get a workout in before the gym had to open. I had just started a jog when I heard a knock on the window. I wasn't surprised to see Colt standing there. Sighing, I unlocked the door and let him in.

"Man, you're here early," he said, walking in. "I'm usually waiting for you."

I didn't say anything as I locked the door.

"You're still mad?" he asked, giving me an exaggerated puppy dog look that did nothing but make me want to slap it off him.

"Dude, it's just been a shitty week."

"So no love from Kyle yet, huh?" he asked as he set his gym bag down next to mine.

"He left town," I explained, not wanting to talk with him about it. "I'm gonna get my run in."

There was silence behind me, and when I glanced, he was holding the balled-up shirt I'd taken off earlier that morning. Fuck! I must have forgotten to zip up my gym bag when I threw my dirty clothes in it.

He looked at me, concerned. "Dude, did you sleep here?"

I grabbed the shirt and shoved it into the bag, zipping it up this time. "You here to work out or to gossip?"

"Man, come on. Just crash on my couch. It has to be better than squatting in a gym. Besides, if Todd finds out, he'll fire you in a second, dude, especially if you didn't tell him."

I hadn't thought about that.

"It's no biggie, man, seriously."

A couch did sound better than another night on that floor or, even worse, in my car.

"'Sides, we're looking for another barback at the club. You can score a ton of cash there in tips and get back on your feet in no time."

It was crash on his couch or go back to Texas like a little bitch.

"Okay, man," I said, smiling a little. "But just for a couple of days until I figure things out."

"As long as you want, bud," he said, slapping my back eagerly.

And just like that, I was sleeping on Colt's couch.

When Todd came in, I told him I was going to need the afternoon off to move my stuff, and he just gave me a lewd smile. "Girlfriend kick you out?"

I growled back, "Something like that."

"Oh! I was kidding," he said soberly. "Yeah, you only had Frank, and he'll understand. Go move your stuff, and I'll see you Monday."

I turned to walk out and then stopped. Looking back at him, I said, "No. My girlfriend didn't kick me out, my boyfriend did. So now I'm going to have to sleep on someone's couch to get back on my feet. Not that I ever started out on my feet, but I figure I should start somewhere. So yeah. I'm gay, always have been, so you can stop with the straight baiting, okay?"

The smirk fell from his face and he looked at me, shocked. When he talked there was no *gurl* in his voice at all; he sounded like a regular guy. "I had no idea. I'm sorry, Brad. I've just spent so much time getting picked on by straight guys that I automatically do it to them. If I had known…."

"If you had known, you wouldn't have?" I offered, and he nodded. "Well then, that makes you a different kind of bigoted asshole, doesn't it? So they pick on you, so you can pick on them? That makes it okay?" I shook my head. "I just wanted to come clean because it was getting old. Tell people, don't tell people. I don't care."

"Brad, look, I'm—" he started to say, but I was over it. I walked out where Colt was waiting by my car.

"So, you ready?" he asked like this was a great thing, and not me begging someone to sleep on his couch so I could have a roof over my head.

"Yeah. I don't really remember where you live, so I'll follow."

"Try and keep up," he challenged with a wide grin.

I was too tired to return it.

Coach Gunn

AS SOON as the elevator doors closed, Gayle said, "No violence."

She saw me roll my eyes because I felt her nudge me after I did it.

"I mean it. This is not the time or place."

You hit one guy and suddenly you're deemed violent.

Last month Gayle and I went to church.

I don't need to spell out that we're together, right? Because what I just did, saying that we were together, is about as much spelling or spilling as I'm willing to do.

So we went to church, and who happened to be there but Jeff Raymond. It was the first time I'd seen him since he "retired" from his job and stepped down as Foster High's principal. I say "retire" because the School Board—notice the capital letters—that means Austin and not the ninnies who crowd around a card table and pretend they're somebody here in town....

Where was I?

Right. Hadn't seen him since he got fired, and I had not been looking forward to it. I mean, for one thing, when I was asked if Jeff Raymond was an effective leader of the school, my answer—"If we're including small-minded bigots who can't find their ass with both hands, then yes, he's a great leader"—didn't help him much. Normally that kind of stuff is sealed and kept off the record, but I know Foster better than most, and there's no way a story like that stays under wraps for long. He knew what I'd said, and it was proven by the way he paused in whatever conversation he was having with two other people and glared at me.

The second reason I wasn't looking forward to this was because the woman I walked in with was responsible for getting him fired. Gayle's son, Chad, works up in Austin, and one word from his mom about what Raymond had been doing down here was more than enough to get his ass thrown out on the street, so the glare was for both of us, I'm sure.

I pointed it out to Gayle, who smiled and waved at someone else as she said under her breath, "Oh, I saw him. This should be good."

I hadn't gone to church in forever, but Gayle went every Sunday, so that meant I was going every Sunday, but this was the first time I'd seen him out and about. Gayle found Dorothy Aimes sitting with the sheriff, and we made our way over to join them.

As soon as we got close, Dorothy asked, "Did you see who came crawling out of the sewer?"

Steve just looked at me and rolled his eyes as the girls began to gossip.

You see, I didn't and still don't much care about Jeff Raymond and what he thought of me. He had dug his own grave and was polite enough to crawl in and begin shoveling dirt on top of himself to boot. He could be as mad as he wanted, but it wouldn't change the fact that he'd been wrong about nearly everything.

The sheriff and I had started speculating about this year's football team when someone cleared his throat in the aisle next to us.

Of course it was Jeff, looking like he was ready to spit on us.

Gayle glanced over at him and smiled. "Jeff, I didn't see you there. It's so nice to see you again."

If there's an Academy Award for fake niceness, Gayle should have a dozen of them on her mantel. If I hadn't known the whole story, I would have believed her words based on tone alone.

"Are you happy?" he asked, his voice louder than it needed to be. It took me a second to realize he was playing to the crowd. "You got me fired and now there's no one looking out for the children."

Gayle turned to fully face him and shined him a bright smile. "Well, Jeff, I'm pretty sure there are still teachers and staff and even a principal there for the kids, so I'm sure they'll be okay."

"No one is going to defend them from the filth that kid introduced to Foster."

Gayle's smile evaporated instantly. "Kyle didn't introduce anything to Foster except tolerance and acceptance."

"He started all this. And he turned the Graymark boy gay and most likely the other one too."

I think Raymond hadn't noticed that Dorothy was sitting next to her.

"I know you did not suggest that Kyle somehow turned my son gay," she said in a tone that could have frozen water.

"None of this happened before Stilleno!" he raged. "I was trying to help us, help this town." His voice got louder again as he played to the cheap seats. "And what did it get me?"

"What you deserved," I said, not realizing I had said it out loud.

"What about you, Coach? I thought you didn't want that kind of crap going on in your locker room."

Looking up at him, I said frankly, "No, you were the one who had a problem with it. I think everyone has a right to participate."

He shook his head. "Maybe I should have checked to see what really goes on in your locker room if that's your answer."

I stood up and he took a step back.

"You know, Jeff, you're shooting your mouth off like you're the victim here. One kid is dead, two kids bullied and beaten, and one so screwed up he brought a gun to school. You can blame Stilleno, but I blame you. You and your small-minded, bigoted, hateful ways. Oh, and if you imply one more thing about what goes on in my locker room, you're going to regret it."

"It's not my fault, Coach," he snapped, looking around to the people listening. "I just assumed you were a God-fearing man like the rest of us." He locked eyes with me. "And not some child lover."

I slugged him.

He went down like Moorer did after Foreman showed him up close and personal what a real punch looked like. There was chaos, some screaming, and the sheriff pulled me away from him. Jeff went scurrying away with a bloody nose and an understanding of what he shouldn't say to another man within punching distance.

One punch and suddenly I'm a menace to society.

Anyway....

"You can't solve problems by hitting people," Gayle went on as the elevator got to the ICU. "Rational people talk things out. They don't use their fists."

"Fine," I grunted. "No fighting."

"Good." She nodded. Before she'd finished that nod, the elevator doors slid open to reveal a tall, lanky-looking hippie who needed a bath.

They looked at each other and an expression of complete shock and total terror crossed the guy's face. "Gayle?"

She didn't say a word. She just hauled off and hit him.

"Billy Stilleno, you no good piece of *shit*," she growled, watching the guy land on his ass. He tried to crab walk away from Gayle, who took a step forward, chasing him back out of the elevator. "If I find you had anything to do with what happened to Linda, I will personally cut your balls off and force you to eat them. You miserable son of a bitch... get the hell out of this hospital!"

I put my arms around her before she started kicking him.

Two security guards rushed down the hall and Billy screamed, "Get that crazy bitch off of me!"

Gayle fought against my grip. "Let me go! You better run, Billy! I mean it!"

The guards helped the guy to his feet, and he retreated into the ICU. As soon as he was out of sight, she stopped struggling, so I let her go.

"What happened to not fighting?"

She looked over at me, and I could see the murder in her eyes. "That wasn't a fight. That was pest control, and I'm not done yet."

She went stomping into the ICU as I followed. This should be good.

Kyle

I PACED the cafeteria like a... like... oh, fuck it. I paced the cafeteria like the frustrated and pissed-off gay kid I was.

I was glad Saturday seemed to be a dead time here, so it was just me raging and two kitchen workers who watched me warily. Why was this happening to me? No, that's not fair. I refuse to be just another self-absorbed product of my environment like everyone else I know who's my age. Why was this happening to my mom?

And the moment I asked that, the answer "Karma" came back really quick.

I suddenly felt like a piece of shit, because I couldn't count how many nights I'd spent crying tears of rage, staring up at my ceiling, wishing she would die. Yeah, I know it sounds horrible, and it probably is, but if you ever had to deal with what I did growing up, you might have wished it once or twice yourself. But why now? She just seemed to be getting her act together, and *now* God, fate, whatever decided to take her legs out?

That's just bullshit.

I felt someone behind me, and I turned around expecting to see Jennifer or maybe Robbie, with that worried look they'd been wearing since I walked into town. Instead I saw Father Mulligan staring at me with a slight smile.

"Hello, Kyle," he said in a comforting tone.

Maybe it was because the ghost of who I thought my father might be had just been proven as wrong as Bigfoot, or that I was worried my juvenile wishes had been made real by a God who had way too much time on his hands, or maybe it was because he had green eyes that made me long for another boy, but whatever it was, I rushed toward him and wrapped my arms around him as I started to cry.

Thankfully he hugged me back instead of asking why a kid he had spoken to, like, once was wrapped around him like a howler monkey. "It's okay," he said, pulling me close. "It's going to be okay."

I pulled back. "You don't know that. Why do people say things like that? You don't know that things are going to be okay—in fact, they could be completely shitty, right?"

He nodded slowly. "They could, but that's not what I meant."

I reviewed his words in my mind. "Then what did you mean?"

He gave me one of those smiles that seemed to make the whole world a little calmer. "You want to sit down and talk?" He gestured to one of the booths, and I realized we were standing in the middle of the cafeteria like we were ready to throw down.

"Sorry," I said, slipping into one side as he took the other.

"No apologies needed," he assured me. "It's a bad time for you; what happened should affect you."

"So what did you mean?" I asked, pushing past him trying to calm me down.

"I said things are going to be okay, which they will."

"But you don't know that!" I snapped, exasperated.

"No, I don't know anything, but I have faith that what's happened to your mom will turn out the way it's supposed to be."

"Oh, perfect. Here we go—let me guess? This is all part of *His* plan and so everything is perfectly fine, right?" He nodded. "So then tell me this: what kind of asshole causes cars to crash? Allows babies to starve? Lets horrible people get away with murder and does nothing? Tell me more about this *plan*, and while you're at it, try to sell me a swamp in Arizona or something."

His expression didn't change from sympathetic. If he was angry, there were no indications of it. "Do you know who Willem Kolff was?" I shook my head. "He invented what we now call dialysis. He also pretty much created the field of artificial organ engineering, for organs like artificial hearts. He was a doctor before World War II and was part of the Dutch resistance that tried to stop the Nazis. He organized the first blood bank in Europe and, while trying to keep his friends and family alive, discovered a way to oxygenate the blood as it passed through a machine."

He stopped talking, so I just stared at him. "Okay, and?"

"And he discovered dialysis during the war. He invented the process with sausage casings and orange juice cans and it ended up saving millions of lives."

"Yeah, but how many millions died in the war?"

"And how many millions more will be saved because of his work? Are you telling me, sitting where you are, that World War II didn't work out for the best?"

"Not for the Jews," I shot back instantly, and he got quiet for a moment.

"Not for all of them, no. But if you were to ask them if their sacrifice was worth saving all those lives...."

I cut him off. "But no one asked them. No one asks anyone; it just happens no matter what you do. What's the point of being a good person if you can just die the next day?"

It wasn't obvious, but I could see a change in his attitude by the way his expression hardened a little. "So if you're a good person, you don't deserve bad things to happen? Is that what you're saying?" I nodded, but I could feel the ground beneath my argument starting to shift. "See, that kind of thinking is what's wrong with the world, Kyle. People do good things and expect some kind of reward, and when they don't get it, they use it as proof there is no God or that God is cruel. God does not reward good behavior, Kyle, the same way he doesn't punish bad. If you were being good for his sake, you're wasting your time."

"Then why bother trying?" I asked him. "Why even go through the motion of being good when it's easier to just get what you want doing whatever you need to do to get that thing, and damn the consequences?"

"Being good is its own reward. You should do good things because it's the right thing to do, not because you think that it will get you brownie points with someone. Doing good things so that God will take your side isn't doing a good thing, it's doing something to get you ahead of others, which is just selfish."

"So then there's no reason to be good? Because no matter what you do, good or bad, God will still just strike you down for fun?"

"God doesn't strike people down, Kyle, and you know it. I know you're upset about your mom, but he wasn't behind the wheel of that car; she was. You want to look at your mother's accident as proof he doesn't exist, yet I see the fact she had a fence post slammed through her neck and is still alive as proof that he does."

My eyes began to sting.

"Horrible things happen, Kyle. It's just that kind of world. Sometimes people do it, and sometimes they just happen, but if all you're looking at is the bad stuff, you're going to miss the good. Yes, World War II was a horrible experience, but we got plastic, radar, microwaves, penicillin, and even artificial organs out of it. You want to blame the war on someone, blame it on bad people, but you ask me where God was, and I'll say he was helping Willem Kolff find orange juice cans."

"She's going to die," I blurted out before I started crying again.

I felt his arms around me as he moved to my side of the booth. "We don't know what's going to happen yet. But we have to have faith that it's going to be all right." I looked over at him, and he gave me a smile. "You want to come pray with me for your mom?"

I nodded.

"Come on, let me introduce you to my boss," he said, putting his arm around my shoulder.

Matt

I HATE flying.

And it's not because I'm scared the plane might crash or some bullshit; I know how safe air travel is. It's because I'm six foot five in bare feet, and they just don't make seats for people like me. Well, that's not true. They make them in first class, but it was sold out, which meant sitting on a Southwest flight to California in a seat that would make Skinny McNoEat feel like she had to lose a few pounds.

Added to this was the fact that Tyler had lured me back into working out with him, which meant I was a little bit wider than normal in the upper body department. That translated into me having nothing that was meant to fit in such a small place. Jennifer and Mr. Crest Whitening Strips found seats together, so I was sitting next to an elderly woman who was either senile and thought she knew me or found it appropriate to share every single detail about her daughter's life with me.

The things I do because I don't like someone.

Honestly, this was a little more than just not liking Sebastian; it was trying to cover Tyler's ass. You see, he loves Brad and Kyle like they were his own blood, so I wasn't going to leave the task of getting Brad back to Texas to a chronological teenager and a mental teenager.

Wow, I really disliked this guy.

You ever meet someone like that? They just hit every single one of your buttons at first sight, and no matter what they do, you just dislike them. I was going to say "hate," but I don't hate Sebastian; I just don't trust him. He's every pretty boy who has ever thought the gay community owed him something because he was young and beautiful. Which, by the way, is not an accomplishment. We're all young at some point, and just because your parents passed on a set of genes that allowed for symmetrical perfection doesn't mean you did a fucking thing. It means you were born and that you haven't aged yet. Period.

When it comes to beautiful people, I prefer people like Tyler. He knows people find him attractive but doesn't let that go to his head. I mean, it's not like every single woman, and a few guys, don't give him a glance when we're at the grocery store or something. He's a great-looking guy and in damn fine shape, but do you see him walking around like the world owes him something because of it? No. If anything, he's a little put off by the attention his looks attract.

Not people like Sebastian.

No. People like Sebastian think you should pay to be around pretty people because they're just automatically better than everyone else. I don't blame Robbie for jumping his bones—I mean, come on, Sebastian is definitely fuckable—but dating him?

That was a bomb just waiting to go off.

I had just settled into the straitjacket that was my seat and Gladys—I had no idea what her name was, but Gladys seemed to work—was just getting to the part where her daughter had ruined her life by dropping out of junior college when Jennifer walked up to our row.

"Everything okay?" I asked, almost hoping there was something wrong so I could get away from Gladys and the train wreck that was her daughter.

"He wants to talk to you," she said in a tone that told me she didn't think it was that great an idea either.

"Right now?" I asked, even though I understood the genius of it. I mean, we were, like, forty thousand feet up; what was I going to do? Step outside to get away from him?

She nodded. "I'll wait here," she said, still not noticing Gladys.

I jumped up before she could. "No problem. Gladys, this is my friend Jennifer." The woman paused for a moment, no doubt wondering who the fuck Gladys was. "Jennifer, this is my friend Gladys. Make sure to ask her about her daughter; it's a great story."

Poor Jennifer wasn't old enough to know the old saying "Never trust a fag bearing introductions," or she would have known I was throwing her to the wolves.

Actually, wolves might have been kinder. Or at least quicker.

My legs appreciated the chance to stretch as I walked back to where Sebastian and Jennifer had been sitting. He was looking at something on an iPad, and part of me wondered if he had talked Robbie into buying it for him.

"You wanted to talk?" I asked, not sitting down.

He didn't look up for a few seconds, and I wondered if he'd even heard me. It was a cute trick, and one I'd seen before. He was trying to grab control of the conversation by making me wait. Obviously he had attended a seminar on how to be the most important person in the room when he was in LA. If he thought his crap was going to work with me, he could think again.

"Fuck it," I said, turning around to walk back to my seat. Gladys was better than mind games.

"Matt," he said quickly. I turned around and saw him pulling a pair of earbuds out of his ears. "Sorry, man, got caught up in this letter, didn't even see you there. Sit down. I think we should talk."

He sounded sincere, but for all I knew it was just another mind game.

"Sure, what's up?"

"I thought I should clear some things up before we land and this whole thing starts to get crazy."

I had to chuckle at that. "The three of us jumping on a plane and heading across the country to hijack an eighteen-year-old kid doesn't seem crazy?"

He paused and put the iPad away. "No. I think Jennifer and me coming is right there on the edge. I think you coming as well makes everything slide right past crazy and into stupid."

"So this is the 'I shouldn't have come' speech?" I snapped at him.

"No, this is the 'you have no idea who I am and just about everything you've said and done in regards to me has been complete bullshit' speech."

I just gave him a half smile. "Oh, is it?"

He nodded. "It is, and I know this little talk isn't going to change your mind because you seem like a judgmental asshole who thinks his shit don't stink, but I promised myself I was going to at least try. This is me trying."

"By calling me a judgmental asshole?"

He gave me a look and asked, "Like everything you've said to and about me has been Miss Manners, right?"

I gestured for him to continue because he was right.

"You don't know me. I'm sorry if some guys were mean to you when you were coming out, but I'm not them. You never dated me, you never fucked me, and I never lied to you and didn't call you back or slept with your best friend or whatever. I never gave you crabs, I never borrowed money and then skipped town. I never said we were a couple and then said I had Grindr on my phone to make friends, and I never, ever, even once did anything to you."

He waited for me to say something, but I just sat there.

"I understand you're protective of Robbie. So am I, but if you think I'm going to stand here and let you bad-mouth me to my face and not say something back, then you're as dumb as you think I am."

We both paused as we tried to figure out that last bit.

"Whatever," he said, waving his hands. "The bottom line is this. I'm not that guy, and you're an asshole for assuming I am. You didn't need to come on this trip, but now that you're here, understand this. I'm not going to let you continue to trash me because you have issues with whatever. Got it?"

"You done?" I asked him.

"I am done, and if you have something to say back, save it. I don't care what you think. Not even a little bit. You said your piece, I said mine, now let's go grab Brad and bring him back and try to act like adults doing it." He put the earbuds back in. "You can go back whenever you want."

And damn if the guy did not just dismiss me.

I thought about making him listen to me, but honestly? What did I have to say? He was right. I didn't believe him, and nothing he said made a damn bit of difference. I got up and walked back to my seat, counting the minutes until we landed and snagged Brad.

Robbie

SO I was sitting in the waiting room, halfway through explaining to Tyler exactly why his boyfriend had bought a ticket and followed mine across the country. Suddenly Billy came barreling through the door like the devil was on his tail. He looked at us with wild eyes and screamed, "Keep her away from me!"

He rushed into the ICU and was gone.

"Was he bleeding?" Tyler asked me, confused.

Before I could answer, the waiting room door opened again and Gayle swept in, looking fifteen different kinds of pissed. "Lemme guess. The little turd went running to hide behind sick people? He's lucky he's already in a hospital, because I am going to kill him."

I'm pretty sure the question was rhetorical because she didn't wait for an answer and just walked into the ICU.

"Did she just threaten his life?" I asked Tyler.

Before he could answer, the waiting room door opened again and an older stocky man came in huffing like he was having a heart attack. "She... get him?" he asked.

Tyler just pointed at the ICU door.

He nodded his thanks instead of talking and followed after Gayle.

We both looked at each other for a second before Tyler said, "Well, I'm not going to miss this!" and got up like a little kid eager to see a fight.

I followed, but I'd like to think I did it with a little more panache.

Still, if there was a fight, I wasn't going to miss it.

By the time we made it inside, Billy was hiding in Linda's room, and the nurse was standing between Gayle and him, trying to keep them apart. Gone was any resemblance of the kind and understanding woman I had known the entire time I lived in Foster. What was left resembled a dragon, or maybe a nightmare brought to life to wreak havoc on Billy's soul.

If he still had one.

"Eighteen years," Gayle was raging. "Eighteen years it took her to get the garbage you put in her head out. Do you know how many times a story of hers starts with 'Billy had an idea…'?"

I looked at Tyler, who nodded in agreement.

"She was *just* cleaning up. Just getting that shit out of her system, and lo and behold, here you are. If I find out that you had anything to do with her accident, I swear on all that is holy—"

And enter the rent-a-cops and the hospital guy again.

Childs looked like he was ready for round two, but when he saw it was Gayle screaming and not a teenage boy, he paused and reconsidered his options. Gayle saw him and her gaze leveled on him. "Barney Childs, you have a lot of explaining to do."

"Does she know everyone's first name?" I asked Tyler in a whisper.

"I think so," he whispered back.

"Gayle, look…." Childs began to stutter.

"What is that man doing in her hospital room? And where is her son?"

"It's not that simple…," Childs tried again.

"He abandoned that family years ago. Tell me why he's in there."

"They're still married," Childs spat out.

"And?" Gayle asked, not even pausing. "He's a criminal, slime who has brought nothing but pain and darkness into her world, and you let him in there with her?"

"It's the law!" Childs tried to rally. "We can't do anything until Monday when we can find a judge."

Gayle looked back at Billy. "I'm giving you one chance right now. Get out of that room and leave this town."

Billy looked like he was going to throw up, but his meathead son wasn't impressed.

"Or what? We ain't going nowhere."

And let me tell you, that was the moment things went south for Billy.

"Later, when you wonder why this is all happening to you," Gayle said to Billy, fury making her voice soft and ice-cold, "I want to you to realize that you had an out and refused to take it. Timing's always been your problem, Billy; you don't know when you've pressed your luck too far and you end up eating shit."

She took a half step toward him, and both Billy and Troy took a step back.

"Prepare to eat shit."

And without another word she did an about-face that would have made a Marine DI take notice and strode out of the ICU.

"And she was worried about me?" the old man said, taking a deep breath before following her.

The nurse and Childs began talking, and I looked at Tyler. "What just happened?"

"Billy is about to find out why no one in this town ever tries to fuck over Gayle."

I couldn't imagine anyone trying, but the tone of his voice made me crack up. "Come on, Tyler, it's not like she's a mob boss or something."

Tyler looked at me, dead serious. "No, she is much, much worse."

And look at that. It's vodka time again.

Brad

So I got most of my stuff into Colt's place in under an hour.

Bruce seemed pretty chill with the arrangement, but then again I couldn't blame him. He probably thought this meant full-time sex options for him since we had already done it. As soon as Colt was out of earshot, I decided to set that straight.

"Look, man, I appreciate you letting me stay here, but what happened before? It isn't going to happen again."

He just smiled at me. "If you say so, but I have a feeling it isn't over yet."

Wow, I thought Colt had an ego on him.

"Dude, no offense, but it's over."

He shrugged with that same smile. "We'll see, but I have faith." I was going to continue arguing, but he patted me on my back and walked away. I swear I was never going to understand this whole gay thing.

I left my clothes in my suitcase and just propped it over in the corner since I didn't have a closet. The bathroom was crammed with hair and teeth products, so mine fit in perfect with theirs. I sat down on the couch and tried not to be depressed while Colt and Bruce discussed what they were doing that night.

"I have the night off, but I'm going because I heard that hottie from Australia is still in town," Colt said from his room.

"His name is Reggie, you know," Bruce called from his room.

"I could care less what their names are when they're facedown in my bed" was Colt's answer.

"He's a nice guy," Bruce argued.

"And he has the perfect ass," Colt tossed back. "It's just begging to be plowed."

I turned on their PS4 and skimmed the games they'd loaded on it.

"Brad, you're coming, right?" Colt asked from the hallway.

"Nah," I yelled back, selecting *Need for Speed*. I seriously needed to hit something hard.

"Oh, come on!" Colt whined. "Dude, you need to get back on that horse—or find a horse to get back on you."

"Dude," Bruce called out. "Too soon."

"Oh, come on. So his boyfriend bailed on him? Look at him. Tell me he can't find a dozen guys willing to crawl through broken glass to suck him off."

"You know I can still hear you, right?"

"Dude, you know you're smoking," Colt shouted. "Ain't no shame in denying your own hotness."

"Yeah, not denying anything, but I'm not going," I said, loading my virtual car.

There was silence, and then Colt stood in front of me in a thong so small it could be called a jockstrap in a pinch. "Dude, you can't stay here and pout."

I wished Colt wasn't connected to his body, because he was ridiculously hot, but there was nothing appealing about him as a person, which I think he didn't get. In a picture, he'd be smoking hot, but the moment he opened his mouth, the whole façade was crushed and you knew he was a douchebag.

"Man, don't you ever wear clothes?" I asked, turning back to my game.

"What?" he said with a lewd smile. "You saying you don't like what you see?"

"I'm saying you need some pants." I still didn't look at him.

"Come on, Brad," he whined, jumping on me. I cried out as he pinned me to the couch. "Come out with us," he pouted, his nearly naked body over mine. "It'll be fun," he added in a tone I figure he thought was seductive.

He just sounded like a dimwit.

"Dude. Get off me now," I warned with no humor in my voice at all. He laughed until I grabbed his shoulders. "I'm not kidding." I pushed him off me and tossed him to the floor.

"Oh, come on! I'm just messing with you," he protested.

I picked up the controller. "Yeah, well, with a dick that small, I assumed it was a joke."

I glanced down at his package, and it was pretty clear he was hard. His face flushed and he stood up, pissed. "Fine, stay here and be a fuck. I don't care." He took a few steps toward his room and stopped. "And it's average, thank you very much."

I glanced back at him and his now half-hard dick. "Yeah, if you did your measuring in junior high." I heard Bruce burst out laughing as Colt stomped off to his room and slammed the door.

I played the game and tried not to think of Kyle.

After about an hour, Bruce came in and sat down in the chair, watching me play. "You're pretty good," he said after a while.

"A friend and me used to play online all the time," my mouth answered before my brain could stop it. The next memory was Kelly's voice over the headset, calling every person we trashed a fag.

I turned off the game and tossed the controller onto the table.

"You were winning," Bruce said, shocked.

"Not in the mood," I said, lying back on the couch. What was I doing there? This was stupid; I had no future there. Well, fuck, I had no future anywhere, but less of one there. I so badly wanted to just call my parents and tell them I was coming home, but I knew my dad would get pissed. Maybe not vocally, but I could hear his thoughts. "You threw A&M away for this? How long are you planning on sponging off of us?"

I shuddered at the thought.

"You okay, man?" Bruce asked, breaking me out of the jail cell I'd thought my way into.

"Nope," I answered truthfully. "Not even a little."

"It'll get better, man. It has to."

Man, it was so sad that he was right.

"So shouldn't you be getting ready?" I asked him.

He shook his head. "Nah, the club thing every single weekend gets old. Always the same guys, always the same music—I mean, what's the point?"

"He seems to like it," I said, jerking a thumb toward Colt's room.

Bruce gave a bitter laugh. "Colt likes anything that gets him attention. If he was a little dumber, he'd just stand in front of the mirror and try to flirt with himself."

"Never work," I said, pausing for effect. "He'd just be pissed the other guy was a bottom too."

Bruce looked at me for a few seconds and then burst out laughing. "Dude, that was a sick burn."

"Thank you," I said, bowing my head in way of a royal acknowledgment.

"He talks all that plowing shit, but trust me, first sign of a dick and his legs are up and spread."

Now I started laughing. "I did not need that image."

"Neither did I, but sometimes his door doesn't close, and trust me, that shit will turn you straight."

I almost fell off the couch, I was laughing so hard. It took almost a minute for me to stop; tears were falling down my cheeks as I sat up. "You know, man, I hate what happened between Kyle and me, but I'm glad it was with you. You seem pretty cool."

He paused and then nodded. "Thanks, I think. I mean, you seem pretty chill also."

"I try."

He smiled. "Well, you succeed."

"So you wanna go in on a pizza if you're staying home?" I asked, knowing I didn't have enough money on me to cover it myself.

"Sure," he said, pulling out his cell phone. "You watch *Doctor Who*? 'Cause the new season starts tonight and I was—"

There was a banging on the door; we both jumped.

"What the hell?" Bruce said, getting up to answer it. "Sounds like the cops are here."

He opened the door and Jennifer barged right in, followed by Matt and some other guy. "Get your stuff," she said to me, ignoring Bruce completely. "We have to get going."

What the fuck?

"What are you doing here?" I asked, getting up slowly. This all felt like a dream; there was no way this could be happening for real.

"Getting you," she said curtly. "Get your stuff."

This was really happening.

"I'm not going anywhere," I said, trying to get my feet under me. "I could have told you that before you came."

Matt put a hand on her shoulder and pulled her back. "Brad, Kyle needs you right now. Grab your stuff and let's go."

I felt the familiar panic in my chest whenever I thought Kyle was in trouble, but the guilt overcame that. "Look, Matt, I appreciate you guys coming out here, but trust me, Kyle is better off without me there. You made a trip for nothing."

"Goddammit, Brad," Jennifer snapped. "This is not the time for you feeling sorry for yourself; Kyle needs you right now. His mother is—"

"I cheated on him," I blurted out, cutting her off.

She paused, mouth open in shock.

"There? Happy? I cheated on him, and there's no taking that back. I fucked everything up, and it's my fault." I felt like crying again. "Trust me, Kyle is way better without me."

"How could you cheat on him?" Jennifer asked, the color coming back to her face.

"I was drunk and…." Somehow telling her I was wasted on drugs too didn't feel like the right move. "I just fucked up, okay?"

"Who with?" Matt asked.

"Him." I pointed to Bruce.

Bruce, who was still by the door, looked behind him. "Are you pointing at me?"

"Dude, you don't need to lie, man. It happened, and I need to own up to it."

He looked really confused for a second, and then his expression changed to anger. "And who told you this?" I opened my mouth, but he held a hand up. "Right, don't tell me."

And then yelled at the top of his lungs. "*Colt!*"

The back bedroom door opened and Colt came charging out, a pair of skinny jeans on and nothing else. "What the fuck do you—" And he saw the living room full of people. "—want?"

"Did you tell Brad we fooled around?"

"You and me?" Colt asked dimly.

"Brad and me! Did you tell Brad that he and I fooled around?"

"Um... didn't you?"

Oh my God, I was so stupid.

"This is low even for you," Bruce said.

"What? I made a mistake," Colt whined. When he saw no one was buying it, he added, "It was an accident."

"Right, like when you *accidentally* dosed his drink. Or when you *accidentally* posted the picture of his underwear on Facebook?" Bruce was livid now and roared, "Fuck this!" as he charged at Colt.

"Okay," the strange guy in the room said, holding Bruce back. "Now that things are starting to make sense, let's all take a breath. Brad?" He looked at me, and I nodded. "Get your stuff together; we need to get going." He looked at Colt. "Walk back to your room. Do not say another word; just turn around and walk." And then to Bruce, "Your roommate is a sleazebag and not worth the effort. If you beat him up, he'll just call the cops, and you'll be the one paying for it. Let this one go."

Colt turned around and half ran back to his room, and Bruce shrugged the guy off and nodded.

"Jennifer, help Brad grab his stuff. Matt, make sure this guy stays here. I'm going to go talk to our criminal mastermind."

Matt didn't seem too pleased, but he nodded, and Jennifer walked toward me and pointed to my suitcase. "That your stuff?"

"Yeah," I said quietly. "Who's the new guy?"

"Robbie's. I'll explain on the plane." She put a few of my things in the suitcase. "You did drugs?"

"Not on purpose!" I shot back.

"Okay, fine, but you're living with the guy who drugged you?"

She had me there.

Ignoring her logic, I asked, more to myself, "I didn't cheat on Kyle?"

She shook her head. "Not sure why you'd think you could."

I gave up for nothing?

Matt

ONE SECOND the apartment was like a Three Stooges movie, the next Sebastian was giving orders like he was a drill sergeant. I mean, sure, they were good orders, but still. I watched Sebastian follow the shirtless guy to his room, and then I looked back at the black kid. "Stay here. Got it?" He nodded.

"Matt," Jennifer hissed at me as I sneaked down the hallway.

I thought I was going to have to listen at the door, but it was partially open.

"Look, you need to listen to me right now. You don't know it, but you're in a lot of trouble, and I can help you get through it."

"Dude, I don't even know who you are," Colt said.

"Sure you do. I'm you in ten years."

There was silence while the kid obviously gave Sebastian a disbelieving look.

"It's true, and though I may not have driven a DeLorean here, I can prove it."

"Go for it."

"Where should I start? You are an only child, you played sports from a young age, realized you liked guys but hid it from everyone growing up. Moved away to a big city, found out you were considered

160

young and hot by other gay guys. Had a lot of sex, broke a lot of hearts, and then found a guy you liked who was a little older but was too busy playing the field to notice you for more than a fuck. After that you said screw it, had a lot of sex because if you can't get one guy to like you then having a lot of guys fuck you is just as good in the long run. You say you just want to have fun, but you see a real couple in love and it kills you because you think you're the perfect guy if someone would just give you a chance."

There was silence from the room.

"I'll take that as a 'close enough.' So, see, I know you because I was you, so let me tell you how this turns out. You keep having random sex with guys, but it gets harder and harder to keep up. There is a new group of fresh-faced, hot-ass guys always walking through the door, and you're just the... stripper? Barista?"

"Barback."

"You're the cute barback who has a rep of being a slut, so no one will think about dating you. So with lack of a love life, you just try to score with the hottest guys you can get and think that shows you have value in the world. Well, listen. It doesn't. See, every time you fuck someone trying to get some kind of value out of it, all you do is give something of yourself away. At first it's not large and most of the time not noticeable, but it's there, and then it's gone. Piece by piece, it just goes away until there's a hole inside of you, an aching hole that's screaming for someone to notice you and to love you. But that's not going to happen, because you're just the cute slut that everyone has fucked and no one is going to date. So you feel worse about yourself, and so you sleep with more guys to try to make yourself feel better."

He paused for a moment.

"But you don't. In fact, every time you have sex you ask yourself, 'Will this be different? Will this guy talk to me? Want to stay after?' But they don't because you're the best-looking moped in the world. People love to ride you, but trust me, they don't want their friends to see them doing it. So where does that leave you? Dosing guys' drinks and trying to break them and their boyfriends up in hope that they'll go out with you? Do you think a guy like Brad would fuck you, much less date you? After you doing all that? What in the world would make you think that was okay?"

I couldn't see in the room, so the kid's sobbing took me by surprise. "I just want someone to love me. How hard is that?"

Sebastian didn't even pause. "Impossible as long as you hate yourself. And you do hate yourself, Colt. It shows with every breath you take. You think people look at you and think you're hot or in shape, but honestly, they look at you and think, 'What a fucking loser.' You know why? Because it's the same thing you see when you look in the mirror."

The kid was bawling now, and I didn't blame him.

"You want to meet someone? You want to fall in love? Then realize it's not about the way you look or how in shape you are. It's about what kind of person you are. Anyone who is going to go out with you because of the way you look isn't going to care about what's inside. You're coming up on your expiration date, when you're going to stop being a cute kid and start being an okay-looking adult and then shift right into a skeevy-looking old man who never settled down and hits on every hot thing that walks into the bar. Maybe you own a gym, maybe you run a club, but you're going to be that pathetic old man who is still chasing tail when everyone else he knew is long settled down and married. Is that what you want?"

A heartbreaking "No" came from Colt.

"Then change. Now. Because if you don't, you're going to find out the harsh truth about being in shape and good-looking."

There was a pause, and I could imagine Colt looking up at him with tear-filled eyes. "What?"

"There is always someone better-looking, and right now is the best shape you're ever going to be in your life. So if that was what you were hoping to coast on for the rest of your life… trust me. You won't be able to."

I heard Colt crying and could not believe what I'd just heard.

Sebastian's lecture had left me as stunned as Colt. A minute later when Sebastian walked out, looking completely unsurprised that I had been eavesdropping, I had not the faintest idea what to say.

"You get all that, champ?" he asked me. "'Cause I'm not going to repeat myself." He walked past me and said loudly, "Come on, people, we're burning daylight, and we have a flight to catch."

I felt my stomach turn, and I knew in my heart of hearts… I had been dead wrong about Sebastian.

PART THREE:
BROKEN HEARTS, HUMPTY
DUMPTY, AND THE BEATLES

Name three things that can never be put back together again.

Kyle

So I felt bad because I went in to pray with Father Mulligan, and at some point I fell asleep.

I couldn't help it! The little room was so quiet and peaceful, and I had been running around all crazy since I left California.... I mean, are you shocked I nodded off? I was sure it meant I was going to hell or something, but I figured the whole liking-guys thing was taking me there anyway.

I wasn't shocked to see Father Mulligan had left.

I was shocked to see Troy in one of the back pews, looking like he was praying silently. I had no idea what to do. I mean, it was like looking at someone while peeing or something. Was it bad taste to talk? Add to that my insane aversion to talking to anyone while my penis was out, and I could assure you if I was on fire in a bathroom, I wouldn't call out for help.

So I wasn't sure what the etiquette was in this case either.

As quietly as I could, I got up and tried to leave the chapel, hoping he wouldn't see me.

"You snore," he said, his eyes still closed.

Fuck.

"Um, sorry?" I offered, since he had talked first, making it okay.

"Doesn't matter to me," he said, doing that cross thing over his chest and opening his eyes. "But you might have insulted the guy upstairs."

My brain told me he wasn't talking about Mr. Childs, so I looked up at the ceiling and offered a sincere, "Sorry." When I glanced back at Troy, he was giving me a questioning stare, so I added, "Amen?"

He laughed, and it made him appear completely different. He went from looking like a Big Dolores to a handsome guy who was built like a brick wall. "I wouldn't figure you'd be the religious type."

My eyes narrowed. "Why, 'cause I'm gay and an abomination?"

164

"No." He looked back at me like I was stupid. "Because smart people have a hard time accepting that the universe might have a higher power that doesn't have normal rules."

"You think I'm smart?" I asked, sitting down in the pew ahead of him and turning around.

He pshawed. "You had to be smart to get into a college like Berkeley. That ain't no small feat."

It was weird, because he sounded like a hick, but he talked like he was most definitely intelligent; it was completely throwing me off. "Why didn't you go to college?" I asked, honestly curious.

"Because I never got through high school." He sounded bitter. "I heard that's a requirement they don't let slide."

"Didn't like school?"

I could see it had been the wrong thing to ask. "Why'd you ask that? Because I come off like a rock to you? Guys like me can't like school because I'm too stupid to understand what's going on around me?"

Now I looked at him like *he* was stupid. "No, because it's obvious you're smart, so the only reason I could think that would cause you not to graduate would be you not going."

It wasn't what he expected me to say, and it took him a second to recover his game face. "My dad travels a lot; no time to settle in one place and attend regularly."

"So you're homeschooled?"

He gave me a glance like he was looking to see if I was making fun of him or not. "Yeah, I was homeschooled. I know how to hotwire a car, so that's electronics right there. I know how to eat loose fruit at a supermarket so you can fill up and not buy anything. That's agriculture and business sense in one lesson. I know how to grab all my stuff and duck out the back window of a motel room when there are guys banging on the door. That has to count as PE or something. And I know how to swallow a sealed gram bag full of dope without gagging when we get pulled over. Extra credit if it's still sealed when I shit it out. Now tell me that shouldn't count as biology credit."

I felt sick to my stomach. I really did.

"So yeah, homeschooled, that's me all over," he said, getting up, obviously upset.

"Hey, you hungry?" I asked to his back.

He looked over at me. "Why?"

"I was about to go to the cafeteria and get something to eat and wanted to know if you were hungry too."

"Nah, I'm good," he said, sounding pretty unconvincing.

"I'm buying," I added.

"I can eat," he said, smiling at me.

We walked out, and again I was stunned by how empty the hospital was. Everything I knew about places like this came from TV, where people were always rushing around, and that lady over the intercom saying "Stat," but not here. It was like an empty building where people had left the lights on.

It felt like the world was holding its breath, almost.

"Y'all are lucky," Troy said as we headed down the hall. "Normally little towns like this are lousy with biker gangs or drug smuggling, but you're so far north, it kinda misses you altogether." He sighed as he looked around. "Kinda nice."

"It's not that nice," I assured him as we walked into the cafeteria. "Trust me."

"Yes, it is," he said back. "Anyone ever get found in the outskirts with his hands cut off?" I paled and shook my head. "Ever have a trailer park go up in flames out of nowhere?" Another shake. "Ever find a whole family shot in their homes, adults and kids?" I stopped and just looked at him in shock. "See? This place is a paradise compared to the places I've been. You may think it sucks, but it doesn't. Places like this are like… oases from the real world. Islands in the middle of nowhere that people hear about but never get to see." He gave another sigh and snagged a tray. "You have no idea how good you have it."

I took a tray and followed him, but I had lost my appetite.

He grabbed two sandwiches and a Coke while I took a slice of meatloaf and some mashed potatoes back to the table. I paid for it, and the woman who took my money looked over at Troy and then back at me. "If you need anything, just holler."

What she meant was, "If the hoodlum you're with tries to cut you, make some noise and we'll call security."

"I'm good," I assured her and walked back to the table to sit down across from him.

"Lemme guess," Troy said between bites. "Blink twice if you're being held against your will or some shit?" He nodded toward the cafeteria ladies. I didn't say anything, and he laughed. "Figures. I told you. Places like this aren't used to people like me."

I wanted to argue with him, but that would have been a waste of time; he'd nailed how they looked at him. "Why do you stay with him?" I asked after a few bites.

We both knew I was talking about Billy. "He's my dad" was all Troy offered.

"And?" I countered with. "You have to know that he isn't a good person."

"Why did you stay with her?" he asked back.

And we suddenly knew where each other was in life.

"Because she's my mom and I had nowhere else to go or I would have. In her defense, she never held someone hostage for money before."

"If the guys that are after my dad were after her, she might." Troy finished his food. "At best, they'll kill him. At worst, they'll cut his hands off and kill him."

If I hadn't been hungry before, I knew I wasn't now. "So then run. Call the police. Do something that doesn't put someone else's life in jeopardy."

He looked away, which meant to me that he agreed with what I was saying.

"Troy, that's my mom up there, and she could be dying as we speak. If the roles were reversed and it was your dad in the bed, what would you want me to do?"

"I'd want you to let him die so I could go and live my own life," he blurted out. "I'd want you to do back what he's doing to you. But you won't, and you know why? 'Cause you're soft. You think the world isn't a giant cesspool of fucks who are just out for themselves, and you can't imagine people like my dad and me living off nothing day after day. You don't have the guts to make the tough choice and let him hang by his own balls. Instead you're gonna sit there and try and find the *good* and *nice* way to solve this."

He stood up and leaned over the table and gave me a serious look. "There is no good and nice way out of this, Kyle. You want my dad to leave? Play his game and maybe lose your mom, or give him the money. Anything else is a waste of fucking time."

He grabbed his tray and began to walk away. "Thanks for the food," he said, tossing his garbage away and walking out.

I didn't want him to be right… but he was.

Matt

BY THE time we all got onto a plane, it was the last flight out for the day. I dunno about Jennifer and Sebastian, but I was exhausted, and Brad didn't look any better. Jennifer and Sebastian got two seats together again since they were using Robbie's miles. I picked up Brad's and my tickets, and we got a couple of seats in the back. I sat by the window and he sat next to me as an older guy grabbed the aisle seat.

"I still don't know what I'm going to do," Brad said as we waited for the flight to take off. "Kyle is not going to be happy to see me."

God, save me from teenagers.

"Look, you're going to have to realize that this whole love thing? It isn't a race." He looked over at me so intently, I could tell he was really waiting for some wisdom to come out of my mouth.

Come on, Matt, time to be smart.

"No, you know what? It *is* a race, but not the kind you're running. It's not a sprint. No one cares who got where first or fastest—that doesn't matter. You'll see people like that with this insane checklist of things that they want done by this or that age. It's bullshit. It doesn't matter when you fall in love or get married or any of that. Love is a marathon, my friend, and trust me, you're about to drop dead because you started pushing for the end before you'd even suited up."

He didn't say anything, but I could tell he was paying attention.

"Love is about taking your time, picking your battles. Knowing when to let the Wookiee win and when to really dig in and fight. You and Kyle, you're both so fucking intense that I bet you guys fought about every little thing in California, right?" He nodded. "See, that's a fool's game. So what if someone didn't pick up the dishes or used the last of the toilet paper? You can't get geared up for that. Just say you're sorry and move on, because you're going to need your strength for the real fight."

"Is this the real fight?" he asked, sounding like he was ready to fall asleep.

"This is the title bout, my man. This is where you come in and let Kyle know he isn't alone. That you love him and you'll stand by him no matter what, and he will draw strength from that and not lose his mind that his dad is an asshole and his mom could be brain damaged. That's going to consume him, so you need to be there for everything else. You get it?"

He nodded, but I could tell he didn't get it all.

"You love him, right?"

Brad nodded instantly. "Of course I do, but Matt...." He paused, and I prompted him to continue. "Everything you said to do, I always do. I'm always there for him and he's always blowing the relationship up. I just don't know how many more times I can convince him that being together is worth it."

"One more time past the last one," I told him and tried to give him a reassuring smile, but I could tell he wasn't buying it. "Things will look better once we land, I promise." He yawned and nodded as he closed his eyes. Within minutes he was out like a light, his head resting on my shoulder.

The man on the aisle looked over and said in a quiet voice, "You're a good father. I wish my dad had given me that advice two marriages ago."

I opened my mouth to correct him and then stopped.

Brad wasn't my kid, but he might as well be Tyler's. Which made me his stepdad in a fucked-up metrosexual way. I looked down at him and could remember vividly disliking this kid for being so close to Tyler because he was so fucking good-looking. Brad was like every single guy I'd lusted after in high school rolled up in a letterman jacket, and there was the guy I loved sharing Cokes with him every day after school.

I had gotten jealous as shit and lost my mind a little.

But looking down at him now, I could see what Tyler saw in him. He was trying so hard, and he meant so well.... How could you not root for this kid even a little?

169

I put my arm around him, and he leaned into me and fell deeper into sleep. "Thanks," I told the man. "He's a great kid."

Now to pray Kyle thought the same.

Sebastian

I WAS halfway through the new *Captain America* movie when Matt walked up to Jennifer and me.

"Jen, can I talk to Sebastian for a few?" he asked.

"Get tired of Brad drooling on you?" she quipped, unbuckling her seat belt.

"I just gave him the window seat. He's out cold."

She chuckled. "Too bad Gladys isn't here. I want to know how things turned out with Kathy." He cocked his head, confused, and she slapped his shoulder. "You asshole. Kathy was her daughter who just left her asshole of a boyfriend."

My hand moved over my mouth to cover my laughing.

Jennifer declared, "I swear, all men are jerks," and then stomped down the aisle to Brad and Matt's seats.

Matt sat down next to me. "I really hope Brad doesn't catch the tail end of that attitude or he'll start looking for a parachute."

I flipped up the screen. "How is he?"

He gave me a solemn look. "Not good, if I'm being honest, which is what I came up here to do."

"Look, man…," I began to say, but he cut me off.

"I was wrong and we both know that." He paused and let that sink in. "I didn't know you and I jumped to the wrong conclusions—at least, I did if that speech you gave the kid was real."

"It was."

"Yeah, it seemed a little too specific not to be. I don't know how much Robbie has told you about everything all of us—Tyler, Brad, Kyle, and me—went through, but let me tell you, it was rough."

I nodded but said nothing.

"I mean, a kid killed himself, another held Kyle in school with a gun, there was Riley dying, and… it was just insane, and though none of us said it out loud, we were a family after all that, which means we would do anything for each other. But then, your boyfriend got on a plane and flew here because of one phone call, so you know that."

I nodded again.

"In my family, we don't let family get hurt. I have three older brothers, and I was taught if one of them is in trouble, you lead with your fists and figure out the rest later. Robbie is my family now, so I came at you with fists, and that was wrong." He gave a nervous laugh and then added, "Funny thing is, I don't think he likes me very much."

"You want to know something?" I asked, leaning toward him. He nodded. "He didn't like me very much either. Robbie has a problem with guys like us."

"Like us?"

"He looks at our physique and our looks and assumes we're assholes, because there's no shortage of good-looking assholes in the gay community. It's a defense mechanism—easier for him to dislike you first than you treat him like a douchebag later. He'll come around."

"We are kinda hot," he said, trying to keep a straight face.

It took all of ten seconds for us to burst out laughing.

"So yeah, let's try this again," I said, holding my hand out. "I'm Sebastian."

He shook it. "I'm Matt."

"I'm dating Robbie."

His face got serious. "And what are your intentions?"

We laughed so loudly the stewardess had to come and ask us to keep it down, which of course made us laugh even more.

Kyle

AS MUCH as I hated to admit it, Troy was right.

There was no way to just *wait* Billy away, which meant doing something. So I went to Mr. Childs' office, counting on the fact he wouldn't go home with all of us causing trouble there. When I got up there his office door was open, and he was on the phone. I knocked on the door and heard the last part of his conversation.

"—to do, Tina? I can't leave here until this is resolved." He saw me, and a look of distaste crossed his face. Not about me, probably just at the whole situation. "I have to go. I'll call you back."

Tina must not have liked that, because from the way Mr. Childs flinched from the phone, she'd slammed it down. "What can I do for you, Mr. Stilleno?" He made it sound like, "Please get eaten by wild animals so I can go home."

"I wanted to go over exactly what the hospital needs to allow my mom to get the surgery she needs."

"Clinically speaking she doesn't *need* it yet, which is the problem. If her life was in immediate danger, then it wouldn't matter what your father—"

"He's nothing to me."

"—wouldn't matter what the other Mr. Stilleno wanted."

I countered with, "If I can prove he doesn't have her best interest in mind?"

He sighed. "You can try, but your evidence would have to be pretty compelling. Without a judge's ruling, any decision we make will leave us open to a lawsuit, so your proof would be our only defense."

"What about extortion?" I asked.

He cocked his head. "In what way?"

"What if I could prove he was only doing this to get money from me? Would that be enough?"

He thought about it for a second. "He would have to say it out loud; inference isn't going to hold up."

I nodded. "If I could get a recording of him telling me or someone else aloud, then it would work?"

"I'd have to hear what he said, but yes, in theory it could."

I had Billy Stilleno's nuts in a vise.

"Fine, give me some time."

"Take your time," he said bitterly. "I can't leave here until one of you leaves, because I can't have the two of you fighting in my hospital all weekend."

"I promise, this will solve it."

He didn't look like he believed me.

172

On my way down to the ICU, I set up my iPhone to start recording. Luckily I had brought some clothes from California; I tossed on a button-up shirt with a pocket on it. It was wrinkled and I looked like a bum, but it held my phone high enough to record what we would be saying.

When I walked into the waiting room, Robbie and Tyler were there. They both looked at me like I was a zombie.

"What happened to your shirt?" Robbie asked, standing up slowly.

"Doesn't matter," I assured him. "I have a plan."

"Kyle," Tyler warned. "Don't do anything drastic."

"Like?"

He blanched a bit. "Like printing up hundreds of Facebook messages and taping them to people's lockers. I don't think those kind of antics will fly here."

"I have a real plan. Trust me."

They looked like they trusted me as much as Mr. Childs did.

I ignored them and walked into the ICU.

I went to my mom's room, and of course Billy and Troy were there. Troy was watching TV while Billy was arguing with someone on his cell.

"—have it. Just give me some more time," he pleaded. He saw me and added, "Can't talk," and hung up. "Come to give me my money?"

I forced myself not to smile; this was going to be easy. "I give you money and you let them operate on my mom?" I wanted this to be as clear as day.

"Yeah. Yeah," he said quickly. "That's the deal."

"Even though you know she could suffer from brain damage without it?"

His face twisted into rage. "Look, punk, I could care less about you or your mother, so if you came in here to guilt me, you're wasting your time. I want fifty thousand dollars, or I sit here until she drools."

"Let them operate, and then I'll pay," I countered.

He laughed. "Don't con a con man. That operation is the only leverage I have. No money, no deal."

Gotcha.

"Let me think about it," I said, backing out of the room.

"Better think fast. She isn't as young as she used to be."

I glanced over at Troy, who was giving me an odd look, like he couldn't figure out what I was doing. Frankly, I didn't care. I had Billy. I had the bastard.

Brad

WHEN I woke up, I was in Texas.

I'm not going to lie; I felt like a complete loser. I had talked so much shit growing up about how I was going to burn out of this town and never look back. How I was going to be the next big thing in baseball, and I promised not to forget the little people.

Now I was the littlest of the little, and there was no joy in my heart at all.

"Who you driving with?" Matt asked once we got to the parking lot. I gave him a confused look, and he explained. "We didn't drive up here together. It was—" He glanced over at Sebastian, who was giving him a shit-eating grin. "—it was my fault, and let's just move past that. You driving with him or me?"

"I'll go with Matt," Jennifer volunteered. "You can get to know Sebastian some."

I gave her a look that she ignored as she walked over toward Matt. "Good luck," she whispered. "He loves the eighties. I mean loves, loves them."

"You're a bitch," I whispered back, and she just kissed me on the cheek and waved.

"You two have fun. See you back in Foster."

I wondered how much of an asshole I'd look like if I said I wanted to ride with Matt too. Sighing, I followed Sebastian to his rental car and tossed my stuff into the trunk.

"So," he asked as he slammed it shut. "Like Whitesnake?"

I. Hate. Everyone.

Kyle

BY THE time I got the recording back upstairs, Childs was locking his office.

"I have it," I said, panting since I had run up the stairs.

He closed the door and sighed. "I'm afraid it will have to wait until tomorrow, Mr. Stilleno. I need to go."

"But I have it!" I said, holding my phone up.

He turned and looked at me, and I could tell he was going to give me bad news. "I need to leave. Now. I will be back early tomorrow morning, I will listen to your evidence, and we can go from there, but nothing more can be done tonight."

"But you said if I got it...." Oh God! I was whining.

"Nothing can be done tonight anyway," he snapped at me and then shook his head. "Even if what you got is enough, there is no way to perform surgery on her tonight unless it is life-threatening, which it is not. I'm sorry, Kyle, but my daughter has been waiting for me to come home for over four hours so she can open her birthday presents, and I need to go. They'll page me if your mother's condition changes, but for right now, nothing can be done."

My first reaction was to yell at him. I was so pissed I couldn't even see straight. Of course he was leaving. Of course he didn't care. My mom could be losing her brain functions, but let's make sure little Susie Childs had a fucking birthday, right?

And then I realized this guy wasn't Mr. Raymond.

He wasn't out to get me, and if I had to be honest, he was kinda on my side. Blowing up at him because he had a life outside of there would be pointless and stupid. It was Saturday evening in Foster, Texas. What did I think was going to get accomplished?

"I understand, Mr. Childs. I'll see you in the morning, and I hope your daughter has a good birthday."

He gave me a weak smile. "We will get this straightened out, I promise." He walked over to the elevator and paused. "You mind some advice?" I shook my head. "Go home. You can't do anything but drive yourself crazy here, and you look like you slept in your shirt. Give the nurse in charge your number and go home and sleep. You'll find things look better tomorrow."

I almost asked, "And if they aren't better?" but I didn't.

"Thanks, Mr. Childs. I'll do that."

The elevator dinged and he got on. "You coming?"

I shook my head. "I'll take the stairs. I need some time to myself."

He nodded and the doors closed. I waited twenty seconds to make sure the car was gone.

And then I screamed at the top of my lungs. I didn't say anything, just screamed and screamed until my throat was hoarse and my eyes were blurred with tears.

Brad

JENNIFER WAS right. This guy *loved* the eighties.

"Now *Kick* is where INXS really broke out. It was like nothing they had done before, and the videos were off the hook." He glanced over at me. "You ever see them?"

"Who?" I asked, not sure what we were talking about anymore.

"INXS."

I just looked blankly at him.

"'Need You Tonight'? 'Devil Inside'? 'Never Tear Us Apart'?"

Just stared.

"Okay, well then, you need to hear that," he said, cycling through his iPod.

So far I had been educated in Whitesnake (good music, crazy ex-wife in the videos), Mötley Crüe (awesome music for complete drug heads), and Van Halen (David Lee Roth and the other guy), and now it looked like it was... oh God, I forgot what band he had been talking about.

"So Robbie thinks Kyle is in such a bad place that he was willing to send you guys out to get me?" I asked, hoping it would distract him from the music.

He nodded. "I didn't get it myself, but he says you guys are better together, so... here you are."

"He said that?" I asked, surprised.

Sebastian nodded.

"I didn't think Robbie liked me all that much," I said, more to myself than to him.

"Hearing that a lot today," he muttered under his breath. "Robbie keeps his cards to his chest—which is a stupid way to play cards, but I don't get to make up sayings."

"I thought it was close to your vest?"

He paused. "But what if you aren't wearing a vest?"

I shrugged. "I thought everyone in the Old West wore vests and stuff."

Sebastian nodded. "Yeah, I suppose. Still a stupid saying. Anyway, Robbie likes a lot of people. He just doesn't show it all the time."

"Or ever," I added.

"Or ever," Sebastian agreed. "But that doesn't mean he dislikes you. It just means…."

"He's wearing a vest?"

Sebastian smiled. "Exactly. Robbie is a vest-wearing motherfucker."

I had to admit, I liked this guy. He was funny.

"So anyway, the year is 1987 and the world is gripped by glam rock."

Oh God, he didn't forget.

Still. Hate. Everyone.

Kyle

BY THE time I got back to the waiting room, I had composed myself.

Tyler and Robbie were both watching something on an iPad. As soon as I walked up, they turned it off. "So, any news?" Robbie asked.

I shook my head. "Nothing." To Tyler I asked, "Can you drive me home?"

"Sure," he said, getting up and then looking at Robbie. "Where are you staying?"

"We got a room at the Motel 6 up past Main. Mind dropping me off too?"

"Nah, the Parker Taxi Company is now in service," he said, trying to make me smile. "You guys want food first?"

"I'm not hungry," I said, fifteen kinds of miserable.

"I am and I know he is," Robbie answered. "Let's grab something at Starr's on the way. I'm buying since you're driving."

Tyler rubbed his hands together. "Oh, you're going to regret saying that."

He sounded like Brad. The realization was like getting hit on the bridge of my nose, and my eyes watered immediately. What was I doing? My mom could be dying, my *dad* was extorting me for money, and I'd told Brad to be gone before I got home. My whole life was out of control. What was I thinking?

Two hands grabbed my shoulder and shook me slightly. I saw Robbie kneeling in front of me. "Breathe," he said firmly. "Kyle, you're having a panic attack. You need to breathe."

I was going to ask him what he was talking about and why he was talking from so near the floor. Then I realized I was sitting on that same floor. My legs had given out and I had kind of slumped to the ground and hadn't even noticed. Looking around, I saw Tyler hovering over me, and there was a nurse too. How much time had passed?

"Kyle," he said, snapping his fingers in front of my face. "Focus on me. Breathe."

I took a deep breath and suddenly color came back into view. It had faded out so slowly, everything was painted with muted colors. I heard Tyler sigh with relief and the nurse let go of my wrist.

I hadn't even noticed she had been taking my pulse.

"He seems okay. After everything he's gone through, can't say I blame him," the nurse reported. "Get some food into him and then let him rest, but I would not suggest him being alone tonight."

"I'm fine," I said, trying to stand up and failing miserably. After about a minute of my best Bambi-tries-to-walk impression, I stopped and just sat there.

"Fine my ass," Robbie said, helping me up. "You can stay in the motel with me; Sebastian isn't going to be back until morning anyway."

"Where's Sebastian?" I asked, realizing I hadn't seen many people there today.

Robbie glanced at Tyler, who jumped in. "He and Matt went to Dallas to get something."

"What?"

"Huh?" Tyler asked back.

"What did they go and get in Dallas?"

"Illicit drugs." Robbie quipped, moving toward the elevator. "Who knows with those two? Either way, you can stay with me so I can make sure you don't fall in a well or something."

"I don't need a babysitter," I growled as we got in the elevator.

"No," Robbie said, giving me a look. "You don't. What you need is a friend and, barring that, a good slap upside your head. You're in pain, you're panicking, and that's okay, Kyle. No one expects you to handle this alone. You think I flew halfway across the country to spend time with this jerk?" He gestured to Tyler.

"You have to lct us help, Kyle," Tyler said, ignoring the jab.

"I'm just so tired," I finally admitted.

"So we get Starr's to go and then to the hotel," Robbie explained.

"I'm not hungry."

Robbie gave me a side glance. "I swear to God, you argue with me again and I'm going to slap the taste right out of your mouth. You need help, so shut up and let us help."

"Doesn't feel like helping," I muttered.

Robbie held a hand up and I shut my mouth. Fast.

Tyler

I DROPPED them off and headed back to the hospital.

So far I had been trying to do the right thing and let people do their job, but it was obvious that wasn't going to get it done. I parked in the front of the hospital and waited. Billy may have been a sleazy asshole, but he was a predictable one. So far the only reason he had left Linda's room was to smoke, and it seemed like he went every two hours or so.

So I waited for him.

People like Kyle, they think the world is run by people with intelligence, so they think that sooner or later people will do the right thing. They think that all things will eventually get better because deep down people are good and will do good. I knew better because at heart I wasn't a very good person. I'd been trying to be a better person, but it was slow going. Not so deep down, I knew what it was like to only think of yourself, to put what you wanted and needed above everyone else. I wasn't proud of it, but it was there, so I knew exactly how far Billy was willing to go to get what he wanted:

As far as he needed to.

I could wait for Kyle to spring some kind of Kyle trap, or I could wait for Mr. Childs to figure out he was putting my best friend in danger, but I would be waiting a long time. Instead, I parked out in the dark and waited. Because if I wanted to get Billy Stilleno dealt with, I needed to do it myself.

Sure enough, around midnight he came out the front doors and lit up a smoke.

He paced around like a…. You ever notice that people with nicotine fits pace like cats? I mean, if they had tails they'd be swishing back and forth something fierce as they smoked. Makes you wonder, what are cats so wound up about? Anyway, he paced and smoked, and I waited for him to wander away from the entrance.

He started to walk around the side, looking here and there like he was ready to bolt at any time, so I got out and moved toward him.

Billy was a problem that could be dealt with real easy. A couple of swings, he'd go down, and I'd tell him to get the fuck out of town while he still had a few of those things that passed as his teeth. With him gone, Kyle could allow the doctors to do the surgery and everything would be better. And I couldn't lie; I'd been waiting to kick the shit out of Billy Stilleno for years.

I must have stepped on a twig, because he spun toward me, his eyes wild with fear. I smiled, thinking that was the way I wanted him, until I looked at the .38 he had pointed at me. His hand trembled, and I froze.

Funny thing was, I wasn't scared. I mean, sure, he could shoot me, but I was more pissed that I had fucked up again than I was scared for my life.

"Tyler?" he asked, peering into the darkness. "Goddammit," he sighed, putting the gun back in his pocket. "You trying to get killed?"

"I'd ask why you have a gun, but I know the answer," I said, wondering if I could still get to him without him pulling that thing again. "What kind of trouble you in now?"

He snarled and turned away from me. "The kind a little money can't fix."

I crossed the distance between us and grabbed his shoulder. "A woman's life is in danger because of you."

He turned and smiled a yellow, rotten grin. "Well, mine ain't so safe either. Guess which one I care about more?" I was about to say something, but he went on. "If you think you're gonna come out here and beat some sense into me, think again. You touch me and I will own that crappy little store of yours when I'm done."

"What makes you think you're walking away?" I threatened.

He glanced down and then back up at me.

I looked down and saw the gun through his hoodie, pointing at my stomach. "What makes you think *you* are, pretty boy?"

I took a step back because I could see in his eyes he was serious.

"Tell that little queer son of mine to give me what I want." He backed away from me toward the hospital. "I ain't playing around."

He walked back into the building, and I stood there, realizing maybe for the first time how bad this whole mess was.

Kyle

I WOKE up in a panic.

One, I had no idea where I was. Two, I had this gripping fear I was supposed to be somewhere. And lastly, because I suddenly remembered where I was and where I was supposed to be.

I sat up and looked around the motel room for Robbie. He had asked the front desk for a rollaway so we didn't have to endure actually sleeping together. The bed sitting in the middle of the small room made the open space seem even more limited. The bed was empty, and it took a second for me to realize the shower was going.

The alarm clock on the nightstand had gone off, playing some radio station way too loudly. I started to get up to turn it off when I recognized the song. It was "What Makes You Beautiful" by One Direction, the song Brad had sung when he took me to prom. It was just another pop song in the total scope of things—just four minutes of random noise. But to me it was the most incredible expression of love that I had ever heard.

He was gone.

I had pushed him away, again. What was wrong with me? Why did I keep doing it? I loved him so much, but somewhere inside, I was so sure he was going to hurt me. At the time I had been convinced he was cheating on me with Colt, but now, looking back....

Robbie walked out of the bathroom and asked in a panicked voice, "What's wrong?"

I hadn't even realized I was crying.

"Everything," I said, breaking down and sobbing. "My mom is going to die, I broke up with Brad, my dad is an extra from *Breaking Bad*. There is nothing that isn't wrong."

He sat down next to me, and I steadied myself for the eventual pep talk these breakdowns produced.

"Well, that's true, everything is wrong," he said finally.

Well, that was peppy.

"Everything does suck right now, and I have no idea how things are going to turn out, but you can't just give up, and you can't just sit and be miserable. Trust me on this. No ditzy godmother is going to float in and make rodents sew you a dress, you can't lie in the middle of the forest and wait for someone to kiss your boo-boo and make it better, and you can't marry a man you just met."

I gave him a confused look.

"Sorry, was on a Disney roll and had to toss it in, but the rest of it is true. You can't give up. This is when real heroes dig in and stand their ground."

"I'm not a hero." I sounded miserable.

"My ass you're not. Kyle, if there were pictures of a hero in the dictionary, there would be a picture of Flynn from *Tangled* 'cause he's hot and a photo of you because you are the only hero I have ever met. Look at what you did to this town. How can you say you are anything but?"

"What did that do for my mom? And I still have a dick dad," I replied.

"I said you were a hero, not an all-powerful god who can stop car crashes or go back in time and rewrite things. Heroes don't fix everything all the time. That's why there's WD-40 and duct tape. Heroes don't back down when it looks hopeless. Hopeless is when they get geared up."

"You're telling me to go get dressed, aren't you?" I asked.

"I am, in an inspirational and emotional way that will help bolster your spirits."

I sighed and stood up. "You could have said 'Hey, Kyle! Get dressed!'"

"I could have, but it wouldn't change the fact you're a hero."

I paused at the bathroom door and gave him a smile. "Thanks."

"Don't thank me yet," he said cryptically. "I have a feeling this day is going to be full of surprises."

That got my spider sense tingling. "Where's Sebastian?"

He gave me a Cheshire Cat grin. "Ask me no questions and I'll tell you no lies."

Robbie

SO WHILE Sir Grump-a-lot was in the shower, I called Sebastian to see where in fuck's name they were. Imagine my surprise when Brad answered the phone.

"Sebastian's phone."

"Oh, I'm sorry, Siri must have dialed the wrong moose," I said dryly.

"Ha-ha," he responded, even more dryly. "He was knocked out after flying across the country twice in the same day, so I took over driving."

"Where are you guys?"

"About an hour away. Matt's jeep had a water pump thing so we had to pull over and fix it."

"Ugh. Men and cars, I swear."

"You *do* know we didn't cause the car to break down just so we could fix it, right?"

"Shut up," I snapped. Partly, of course, because I'd been about to accuse him and the other two of doing just that. "Just hurry and get here." I listened to the music in the background and hoped neither Brad nor Sebastian suspected me.

"I told Sebastian this, but I don't think this is a good idea."

I rolled my eyes. "Imagine my surprise. Well, I do, so get your doubting butt in gear and get here!"

He muttered, "Wow, someone got up on the wrong side of the broom today."

"You know I can hear you, right?"

"You know I don't care, right?"

"Drive. Faster. Now," I ordered and hung up.

The bathroom door cracked open, and I saw Kyle peek out just far enough to spot me with his left eye. "Who are you yelling at?"

"Judge Judy; the woman is a moron."

He paused and opened the door a bit to stare disbelievingly at me. "You do know the TV isn't on."

"I don't need a TV to tell me that old woman is insane. Change, now!"

He slammed the door, and I took a deep breath.

And this was why I hated Foster.

Troy

SO YEAH, this town sucked.

I know I'd only been there a couple of days and you shouldn't be judging books by their covers, which is a bullshit saying. What else could you judge it by if you'd never read the book? Its sparkling personality? I didn't like this town, and I'm pretty sure it wasn't sweet on me either. Either that or everyone here learned manners on the wrong side of the Berlin Wall and believed everyone not born and raised here was a spy.

If what I just said shocked you because you didn't think I would be able to pull up a Cold War analogy, then fuck you because you're as bad as this town.

I know what I look like. I know what my dad looks like, and I know what the Brady Bunch looks like. So I get we didn't fit in here, but for fuck's sake, people! Could you at least not watch me like we were going to steal the nearest church's silver stuff?

Maybe the reason we were there was making them all hostile toward us. I mean, it wasn't like we were the good guys here.

My dad had been pulled over crossing the border in Laredo and had to dump about a kilo of coke or get caught with it. Now, for those of you not in the know, let me break it down for you. On the border that kind of powder would go for around twenty-five grand wholesale. That means before it was cut and other stuff is added to it to dilute its potency and then marked up, the best price you could hope for was maybe twenty grand, if you knew someone.

Once that was cut with something else, like baby powder or something, the value could double easily. So my dad didn't just owe them the twenty-five grand; they were going to want the street value of it. And I can assure you, that was money my dad didn't have.

So now the Vasquez brothers wanted to know where their coke was. The answer they did not want to hear was that it was killing fish in the Rio Grande. Worse, most of that coke was already sold before my dad ejected it out of the car, so he didn't owe them the wholesale cost of the coke. He owed them the street value plus.

Plus whatever value they wanted to add not to break both his legs.

To tell the truth, breaking his legs would have been nice, because this wasn't the first time my dad had come up short for them. Now you might be saying, "Troy, you sound rather calm for someone discussing the possible murder of your father."

If you are, you're right.

This wasn't the first time or the fifth time we'd been in this situation. I suppose I'd grown a little numb to my father's impending doom. He was a survivor, and it was an odd form of reality television for me to watch him get out of these jams. I was growing a little concerned, though, because I suspected the Vasquez brothers had figured out where we were. My dad took off across Texas once he was clear of customs; I wasn't sure he had a destination in mind before the call from the hospital came in.

I didn't know this lady, but she had some shitty luck, let me tell you.

The hospital had my dad still listed as her husband, so when she was brought in, they did a search for a way to contact my dad and somehow came up with his cell phone. Next thing I knew we were squatting in her hospital room while my dad plotted his next move. I expected him to get her house keys and take anything he could pawn to raise some cash, but it turned out that his other son, Kyle, had come into some money, so he started scheming.

So yeah, hard to figure why the local population hadn't warmed to us yet.

I was watching *Supernatural* on TNT when the nurse came in. She and those other nurses had been giving us the stink eye for days, but so far she hadn't been able to kick us out. Something about spending as much time as possible with the dying family member. Leave it to my dad to figure out a way to outsmart the rules. I thought this was just the ordinary change-of-shift checkup, but instead she stared straight at my dad. "Mr. Childs would like to see you up in his office."

Again? What was going on now?

He got up and I followed, but he shook his head. "Stay here."

If you're curious, it was the same way he'd tell a dog to stay.

He walked out and I waited. The next commercial break, I made my way upstairs to Childs's office. When I got there, I could hear my dad's voice coming from a recording, and I knew I'd been right about Kyle after all. When he came in yesterday ready to deal, I knew something was up. The questions he was asking were so simple, they had to be a trap. And sure enough, they were.

"*I give you money and you let them operate on my mom?*" Kyle's voice asked.

"*Yeah. Yeah. That's the deal.*"

"*Even though you know she could suffer from brain damage without it?*"

"*Look, punk, I could care less about you or your mother, so if you came in here to guilt me, you're wasting your time. I want fifty thousand dollars, or I sit here until she drools.*"

Kyle's voice came next. "*Let them operate, and then I'll pay.*"

My dad's laugh was as malicious as it was damning. "*Don't con a con man. That operation is the only leverage I have. No money, no deal.*"

"*Let me think about it.*"

"*Better think fast. She isn't as young as she used to be.*"

Kyle sounded pissed. "You see, Mr. Childs, I told you he was here to extort money from me."

"You have an explanation for this, Mr. Stilleno?" Childs asked my dad.

"I didn't know I was being recorded," my dad started with, which was not the best comeback.

"This isn't a court of law," Childs responded coolly. "I don't care about the legality of the recording. I'm more interested in whether you dispute it."

No one spoke, and I could imagine my dad glaring at Kyle. "Okay, yes, I did say that. But you have to understand why."

"Go on," Childs prompted him.

This should be good.

"It's my son. He's gotten himself in trouble."

I felt my blood turn to ice.

"He has a drug problem, and he owes some men money. I know I'm trying to get money out of you, but I'm trying to save my son's life." His voice was so distraught, I would have bought it if he hadn't been talking about me. "I know it's wrong, but I'm just a father trying to do the best by his son."

I was so glad no one was looking at me because I probably looked like the biggest idiot alive. My jaw dropped until my mouth hung open like a freshly caught trout.

"You have kids, Mr. Childs. You know the things you'll do to save them. I've tried to get him off it, but he messed around with the wrong people, and I'm afraid for his life."

"I see," Childs said, and I knew my dad had done it again.

I didn't want to hear anything else, so I went back to the ICU and tried to figure out what to do next. So, worse than everyone thinking I'm a hood, they're going to think I'm a druggie hood. The ironic part is that I didn't even drink. If you grew up around that shit, you fostered an aversion to it that never really went away. Most kids looked at booze and drugs as forbidden fruit; I saw it as part of the family business I didn't want to get into.

About fifteen minutes later my dad came back. I could tell he was proud.

"So what happened?" I asked, feigning ignorance.

"Fucking faggot tried to set me up," he growled, pulling his cell out. "Showed him who was boss."

Yeah, by throwing me under the bus.

"So then everything is okay?"

He shook his head. "He said he was going to call their lawyers and see what the deal was, but I'm willing to bet they aren't gonna do a thing. He's gonna pay."

I said nothing.

"Go get lost; I need to make a call," he ordered.

"So? Make the damn call, what do I care?"

He crossed the room and grabbed my shoulder hard. "Did I ask if you fucking care? Go get a Coke, go downstairs and smoke, do anything but be here."

I pulled away and moved back toward the bed. "You really wanna get caught roughing your poor, pathetic son up?" I asked him. "That won't help your case any."

He paused because he knew I was right: this all hinged on him looking like the not-so-bad guy, which meant me going along with him. "Get out of here if you know what's good for you."

We both knew he wasn't a physical threat to me, but I still walked out because I'd been conditioned to do so. I was a trained dog with nowhere else to go, so what choice did I have but beg for table scraps? I walked away from the room and waited about a minute before going back. I pressed my ear tight against the door, near the hinges so it wouldn't accidentally open. I could barely make out my dad's voice.

"—tter of time. Look, Carlos, I can get you your money," he pleaded.

Silence, which was probably Carlos screaming at him that he was out of time.

"I can pay you more than what the junk was worth, I promise."

I could just imagine Carlos tearing him a new asshole.

"This won't be like Chicago. That was a mistake."

Chicago was when my dad got fronted some crank for a weekend and then skipped town when Carlos tried to get paid. They got that settled, but I could guess Carlos was telling my dad no because he would just run again.

"Look, I can prove it. What if I give you some collateral?"

Pause.

"Tell your guys that if I don't have the money when they get here, they can hold my kid as promise I'll get the money."

My blood turned to ice water.

"You know I won't let anything happen to the kid! What kind of guy you think I am?"

The kind of guy who would let a drug dealer hold his son as a promissory note.

"Just one more chance, please, Carlos."

I didn't hear anything after that because all I could hear was the pounding of my heart. He'd just said that. He really just bargained me away like I was a poker chip. My first instinct was to run, but where? With what? I was as fucked as my dad—well, worse, because I couldn't offer him up as a down payment on a debt.

Kyle

ROBBIE AND I paced the waiting room waiting for Mr. Childs to make his decision.

"He blamed the kid?" Robbie asked for like the fifth time.

"Of course he did," I said, scowling. "What else was he going to do?"

"I don't know, be a man," Robbie muttered as Tyler walked in.

"What did I miss?" he asked.

"Encyclopedia Brown here confronted the crack addict, and the hospital official needs to think about it," Robbie said sighing.

"What does he need to think about?" Tyler almost shouted.

"Mr. Parker," Childs said, coming in from another door. "Do I have to eject you from here again?"

It was slightly amusing to watch Tyler go from grown-up jock to looking like a kid being scolded by the principal. "No, sir."

"Mr. Stilleno, this way," he said, gesturing toward the ICU. I followed him in as he asked the nurse to get Billy.

Billy came out looking pissed. "Well?" he asked Childs.

"Before I say anything, I need both of you to promise me there will be no yelling. This is a hospital, and I am this close to throwing both of you out."

I nodded and saw Billy do the same.

"I talked to our lawyers and they advised that, to protect us from possible litigation, we don't do anything at this time."

It took both of us a second to comprehend his words.

"That means I win?" Billy asked.

"You're fucking kidding me!" I said at the same time.

"Kyle," Childs said, looking guilty. "If he sues us, it is going to be a jury trial, and our lawyer assured me even though his actions are deplorable, his motivation of saving his son would be enough to sway certain jurors. If that happens, it could cost this facility far too much money."

"So how much money is my mom's life worth?" I demanded.

Childs looked like he was going to hurl.

Robbie pulled me back, and I was about to go with him when Billy had to open his mouth. "You know the price. The question is, how much is your mom's life worth to you?"

And that was it.

I turned around and threw myself at Billy. He wasn't ready for me because I hit his stomach and we both crashed to the floor. His confusion didn't last for long, because he slammed both fists into my back as we rolled around. This wasn't going to be like with Tony Wright where being in an actual fight was an alien concept. I could tell Billy had been in more than a few scraps from the way he moved to protect his balls while whaling on me.

Childs was yelling, Robbie screamed something, and then I was picked up like a rag doll.

Tyler pulled me off him and then kind of tossed me back to get me out of the way. Billy scrambled to his feet, and a wicked grin spread across Tyler's face. "Come on, Billy. I told you this was going to happen. Why don't you pull the same stunt you did last night?"

I had no idea what he was talking about, but I didn't care. I ran at Billy, ready to kill him if I could. I was not in any way intimidating, evidenced by the way he almost casually backhanded me to the ground. It hurt, but it was nothing, I'm sure, to the right hook Tyler slammed into his chin. The sound was like a fleshy gunshot and Billy's feet literally left the floor. For a second he floated there. Then gravity hit and he fell down like a bag of potatoes.

I got up and was ready to kick him until he bled, but as soon as I got to my feet and took a step, I was tackled from behind. Troy hit me hard, and once again I ate linoleum.

"Get the fuck off my dad!" he roared as he began to hammer a fist into my head.

I curled up into a ball and tried not to die.

"*Get the fuck off him*," a voice bellowed through the ICU. I must have been hit harder than I thought, because it sounded just like Brad.

There was one more blow and then nothing. I lay there with my eyes closed.

I cracked one eye open finally. Sure enough, Brad stood there with his hand wrapped around Troy's throat.

"Listen up, G.I. Joe. The last guy who tried that with me around walks with a limp, and he was a Marine. Touch him again and there won't be enough of you for dental identification."

Troy was petrified.

"I'm going to let you go. Even look at him wrong, and we're going to have a different kind of conversation. Got it?"

Troy nodded.

Brad released him, and he inhaled frantically as he stumbled back.

"You okay?" Brad asked, holding out a hand to me.

"I have never been more okay in my life," I said in complete awe as I stood up.

"Need your boyfriend to fight for you?" Troy spat at him.

"I ain't his boyfriend. Keep talking, and you'll find out what my fist tastes like up close," Brad fired back.

"You're not?" I asked Brad, completely not caring about what was going on around me.

"Not now," he said back to me, refusing to make eye contact.

"Stop this at once!" Childs exclaimed.

"I wanna press charges," Billy said around the blood coming out of his mouth.

Robbie fired back at him, "Try it, crackhead. Want to bet not one person in this room saw a damn thing?"

"I saw it," Troy protested.

"Shut up, boy," Billy snapped automatically, and Troy scowled. "Call the cops; I'm pressing charges against both of them."

Before anyone could answer, Tyler said in a low voice, "Yeah, Billy, call the cops. I'm sure the pistol in your hoodie is registered all legal-like, right?" Billy paled and looked over at him. "And you can't be on probation, so just carrying it can't be a violation, right?"

Billy visibly deflated in front of us.

"What did that mean?" I asked Brad.

He gave me a side glance and said, "You know exactly what it means. This was your idea."

Childs started talking before I could respond. "I want everyone out of here now. No one is to be in that room unless it is visiting hours, and even then *one* person at a time will be allowed in for no longer than thirty minutes. If you want to call the police, you may, but not from in here. As of now, the ICU is off-limits."

No one moved until Nurse Redmon came rushing toward us. "You heard the man. You two," she snapped at Billy and Troy. "Collect your stuff out of that room and get." She looked at Brad, Tyler, and me. "That goes for the three of you too. Door's that way."

We all started shuffling away in our respective directions when Sebastian came barging in. "What did I miss?" he asked, looking around. "Oh, man, did I miss it?"

"Out!" the nurse barked, and we all picked up our paces.

Brad still wouldn't look at me.

"Can we talk?" I asked him as soon as we were out of the ICU.

He shrugged. "Sure."

"You know I hate violence," Robbie said to Tyler.

"Coming from the guy who racked me on our first date," Sebastian muttered.

Robbie shot him a death glare and then went back to Tyler. "It is never the answer and you know where I stand." Tyler nodded. "That being said, you should have hit the bastard again."

Matt and Jennifer walked in, looking confused. "Why is everyone out here?"

"Come on," I said to Brad, motioning to the exit.

As Tyler filled them in, we walked out and found a bench in the hall to sit down on.

"How are you even here?" I asked once I had my thoughts settled.

"Robbie thought you needed me here." His voice wasn't cold; it was apathetic.

"I do. Thank you for coming." I was too scared to even touch him.

"You needed help. Of course I came."

"I'm sorry about what I said in California."

He looked over at me. "Let's not do this now. Your mom is still in there, and you need to be worrying about that. We can talk when this is all over."

He didn't sound like the Brad I knew at all.

"Promise?" I asked as everyone else was coming out of the ICU.

He looked at me, and I could see the hurt in his eyes. "I've never broken a promise to you, Kyle. I don't plan on starting now."

His words hurt more than any physical blow could have.

"So now what?" Tyler asked me like I knew what I was doing.

"I don't know. That was my last plan," I admitted.

The doors slammed open and Troy came rushing out with Billy hot on his heels. "I was trying to help you!" he screamed at his father.

"I need you to do what I say!" Billy screamed back and then saw he had an audience. Discretion being the better part of being a fucking coward, he looked at the crowd of people scowling at him and just turned and left. They both exited toward the elevator.

I needed to finish this.

"Billy, wait," I said, standing up, garnering a whole slew of shocked looks from everyone else. He turned around and looked at me expectantly. "Can we talk for a second?"

"You ready to end this?" he asked.

I walked over to both of them. "I am. You win. Sign the papers and let my mom get the surgery."

"Get me my money first."

"It's Sunday, but I can go to the ATM and grab some money out."

"I don't need no four hundred bucks. I need fifty grand, and I want it now."

"Well, unless you want to rob a bank, I can't get it, and she needs that operation."

"Then you better hope she can hold out until tomorrow" was all he had to say.

"Can you please just try to be a human being," I pleaded.

"I am a human being," he answered. "A human being that needs fifty thousand dollars." The elevator opened and he and Troy walked in. "Be here tomorrow morning if you want to do business."

Troy jabbed a button and the doors closed on me.
I was officially out of ideas.

Brad

I HAD never seen Kyle look so low in my life.

He came back from the elevator looking like he had just been shot.
It was pretty obvious his dad was every bit the asshole Matt had made
him out to be. "He won't do anything until he has the money in his
hands," he told us.

"You're going to pay him?" Robbie asked, sounding shocked.

"You want me to wait until my mom is a vegetable?" he almost
screamed.

I walked to him and put an arm around him. "He's just asking," I
said quietly.

He shrugged my arm off. "And stop trying to handle me. I'm not a
crazy person."

"You're acting like one," I replied, taking a step back. He gave me
a hurt look and I added, "I'm sorry, but you are. Everyone here, we're on
your side. Yelling at us isn't going to help."

He looked like he was ready to fight; then he sighed. "I know. I'm
sorry."

Every part of me wanted to pull him into a hug, but I knew that was
the wrong move, so I looked at everyone else. "So, food?"

"Hell, yeah," Sebastian said, his voice booming. When everyone
stared at him, he smiled, obviously embarrassed. "Sorry, my inside voice
is broken."

I smiled and looked at Kyle, who just shuffled into the elevator like
he was a cow being led to a slaughterhouse. No one talked during the
elevator ride down; the next thirty seconds were the longest of my life.

"Who's going with who?" Tyler asked once we hit the main floor.

"Who are you going with?" Kyle asked me.

The question shocked the hell out of me. "I guess Tyler."

He turned and looked at Robbie. "I'll go with you."

So that was how it was going to be.

Matt and I climbed into Tyler's jeep. Once we were buckled in, Matt turned around and said, "Give him some time. This has to be the worst possible of situations."

"Time isn't going to change much," I answered, feeling the ache in my chest. "Once Kyle has made up his mind about something, nothing short of a nuclear war will change it."

"Well then, you're in luck," Tyler said as we pulled onto First Street.

"Why?"

"Because Robbie is a one-man walking, talking, rainbow-colored nuclear bomb. Once he starts talking to Kyle, he'll agree to marrying you as long as Robbie gets off his back."

Matt glanced over at him. "Speaking from experience?"

Tyler gave him a shy grin. "Remind me to tell you about *Hollywood Squares: Get Tyler a Man* edition. Robbie almost had me dating a fifty-year-old ranch hand just to get some release."

"Oh, we're coming back to that subject," Matt said knowingly.

We pulled up in front of Nancy's Diner and waited for Robbie and everyone else to join us. Kyle just walked by me without a glance. Robbie patted me on the back and advised, "Ignore everything he says today."

They ended up putting three two-person tables together to seat us all. I sat at one end near Tyler while Kyle was at the other near Robbie. Matt, Sebastian, and Jennifer sat between us. It felt like it was a meeting of two warlords coming together to work out a peace treaty. Everyone sat next to their liege and waited for the inevitable fight to begin.

Man, I gotta stop watching so much *Game of Thrones*.

Everyone made small talk, mostly with the person next to them, which left me with Tyler.

"So how did you like California?" he asked after the waiter had gone to put our order in.

"It was...," I began and then paused as the kaleidoscope of feelings that made up my time in California swirled around in my mind. The first weeks with just Kyle and me in the apartment, the days of endless sex and goofing around online, finding a new place to eat every night... my eyes got misty just remembering how happy we were. Then there was getting the job at the gym and the feeling of pride I had knowing I could do something besides play baseball. Meeting Colt, then Kyle going to school, and the distance and the coldness, spiraling out of control while I tried anything to keep us together.

And then the numbness when Kyle told me to get out.

"Different" was all I said to Tyler.

It looked like he wanted to say more, but instead he shook his head and asked, "So, you see who the Rangers are looking at?"

Thank God for sports, or men would have to actually talk with each other about shit like their feelings.

Kyle

SO DANTE, the one who wrote that bullshit book about Hell, that one? Dante was a liar and a little bitch. Wanna know why? Sitting at a table with someone you fucked it up with and not being able to scream at the top of your lungs is Hell. Knowing that you had the best guy in the world completely devoted to you and throwing it all away? *That's* Hell. If someone walked in and threw gasoline on me and set me ablaze, it would hurt less than looking down the tables and seeing Brad talk to Tyler.

"You're staring," Robbie whispered to me.

"Oh God, it's that obvious?" I asked him, mortified.

"It is if you speak Kyle," he said, handing me a menu. "If you're going to stare, at least put some effort into looking like you're hiding it."

I picked up the menu and hid my face.

"What are you going to do?" Robbie asked.

"About what? Brad or Billy?"

"Either."

Good question.

I didn't have any answers.

We ordered food, and I watched Tyler and Brad make small talk about something. How could he just sit there? Did he hate me? I know *I* hated me. Nothing in life had made sense since I graduated high school, and let me tell you, life didn't make sense then either. Matt joined in and then Sebastian. It took me a few seconds to realize they were talking about sports.

"Ugh," I muttered to Robbie. "Really?"

He rolled his eyes. "Don't ask me."

And yet another level of Hell. Being stuck at a table with a guy you fucked it up with while guys talk about sports. At least they weren't going on about cars....

When the food arrived, at least they couldn't talk and eat, so that helped, but I wasn't hungry at all. All I could think about was my mom lying in her hospital bed. I pushed my plate away.

"You should try to eat something," Robbie urged.

"Not hungry," I sighed.

"Well, you need to keep your strength up, and.... God damn, I sound like my mother!" he announced, pounding the table with his hand.

"I wasn't gonna say it," Sebastian said between bites.

They gave each other a look as Troy walked into the diner.

He saw us all at our tables and paused. We made eye contact before he went to the counter to pick up a to-go order.

"I'll be right back," I said, getting up.

Brad asked with his eyes if I wanted backup. I shook my head and sat down next to Troy at the counter. "So I tried it his way."

Troy kept looking forward. "Yeah. Nice try."

"I don't know what to do." I tried not to sound as desperate as I felt.

Troy turned and looked at me. "You do know that even when you find a judge tomorrow, my dad will drag this out as long as he needs to, right? You're going to need a judge to make a court order. Even then my dad will find some way to fuck things up. If he can't get the money from you, he'll sue that big guy for hitting him or whatever. He's dangerous, Kyle. Are you getting that?"

I'd figured that out a while ago.

"So what do I do?"

He thought about it for a few seconds and then said the last thing I expected from him.

"Don't give him the money. Just don't do it. He's going to make all these excuses like it's for me or for something I did, but it's not, and we both know it. I'm not going to see a dime of that money. You want advice? Don't give it to him. He needs it more than your mom needs an operation. The worst that can happen to her is that the swelling gets bad enough that they'll operate to save her life."

"But she could have brain damage!" I protested.

"Yeah. My dad is going to get worse if he doesn't get that money. He deserves to get worse." I looked at him, shocked, but he kept talking. I think he was talking more to himself than to me. "I'm tired of covering for him, of putting up with his lies. I just want out."

And that's when it hit me.

"He trusts you, right?" I asked Troy as my mind raced.

He nodded slowly. "I suppose."

"I mean, if you told him something, he would believe it, right?"

"Yeah, why?"

"Look, tell your dad I'll get him the money in the morning. Tell him to go to the hospital, and the second I give you the money and you call him, he has to tell them to operate. That's the only way this is going down."

Troy looked confused. "So you're going to give him the money?"

I smiled at him. "Just tell him that. Then you meet me here tomorrow morning at a quarter to eight."

He shrugged just as his food showed up. "Okay, man, your money. But this is a bad idea."

"Just tell him that's the only way I'm going to do this. He's at the hospital; the second you have the money, he signs away his right to decide about her care. I don't even want to wait for the time it takes to drive back to the hospital. And Tyler will be there to make sure he signs. If not, he won't get a dime."

"Don't give him the money, Kyle," Troy warned me. "You pay him once, he'll never go away."

"Quarter to eight," I repeated, getting up. I looked over at Ricky, the guy working the counter. "Put his food on our tab," I said, gesturing toward our table. "We got it."

Troy picked up the food and sighed. "Okay, I tried."

I watched him walk out and then rushed over to the table and tapped Brad on the back. "Can I talk to you over here?"

He made a face but got up from the table and followed me to a corner booth. He sat across from me, and all it did was remind me of how much things had changed.

"What's up?" he asked.

"I'm going to give them some money," I told him.

"Um, okay."

"Well, I want to make sure you're okay with it."

He cocked his head. "Why?"

"Because it's part your money too."

"No it's not," he countered instantly.

"Robbie gave it to both of us."

"He gave it to you so that we could be together. We're not together, so the money stays with you. I don't want any of it."

"We can still be together," I said, sounding panicked.

He just stared at me for a series of agonizingly long seconds. "Was that it? It's your money; do what you want with it."

"Brad, please."

He got up. "Not now. Not here."

"Then when?" I asked.

"When this is done." And he walked back to the table.

This was going to be done tomorrow morning. Count on it.

Tyler

THE THINGS I found myself doing.

I mean there it was, Monday morning, and I was at the hospital watching Billy. Kyle had assured me that everything would make sense soon. I hated to admit the teenage boy might be the smartest one out of all of us, but there I was, waiting.

"So is this some kind of scam or what?" Billy asked me through his second cigarette. We had been standing outside, since neither of us was very welcome in Foster General right then. "Because if this is a waste of time...."

"You'll what?" I barked at him. "Go back to your busy life of extorting family members for blood money?"

"Easy to judge when you've never been where I am."

I gave him a shocked look. "You're right, Billy, I have never been where you are. I have never become so addicted to drugs that I'm willing to hold an innocent woman's life over my son to force money from him to pay off my debts."

We didn't talk after that.

Ten minutes past eight, both Billy's and my phones rang.

"Yeah?" I answered, knowing it was Kyle.

"Make sure he signs the paper releasing his rights over my mom." He sounded angrier than I had ever heard him.

"Okay, then what?" I asked.

"Nothing, just make sure he signs it." And he hung up.

I looked over at Billy, who was hanging up too. "Okay then, seems we're almost done here."

"You need to sign that paper," I reminded him.

"I know, I know, man. Let's get this over with."

We walked in and the security guard sighed and stood up. "Help you gentlemen?"

"Yeah, I need to sign some papers," Billy said like he was a businessman instead of a crack addict talking to a secretary.

"Let me call Mr. Childs," the guard replied. He picked up the phone.

"How much is he giving you?" I asked, hating that Kyle had to give in to this fuck.

Billy flashed a nasty, yellow-toothed smile at me as the guard hung up. "He's on his way down."

It was pretty obvious we were to wait in the lobby and not cause a scene.

Childs walked out of the elevator, looking like he'd gotten no sleep last night either. "Mr. Stilleno, I was informed there is going to be a motion made this morning on behalf of Kyle Stilleno and Linda Stilleno, challenging your rights related to Ms. Stilleno's care."

"Don't need it," Billy said. "I'm here to sign away my rights. Kyle can call the shots now."

Childs couldn't have looked more shocked if Billy had pissed on him. "Once you sign the waiver, you have no legal right to say word one about her condition."

"Yeah, yeah, give me the paper and I'm outta here."

"Wait here," Childs ordered eagerly.

Another five minutes passed and Childs returned, followed by a woman in an expensive-looking suit. She walked up to Billy and said in a clipped, no-nonsense tone, "Mr. Stilleno, by signing this you are effectively surrendering your legal right to have any opinion whatsoever in regard to your wife's medical procedures. If that is the case, all such decisions will be made by her son, Kyle. Do you understand?"

"I know that," Billy snapped.

"Be that as it may, I want to make it crystal clear. Further, Mr. Childs, Mr. Parker, security guard Drake, and the head of hospital finances will sign as witnesses. The document will be notarized in your presence by Mr. Childs's secretary. You will remain until the signatures are complete and notarized. A copy will be placed in public record, you will take a copy with you, and Hospital Records will retain the original."

"You're the lawyer, huh?" Billy asked with a lewd smile.

As cold as a glacier, she stared at Billy until he looked away.

"I got it. Give it to me already."

She handed him a clipboard and he scribbled his name on the bottom line.

"Initial here," she said when he tried to hand it back to her. "And there."

He repeated the signatures on the three other original copies. Everyone signed as witnesses, and a quiet woman carrying an old-fashioned notary's seal sat at the security guard's desk to properly notarize the documents. By the time everything was done, Billy looked about ready to chew paper himself.

"Mr. Stilleno, your copy. Since you have caused several severe disturbances while on these premises, and since you have no valid reason to be here, please leave at once or prepare to be escorted out." Never once did her tone change, and I realized something. Although she seemed to be looking at Stilleno, she was, in fact, looking straight through him as if he didn't exist.

"Fuck it," Billy laughed. "I don't want to be here anyways." He looked at me. "Well, there you go, jocko. Tell your boy it's done." With that he walked out of the hospital.

I called Kyle. He didn't even say hello. "Did he do it?"

"Just watched him with my own eyes."

"I just pulled into the parking lot. I might need some help."

That didn't sound good. "I'll meet you outside."

When I walked out, Billy was standing to the side of the walk, calling someone.

Kyle came running up. He had a grin on his face. A grin like a big cat that's just eaten… which was no grin at all.

"Help with what?" I asked him.

"This might get physical," he said under his breath as he watched Billy.

"What did you do?" I asked as Billy saw Kyle.

"Hey! Where's Troy?" Billy shouted.

Kyle looked up like he was thinking about it. "I don't know; he's not here?"

Billy growled and took a step toward Kyle. "Where's my money?"

"I gave it to Troy," Kyle said, sounding as innocent as he could. "Why?"

Billy opened his phone and dialed again.

There was a muffled ringing from Kyle's rear pocket.

"Oh yeah," Kyle said, pulling out a phone. "Troy wanted me to give this to you."

"Where is my son?" Billy asked, snatching the phone.

"I don't know," Kyle said, his whole demeanor turning serious. "I mean, he wouldn't take the money and just run, right?" I saw Billy's face go pale. "I mean, where would he learn such deplorable behavior as to say 'fuck it' to family and just think of himself? Where in the whole wide world would he learn that from? Huh, Billy?"

"He wouldn't," Billy choked out.

Kyle shrugged. "Maybe he would. Maybe he heard that you were ready to leave him with those creeps as collateral and figured it was every man for himself. Maybe he got sick of you blaming him for being a drug addict when he isn't. Or maybe he was sick of your shit and left."

"You can't do this," Billy protested.

"I didn't do anything. I gave Troy the money, just like we agreed."

Billy reached out to grab him, and I slapped his hand away. "You little fuck. You can't do this. I'll…."

"You'll what? Threaten not to let them operate on my mom?"

I chuckled as I realized Billy was fucked.

"You better start running, Billy," I said, making sure Kyle was behind me. "Those guys who're looking for you have to be on their way."

"I'm going to fucking kill you!" Billy raged as he reached into his hoodie.

Sheriff Taylor's voice boomed from across the street. "Take your hand out of your pocket or I will open fire."

The sheriff and two deputies huddled behind an unmarked car. Their guns were drawn.

"Yeah. I might have called the cops and told them we were meeting," Kyle said. "I mean, you never know who you can trust."

Billy slowly took his hand out of his hoodie and raised his hands even before the cops ran across the street.

"You come into my town and threaten my family?" Kyle said in a low growl. "You really thought that was how it was going to go down?" I saw Billy blink twice, as if he was seeing his son for the first time. "Want to know the fucked-up part? All you had to do was ask. Be a human being and ask for my help, and I might have done it. But instead you wanted it this way, so congratulations."

"On what?" Billy asked as the cops got closer.

"On losing both of your sons in the same day."

"Billy, what's in your pocket?" Sheriff Taylor asked in a casual tone.

Billy sighed. "A pistol."

The two deputies moved like they were blurs. One grabbed Billy's arms and yanked them behind him to cuff him, and the second pulled the same gun he had drawn on me out of his hoodie.

"Loaded," the second deputy told the sheriff.

"Tell me you have a permit."

Billy said nothing.

"You're under arrest."

"Big mistake, you little fag," Billy snarled at Kyle.

"You don't know this, but I just did you a favor," Kyle said without an ounce of fear in his voice. "The guys who are looking for you, they can't get you while you're in lockup. So pray they keep you locked up for a long time."

Billy said nothing as the cops dragged him away.

The sheriff looked at Kyle. "You okay?"

Kyle nodded. "I am now. I need to go in there and tell them to operate on my mom."

"Don't let me stop you," the sheriff said with a smile.

Kyle ran into the hospital while we watched.

"That kid really is going to take over the world, isn't he?" he asked me once Kyle was gone.

"Oh yeah, big-time," I agreed.

Troy

AS THE cops put my dad in the back of the car, I felt a twinge of guilt hit me.

I'm not gonna lie, my first instinct was to run out there and do something. But before I could, Kyle's words from that morning came back to me and I paused.

"So let me ask you this. If you could do anything with your life right now, what would it be?"

I had a feeling my answer wasn't the words he'd been expecting. "What does it matter? What you want to do is always trumped by what you have to do."

There was sadness in his eyes, and for some reason it didn't look like pity. "Let's imagine, then. Pretend that you can do anything. *What would it be?*"

"Look, Kyle, no offense, but I'm here to get money. I appreciate the effort, but I hate fairy tales."

He made a face, no idea why, but I really didn't care. I just stood there outside the bank with him, waiting for him to get this done with.

"Wait here, okay?" he asked.

"Is this a scam? Because I don't have time for—"

He held his hands up. "Trust me, just wait here. I'll be right back."

I watched him go up to the teller and hand her a slip. For all I knew, it said he was being robbed and to call the police. A couple walked by and gave me a look, no doubt horrified that their perfect little town had been invaded by a hoodlum.

Kyle came out with an envelope in his hand.

"There's five thousand dollars in here," he said, not handing it to me.

I cocked my head. "My dad needs a lot more than that."

"I know, so I'm going to leave it up to you," he said. "You can take this money." He handed me the envelope. "And just go. Get in your car and drive away and start a new life somewhere. Get a GED, join the Army, anything you want." I opened my mouth but he stopped me. "You need more? I'll go back in and get it. But that money is yours."

"What do I have to do?" I asked skeptically.

"Nothing. Just leave. Your dad is going to end up in a bad place, and if you continue to stick by him, you'll end up there too. I'm giving you an out right now."

"You want me to just abandon my dad?"

"Do you have a drug problem?" he asked. I had to look shocked, because he added, "Are you the one with the drug problem and the reason he needs money? Because you know that's the excuse he told Childs. Do you have a drug problem, Troy?"

"No."

"Didn't think so. So, then, how long you going to stand by a guy who will sell you out every chance he can get?"

"Your mom never used you as an excuse?"

"My mom never used me as a reason or an excuse while she was holding someone's well-being over their head. He's a bad man, Troy. I know he's your dad, but he is bad. This is your chance."

My eyes stung. "To do what? I have nowhere to go, no family, no nothing."

He smiled and put a hand on my shoulder. "Well, you have a brother. You have a car, and you have five thousand dollars. You need anything else, call me."

He was serious; this guy who had known me all of two days was giving me five grand and an exit strategy. And, yes, I know what an exit strategy is.

"I mean it. You don't have to do this alone. And you don't have to do it with him."

205

"What's going to happen to him?"

"He's going to go to jail, and if he's lucky it'll be for a long time. Long enough so the people who are looking for him will realize that there is nothing gained from hunting him anymore. See, Troy, you're going to be alone no matter what goes down. The difference is, you can be gone and not have to deal with any of your dad's crap. The choice is yours."

And I did make a choice.

I rolled up the window and pulled out of the hospital parking lot. No one saw me, no one missed me, and that was good. I had a life to figure out. And who knows… maybe I'd get used to having a brother out there who really cared about me.

Life was full of possibilities.

PART FOUR:
JEAN GREY, LOVE,
AND DISCO

Name three things that will always come back no matter how many
times you think they're dead.

Kyle

"So let's talk."

I was standing in front of Brad's house at the crack of dawn. He was staring at me, hair completely jacked, sleep still in his eyes, wearing a pair of green sweatpants and nothing else.

It was a sight to behold.

"Really?" He yawned. "You couldn't wait until... I don't know, morning?"

"It's morning," I said, holding out a Red Bull because he hated coffee.

"It's morning somewhere, I agree," he said, popping the top open and downing it in one gulp. "Let me change. I'll be right back."

"Can I come in?" I asked, sounding like a beggar from a Dickens novel.

"I'll be quick," he said and closed the door.

I already didn't like where this was going.

About ten minutes later, he came out in jeans and his old letterman's jacket. I realized he must have left all his stuff back in California. "Where's your car and stuff?" I asked.

"Well, all my stuff was already packed," he said as calmly as if he was talking about the weather. It still hurt me to hear it. "We put my car in long-term parking. I'll figure things out in a few."

"You could come back to California with me and you wouldn't need to figure anything out." I gave him a smile.

He didn't return it.

"Look, Kyle, I'm not going back to California."

"Why?"

He looked at me in disbelief. "Because there's nothing for me there."

"There's me," I offered and instantly knew it was the wrong choice.

"I'm not getting back together with you either."

"You don't love me anymore?" Every word I said hurt like pulling a tooth out of my skull with a pair of pliers.

He sighed and ran a hand through his hair, a sure sign he was frustrated. "Of course I love you, Kyle, but that isn't what this is about."

Him admitting he still loved me was the tiny ember of warmth in an otherwise cold, cold place in my life.

"Then what's it about? Explain it to me."

"This doesn't bother you?" he asked suddenly.

"Us not being together? Of course it bothers me."

"No, the fact that we broke up. Again. This is tiring, Kyle. I mean, we're a fucking Taylor Swift song on repeat, and I can't do it anymore."

"It won't happen again! I swear it won't!" I pleaded with him.

"You say that now, but what happens the next time you think we aren't going to work out? Or that you think I'm going to leave you? Or that I have a friend who you think is better-looking than you? You're fine now and you want to get back together, but then you end up snapping and I'm the one who pays. Every time, I have a ring thrown at my head or I'm kicked out and forced to find another place to live. I can't do it. I can't keep doing this when you don't have faith in us."

I was wrong: *this* was like getting your teeth pulled out with pliers.

"This is the same fight we've been having since the night I dropped you off," he said. "Where I stand very still and try to convince you I love you, and you think this is insane and isn't going to last. This is the same fight we had that night at the lake. The same fight we had in the parking lot. And I'm sorry, Kyle. I can't do it anymore."

People say I'm smart, which isn't true. I don't think I'm smart at all. What I have is a quicker processor than most people. Time moves differently in my head, which means what sounds like a brilliant comeback off the top of my head is really me mulling it over for five or six Kyle seconds and then saying the best thing I can think of. To the outside world it appears I'm clever; the truth is I'm as stupid as they come. It's times like this that I'm reminded of it in a big, bad way.

Brad was right, of course. We *have* been having the same fucking fight since he dropped me off and I told him he didn't have to talk to me at school. Then we'd make up, but not really. All we've done with kisses and hugs and finally sex is try to cover up the fact that the way we are isn't working. This entire time it had been my fault, and I had no idea.

See? Pretty stupid.

JOHN GOODE

"I'm sorry," I said after a few seconds. "I'll leave you alone."

He looked like he was going to say something to stop me, but he didn't, and I probably wouldn't have stopped anyway. I got in my rental car and drove away, knowing I was leaving the best part of my life behind me.

Brad

WATCHING HIM drive off was the hardest thing I had ever done.

But I was right, and we both knew it.

Hooray me for being right.

Kyle

ROBBIE AND Sebastian met me at Nancy's for breakfast. Still no Gayle.

"So no dice, huh?" Sebastian asked, sipping his coffee.

"Nope, he said we were broken up, and that was that."

"Sucks," he said, grabbing some sugar to stir in.

Robbie slapped his arm. "Sucks? Really?" To me he demanded, "So what are you going to do?"

"What is there to do? He made his choice, and as much as I hate to admit it, he's right. I've been so screwed up about him leaving me that I ended up driving him away. I've got no one to blame but myself."

"And that sucks," Sebastian added pointedly. "Not sure how me saying that it sucks was inappropriate."

"You can't just give up," Robbie said, glaring at Sebastian.

"It takes two to save a relationship, and Brad isn't interested anymore."

"Bullshit," Sebastian grunted, his eyes on his phone.

We both looked at him; a few seconds ticked away before he realized we were staring at him.

"If you tell me that 'bullshit' was something you read on Facebook, I'm taking your phone away from you," Robbie warned, grabbing Sebastian's phone.

210

The way Sebastian pulled his phone away from Robbie was cute. "One, don't do that. Two, I was saying 'bullshit' about Brad. If he wasn't interested, he wouldn't have flown here at a moment's notice."

"He has a point," Robbie agreed.

"It was guilt. What was he supposed to do? Say 'fuck off'?"

"Yeah," Sebastian said without a second's hesitation. "Some people come telling me my ex needed me? I would not just tell them to fuck off, I would send them back with several pictures of me flipping the camera off saying 'fuck off.'"

"Okay, then," Robbie said after a few seconds. "Brad wouldn't have come if he didn't care."

"He cares," I snapped. "But he doesn't want us to be together. Caring and knowing that something isn't working aren't mutually exclusive things."

Robbie opened his mouth to reply when two people walked up to our table.

They were high school students, and the fact they looked so young to me was like sunlight to vampire. I was barely nineteen, but I felt like I was fifty. They both had these weird grins on their faces as they looked at me.

"Um, help you?" I asked, concerned.

"You're Kyle Stilleno, right?" the dark-haired one asked.

"Are you serving me a summons or something?" I asked, wondering if they could hire high school kids to do that.

They both laughed, and the blond-haired one said, "I told you he was funny."

"Yes, I am," I said, trying to get whatever this was over with.

"I'm Jared," the dark-haired one said, holding his hand out. "And this is my boyfriend Joel." The blond one waved.

I shook Jared's hand slowly. "Okay, cool. Do I know you guys?" I asked even though I was pretty sure I didn't.

"I was a freshman last year," Joel answered. "You wouldn't know me."

"And I just moved here," Jared said. "My dad is Mr. Fisher, the new principal."

The guy who told me to stand up at graduation and tell the truth.

"I remember him," I said. "Um, welcome to Foster."

They both giggled, and I still had no idea what was going on.

"I just wanted to say we're big fans."

"Of?" I prompted, expecting 1D or Cody Simpson.

"See?" Joel nudged Jared. "Funny."

"Of you, man," Jared explained. "If it wasn't for you, we would have never gotten together."

That didn't make sense. "How's that, now?"

"'Cause no one cares about people being gay anymore," Jared said, and I gave him a look. "I mean, sure, there are always going to be haters, but that's everywhere. You changed things."

"And I have your graduation speech poster," Joel added.

"Poster?"

"Yeah, the AV club made a WordArt poster of it and sold them for a charity drive. They went like crazy."

What in the fuck was going on?

"Wait, people bought a poster of my speech?"

They both nodded like they were a pair of bobblehead twinks. "How cool is that?"

It didn't feel very cool to me.

"Well, uhm, you're welcome," I said distractedly. This could not be real.

"Do you have any advice for us?" Joel asked. "I mean, how did you make things work with Brad?"

Something inside me cringed. "You want advice? On dating in high school?" They both nodded. "Don't. Just don't do it. I mean, sure, it's fine to get together and make out and all that, but after senior year, trust me, it's like a soap bubble and is going to pop so fast...."

"You know what, boys?" Robbie interrupted me. "It's been a long morning, and Kyle here has low blood sugar. Can we do this after he eats?"

They looked concerned, but they nodded nonetheless. "Sure, sorry to bother you, man," Jared said, backing away.

"Say hi to Brad for us," Joel added, and they turned and ran to the back of the diner.

"Well, congratulations," Robbie said once they were gone. "If you were trying to do an impression of bitter and jaded me, you pulled it off perfectly. Though I compared high school love to glitter."

Sebastian and I looked at him, dumbfounded.

"Never mind, made sense in my head. The point is, you can't be that bitter. Those kids are in love, just like you and Brad were... like you and Brad *are*, and it's bad enough if you want to give up, but you can't jump out at unsuspecting teenagers and warn them never to love again."

"Why not? It doesn't end well," I grumbled.

"I think you want it to be over," Sebastian announced out of nowhere.

"What?" I almost choked.

"I think you want it to be over because then you know you were right. I think you aren't fighting because you want it to be over and your own prophecy to come true so you can then use that to make sure you never put yourself out there again. I think you're scared, and I think this is an excuse for you to be alone."

My jaw literally dropped as I stared at him.

"Because from what everything this one has told me," he said, gesturing at Robbie, "there's one question you should be asking yourself, and you're not."

"I didn't tell him to say any of this," Robbie assured me.

"What question?" I almost dared Sebastian to say.

"What would Brad do?"

Fuck. I guess it was the day for me to be wrong.

Brad

SO I took a shower and had some breakfast while waiting for my parents to wake up.

My dad was first. He looked worse than I did in the morning, and it was kind of funny. He looked better than when I left—he'd lost some weight, got some color on him... it was kind of weird.

"You go to sleep yet?" he asked, pouring himself some coffee.

"Yeah, Kyle woke me up this morning."

"How'd that go?" he asked, sitting down across from me.

"It's just not going to work out," I said, trying not to sound like I was pouting.

"You sure?" he asked, one eyebrow raised.

"Yeah, why?"

He shrugged. "Dunno, you guys seem like you had it figured out. I would have put money on you guys for the long haul."

"Well, that would be wasted money." Now I *was* pouting.

"So then what's the plan? After getting your car back here."

"Well, I could ask Tyler for a job and enroll in online courses to get my basics out of the way?" I threw it out there.

"And you didn't do this in California, why?" he asked. In the past I would have expected that question to be asked with scathing sarcasm or judgmental tones, but it was just a question now.

I didn't have an answer.

"I know you said the reason things didn't work out was Kyle sabotaging everything, but do you think it might have had to do with the fact that you followed him with the plan of just being with him? I mean, that sounds romantic and all, but this is real life, kiddo. Moving cross-country so you can be with someone is fine, but there has to be more to your life than that."

I sat there, stunned at his revelation.

"Anyway," he said, getting up, "figure something out. You can stay here as long as you have a job and are doing something with your education, but you are not going to sleep and eat here and end up doing nothing. That is not an option."

"Yes, sir," I said a little too bitterly, and he looked back at me.

"Look, Brad, either you're an adult and get treated like one, or you're a kid and you get treated like one, but you don't get to straddle that line anymore. I'm treating you like a man, not some little kid. I am telling you the rules you have to follow if you want to stay here, and that's it. I'm not going to make you pay rent or pay me back for the car, as long as you're moving forward. I have your back, but the second you give up and just sit around and mope... then you're a little kid again and those aren't rules anymore; they're orders. Got it?" I nodded. "Good.

There's an opening at the dealership for a salesman too. I don't think you'd ever take it, but I am putting it out there."

"Thanks."

He smiled. "Real life can suck, buddy, but you know at the end of the day what makes it all worthwhile?" I shook my head. "Knowing real life can suck, but you still get up, get dressed, and go to work because that's what grown-ups do."

"That makes it better?" I asked honestly.

"No; it makes life worth it, though, because what you make of even the parts that suck is yours, and no one can take that away from you. Ask yourself this—what do you have that no one can take away from you?"

I couldn't think of a thing.

"See? When you're an adult, you say, 'That's my car because I paid for it. This is my house because I bought it, and this is my life because I made it with my own two hands.' That makes getting up worth it. Just find something you want to wake up for."

"I will!" I said, feeling better than I had in days.

"Good. And until you do get a job?" I nodded. "Take out the trash for your mom."

Some things never change.

Kyle

"So I don't know what I'm going to do. Any thoughts?"

My mom lay there, breathing through a tube.

"No? Well, that's okay. I've heard I am lousy at taking advice."

The room was quiet save for the small sounds the machines surrounding my mom made. The operation had been a success, but the doctors had no way of telling how impaired she would be until she woke up. So I sat next to her, babbling, wishing she would open her eyes.

I was scared.

What if she was bad? I mean bad, bad? She couldn't stay on her own, and I had no idea how much a live-in nurse would cost. I mean, I was boned on several levels. Of course, the second I thought it was as bad as it could get, fate reminded me it could get much worse.

215

My phone rang, and I saw it was Teddy from California.

It seemed like a year since I'd last talked to him instead of a week. "Hey, what's up?"

"How's your mom?" he asked, real concern in his voice.

"Resting" was all I was comfortable saying.

"Well, I hate to be this guy who makes things worse...."

But he was going to.

"Professor Madison's midterm is Friday, and he wanted me to tell you there are no excuses."

Fuck. Even Madison had given me time off because my mom was, like, almost dying, but it seemed sympathy only went so far.

"You there?" Teddy asked after a few seconds.

"Yeah, I don't know if things will be done here by then," I said, truly realizing how bad things were. "There's no way to tell how bad she'll be until she wakes up, and no one knows when that will be."

"Dude...," he said, picking up the smallest inkling of the drama I'd been dealing with all weekend. "You can't just fly back for the test and then go back?"

"Teddy, I don't even know if I'm going back to school."

"Oh," he said, sounding as depressed as I felt.

"Yeah, but thanks for the call, and I appreciate the information."

"Let me talk to Madison. Maybe I can convince him to let you take the test over Skype or something."

"It really won't matter if I'm dropping out, will it?"

He had no answer to that.

"Let me know what he says. I'll try to do something here."

"Hey, at least you don't have your douche of a boyfriend there fucking you up."

I felt a protective surge flare up at someone calling Brad something derogatory, but before it got to my mouth, I realized he wasn't someone I needed to defend anymore.

"Talk to you later," I muttered, hanging up before I said something stupid.

I glanced over at my mom. "Any chance of you waking up now?"

Nothing.

"Didn't think so," I said, feeling defeated.

"They say talking to yourself is a sign of intelligence."

I stifled a yelp and stopped before I jumped out of my seat. When I looked behind me, I saw Riley's mother standing there in a long wool trench coat. "Sorry," I said, holding my chest. "You scared me."

"I have that effect," she agreed. Coming in, she looked around the room. Finally, her stare rested on me. "You are Kyle."

It was a statement, not a question.

"And you're Riley's mom."

As soon as I said it, I knew it was a mistake. She glanced over at me, and I could see the pain in her eyes. Just as quickly as it had flashed, it was gone, and she gave me a weak smile. "I'm sorry. No one has called me that in a long time. I am Dolores Mathison." She held out a gloved hand, and I shook it lightly. Nodding at my mom, she asked, "How is she?"

"Better now." Again I was unsure how much information to share with anyone.

"So, I heard an undesirable person was trying to extort money from you so she could get help."

I nodded.

"You figured a way around it and still gave one of them money?"

Another nod.

"Why?"

Normally some stranger coming in and asking me questions would piss me off, but she carried herself with such an air of inborn authority that I found myself answering automatically. "Why not? It's just money. He was my half brother and in a bad place, and I had the means to make his life a little better."

"Money doesn't solve every problem," she countered.

"It solves a bunch more than you think when someone is poor. Things like food, a place to sleep, a car—having those things are insurmountable problems when someone's poor. The solution is just a little money. So I gave him some and hoped he would do right by it."

She raised an eyebrow and glanced over at my mom for a second.

"The money you gave him, it came from the money Riley left, correct?"

I felt a cold chill in my spine as I wondered if she was here to take the money back.

217

"Robbie gave it to me," I said, sounding defensive.

She flashed another brittle smile. "Calm down, Kyle. I'm not here to take anything away from you. I did not come off my mountain just to swoop down and attack the locals."

"Then why are you here?" I asked. I swear, the question just jumped out of my mouth.

"A friend asked me a favor, so I came," she explained distantly as she finished examining the room and sat down on the chair in the corner. "These rooms are so depressing. They need a new décor."

I barked a laugh. "The people who are in here don't care about the décor, trust me."

She stared at me for a long time as I held my breath. "You're right, that was a crass statement for me to make. What I meant was that the people who have to be in these rooms are depressed enough by their situation, the furniture shouldn't add to their misery."

"Not sure what you can do about that," I said, sitting down on the other chair.

"I could buy better furniture. After all, it is my hospital."

I cocked my head as I ran that sentence back and forth in my mind a few times. "Excuse me?"

"The hospital. My husband and I built it decades ago for the town. Before this place, there was a tiny clinic that I wouldn't have trusted to groom a dog, so we made the initial investment. Others followed and voilà! One hospital!"

I just sat there, stunned. I had never heard someone say something so incredible in my life. "I'm sorry. I guess there would be something you can do. About the furniture, I mean."

She pulled her gloves off and folded them on her lap. "So, do you go to school?"

"UC Berkeley," I said, still wondering what she was doing there.

"It's an excellent school," she said like we were old friends.

"I don't know, only been there a few months, but it seems like it."

"You earned a full scholarship based on your academics alone. That is impressive."

I had to ask. "I'm sorry, but you seem to know a lot about me."

"I do; I make it my business to know things. However, in your case my friend has told me a lot about you. That's why I am here today, but it seems I was too late."

"For?" I asked.

"I was going to tell Mr. Childs to do the operation despite your father's protests. I mean, if there was a lawsuit, I was going to have to pay for it anyway."

"Wait, what? You came here to help me?"

She nodded. "But by the time I got here, it seems you took care of it yourself. Ingenious solution, by the way."

"Who told you to come?" I asked, confused as hell.

Ignoring my question, she asked, "Did Robert tell you what was in the letter Riley left him?"

"I read it." She paused when she heard that, but the only sign of surprise I could see was the slightest lifting of one eyebrow.

"Then you know the money was to be used on their children if they had any."

I nodded.

"Yet Robert gave it to you."

"To me and my boyfriend," I said before I could stop myself. There was no boyfriend anymore.

"But mostly you, am I right?"

Another nod.

"I see. Then, in some way, Robert sees you as a son?"

That made me grin. "I wouldn't say that in front of him; I think he thinks of himself as my not-so-older brother."

She gave me a smile back, and I could tell it was her first real one of the day. "I promise not to tell if you don't."

"I suppose so," I said, thinking about it. "I mean, I never thought about it that way because I never had a dad, but Robbie has been there to give me advice, get me out of jams, and slap me silly when I screw up."

"That indeed sounds like a father," she commented. "The club at school—that was your idea, correct?"

"The alliance? Yeah, I kinda screwed that up."

"Last I heard they were going strong, and more than a dozen students from both schools attend. They all say they owe it to you."

"How would you know that?" I asked. This lady was spooky.

"I was the person who shut the first one down when Ms. Axeworthy started it. I was the person who also told Mr. Raymond to allow this one to start. So I have a vested interest in the matter."

"You did that?" I asked, shocked.

"I did. Shutting down the first attempt was not my proudest moment, but I am trying to fix it."

"How?" I asked, realizing it was really none of my business.

"In many ways that aren't nearly enough," she answered sadly.

I had no idea what to say to that.

"So you need to be back in California on Friday." Again she made a statement instead of asking a question.

"You were listening?"

"When you get my age, you'll find there is little else to do but listen at doors. I didn't want to interrupt you, and I have to admit, I was intrigued by what kind of young man you are. My friend has very exacting taste; I wanted to see what she saw in you."

"What did you see?"

"I see a young man who did not have a pleasant childhood, who spent most of it formulating a way out of his predicament yet was ready to throw all of his plans for a bright future away to stand by the side of the person who made much of his early life unpleasant. It is not easy to exchange dreams for duty. Not many people today understand that."

"She's my mom," I said, my eyes stinging with tears. "I can't just leave her."

"Yes, you could," she corrected me. "And many young men in your situation would do just that. You don't plan on putting your dreams ahead of your family, which tells me my friend was right."

"Who is your friend?"

Again she ignored the question. "I'll make you a deal. You go back to school, and I will not only take care of your mother's hospital bill but make sure she has the care she needs to recover completely."

I know my jaw hit the floor.

"Why would you do that?"

She gave me a wry grin. "It's just money; why not?"

"Seriously, why would you do that for a stranger?"

She looked down, and I could tell she was composing herself as well. "Well, I suppose because if Robert gave you that money, it means he sees you as a son. If that is true, that makes me in a sense your grandmother, and this is what grandmothers do. They spend exorbitant amounts of money on their grandsons to make them happy. And I have to agree, if Robert and Riley had a son, I would have very much liked him to be like you."

It was like a huge weight was lifted off my chest and I could breathe again. The emotion swelled up inside of me so fast it was like being drunk for a second, and I lost all sense of self-control.

At least I think so, because it is the only reason to explain what I did next.

I got up and threw my arms around her. "Thank you," I sobbed. "Thank you so much."

She froze. I could tell she had no earthly idea how to react to me, but her arms slowly embraced me, and I felt her pat my back. "Just do not give up on your life, Kyle," she said, her voice cracking with emotion. "Do not let money or circumstance change who you are. Don't ever let that happen."

So I stood there crying into an old woman's chest as I tried to realize things might not be that bad after all.

Brad

SO AFTER taking out the trash, I headed down to Tyler's shop.

He and Matt were unpacking boxes and looked like they were seconds away from having a popcorn fight with the Styrofoam packing peanuts. As soon as I walked in, they sobered up and tried to look like adults. Not that they succeeded, but they tried.

"Hey, Brad," Tyler said. His attempt at casual sort of flopped because he had two peanuts tangled in his hair. Matt snickered, although he kept his mouth covered until he could control himself.

"You guys need a minute?" I asked, pointing back at the door. "I can walk around the block or something."

"Shut up and get in here," Tyler ordered, laughing himself.

"In my defense," Matt said, "he started it."

"You want a Coke?" Tyler asked, brushing the peanuts out of his hair. Both of us nodded. "Two Cokes coming up."

"How you doing?" Matt asked.

I shrugged. "Kyle came by."

"How did that go?"

"Bad," I admitted, grabbing a stool and sitting down.

Tyler reemerged from the back room with three Cokes in hand and asked, "What did he say?"

"He wanted to get back together and...." I paused, not ready to show how much this upset me. "Well, I told him that wasn't happening, and he just looked like I had kicked him in the balls."

"You did?" Matt said, taking a sip from the bottle. When both Tyler and I looked at him, he said, "What? Getting dumped feels like shit."

"What are you going to do?" Tyler asked, looking back to me.

"I dunno. That's why I came by."

Tyler nodded and took a stool himself. "Okay, shoot."

"Any chance you're hiring?"

"Yep," he answered, sounding way too chipper.

"Any chance you'd hire me?"

"Nope," he answered, just as chipper.

"What? Why?"

"Because if I give you a job, then you'd resign yourself to living here and you wouldn't get back with Kyle."

I needed a second to process that. "Wait, you're not going to give me a job because you think Kyle and I should get back together?"

He nodded.

"I don't want to get back together with him."

"Yeah, you do," Tyler corrected. He definitely sounded like an adult.

"No, I don't," I assured him.

"Yes, you do," Matt chimed in.

"I think I know what I want," I snapped... well, I whined.

"Did you know what you wanted at eighteen?" Tyler asked Matt.

"Besides sex? Nope."

Tyler looked back at me. "So yeah, you don't know what you want."

222

I stood up. "I don't want to be with Kyle."

"Do you love him?" Tyler asked.

"That's not the point."

"Yeah, it is," he argued and gulped another swig of Coke. "See? You don't know what you want."

I slammed my Coke down on the counter. "I am not a little kid! I know what I want do to with my life."

"And that's working at a sporting-goods store?" Tyler asked.

"It's a start," I challenged him.

"Nope, it's you making a mistake. Sorry, no job here."

"You're serious?" I asked, not believing what was happening.

"As a heart attack," he answered.

"I don't want to be with Kyle!" I raged.

"Yeah, you do," they both said simultaneously. They sounded like grown-ups. In stereo.

I turned around and stomped out.

I hated it when people said they knew what I wanted more than I did myself. I mean, I'm the one inside my brain; I should know better, right? I walked across the street to Nancy's. Maybe something to eat would settle me down. Gayle waved at me as I sat down and glanced at the menu.

"Kyle joining you?" she asked, walking up.

"We broke up," I said, wondering how she didn't know that already.

She grabbed the menu out of my hand. "Then go make up with him."

"He broke up with me in California, and I don't want to get back together with him." Was this shit for real?

"Yes, you do," she said, still holding the menu hostage.

"Please don't do this," I not quite whined. "Tyler and Matt just started in on me."

"Do you love him?" she asked me.

"Why do people keep asking me that? Love is not the problem!" I almost screamed.

"Nope, it's the solution. Go work it out," she said, walking away.

"I can't order?" I called after her.

"Not while you're single."

Growling, I got up and stomped out.

This was getting ridiculous.

Kyle

AFTER MRS. Mathison left, I drove over to the hotel where Robbie and Sebastian were staying.

I knocked twice before Sebastian, shirtless, opened the door. *Jesus Christ*, he was built.

"Oh! Hey, Kyle," he said, clearly out of breath. I didn't want to know from what. "He's in the shower."

"I came to talk to you, actually."

"Okay." He backed away from the door and added, "Come on in."

The room looked a little trashed, and I wondered what had happened in here. When I saw that most of the covers on the bed were torn off, I got it. "If this is a bad time, I can come back," I said, suddenly feeling way out of place.

"If you'd shown up ten minutes ago it would have been a bad time. Now is okay," he said, grabbing a shirt and pulling it on. "So speak."

I sat down on one of the chairs. "What did you mean 'what would Brad do?'"

"Ah, so we're having this conversation," he said to himself, nodding. Then he looked straight at me. "What do you think I meant?"

"What conversation? You were expecting me?"

"Kinda, but answer the question. What do you think I meant?"

How had this guy who'd never met me known I was coming back?

"I dunno, I mean… what would he do if I wouldn't take him back?" He nodded. "Um, keep trying?"

He gave me a small smile. "Is that your final answer? Have you ever broken up with him before?" I nodded. "And what did he do?"

"Kept calling me and begging me to take him back."

"Right, so is that what you're doing?"

I paused.

"Robbie filled me in on what went down when he lived here, and every story seemed to be this incredible thing that Brad did for you. I really never heard something *you* did for *him*. Did Robbie forget to tell me a story? Did he leave out an event?"

I felt myself shrinking into the chair.

"See, guys like Brad, they're fiercely loyal and will go to the ends of the Earth for the people they love. But that loyalty only lasts so long if it isn't reciprocated. He gave it his all trying to be with you, and you still dumped him. He's hurt and he doesn't want to be made a fool of again."

"I didn't call him a fool!" I protested.

"No, but you rejected him. You didn't trust him, right?" I nodded. "Well, that's the same thing. You want to get him back? Ask yourself, what would Brad do?"

"Anything."

"There you go."

He was right. Brad had always been the one doing all the romantic things, while I was the one he chased. And that was just wrong. He'd never complained, but that was Brad; he never would. God, I'd fucked this up pretty bad.

"What if he doesn't love me anymore?" I asked, suddenly scared.

"He loves you, trust me. He just doesn't *like* you that much right now."

"I don't like me that much either," I mumbled.

"Don't blame you," he said, getting up. "Look, Kyle, you're both young and things like this seem insurmountable, but trust me, they aren't. If you guys are really meant to be together, you will be. It's just your turn to convince him."

"I will," I said, standing up myself.

"Are you getting in here?" Robbie yelled from the bathroom.

"*Now* it's a bad time," Sebastian clarified wryly.

"Thanks for the advice."

"My pleasure," he said walking me to the door. "Just remember, you hurt his ego and his pride, so make sure whatever you do, you're willing to sacrifice your own."

I nodded. "Any suggestions?"

225

He glanced back to the bathroom and then to me. "I'm not going to lie, my mind is somewhere else. You're a smart guy. You'll get it."

And he closed the door.

Ego and pride? I began to think on it as I walked back to the car.

Brad

I HADN'T walked First Street in years.

Before I got my car, my two feet were my only form of transportation. I have no idea how I got around then. Now I had no idea where I was going; I was pissed, hungry, and just walking. So I was kind of shocked when a car honked at me and pulled over.

It was weird how my mind had changed. Before I would have just assumed it was someone I knew and jogged over to the car; now I wondered if I was being cruised. Did they cruise in Foster? I can't imagine things had changed that much. My fears were dismissed when I saw Josh Walker get out of the car.

"What the fuck, man?" he called out with a huge smile on his face. "Since when does Prince Graymark walk anywhere?"

I hadn't realized how much I had missed Josh, and I walked over and gave him a huge hug. "Dude, it's a story, trust me."

He pulled away. "Yeah, Jennifer told me everything. You should get back together with him."

God fucking dammit!

"Can I have a conversation with someone today without them telling me how to live my life? Just one?" I almost screamed.

"Okay then," he said, shaking his head. "This is a no-Kyle zone," he decided, gesturing around us. "Promise."

"Thank you!" I sighed, relived. Then I glanced over at his car, did a double take, and felt my heart flip-flop. "Is that yours?"

An electric blue Dodge Challenger with a spoiler and rims... I mean, this car was fucking sex... and it lounged right at the curb. Briefly I wondered if being charged with carjacking would be worth it.

"Yeah, the alumni get us cars to use during the school year. They say it's an incentive for us to play harder." Josh leaned against the car and grinned. "You wanna drive it?"

"Me?" I squeaked, sounding like a twelve-year-old. Shocked. "You'd let me?"

"Dude, you got me into A&M; as far as I'm concerned this is half your car too." He tossed me the keys. "Come on, let's get the fuck out of town."

I hadn't heard a better suggestion in my life.

It purred like a saber-toothed tiger, and I felt instant jealousy because Josh got to drive it all the time. I mean, I loved my car, but this, this was just… let's say I wanted to have relations with this car in a big, bad way. Two seconds later I slid behind the wheel, waited for Josh to climb in, and started the engine. I pointed us toward the lake and let the road disappear beneath us. I had a strange sense of déjà vu as we came up on Old Man Wilson's bait-and-tackle shop. It was the only store out there, and most of us had bought booze there before heading up. As far as Old Man Wilson was concerned, money was money.

"I haven't been here in…," I began to say and then stopped. I hadn't been here since I brought Kyle out here to cut school. "In a long time," I finished, pulling into the parking lot.

"You wanna grab some brews and hit the lake?" he asked, purposely ignoring that I was suddenly as depressed as shit.

"College has made you wise, son," I said, nodding.

He laughed and got out with me hot on his heels.

"So how is it?" I asked as we grabbed supplies.

"It's okay," he said nonchalantly.

"Dude, I am not going to get mad because I turned it down."

He spun around. "Dude, it's fucking epic!" he roared with a huge smile.

"I figured," I said, smiling back. I wasn't upset about my choice. A&M had wanted me to hide who I was, and I wasn't going to do that again, ever. "Parties?"

"Insane! It's basketball season, so those guys throw a fucking party every week after the game."

"I went to one of those," I exclaimed, putting my stuff on the counter. "That was when one of the guys hit on me."

Josh pulled out a wad of bills. "Danny?"

I did a double take. "You know him?"

He nodded as he got his change. "He's best friends with my cousin. They're both on the team."

"Wait, who's your cousin?" I asked, confused.

"Nathan Walker?" He saw I had no idea. "He's a good guy, but yeah, Danny is a trip."

"He ever get together with his guy?" I asked when we got into the car.

"No idea, man. I go to the parties, but he and Nate are the close ones. I mean, I know he's at least bi, 'cause he was dating a girl, but Nate says he's gay."

"He told me he was bi too," I said, driving out to the lake.

"Yeah, he has issues," Josh agreed, opening a beer. "So what's going on with Kyle?"

"You said this was a no-Kyle zone," I protested.

"Yeah, back on First Street; this is a completely different zone."

That made me laugh despite being upset.

We parked at one of the campsites and got out. Then, leaning against the hood of his car, we watched the sun reflect off the lake as we drank. For a second, we were both back in high school, nothing more pressing than the next game and who we thought liked us or not. No moving across country, no college, no trying to earn a living. Just two guys drinking beer by the lake.

And then he had to talk.

"So, Kyle?" he asked.

"It's over, man," I said, sighing.

"So you don't love him anymore?"

I turned around. "What the fuck? Are you all reading off a script or something?"

He looked away, and I realized I was right.

"Did he put you up to this?" I asked, almost throwing the beer at him.

"Who? Kyle? No, man, but Jennifer said they all got together and had a talk and thought you guys were being stupid."

Awesome—it was, in fact, a conspiracy.

"He kicked me out!" I raged at Josh. "He thought I had slept with a guy and kicked me out."

"Um… didn't you think you slept with that guy too?"

"Shut up," I said, ignoring him. "He kicked me out and left me to rot in California. You think getting back together with him is a good idea?"

Not even a pause. "Yes, I do."

"If you like him so much, you go out with him," I said, finishing my beer and tossing it in the lake.

"I would, but he is in love with you. And if I did, you'd kick my ass because you're in love with him."

"I can't trust him, Josh."

"No, you're afraid to trust him. Big difference."

He walked around to the trunk and pulled another couple of beers out. "Nothing wrong with being afraid, man. Letting that fear ruin your life? That's some bullshit."

I took the beer and tore the top off. "When did you become Yoda?"

He gave me a shit-eating grin and said, "Look, man. I've gotten laid more times than any three people I know. I have had guys, girls, parents—hell, I think a dog came on to me one time—so when it comes to matters of the heart, I am wise beyond my years. And what you and Kyle have… dude, that's rare. So yeah, he fucked up. And? You really going to throw in the towel on one play?"

"This isn't the first time," I protested.

"So you've been keeping score?" I looked away. "See? Come on, dude. You know what your problem is? You went out there and you found out that you had zero life skills. Kyle was going off and being all Joe College and you were, what?"

"Personal trainer," I mumbled.

"You were the guy telling fat people how to exercise, and it scared you. And the second the security blanket was torn off, you freaked and realized you had nothing left but to come home and be a bum. The one thing we all feared the most growing up. That's not on Kyle, man, that's on you. You were the one who just hitched a ride on his star without a plan. You have tons of talent, man, and you're wasting it as a personal trainer?"

"Really, Josh? What talent am I wasting? My mad baseball skills? Last time I checked, those don't pay the bills."

"No, not playing baseball, but I bet you would make a fucking awesome coach."

I froze.

"Hell, man, you coached me that last season and got me into A&M. We wouldn't have made it to State without you."

"That was Coach Gunn," I protested.

"That was Coach Gunn and you, dumbass."

I sat there drinking my beer and thinking about it. Coaching? Why hadn't I thought of that before?

"So, yeah, this is less about Kyle and more about you being scared. So get over it already."

"Shut up and drink your beer," I said, grumbling, but he saw the smile on my face. He was right, I needed a direction. A real one.

Kyle

I CALLED the hospital and there was no change with my mom, so I went....

Wow, I was going to say "home," but that wasn't true, is it? I went to my mom's house to get a shower and a change of clothes. I was mentally exhausted, and some downtime would do me good. When I walked in, the whole place looked like it was a museum replica of the apartment I had lived in growing up. Everything looked the same, but something felt off, like someone had built a replacement Kyle's Home to specs, but no matter how well the builder tried, whatever had made the apartment my home was gone.

I felt like an imposter in my own life.

If I'd thought the living room was bad, my room was worse. Everything was pretty much the same—my bed, my dresser, the clippings on the walls, it was exactly the same, yet it looked completely wrong to me. I sat on the edge of my bed and looked around, wondering how I had ever lived here. It was so small, so cramped; the things around me seemed so... useless? No, that's not it. Juvenile, that's better. I mean, there were pictures of bands I could care less about now. Now I have school and rent and a life; what the fuck did I care about music? Pictures of actors who starred in movies I used to watch all the time stared at me from my walls, and I realized I hadn't watched those movies since I moved.

I guess you can go home again, but it won't ever feel like home.

Taking a shower was even worse. I felt like a stranger breaking into someone's house and then getting naked. I mean, between you and me, I had spent hours jerking off in this shower. This shower and I were close, like biblically close, and now I felt like keeping my underwear on as I showered in case someone walked in on me.

My instincts were right, though. I badly needed a shower and a second to take a breath. By the time I got out, I felt like I had run a marathon and just collapsed on the couch in a pair of boxer briefs and nothing else. I wanted to sleep forever. No, scratch that—forever and a day, please.

I should have ordered a pizza, but that would require me moving, and that shit wasn't happening any time soon. Instead I imagined eating pizza and tried to relax.

I must have dozed off, because someone knocking startled me both awake and into a half scream. I was pretty sure I had actually broken into someone's house and was about to get caught in my underwear.

I *was* in my underwear. Fuck!

"Hold on!" I called as I ran into my room and pulled on a pair of jeans. Thankfully my hoodie was close by and I slipped that over my head before I ran to the door. I opened it and saw Jennifer's dad standing there.

"Did I wake you?" he asked with a smile.

"Um, no, why?" I asked, trying to play it cool.

"Because you look like you stuck your finger in a light socket," he said, pointing to my hair.

Fuck, I fell asleep with wet hair.

"I might have closed my eyes," I said, retreating to the bathroom. "Come in."

"How're you holding up?" he called from the living room while I threw copious amounts of water on my hair.

"Better—I mean, waiting for her to wake up, but at least she got the operation."

"I heard Dolores Mathison paid you a visit."

"Yeah, she came by." I finished patting my hair down to a tolerable disaster. "You know her?" I asked, coming out of the bathroom.

He chuckled. "Son, everyone knows her one way or another. Mind if I ask what she wanted?"

Worry started to creep into my mind. Well, not worry exactly. Something more like… concern.

"I guess someone told her about what was going on, and she came by to see if she could fix things," I explained.

"Fix things?" he asked, his brow furrowing.

Now concern was upgraded to worry.

"She was going to tell Mr. Childs to do the surgery on my mom no matter what Billy said."

Sheriff Taylor looked shocked. "She said that?" I nodded. "Well then, that's new."

"I don't get it. Why does everyone act like she's one bucket of water away from melting?"

That made him smile. "Because the Mathisons don't get involved in the problems of lesser folk." The way he said "lesser" made it pretty clear he was not a fan. "That all she said?"

My mind clamped a hand over my mouth before I could tell him about the offer to pay the medical bills. "She might not be all that bad," I suggested.

"You ever hear the saying 'a leopard can't change its spots'?" I nodded. "Well, Dolores is incapable of getting rid of the fin on her back. Once a shark, always a shark in my book."

That didn't sound like the nice old lady I'd met earlier.

"Well, she seemed cool to me."

"Okay, well, that's not why I stopped by. I wanted to know if you were going to press charges against your dad."

My stomach did a barrel roll at the thought of Billy.

"Isn't there enough for him to be put in jail without me?" I asked hopefully.

Taylor nodded. "He was on parole and carrying a loaded gun that he doesn't have a permit for. That is more than enough to send him away for a couple of years. I'm just making sure you don't want to have your say."

"I'm good," I said truthfully.

"That's something of a habit, isn't it?" he asked, and I looked at him, confused. "First Jeremy and now your dad. You know, Kyle, sooner or later you have to hold people accountable for their actions."

"I do! Jeremy was sick and my dad is already going to jail. One didn't deserve jail, and the other is well on his way without my help."

He held his hands up in surrender. "Okay, just saying." He took a step toward the door and paused. "Say, what's going on with you and the Graymark boy?"

I cocked my head at him. "Did Jennifer tell you to ask that?"

He gave me a small smile. "Guilty. Can we just say I asked and be done with it?"

"Deal," I agreed.

"You're a good kid, Kyle. I don't know if people tell you that enough, but you are."

I was kind of speechless. "Thank you."

He tipped an imaginary hat to me. "Just keeping it real." He walked out, and I watched him get in his squad car and drive off.

I needed food, and then I needed to call Robbie.

Sheriff Taylor had me terrified of Dolores Mathison.

Brad

JOSH DROPPED me off at Nancy's. I was kind of buzzed.

Hanging out with someone from my old life had been great, and that car… but Josh had brought up some good points about what was going on. I had gone out to California with no plan, and that had bitten me on the ass. I walked into the diner, hoping Gayle was already off shift so I could actually order something without getting hit in the head. I needed something in my stomach to sober me up before I went home.

I was floored to see Coach Gunn sitting in a booth reading a newspaper.

For half a second I felt like turning around and running away before he saw me buzzed. Then I remembered I was no longer in high school and could get as drunk as I wanted. I still popped a breath mint in my mouth before heading over there.

"Hey, Coach," I said, trying to sound as sober as I could.

He glanced up. "Graymark? When did you get into town?"

Oh thank God, someone who hadn't been given the "Get back together with Kyle" speech.

I sat down across from him. "This weekend. It's a long story."

"Kyle's mom?" he asked, and I paused.

"Oh, you know about that?"

He nodded and folded the paper up. "Gayle and I went by.... It didn't go well."

"What happened?" I asked, unsure if I had ever heard of drama in direct connection with Gayle.

"She knew the guy—Kyle's dad?" I nodded. "She tore him a new one and then spent the rest of the weekend calling in favors. Never seen her so pissed at someone before."

"Favors from who?" I asked, intrigued as fuck.

"From friends," Gayle said, no longer dressed in an apron and carrying her order book. She gave me a look. "Have you made up with Kyle yet?"

"Oh come on, Gayle! I'm hungry."

"And? Feed your heart and your mouth will follow." She looked over her shoulder. "Carlos, do not serve this one. He knows why."

"You're serious?" I asked with my mouth open in shock.

"Honey, I am always serious." She looked at Coach Gunn. "You ready?"

He paused, staring across at me and then back to her. "Stop meddling."

If he had slammed his foot down on hers, he wouldn't have gotten a bigger reaction from her. "What?"

"You heard me. Stop meddling. What you did for the boy was admirable—he was in a tight spot and you helped—but this is crossing a line. If they aren't going to get back together, you can't make them."

"They're supposed to be together."

Coach Gunn nodded. "Yeah, and the Cowboys should be a number-one team, but what you're supposed to be and what you are rarely ever meet." He glanced at me. "I don't know what is going on between you two, and I'm going to be honest, I don't want to know. But if you're going to get back together with him, it should be because you want to, and not because some nosy woman withholds food."

"Are you done?" she asked, her voice sounding like she was clearly not enjoying the conversation.

"Almost," he said curtly. In full Coach Gunn mode, he turned back to me and stared straight into my eyes. "You were ready to run into the school even though you knew someone had a loaded gun just to protect that boy, so I know the reason you aren't with him isn't lack of courage. But if it's from lack of conviction or it's just too hard, well, then she"—nodding at Gayle—"is right. You should talk to him because later on in life, you'll regret not doing that until the day you die."

He looked over at her. "Now I'm done." He got up and tucked the paper under his arm. "I trust you to do the right thing, Brad."

Suddenly, I was no longer sure what I felt.

"Nosy?" she asked him as they walked out.

"Stifle it… you look up 'gossip' in the dictionary, there is a signed eight-by-ten glossy photo of you."

She slapped his arm and laughed as they walked out. While I watched them stroll down First Street together, out of nowhere all I could feel was missing Kyle something fierce. Was I making a huge mistake?

Kyle

THE NEXT morning, I called Robbie and asked if he had time for breakfast before he and Sebastian flew back home. He agreed to meet me at Nancy's, which was fine with me. I tossed on some clothes and tried to banish the fact that I had slept in my old bed in my old room and had opened my eyes to the thought that I had to go to Foster High. Then reality hit. I got dressed and took off.

They were sitting down by the time I got there; Sebastian was at the counter while Robbie waited in a booth for me. "Why's he over there?" I asked, sitting down.

"You sounded like you just wanted to talk to me, so he's ordering food."

"Oh, well, not really, but maybe." He gave me a look, and I took a deep breath. "So, Riley's mom came to the hospital to talk to me."

"Of course she did. You know she owns the hospital, right?" I nodded. "So what did she say?"

"She was actually really nice," I said, waiting for him to explode.

"Yes, and a house made of candy might seem kid friendly, but the truth is something completely different," he quipped while stirring his coffee.

"She offered to pay for my mom's hospital bills," I blurted out.

He kept stirring but his gaze locked with mine. "In exchange for?"

"Nothing," I answered quickly. "She just wanted me to go back to school and not worry about my mom."

"You can't take it," he said after a few seconds.

"Why?" I almost whined. "After what I gave to Troy, I don't think I have enough to cover her bills."

"Taking money from her is a bad idea."

"Easy to say when *you* have money," I muttered. "She said she considered me like the grandson you and Riley never had. Maybe she has changed."

"Uh-huh, and maybe she's trying to make a coat out of shaggy-headed teenagers and you're the first."

We were getting nowhere, and I had nothing to add that wouldn't just start a fight.

After a few seconds he asked, "How did she even know who you were?"

I shrugged. "She said a friend told her about what was going on. She was there to tell them to operate on my mom no matter what Billy said."

"And she couldn't do that over the phone?" he asked. I had seen Robbie upset before, but this was a whole new level.

"I don't know," I admitted. "I don't even know if I'm going to bother, anyway."

"Bother what?"

"Bother going back to California, at least not without Brad."

"You have to go back to school," he snapped instantly.

"I don't *have* to do anything except get the man I'm supposed to share my life with back."

"You can't give up your future for one person. I mean, honestly, Kyle, who gave you that idiotic idea?"

I pointed at Sebastian. "He did."

Sebastian looked over at us and smiled. Robbie's eyes narrowed in anger, and all he got was a goofy wave back.

"Did you tell him not to go back to school?" Robbie called out across the diner.

"Um, no," he answered, confused.

"You said I should do what Brad would do," I called back.

"He'd pass up going to college for you?" he asked. I nodded. "Oh, well then, yeah. I guess I did say that."

"Sebastian!" Robbie almost screamed.

He stood and walked over to the table. "No. No siree, Bob. You," he pointed at Robbie, "sent me across the country to get this kid so they can be together. You don't get to come back now and say there is a limit on crazy. If he doesn't want to go back to school"—he looked at me and added—"which is a terrible idea, just saying"—and then back at Robbie—"then he doesn't have to go back to school. You're the one who piled this whole set of events up. You get to just sit there and watch it play out now."

"Oh, I do?" Robbie asked, almost daring Sebastian.

"Yes, you do," Sebastian fired back. "And you can cop whatever attitude you want and threaten to withhold anything you can imagine, but you know I'm right."

They just glared at each other for a few seconds, and then Robbie looked back at me. "He's right. It's a terrible idea."

"I've made more than my share," I said, forcing myself not to sigh. "What's one more on the pile?"

"So do you have any bright ideas how to get Moose back?" Robbie asked me.

I didn't. Then, right at that moment, Jared and Joel walked in holding a stack of yellow papers. They headed over to the counter and started talking to the guy working there.

"No. But one is coming to me." I stood up, said a quick goodbye, and then headed toward Jared and Joel.

Brad

AFTER MY morning run and taking out the trash, I headed over to the high school.

Josh's idea about me coaching had nested in my ear, and I couldn't shake it loose. I should have asked Coach Gunn when I saw him at Nancy's, but I'd spaced out. If he thought I could coach, then maybe there was something to it.

I don't know why I expected the place to look different.

Foster High had always looked like Foster High in my mind; six months wasn't going to change that. It was weird walking around without the pressure of having to go to a class. All the people rushing around me heading in one direction or another kind of made me laugh. I used to be one of them; nothing else but this school and these people mattered. Now it looked like a bunch of little kids playing tag, and I just laughed.

I found Coach Gunn's office and knocked on the door.

He opened it up with a scowl on his face before he saw who it was. "Brad? Thought you were one of the freshmen." He moved aside. "Come in."

I walked into his small office and looked around at all the history on the walls. There was a framed picture of every team he had coached since he arrived at Foster. I saw our picture at the end, the state champion banner over our heads.

"What brings you back to school?" he asked, sitting down.

"I wanted to ask you a serious question, and I need you to be honest."

He sighed and shook his head. "Son, if your question has anything to do with your love life, I swear by all that is holy—"

"No no no no!" I said, interrupting his threat. "It's about baseball." Small pause. "Kinda."

"Questions that are 'kinda' about baseball are fair game," he said, smiling.

WHEN I GROW UP

"Am I good player?" I asked after a taking a deep breath.

He looked at me, confused. "You're a fine player, Brad; why?"

"No, I don't mean for high school. I mean period. Am I a good baseball player?"

He didn't say anything for a little bit. "You're talking professional?"

I nodded.

"You're asking me if I think you're good enough to play professional baseball?"

Another nod.

"And you want me to be completely honest?"

Nod as my stomach turned.

"No, you're not."

I waited for the crashing feeling of failure to come raining down on me, but oddly it didn't.

"You have the hustle for high school level, and I think you would have done okay in college, but at your very best, I don't think you'd even make a farm team. And if you did, you'd spend your life playing there."

Again I waited for the misery to sink in, but instead it was like a weight lifted.

"Son, you okay?" he asked carefully.

I smiled. "I'm great. I'm serious. Why didn't you tell me?"

"Because I could be wrong. I'm not, but I could be. And it isn't my job not to let teenage boys try to follow their dreams. My job is to make them as ready as they can be if they ever get the chance."

"Do you think I have a chance of scoring a scholarship?"

"Now? After half a year not playing? Very doubtful. I mean, on paper you look like the real thing, but playing baseball doesn't have your heart."

I cocked my head. "Why do you say that?"

"Because you gave it up too easily. If you were meant to play it, I mean in your blood, you would have been all over every single college in the country the moment you turned A&M down. Instead you were happy to leave it all behind and go to California, which I thought was what you really wanted."

And here I thought we weren't going to talk about my love life.

"Okay, so I don't have a future playing. What about coaching?"

He gave me a big smile. "I'm out of coffee; come on with me while I get some."

I wanted him to answer the question, but he wanted to do that *I am an adult, so walk with me as I lay some Yoda shit down on you* instead. I forced myself not to sigh and walked with him.

"Do you know what the number one job of a coach is?" he asked me as we walked out across the quad.

"Um, to win games?"

He chuckled. "You'd think so, but nope."

"Um, to teach the guys how to play?"

"Nah, most already know the game. You can go over fundamentals and teach them plays, but honestly, anyone can do that. Don't need to be a coach."

We walked into the main building, and more kids rushed by us, most trying not to make eye contact with the coach since it was past the tardy bell. "I dunno," I admitted.

He held the door to the teacher's lounge open for me. "A coach really only has one job," he said, gesturing for me to go in. I'd never been in there before, and I couldn't help but feel like I was breaking a rule. "You can't make people win; that's on their shoulders. Most of them already know the game, and teaching plays is the job of an assistant coach at best."

He poured himself a cup of coffee and then offered me one. I shook my head.

"So then what does a coach do?"

"A coach has to make the team think they can win."

Say what now?

"Sometimes they *can* win, and then the job is incredibly easy, like you guys last year. You all had more than enough talent and drive to make it. What I needed to do was make sure the talent and drive were pointed in the right direction.

"The worst is when you know the team doesn't have what it takes, but you have to motivate them anyways. Nothing can kill a season quicker than a group of guys thinking they can't win. Doesn't matter if you had Nolan Ryan on the team, if they don't think they can win, they won't."

"So you have to lie to them?"

"Yes and no. Sometimes you're wrong; sometimes you think they don't have it, and out of nowhere they pull it out of their ass and win. Sometimes it's luck, and sometimes it's because they don't know any better. You don't lie to them; you simply get them to believe a different truth. A truth that they can win, and sometimes it comes true."

"You think I can do that?" I asked him, holding my breath.

"I do not," he said with indifferent certainty.

"Why not?" I asked, a little pissed.

"Because if you can't convince yourself you can do it and need to come to me to convince you, what chance do you have of convincing a team?"

"But I…," I started to argue and then stopped. He was right; I didn't have any faith I could do it, which pretty well ensured I could never do it. I wanted to give up and just leave, but there was a small part of me that was too pissed to let it go. I knew I could coach—I did. Ever since the words came out of Josh's mouth, I knew it, and damned if I was going to let even Coach Gunn's opinion stop me.

"I think you're wrong," I finally said. "I think I can do it, and not only that, but I think I can be great at it." He arched an eyebrow at me but said nothing. "I love baseball and I love watching people learn to love it as well. I respect your opinion, Coach, but you're wrong and I know it."

He took a sip of coffee and then smiled. "See? You almost convinced me. I think you'll do fine."

My anger hit a wall in my head. "Wait, you didn't mean that?"

He shook his head. "Nope, but I wanted to see if you were willing to fight for what you want, because that's what coaching is, son. It's fighting against what life has in store for your team and willing that something to be something else. It's fighting against a team of guys who don't think they have a snowball's chance in hell. And it's fighting your own fear that maybe, just maybe, you can't turn them around."

"So you *do* think I could be a coach?"

"I think you can do whatever you want to do, Brad. Your speech in front of the school board showed me that. When you put your mind to something, you get it done, and that is the most anyone could ask for out of a coach."

I sat there basking in the fact that I got a compliment from Coach Gunn. It was kind of overwhelming. That was when I saw the yellow fliers all over the place. They had been in the halls, too, but I was so busy talking with Coach, I spaced them out. "What's all that?" I asked, pointing to one.

"Winter Ball, which is a fancy way of saying the last dance before the end of the year. We used to have them all the time, but Raymond nixed them when he took over. The new principal brought the ball back. Says the students deserve a celebration."

"So what's the first step in becoming a coach?" I asked him, going back to the task at hand.

"You just did it. You decided you can be a coach."

That made me laugh. "Okay, what's next?"

"School," he said without hesitation. "Lots of school."

"Great, just great," I said, sighing.

Kyle

AFTER TALKING with *Me and Brad: the Next Generation*, I went back to the booth with a plan. "When are you due home?" I asked Robbie.

"We're supposed to leave tonight. Why?"

"Because I know how to get Brad back. I just can't do it until Wednesday."

"What's happening Wednesday?" Robbie asked, suspicious.

"I'm getting Brad back," I answered, smiling.

He looked over at Sebastian. "We can leave if you want to, but I think I need to suss out what Cruella De Vil's eviler sister is up to."

Sebastian shrugged. "I'm game if you are. I'm kinda curious how this turns out."

Robbie rolled his eyes. "Welcome to Foster, home of the Dumb and the Useless." He looked at me. "So if I can prove that Dolores is up to no good, will you turn her money down?"

"If you can prove it, yes," I said truthfully.

"Fine. You go set up whatever Ferris Bueller-like scheme you're hatching, and I will find proof."

I impulsively gave him a hug. "Thank you for staying."

He sighed as he hugged me back. "What else do I have to do? Live an actual life that doesn't involve Foster, Texas?"

"I'm staying too," Sebastian said, half pouting.

I moved over and gave him a hug too.

When I let go, I saw Robbie staring at him. "What?" Sebastian whined. "I like hugs."

"I'm going to go," I said, backing away.

"Yeah, that's a good idea," Robbie said, not taking his eyes off Sebastian.

I ran out the door giggling. I knew how to get Brad back.

Brad

I LEFT school and headed home. I needed to do some homework.

As I was walking, a car honked behind me. I turned, expecting to see Josh again, but instead of the Challenger, an old beat-up pickup coasted up next to the sidewalk. I saw Aaron White smiling at me from behind the steering wheel. I hadn't seen him since the school board meeting where he stood up and tried to defend me. From the uniform I'd seen that night, I had guessed he'd joined the Navy, but I hadn't heard anything about him since.

Aaron was a year older than me and insanely hot, a fact driven home when I realized he was wearing only a pair of Wranglers.

"I thought that was you," he called, reaching over to open the passenger-side door. "Need a ride?"

Why walk when you can ride with a hot-ass military guy?

"Sure," I said, getting in.

"Sorry about the mess," he said, grabbing some trash from the floorboards. "I'm on leave, and my dad doesn't keep his truck all that clean."

"It's okay; I'm used to it," I lied. The thought of trash on the floor of my Mustang made me shudder.

"So why're you walking down First Street in the middle of the day?"

"Was heading back to my folks' house, and my car is in California."

"Oh… you move?" he asked as we drove.

"I did, but I'm back now. Just haven't got all my stuff here yet."

"With your boyfriend?" he asked, as casual as all get-out.

"Um, yeah."

"Didn't work out?" he asked, sounding sympathetic.

"You can say that."

"That sucks, man, but these things happen. Takes a while to find the right guy."

I nodded and then paused. "Or girl in your case?" I asked cautiously.

He chuckled. "Nope, I'm gay too, man. In fact, going to that school board meeting was kind of my coming out."

"Really?" I asked with my mouth open.

"Yep, I heard what they were going to do and I just couldn't keep my mouth shut. I knew if I did it, people would talk, so I just said 'fuck it' and came out to my folks."

"How'd they take it?" I asked, blown away. Aaron White had been, like, an überjock around town. Whenever Tyler talked about how it was when he was a kid, I imagined him looking a lot like Aaron.

"How does anyone take it in Foster? Slowly and one day at a time. It was touch and go at first, but it's gotten better. It also helps I'm stationed in Hawaii, so it's not something I have to throw in their faces."

"Hawaii must be cool."

He shrugged. "Not really, but it's okay on the Navy's dime. I'm in for two more years, and then it all pays off."

"How?"

"I get out and they pay for college," he explained. "Reason most guys go in."

"Oh. Then the ads aren't just faking about money for college."

"Nope. Plus I've saved some of my pay. It's all worth it." We turned onto my street, and Aaron asked, "Where you going to school?"

"I'm not," I muttered dejectedly. "'S part of what I am trying to deal with today."

"I would have thought you would have had a baseball scholarship or two offered."

"I had one, but I guess no one else wanted to bet on a gay player yet."

"Man, that blows. Well, if you're looking for an easy way to pay for college, the military is always hiring."

"I couldn't do that," I said as we parked in front of my house.

"Why not?"

"I couldn't handle hiding the fact I was gay from everyone."

He smiled. "Then don't. It's a different world, man. You'd be surprised how many people don't care. The guys on my ship know about me and couldn't give a fuck." I shot him a look and he laughed. "No joke, man. I thought I was going to get killed, but they are super cool about it, and most of the other gay guys I know on the island say the same thing."

"Really?" I asked, amazed.

"Scout's honor," he said, holding up a hand to his heart. "Just saying, man, don't think you're stuck here in Foster forever. There's always a way out."

"I was starting to feel that stuck," I admitted.

"Yeah, this town does that to you. You're a stand-up guy, Graymark. Trust me. You have better things to do than rotting in this town."

I felt a thousand times better.

"Thanks, Aaron. I needed to hear what you just said. Man, did I need to hear it."

"No problem, man. By the way, if I was single, I would so completely hit on you right now, but I'm pretty serious with someone, so just take this as a compliment and nothing more. You look fucking fantastic."

I felt my face redden. "Thanks, man, same to you," I said, staring at his abs.

He slapped his stomach, and I saw the muscle ripple under the skin. "What can I say? It helps to get paid to stay in shape."

"Sounds like you love your new life."

He considered that for a second. "You know what, man? I do. I really do. I was so miserable when I was in school, the second I had my own life, I just took it and ran with it as far as I could. And now—now I have a steady job, I have money in the bank, and I'm seeing a great guy. My college is taken care of, and my car is paid off. I mean, what is there not to like?"

I had to admit, I could definitely see his point.

"Well, thanks again, man," I said. We shook hands, and Aaron chuckled.

"Damn, you really make me wish I was single."

I laughed and got out of the truck. "Thanks, man. Have a good one."

He waved and took off, leaving me a lot more to think about.

KYLE

I MADE a few calls around town before I headed back to the hospital.

The room was as quiet as ever, so I pulled a chair up next to the bed and started to play some soft music on speakerphone. I've heard that people who were unconscious for long periods of time could hear things in the outside world and sometimes it helped them come back.

After I clicked open my eighties playlist, I put together an email for Professor Madison. I explained what had been going on and made my mom's condition sound much worse than I hoped it actually was. I was begging him to give me another couple of days to get back to class. I emailed my other teachers, too, but they were good; I had been so far ahead that they were more than willing to cut me some slack.

Madison had made it clear the first day what I was asking for was impossible, and I doubted he was going to budge off his position, even in the face of things like life-threatening illnesses. He'd turn me down, I'd fail and have to come back to Foster… maybe I just wasn't meant to be at college in Cali. Thinking that brought up another question: did I want to go back? I mean, sure I did, but what if Brad still said no? Was I willing to throw away college and a life outside of Foster just to be with him? I didn't know which answer scared me more. If I was willing to give everything up to be with Brad, didn't that mean I was a crackpot? But if I wasn't, did that make me a cold bitch who wasn't willing to try to be with the person I loved?

I was so tired and wound up, I wanted to scream.

No, scratch that. I wanted to have sex. I wanted to have crazy, wild, monkey sex with Brad and just get all this doubt and stress out of my system. I wanted to sit on the living room floor eating Mrs. Phan's noodles while we argued about what to watch on Netflix. How had I let all that go? What the hell was wrong with me?

I felt the voices in my head rising to a crescendo, and I needed to do something before I actually screamed. So, taking a page from Father Mulligan's book, I decided to see if the guy upstairs was taking requests.

Closing my eyes, I said to myself, "Okay, look, I know this seems shitty, me talking to you only when I need something, but I've tried to do right by you, and I think you know that. I'm not asking for you to change Brad's mind or to magically make me sane. I just need a sign, a small sign that tells me everything is okay. That this is all part of your incredibly complicated but well-meaning plan, and that I have nothing to worry about." I paused. "I don't know if you want me to offer you anything at this point, but I will. I mean, I don't have much, and it would seem petty for someone who can literally do anything to ask for payment, but maybe you want some kind of collateral so I'll continue to be a good guy even if you don't do this for me. So here it is. Just one sign, one tiny sign, and I promise, I'll spend my life doing good. I don't know how, but I will make it my goal. I want to make the world a better place, and I think you want that too. So please… one sign, and I am your guy for life."

The room was silent save the subdued tones of Laura Branigan going on again about her idiotic friend Gloria. I opened one eye and looked up, waiting for something, anything to happen, but nothing did.

"Oh well, it was worth a shot," I mentally said. "Doesn't matter, I'm still your guy either way."

Which was when my mom started to cough.

It was so startling, I almost fell out of my chair. They had removed the ventilation tube yesterday, since she was breathing fine on her own, but it looked like she was trying to gasp air something fierce. I pushed the call button a few dozen times and then screamed for someone to help me. Her eyes opened and she kept coughing even when she reached out to me. I took her hand, terrified, and she gasped what sounded like "water."

I slopped some into a glass from the pitcher that was always beside her bed, steadied her with one arm, and waited while she took a deep gulp. Nurse Redmon came charging in with two other nurses behind her. My mom coughed a couple more times and then finished the glass while they checked her vitals.

After almost a minute of her drinking and them checking, even I could tell she wasn't in any distress. She was just thirsty. Redmon looked at me and smiled. "She's okay. She's just groggy."

They moved aside, and I stepped closer to the bed. My mom looked ten years older than when I left for college, and I felt a swell of emotion flood my throat.

"Do me a favor," she half whispered. I nodded, ready to promise anything. "Turn that off. I've always hated that fucking song."

I began to laugh as tears fell from my eyes. "I hate it too."

Okay, God, you got your guy.

Brad

SO WHEN my parents got home, we had a conversation about my future.

I don't want to get into the details because it was long, messy, and emotional, but in the end I think it was for the better. They tried to talk me out of what I had decided, but I insisted this was my life and I needed to do what I thought was best.

My mom looked like I had said I was going to jump off a bridge.

When I got back to my room, I saw a missed call from a number I didn't know and a voicemail. I checked it, and it was Coach Gunn asking me to call him back. For half a second I wondered what I had done that was so bad he needed to call my phone. Then I remembered I wasn't in high school anymore, and he was just calling me like a normal person.

As the phone rang, I still mentally went back over the last few days, just in case.

"Good. You got my message," he said as way of a hello. "I need a favor this weekend."

"Um, sure," I said, not sure at all.

"A couple of people have backed out of chaperoning the Winter Ball, and I need some warm bodies to make sure no one does anything stupid." Small pause. "Well, stupider than normal."

"You want me to be a chaperone?" I asked, kind of shocked he would think I was up to the task.

"Yeah, I already asked the sheriff's daughter and she said Josh is in town, so they're doing it; I need a couple more. Can I count on you?"

He asked the same way a mob boss would remind you that you were family.

"Sure, no problem."

"Good. Thanks." And he hung up.

"So much for small talk," I mumbled, slipping my phone into my pocket.

Kyle

So THE day of the dance, Robbie held an intervention for me.

I'm sure he thought he was getting a group of my friends together to try to talk some sense into me; nonetheless, I felt like I was a crack addict who had ripped each one of them off. Tyler, Matt, Robbie, and Sebastian were there, along with Jenifer, Josh, Gayle, and the surprise guest of the day.

Dolores.

Gayle had closed Nancy's down, so we were all sitting at a bunch of tables moved together for the occasion. Mrs. Mathison looked like she was going to get common dirt all over her; she sat in her chair trying to make as small a target as possible. I sat down in the only other vacant chair and waited. Everyone knows that a person being prosecuted as a witch doesn't speak first.

Robbie started it off. "So you must be wondering why we asked you here."

"Nope," I answered truthfully.

That made him pause. "You aren't?"

249

"Nope," I repeated. "I'm sure it's some well-meaning attempt to tell me I'm wrong about something, but no, I wasn't really wondering."

He gave me a sour look, and Tyler took over. "Look, Kyle, you know we want you and Brad to get back together, and we all tried to help you out with that, but you can't be seriously thinking about not going back to school if he turns you down."

I pointed at Sebastian. "He told me to ask myself 'what would Brad do?' This is what he'd do."

"Sebastian"—Robbie said the word as if he wanted to use Sebastian's name to beat him over the head—"says a lot of things. You have to learn what to listen to."

"Thanks," Sebastian said, shaking his head. "Yes, I gave you that advice, but I didn't mean to flush your future down the toilet because of it."

"Honey," Gayle said softly. "You have to go back to school, with or without him."

And that was when Mrs. Mathison figured out what we were doing there. "Who is not going back to school?" she asked the room.

"Nice of you to join us," Robbie mumbled under his breath. "Kyle is thinking of not going back to college if Brad turns him down tonight at the dance."

She looked at him and then at me. "You can't stop going to college because of a boy. That's ludicrous." I didn't say a word. "You have to go back to school, that's all there is to it."

I silently counted to ten before I answered everyone at the same time. "Thank you for your concern, but the choice is mine."

Everyone started talking at once. Each one of them was telling me I was being stupid and making a mistake and that this was not the way I should go about it. I mean, I assume that's what they were saying, because they just sounded like a flock of geese to me, all honking at the same time, making noise to make noise.

Tyler stood up and put two fingers just past his lower lip... I plugged my ears because I had seen his trick before.

A sound came out of his mouth that was in no way unlike a pterodactyl trying to yodel. I was pretty sure that he could shatter glass if he put enough force behind that whistle. Everyone stopped talking, a few made faces, and Jennifer and Josh covered their ears.

Once everyone was silent, he commanded, "One at a time or not at all."

Robbie shot him a dirty look and then looked back to me. "This is a mistake."

I looked at Sebastian. "This isn't what I meant by 'what would Brad do.'"

Tyler: "I know what it's like wanting to go to the mat to get the guy, but seriously, Kyle, you can't throw away college on that."

Matt shook his head and indicated that we should move on.

Jennifer: "You can't blackmail someone to get back with you, and that's basically what you're doing. 'Get back with me or I will drop out of college.' You know what Brad will say to that."

That one hurt.

Josh: "Dude, Brad is a great guy, but if it's meant to be, it will be. You can't force things like this."

Gayle: "Honey, you have to trust that life will get you where you need to be."

And finally Dolores: "If you don't go back to school, find another way to pay for your mother's hospital bill."

That got a reaction out of me. "Seriously?"

She gave me a small smile. "Trust me, young man. I don't waste time with frivolous activities. When I say something, I mean it."

I looked back at Robbie, and he seemed sad and pleased at the same time. "I told you."

"You told him what? That I was an evil woman who was trying to taint his soul?"

"I told him that no gift from you comes without strings."

"There are no strings. Our arrangement was that if he went back to school, I'd pay for her hospital bill. If he isn't going, the deal is off."

"That wasn't the intention of me bringing you down there," Gayle said, standing up.

"Your intention was for me to help the young man, and I am." She looked dead-on at me. "Go back to school, earn a degree, and become a better person or stay here, wallow in poverty, and know you're trapped here only because of your own choices."

Robbie took two steps toward her, no doubt ready to read her the riot act. I stopped him. Cold.

"You have no idea how to use the word 'wallow.' You're trying to imply I am going to wallow in the mud like some kind of pig, which, by the way, is how they stay cool, since they have almost no sweat glands. So wallowing like one is a pretty smart way to keep cool and survive when it gets too hot. The second definition is to indulge in an unrestrained way, which is not what I would be doing, because I would be taking care of my mom and trying to win back the heart of the guy I love. Only a woman so far removed from reality that she thinks living in Foster is a bad thing would use the word you did."

She glared silently at me.

"Keep your money. Robbie was right; it comes with too high a price." I turned around and looked at Matt. "Come on, Matt. Everyone else got a chance to swing at the piñata. You don't want to miss out on the fun."

He shook his head again. Tyler nudged him and said, "Go ahead, say your piece."

Everyone looked at Matt and he sighed, defeated. "Okay, do you want me to say what I think?" I shrugged and nodded. "I think you should not stop until you get him back." The geese started honking again, and Matt put his fingers up to his mouth. The geese stopped. "I'm sorry. You guys make sense, but this isn't a matter of sense. This is a matter of the heart. Logic and reason don't always have the weight they do in real life once the heart is involved. Kyle, you want him? You think you can't live without him? Then go and tell him that. Go and don't stop until you can make him believe, and don't listen to anyone in this room. Don't listen to anything, period, except the voice in your heart."

Tyler was giving him an odd look, and Matt smiled at him. "You're talking to the guy who couldn't date anyone else because I saw you mow the lawn shirtless one day. I believe in true love, and I think he should go for it."

Tyler's expression softened, and he looked like he really wanted to kiss Matt. Instead he looked at me. "I changed my mind. Go get him."

"Oh, for fuck's sake," Robbie exclaimed. "Has everyone gone nuts?"

"I'm with them," Sebastian said. "Go get 'im."

"How odd," Dolores said to Robbie with no humor in her voice. "We seem to be in agreement for once."

"Well, now I know I'm wrong," he said, throwing his arms up in frustration. "Fine, you want your moose? Go get him. We'll be there cheering you on."

I looked back at Dolores and said, "Thank you for the offer, but I'm not interested."

She slowly got up and again tried not to touch anything around her. "Happy wallowing," she said and walked out of the diner without a backward glance.

Robbie waited for the door to close before he added, "I'd sing 'Ding Dong! The Witch is Dead,' but it's been done."

We all laughed, but I knew this was the start of the hard part. This was it: do or die time.

I really didn't want to die. I mean, seriously.

Brad

WHEN I walked in, the dance was in full swing.

I checked my watch because I always thought chaperones were supposed to arrive before the kids. From what I could see, I was the last one there. Jennifer and Josh stood talking by the food table, so I made my way over there to see what was up.

"—not manipulating people. We are just trying to...." Jennifer paused when she saw me. "Hey, you."

Wow, she was a bad liar.

"What's going on? Coach Gunn told me to be here by seven. When did the dance start?"

Josh shook his head and handed me a cup of punch. "Here. You're going to need this."

I smelled it and would have been shocked to find any actual fruit punch floating with the alcohol. "Did the kids do this?"

"Nope," Josh said, opening his coat, showing me his flask. "Trust me, drink."

I saw Jennifer shoot him a dirty look and knew tonight was going to be a clusterfuck. I chugged what was in the cup and, when my brain got over the shock, wondered if I could clean fuel injectors with what Josh had in his flask. "So what's really going on?"

"What?" Jennifer asked, looking back at me. "What do you mean? It's a dance—what else would be going on?"

Oh God.

Josh looked like he was going to spill the beans but was interrupted and stayed silent when Robbie and Sebastian walked up. "Now I know why I didn't go to any of these things when I was in high school," Robbie commented dryly. "This is about as exciting as watching paint dry."

"What are you guys still doing here?" I asked, knowing the answer already. "Thought you were heading back to New York."

Sebastian looked away, and Robbie just leveled a gaze at me. "What? I can't stick around and enjoy the Foster nightlife?"

I glared back at Josh. "Okay, what the hell is going on?"

The song finished, and the lights on the stage came up. "Now for something completely different," the DJ announced. A dark-haired kid came out with a guitar in his hand. He sat down on a chair and began to tune the instrument.

Oh freakin' no: whatever was going to happen was worse than I could have imagined. "Josh, what is happening?"

The lights on the stage went dark and a spotlight hit where the kid was sitting next to a lone microphone. I knew he was there a second before he stepped into the light. Kyle looked like he was about to throw up, and he grabbed the microphone stand as if it was a life preserver.

"This is for love," he said and then took a deep breath.

"Oh God," I said under my breath as he waited for the guitar.

"Come on, baby...," he sang, his voice cracking slightly from nerves.

I had always told Kyle he had a decent singing voice when I heard him crooning in the shower, but he never believed me. I never thought it was about him not thinking he could sing; it was about him being terrified of people hearing him sing. He hated attention, especially attention like this, but there he was, singing "You Can Sleep While I Drive" in front of everyone.

He had shared the song on our trip to California as one of, if not the most, romantic songs he had ever heard. I had listened with an open mind, but what was romantic to Kyle was sad as fuck to me. Melissa Etheridge's voice sounded like she was on the verge of crying as she begged this person to go with her.

Which was what Kyle was doing right now.

He told me he had a full tank of gas and his hand shook slightly. Everyone looked up at him, captivated. Not by the singing, though it was good, but by the human drama of the moment. Glancing around, I saw more than a few people looking at me as well, and I knew I'd been right: I'd been set up. Of course, I wish I had figured that out before I came there, but what could I do about it now?

He sang about his bags and guitar, and his voice warbled again, and it was like nails on a chalkboard to me. He was dying of fear up there, and no one else could see it. When he started going on about Santa Fe, I started toward him, not sure what I was going to do but knowing Kyle was in pain and I needed to do something about it.

He sang about the morning and my dreams, and he looked up and saw me. I heard the change in his voice as he fought off tears.

As he went on, his anguish was washing off him like radiation off a bomb. I took another step, and I could see his whole body was trembling slightly.

I jumped onstage, just wanting him to stop, to stop being in pain.

"Please, my intentions are true," he sobbed no longer singing, and then in a tiny voice added, "Won't you come home with me?"

And that was it; he lost it.

He let go of the mic, and I rushed to his side and pulled him into an embrace.

"Please, please don't leave," he said as the mic stand fell over, causing a small explosion of sound and feedback until the DJ cut the feed.

"Please don't leave," he said, looking up at me, already drowning in panic.

"Okay," I said softly. "It's okay, I'm here."

"I don't want... I can't...." And he began to cry again.

I scooped him up. His arms tightened around my neck as I walked off stage. Behind us people began to clap, thinking they had seen some incredible romantic gesture where two souls came together and true love was saved.

They had no idea they had seen the strongest guy I know completely crumble in front of everyone.

I carried him backstage and found a couch to lay him down on. He refused to let go of me, but that was okay. I knelt next to him and waited for him to calm down some.

"I'm sorry," he said after a minute or so. "I didn't mean to lose it like that."

I gave him a smile. "Did you really go up there and try to Ferris Bueller me back?"

"You danced and sang to get me to prom. I thought it would work." He looked down and then back at me. "Did it work?"

I sighed as I struggled to find the right words.

"Please don't dump me," he begged, seeing my hesitation. "Please, just don't break up with me."

"Okay," I replied after a slight pause.

"What?"

"I said okay, I won't break up with you."

He just stared at me. "You're serious?"

"I am. I will not break up with you."

"I love you," he sighed, reaching over and hugging me.

I hugged him back tightly. "I love you too."

We stayed there just holding each other for who knows how long before he looked me in the face. "So we need to get back to California by Friday, I have a test, and if I'm not there I'm in—"

"I'm not going back to California."

He paused, and I could see his brain working the math out in his head. "You want to stay here? Because we can. I don't care anymore, I just want to be with you. I can handle Foster well enough, and I bet I can take classes at...."

I cut him off again. "I'm not staying in Foster either."

He paused again, and I could see he thought I was somehow conning him. "What are you talking about?"

"Now, I'm going to say something and you're going to thir means something else, and before we even go down that road, I'm tellⁱᵃ you this right now. You're wrong. Got it?"

He said nothing back.

"Okay, here we go." I took a deep breath. "You remember Aaron White?" He shook his head. "He was the Navy guy who stood up at the school board meeting?" He nodded. "Well, I ran into him, and we got to talking…."

"You're going out with Aaron White?" he asked, sounding a little pissed.

"What? No. He's seeing someone. He took me to take the ASVAB."

"The what?" Kyle asked. I think it was the first time in his life he didn't instantly understand an acronym.

"It's the test you take to get into the military," I explained. "I joined the Navy. I leave for boot camp in a couple of weeks."

He looked like I had just told him I had cancer.

"Why?" he asked, shocked.

"Because they'll pay for college, and I need a direction in my life—" I started to explain.

"I can pay for college!" he interjected quickly. "We have money from Robbie! I wanted to pay for you before."

"I don't want you to pay for it," I said firmly but gently. "I don't want you, Robbie, my dad, or anyone to pay for it. I want to pay for it myself. I need to know I can do it myself."

He just stared at me for a long time, and then he pointed an accusing finger at me. "So you *are* breaking up with me."

There it was.

"I covered this; you're wrong," I said, trying not to smile.

"But you're leaving! How is that not breaking up with me?"

I sat down next to him on the couch and faced him. "Okay, look. This isn't working, the whole you and me thing. I don't know who I am, and you can't be the guy you want to be. At least, not right now."

"I want to be with you," he insisted.

"No, you want to be the best at whatever you try to be, and that was going to college and doing the best you could, and you wanted that before you met me. When you tried to be that guy around me, you felt guilty because you're weren't paying attention to me, and I got t because I didn't have a life and wanted you to myself. Don't you ?"

He didn't even blink as he stared at me.

"We aren't the people we're going to be yet. You're going to go and be this incredibly successful guy, and I have no idea what I want to be, and right now we just can't do this because all we're doing is holding each other back."

"You're not holding me back," he said, sounding like he was going to start crying again.

"Kyle, we both know I am. But that's not the point. The point is that I have absolute faith in us."

"So much faith you're leaving?" he asked sarcastically.

I had known he wasn't going to take my decision well.

"Okay, look, that whole thing." I nodded to the stage. "The whole singing thing was to prove to me that you were willing to fight to keep us together, right?" He nodded. "Okay, fine, then here's your chance to prove it. I am so sure that you're the guy I'm going to spend my life with that I am willing to walk away for a few years to become a better person for me and for you... for *us*. This isn't me breaking up with you. This is me telling you that I'm so invested that I'm willing to forgo the now to make the future better."

I could tell some part of him agreed with me, but he was still fighting it. "But what if you go out there and find a better guy? What happens if you fall in love with someone else?"

I flashed him a smile and said, "Never happen—already found my guy. What if you find someone else? What then?"

"I won't," he said softly.

"Then have faith in that. I know I do."

"So you just leave and, what? How am I going to know you'll come back? I'm just supposed to wait around forever?"

There was no way to stop myself from laughing. "Okay, fine, you want proof?" I said, digging into my pocket. "I am so sure that I'll be back that I am willing to leave the second most important thing in my life with you for safekeeping."

I handed him the keys to my car. He stared at them openmou[

"Make sure you take her out for a drive now and then and kee,
clean."

"You're giving me your car?" he asked, clearly not believi\
anything that was happening.

"If that's what it takes, sure. I'm leaving my car with you becaus\
you know how I feel about it. I assure you, the way I feel about the
Mustang is nothing compared to how I feel about you."

"I don't want your car," he choked and tried to give my keys back
to me.

"And I want you to understand that I'm telling the truth," I said,
closing his hand over the keys. "You're who I'm going to grow old with;
we just need to grow up first."

"So when would I see you?" he asked, leaning against my chest.

"Every single chance I have," I reassured him, putting my arms
around him. "Every second of every leave is yours. And who knows?
Aaron got stationed in Hawaii. If I got that lucky, maybe you could come
and visit me. The thought of you in board shorts is too hot for words."

He nudged me, but I knew he was smiling.

"This isn't goodbye, Kyle. This is just 'hold on.' Go and become
the amazing man we've all known you have inside of you, and let me go
figure out who the hell I want to be. And then some day you're going to
turn around and I'm going to be just standing there."

He looked up at me. "And?"

I looked down at him and felt the same fire in my heart that I had
the first day he kissed me. "And I'll ask if you want to spend the rest of
your life with me, and that's it."

"Someday?" he asked.

"Have faith," I said, leaning in to kiss him.

"I have faith in you," he whispered.

"And I have faith in us," I said before kissing him.

We kissed for a long time before we could stop. "So what now?"
he asked, and I realized he was looking to me to guide us through this.
Usually it was Kyle with the plan, but now… now this was all me.

"We go out there, talk to the other conspirators, and then you need to
get home because you have a flight to catch or you're going to flunk civics."

He paused and gave me a look. "How do you know that?"

Normally I would say something like, "'Cause I got mad skills" or "now everything," but I could tell he wasn't in the best of moods, so I ed for the truth. "Your friend messaged me on Facebook and went off me. He was under the impression that I was the one keeping you from aving, and that made me a grade-A douche."

He looked embarrassed. "Yeah, Teddy is not a fan of yours."

"He likes you, so I like him."

He just gave me that bewildered look again.

"So we go out there, smile, thank everyone, and then get you home."

"And that's it?" he asked, sounding hurt.

"I said get you home, not drop you off," I said, leaning in. "This is our last night together until the next time. I don't want either of us walking straight for the next week or so."

He smiled back and pressed his forehead against mine. "That sounds good."

The words fell out of my mouth. "I love you."

He looked up at me, and I saw the old sparkle back in his eyes. "I know."

"Oh, now you're Han?" I teased.

"I'm the guy in love with you," he said, putting his hands over my shoulders.

"Hi, guy who is in love with me," I said in almost a whisper. "I'm the guy you're going to spend your life with."

"Pleasure to meet you," Kyle said before he kissed me.

It was a while before we left backstage.

Just saying.

Kyle

SOMETIME THE next morning, I half limped into my mom's hospital room.

Brad had left somewhere around six that morning to change and grab a shower before taking me to the airport. And he didn't look like he was walking any better than I was. Neither one of us wanted the other to leave, but time has a nasty habit of moving on no matter how badly want it to stop. So there I was, making sure my mom was taken ca. before I went back to California.

I wasn't shocked to find Tyler there sitting by her bed making laugh. They tried to sober up when I walked in but failed pretty badl "Oh, hey, honey," my mom said.

"What's so funny?" I asked, pulling up a chair.

"Tyler was telling me about Matt and him trying to get down at the dance last night."

"After you left Matt actually wanted to dance," Tyler explained. "It was horrific."

"I wish I had seen that."

"Trust me, I'm glad you didn't," Tyler admitted.

"So you heading to the airport?" my mom asked.

I nodded. "You sure you're going to be okay?"

She gave me a smile. "I *am* a grown woman. I can take care of myself."

I looked at Tyler and he added, "What she means is that she has grown friends who will take care of her crippled ass while she gets better."

That made me chuckle. "That's more like it. If you need anything, call me; my classes are over week after next for the break, and I can get back here."

"I'm fine," she insisted. "Just go and live your life. Have fun, graduate, hang out with Brad. I'm going to be okay."

I must have made a face because Tyler stared at me.

"You guys left pretty quick last night. Everything okay?"

I nodded, not sure how much I wanted to share. "I'm going to go make sure the hospital has my contact information and then get my stuff packed." I leaned over and kissed my mom. "I'll call you when I land."

"Thank you for coming," she said. "I am so proud of you."

"I haven't done anything yet. Let me graduate first."

"You've done plenty, Kyle, don't kid yourself."

As with every other time I've received a compliment, I felt uncomfortable and wanted to run out the door. "Make sure she gets better," I said to Tyler.

261

He gave me a mock salute and then stuck his tongue out at me.

I rolled my eyes. "God, you guys are so alike."

"That better be a compliment," my mom called after me as I walked

I found Nurse Redmon at the nurse's station, filling out charts. Who do I talk to about billing? I want to make sure it's taken care of before I leave."

She gave me a confused look. "It's already taken care of, Kyle."

Now I gave *her* a confused look. "What?"

She nodded and pulled my mom's chart out. "I thought you knew; her bill was taken care of a couple of days ago." She opened the chart up and showed me the space at the top of the page where insurance information was usually put. No insurance was listed, of course, but someone had stamped Paid In Full in the space. "There's also an order here for PT three days a week that's paid for as well."

"Who did that?" I asked, already knowing the answer.

"All I know is that the hospital is picking it up."

I wondered if this was Mrs. Mathison trying to say sorry. If it was, it was a pretty good way of doing so.

EPILOGUE ONE

Brad

I WALKED Kyle into the airport and felt my resolve slipping.

Was I making a mistake? Signing my life away for four years just to find out who I was. Praying that when I got out Kyle would be waiting for me. What the hell was wrong with me? And then he looked at me and gave me a smile.

And just like that, my fears were dispelled.

"So, last chance," he said as we stood in front of the security gate. "Come with me?"

I wanted to so bad, but I also knew if I did, we wouldn't last. Things would be good for a while, but sooner or later it would become exactly what it had been when we broke up. And I knew if that happened again, there would be no fixing it. This was the only way I could think of to make it better.

Even if it sucked.

"You going to write me in boot camp?" I asked, sidestepping his question.

"Of course."

"Send me naked pictures in boot camp?"

He burst out laughing. "You're crazy."

I reached out and pulled him close. He dropped his suitcase and embraced me. "I am insane about you, I agree."

"Are you sure about this?" he asked, the fear in his voice echoing my own.

"I'm sure about us," I answered truthfully. "That's all that counts."

He nodded and leaned in to kiss me.

As with the first time in my room, I felt my heart skip a beat as I kissed him back.

It was that good a kiss.

"Call me when you get home," I reminded him once we came up ir.

He nodded and then paused. "I am going home, aren't I? I always ,ught Foster would be home."

"Not anymore."

"And where is your home?" he asked me, his voice teasing but his intent deadly serious.

"Right now I don't have one. Hopefully it will be with you when I'm done."

He smiled and nodded at me. "Good answer."

"I love you," I said, almost losing it.

"I love you too," he echoed, picking up his suitcase.

Everything in my head was screaming to not let him go.

Everything in my heart was telling me he wasn't going anywhere, not in the way that counted.

"Bye," he said in a tiny voice.

I grabbed his hand. "No. No goodbyes." He looked at me questioningly. "Until next time."

He gave me a sad smile. "Until next time."

His hand pulled out of mine as he turned to the security gate.

I watched him walk down the concourse. He turned back once and smiled at me.

And then he was gone.

God, I hope I'm right about this.

EPILOGUE TWO

THE DOOR to the cell block opened and Billy looked up, expecting to see one of the deputies who had been bringing him his meals.

Instead he saw an old woman walk in and the door close behind her.

"You lost, lady?" he asked, wondering who the fuck she was.

She gave him a brittle smile and stopped in front of his cell. She gazed at him in silence for a long while. Finally she said, "I love what you've done with the place."

He gave her a chuckle. "Who the hell are you supposed be?"

"I am your best friend," she said in that same pleasant voice.

"Oh, are you? Why is that?"

"Because I am the person who just paid your bail."

Billy felt the blood in his veins turn to ice water. "What?"

"I just paid your bail; you're free to go."

He shook his head. "Bullshit. I have warrants in three states. No way a judge would set a bail."

"Oh, that's one of the many benefits of being close personal friends with so many judges. They will do all kinds of things for you if you ask nicely enough."

"Why would you do that?" he asked, inching toward the bars.

"You are free to go, Mr. Stilleno. You are free to walk out of here and do whatever you want to do. Of course, the people who are after you will have access to you as well, but one must take the good with the bad."

"You've killed me," he realized, his hands gripping the bars tight.

"No." Her voice sharpened, and she skewered him with a gaze that could have cut through corundum. "You killed yourself the second you came into my town and threatened people I care about. This is what is going to happen. You're going to go get out of here and run far away. If you try to talk to Kyle, if you try to talk to Linda, if you stay one second

than you need to in Foster, I will make sure 'those people' find
his is your only chance to run, Mr. Stilleno. I suggest you take it."

"You can't be this heartless," he pleaded with her. "Why are you
ıg this?"

She gave him another smile. "I have been reminded lately that I am
ıt a very nice person. As it turns out, I'm quite all right with that. People
ıke you can't be reasoned with. You put a woman's life in jeopardy to
force your own son to give you money. You are beneath contempt. This
is your reward. Run and never stop."

"Please, have mercy." Billy had honed his wide-eyed suffering look
to perfection, but he realized a heartbeat later his best efforts weren't
going to help in this case.

Dolores rolled her eyes as she turned around and walked toward
the door. "Mercy is for those who deserve it." She paused and looked
back at him. "Trust me, Billy, this is exactly what you deserve."

And with that she walked out.

THE STUFF AT THE END OF THE BOO

SO THAT happened, huh?

There are a lot of people I want to thank in this book for making sure it got where it was supposed to on time and all that. I first want to thank my editor since, without her never-ending attention to detail, I could never get a word written.

What?

Why are you looking at me like that? Mind if I finish?

Also I would like to give a shout-out to Gayle, who once again really helped flesh out....

You seem upset. You sure everything's okay? Hey now, that language is not necessary. I mean, why are you so mad?

The what?

Oh, the ending? Really? That has you so mad you're white-knuckling your Kindle right now and want to throw it at my pumpkin-sized head?

Wow, that was mean even for you.

Okay, fine, but what do you want me to do? The story is over. Yes, it is. Look back and read again; there was a resolution and....

Okay, one, you don't even know my mom, so that was uncalled for.

Wow, you're really mad. I can tell by the way your one eye twitches a little when I talk. So what do you want? Another ending? Oh, come on, the only way that could happen was if we....

SIGH. FINE, will this make you happy?

Epilogue Three:
Time, Your First
Heartbreak, and True Love

Name three things that never end.

Kyle

"DID YOU put the Kansas vs. Staler ruling in here?"

Teddy looked over at me with a withering stare. If I hadn't become immune to it over the last three years, I would have fallen down and collapsed into a ball of screaming pain. I was being anal-retentive, which was okay because that was who I was, and he was trying to deal with it because that was who he was, but from the look, I was pushing it.

"So that's a yes?" I asked as the elevator opened into the lobby.

"You know, one of these days you're going to have a heart attack and just die, but your body will still run around for a couple of weeks finishing errands."

"Well, duh," I said, giving him a smile. "I mean, why let a little thing like death stop me?"

He sighed, which meant he understood I was joking but in no way thought I was funny.

"What do you care?" I asked as we headed toward the lobby. "If I drop dead, then you're a shoo-in for the next job that opens up here."

We were both interning for Adam Kardia, the youngest full partner of the law firm Lupus, Ovis, and Kardia. Teddy and I had both been awarded internships based on four years of academic brilliance and a glowing letter of review from Professor Madison, our freshman civics teacher. If we did well on our LSATs and lived at the top of our classes in law school, then it was a mortal lock that they would hire at least one of us to join the firm. That action alone pretty much ensured a future for one of us.

Of course, I had to get into law school first, but you know me; I like to worry about things in advance.

"Like I want to win like that," he scoffed. "When I beat you and take that job, and I will, it will because I'm the better man and a full Jedi and you were the deluded but well-meaning Padawan who lost."

"You are such a nerd," I said as the elevator opened on the lobby.

"And yet you understood every single word. That sure makes you a nerd too."

269

We walked across the tastefully decorated lobby of the firm. The
as Italian, the sculptures were from Rome, and I was pretty sure the
in the inlays was real. Getting in here, doing this? This would be
ticket to a life I could have never dreamed of growing up in Foster.

"'Sides, if I wanted to cheat to win, I'd pull the minority card on
our ass." I glanced over at him. "Bitch, please; I am a gay black man
who was raised by two adoptive lesbian mothers. I am, like, one bad day
away from my own reality show, and you are still a skinny white boy
from Nowhere, Texas."

I shook my head, knowing he was trying to make me smile.

"If you're so sure you're going to win, why don't you let me drop
those papers off?" he asked with a sly grin.

Adam was heading up north for a party that weekend, and there
were some cases I thought he should go over in his spare time that might
help with the case he was preparing for. It was busy work, but he had
asked me to do it, which meant I got to drop them off and get some
valuable one-on-one time with him.

Something Teddy and I knew was worth its weight in gold.

"I'm sure I'm going to win because I don't fall for cheap-ass Jedi
mind tricks like that one."

We both laughed as we headed toward the front desk to check
messages before we left. It was one of Adam's immutable rules: check in
and out with the front desk to see if there were any instructions waiting
for us. Of course, he could have just texted us, but I think he liked the
routine because it was a pointless rule and he wanted to see how strictly
we would follow it.

We followed it like it was handed down from on high.

"So you want to come out with us after you drop that off?" he asked.

"Nah, I think I'm going to stay in."

"Big shock," he said under his breath.

"What? I'm fine."

"Fine and you have never met," Teddy said, pausing to check
messages. "I bet you don't even know what fine looks like. You may
have written a book report on fine and even went to fine's Wikipedia
page, but you and fine have never even sexted, much less got it on."

"Um, I'm okay, then?"

He gave me another withering glare, and I had to laugh.

"What? I'm focused. You can't say you're any different."

"I can say I'm different," he said, giving the secretary a small as we walked away. "I'm in a relationship and go out and socialize all time, while you are worse than a monk most of the time."

"Oh please," I said, pushing the door open. "Just because Colt like you for the one black stereotype you do possess does not mean you're any less focused than me."

"All work and no play makes Kyle an asshole," he said, squinting as the afternoon sun blinded us walking out. "Fuck," he exclaimed, digging in his satchel for a pair of sunglasses. "I swear, I always forget walking out of that building is like walking out of a darkroom."

"I am fine," I said, continuing the conversation. "It's just this job is the most important thing in my world right now."

"And that is my point," he said, head still stuck in his bag. "It's just a job. There's more in the world, you know?"

"Not to me," I said under my breath.

While he kept looking for his sunglasses, he asked, "This is because you have a gigantic stick up your ass, and not because you still hate my boyfriend?"

"Wow, so many things wrong with that statement," I said, sighing. "One, I do not have anything stuck up my ass, which I believe you think is the problem; two, just because I don't want to go out to a club, it doesn't mean there is something wrong with me; and three, your boyfriend is a major douche."

"That was then. He's changed."

"'He's changed,'" I muttered under my breath. "Words said by every single shallow gay guy who doesn't want to believe his stripper boyfriend is a douche."

Teddy said nothing back to that.

I waited, knowing his bag and the TARDIS had more in common than being from the UK, so this could take a while. I looked around, part of my mind noticing how beautiful a day it was in San Francisco and the other part wondering how much time we were wasting. I was so preoccupied that I missed him at first. My eyes moved right over him leaning up against a light post, just waiting.

I glanced back at him and stared for a long time.

If I was in a cartoon, I would have rubbed my eyes to make sure I 't imagining him, but I knew better. His hair was still short, and he e a dark brown leather jacket that looked like he had robbed Indiana .es for it. The gray shirt under had the word Navy stretched over a air of pecs that looked like they were drawn for a comic book hero. He as fully dressed, but the clothes did nothing to hide the incredible body underneath.

All that was logged instantly, but what stuck with me was his smile. That same smile he'd had when he was eighteen, leaning against the locker next to mine, waiting for me to notice him. He didn't say a word. He didn't budge. He just stood there, staring at me, waiting.

"Make sure Adam gets this," I said, pushing the briefcase into Teddy's hands. He fumbled with his bag and the briefcase and both fell to the ground as he cursed.

"Kyle, what the hell?" he asked, looking over to where I'd been.

But I was no longer there.

"Hi," he said as I got closer.

"Hey," I said, still moving toward him.

"Wanna spend the rest of our lives together?" he asked, the twinkle in his eyes telling me it was taking all his concentration not to just explode with happiness.

"Thought you'd never ask," I said, putting my arms around him and kissing him hard.

He kissed me back, and for the first time in a long time… the world stopped moving for a second.

And I was okay with that.

Never the end.

THE STUFF AT THE
REAL END OF THE BOOK

BETTER? I had you convinced it was over, and you know it.

This was a challenging book to write because what it started as and what it finished as were two different things. I set out wanting to tell a story about that time when you're first out on your own. You know, the apartment that had milk crates for shelves and you ate a lot of ramen for meals? Yeah, that one. The one place that, if you had to live there now, you'd most likely throw up but at the time was just perfect.

It's also that time in life when you realize that the person you were in high school has very little to do with the person you're going to become one day. I wanted to write a story about those moments just before you break out of that cocoon youth wraps around you and you take flight on your own. I thought it would be a cool time to look in on our guys.

Which was the moment I realized there was something wrong.

You see, this is one of the problems I have with romances that are made for entertainment reasons: they don't really capture the complications of real life. It was a conversation real-life Robbie and I had about Disney characters once. You can watch those movies as a kid and think it's incredible, but in real life those princesses are messed in the head. I mean, some guy comes and kisses your seemingly dead body in the middle of the woods and you think that's cool? Really? My first question would be, "Dude, why were you kissing a corpse anyway?"

There's something comforting about reading these fictional relationships, but they ingrain this impractical belief that that is how things should be, and they aren't. Music isn't going to play the first time you see that guy, and the lighting won't get all soft and focus in his eyes as you make your way across the room. That's not how you meet people in real life, and even if you love someone wholly and completely, it doesn't ensure that things will work out.

273

Of course, that doesn't mean give up; it just means be ready for hard work.

Brad and Kyle, if they kept on their prospective tracks, would have er worked out because Brad would have always been the last part of yle and," and Kyle would have never stopped doubting if they were pposed to be together. They needed to grow up if I was going to write hore of them, and I do want to write more of them.

So you get this book.

First loves are incredible things, and you will never forget your first. Never. No matter how many people you may be with, how many you fall in love with, that first is always the one your mind comes back to. That doesn't mean it was your best love; it just means it was your first. I wanted to give Kyle and Brad both. I wanted to give them their first love and make it their best, because it does happen in real life, and those two boys deserve each other.

I don't know what is next for them. I really don't. As I write this, I have no earthly idea what comes next. I just know one thing.

They will do it together, and in the end, isn't that the happiest ending you could ask for?

Drinking a coke while I use Tyler's laptop
Foster, Texas
2014

Keep reading for an excerpt from
A Way Back to Then
Tales from Foster High: Book Six
by Robert Halliwell

PREFACE

I ADJUSTED the rearview mirror and saw the reflection of a blond-haired boy wearing a graduation gown grow smaller as I drove out of the high school parking lot. When I knew I was a safe distance away, I pulled the car to the side of the deserted road and cried for what seemed like hours. Fortunately, most of the town was at Foster High, so there was very little chance that someone would spot a middle-aged gay man bawling his eyes out in a lime-green VW Bug.

I opened the glove compartment for some Kleenex and a stack of napkins from the Bear's Den fell out. I watched them fall to the car floor. Each represented a memory I had of that place. Good, bad, and horrific. I met some of my best friends at that little hole in the middle of nothing. It was where I was the real me without any judgment.

It was the place where my worst nightmare became a reality.

I stuffed some of the napkins back into the glove compartment, not wanting to lose the memories or even the smell of the Bear's Den. I wiped my face and nose, thinking not about that night which happened a lifetime ago. Instead I thought about the mini-bon-voyage party that my friends Tom, Tyler, and Tyler's boyfriend, Matt, were throwing for me only a couple of hours ago.

"To Robbie," Tom said as we all raised our glasses, "one of the biggest bitches and best friends a man could ever want."

I was about to protest the bitch part, but the tearful wink Tom gave me told me he was joking and serious at the same time.

We each took a sip of what passes for champagne in this godforsaken part of town. Tyler downed his glass in one gulp.

"Slow down there, babe," Matt said to his boyfriend. "I don't want to have to carry you out of here tonight."

Tyler smiled gently and looked at me before quickly turning back to Matt.

"So—" Tom cleared his throat. "What time are you leaving s[ ]
munchkin parade can start?"

I flipped him off and his belly shook with laughter.

"The moving company is coming to pick up my car l[ ]
tomorrow afternoon to be shipped up to New York, and my flig[ ]
is the following morning." I turned to a rather uncomfortable an[ ]
slightly intoxicated Tyler. "I'm going to have to cut out before th[ ]
end of graduation."

Tyler looked like I just kicked him right square in the balls and then
ran over his dog.

"You can't do that to the kids!" He shouted as he tried to get up but
slumped back down immediately with Matt's help.

"They'll live, Tyler," I said calmly. "They're young and will get
over it quickly."

"But…," Tyler said as the tears started to flow. "But what about the
kids?"

Matt looked at his boyfriend like he was a five-year-old complaining
about the socks he got for Christmas, while Tom wiped his own wet face
with a dirty bar towel.

We all knew this wasn't about the kids; this was about Tyler and
me.

I took a deep breath and walked over to Tyler. I wrapped my arms
around him. I saw Matt tense up out of the corner of my eye as Tyler
buried his head into my shoulder and cried. I didn't say anything. I held
him tight, rubbing his back until he calmed down and stopped using my
shirt as a snot rag. I tried not to look at the pair of eyes that were staring
at me from the bulletin board in front of me.

I failed.

Tyler raised his head a little and rested his chin on my shoulder.
"You promise you're going to call me? Or TimeFace me when you're
up there?"

I laughed and pulled away from Tyler, making sure I gave Matt an
"At ease, soldier" glance. "Yes, Tyler, I will call or FaceTime you when I'm
back and settled. And you can do the same when you get sick of constantly
talking to your fellow moose over here." I smirked at Matt, and he laughed
nervously. It was still a mystery whether we liked each other or not.

Tyler smiled. At my little jest or because he was head over ass in vith said moose, I would never know.

"All right. Enough of this fairy shit," Tom bellowed. "Another ad, and no more goddamn crying."

Thank God Tom wasn't here to see me now.

I picked up the rest of the napkins, shoved them back into the glove compartment, and shut the door.

I looked at the time and saw that the car movers would be at my house within the hour. I pulled myself together as best as I could and drove to my old store. I parked in my usual spot for the last time and got out. I unlocked the door to my second home for the past decade and slowly opened it.

The place was dark and empty except for a few racks and hangers scattered on the floor. I closed my eyes and took a deep breath. Memories filled my head of Foster townspeople coming in here, not knowing what the hell just sprang up in the middle of their beige lives, with a colorful homo standing behind the store counter giving them all a welcoming but evil look.

The act I put on became a lifestyle. I packed my old, real self into a small cage inside my bitter and angry heart. And it wasn't until a floppy-haired, terrified teenager with worn-out clothes came through that very same door that the bars of my cage started to melt.

After that, everything in my life had been a butterfly effect—right up until to now.

I opened my eyes and knew I had one last thing to do before I closed this part of my life for good.

I found an old sign, flipped it over to the blank white side, and placed it on the counter. I went to the storeroom and found a red Magic Marker and brought it back to my makeshift canvas.

I carefully wrote the words out in big, bold print and colored in the letters. Satisfied, I gave my creation a nod of approval and hung it in the window. I wasn't sure how long it was going to be up there, but I hoped the people it was meant for would see it before someone took it down. I took one last look around and before I started to lose it again, I walked out of the empty shell of a store and locked the door behind me.

I started my car and looked at the sign I had hung in the win
"Make your own happy ending," I read out loud.
I smiled proudly.
"You're damn right I will."

JOHN GOODE is fifty years old and was found in his floating crib by a strange man… wait, no that's Baby Yoda. I am a cat that gets constantly screamed at by a blond woman while I'm trying to eat… wait, no, not me. I am inevitable, nope. I am Iron Man? More no. I'm not bad, I'm just drawn that way? I can't pull that dress off. Okay, I am and shall always be your friend. Sigh, I think I stole that from somewhere. Let me try again. WHEN I WAS A YOUNG WARTHOG! Too much? I agree. Okay, how about a little Fosse, Fosse, Fossee, a little Martha Graham, Martha Graham, Twyla, Twyla, Twyla and then some Michael Kidd, Michael… I lost you, huh? Well whoever he is, I can assure you he isn't a black cat that wears glasses. Okay, how about this?

He is this guy who lives in this place and writes stuff he hopes you read.

Twitter: @fosterhigh

Facebook: www.facebook.com/TalesFromFosterHigh

Follow me on BookBub

By JOHN GOODE

Last Dance with Mary Jane

TALES FROM FOSTER HIGH
Tales From Foster High
End of the Innocence
151 Days
Taking Chances
When I Grow Up
What About Everything

Published by Harmony Ink Press

Jordan vs. All the Boys

FADEAWAY
Going the Distance

LORDS OF ARCADIA
Distant Rumblings
Eye of the Storm
With J.G. Morgan: The Unseen Tempest
With J.G. Morgan: Stormfront

Published by DREAMSPINNER PRESS
www.dreamspinnerpress.com

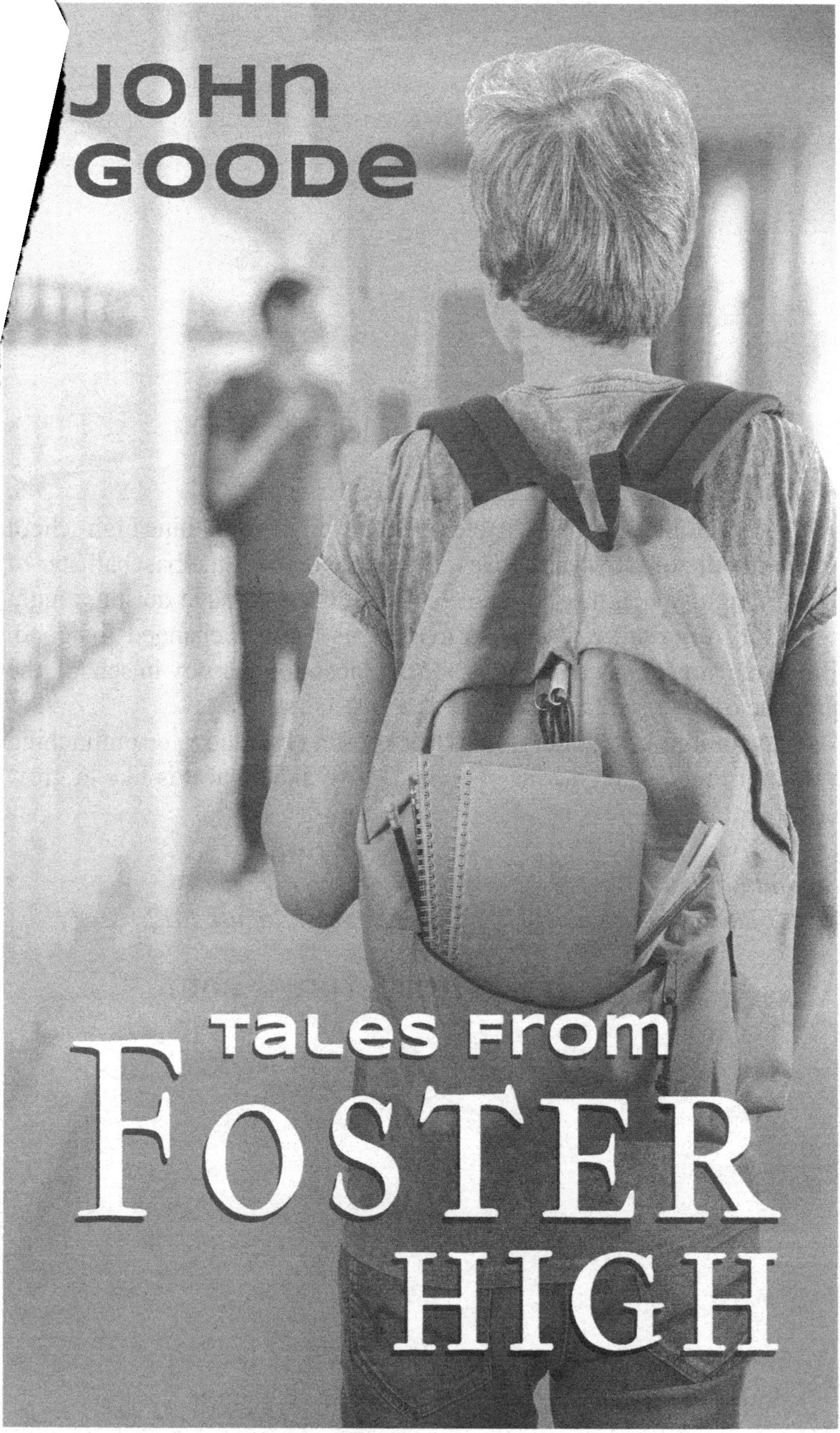
JOHN
GOODE
TALES FROM
FOSTER
HIGH

Tales from Foster High: Book One

Kyle Stilleno is the invisible student even in his nothing high school in the middle of Nowhere, Texas. Brad Graymark is the baseball star of Foster High. When they bond over their mutual damage during a night of history tutoring, Kyle thinks maybe his life has changed for good. But when you're gay and falling for the most popular boy in school, the promise of love is a fairy tale, not a reality. Isn't it?

A coming-of-age story, Tales from Foster High shows an unflinching vision of the ups and downs of teenage love and what it is like to grow up gay.

Second Edition
First Edition published by Harmony Ink Press, August 2012.

www.dreamspinnerpress.com

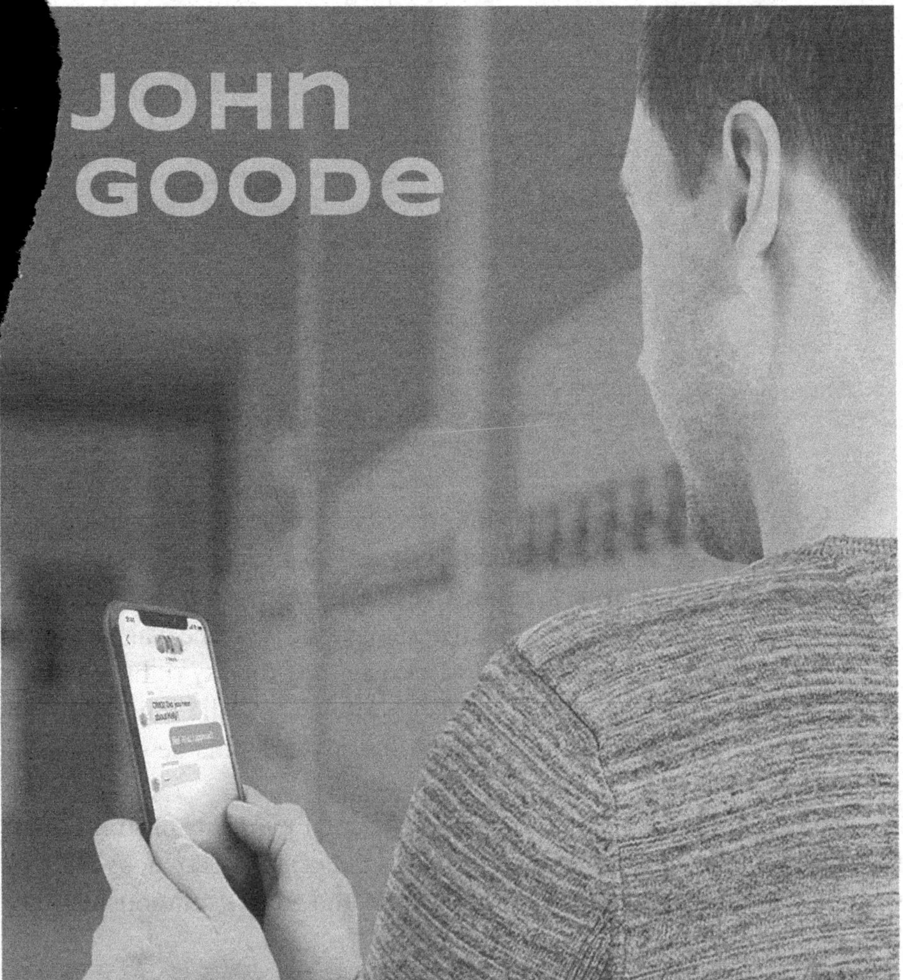
JOHN
GOODE
END OF THE
INNOCENCE

Tales from Foster High: Book Two

Kyle Stilleno is no longer the invisible boy, and he doesn't know how he feels about it. On one hand, he now has a great boyfriend, Brad Graymark, a handful of new friends, and even a new job. On the other hand, no one screamed obscenities at him in public when he was invisible.

No one expected him to become a poster boy for gay rights either—at least not until he stepped out of the closet and into the limelight. But with only a few months of high school left, Kyle doubts he can make a difference.

With Christmas break drawing closer and their trials far from over, Kyle and Brad have each other to lean on. Others are not so lucky. One of their classmates needs their help—but Kyle and Brad's relationship may be too new to survive the strain.

Second Edition
First Edition published by Harmony Ink Press, November 2012.

www.dreamspinnerpress.com

JOHN GOODE

151
DAYS

Tales from Foster High: Book Three

With just 151 days left until the school year ends, Kyle Stilleno is running out of time to fulfill the promise he made and change Foster, Texas, for the better. But he and his boyfriend, Brad Graymark, have more than just intolerance to deal with. Life, college, love, and sex have a way of distracting them, and they're realizing Foster is a bigger place than they thought. When someone from their past returns at the worst possible moment, graduation becomes the least of their worries.

Second Edition
Previously published by Harmony Ink Press, March 2014.

www.dreamspinnerpress.com

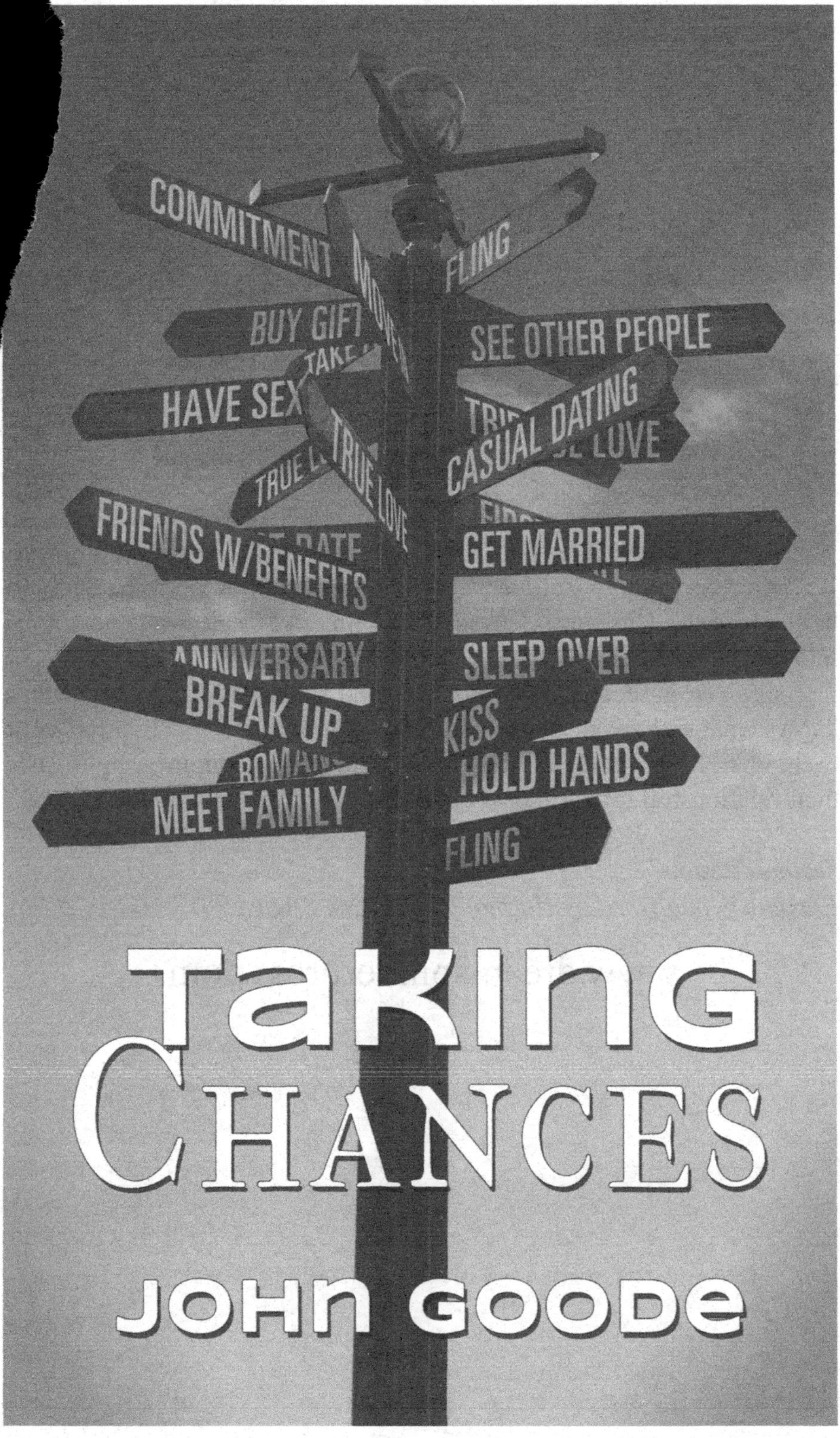
COMMITMENT
FLING
BUY GIFT
SEE OTHER PEOPLE
HAVE SEX
CASUAL DATING
TRUE LOVE
FRIENDS W/BENEFITS
GET MARRIED
ANNIVERSARY
SLEEP OVER
BREAK UP
KISS
HOLD HANDS
MEET FAMILY
FLING
TAKING
CHANCES
JOHN GOODE

Tales from Foster High: Book Five

Fearing the backlash of living as a gay man in Foster, Texas, Matt
Wallace runs away to California, only to find it isn't the Promised Land
he'd hoped for. Christmas sees him returning to Foster, where he bumps
into his old high school crush, jock Tyler Parker.

It's love at second sight—for Matt and Tyler. The problem is neither
knows what to do next. Between running from the past and running from
each other, Matt and Tyler need to do some reverse engineering to spur
their relationship forward, or they'll never get their love off the ground.

Second Edition
Previously published by Harmony Ink Press, August 2013.

www.dreamspinnerpress.com

WHAT ABOUT ABOUT EVERYTHING?

a tales from foster high story

Sequel to *Taking Chances*
Tales from Foster High: Book Eight

No matter how fast you run, the past has a way of catching up with you.

When an accident ruins Matt's parents' anniversary party, Tyler and Matt decide a vacation is in order, and they book a gay Disney cruise with Robbie and Sebastian. It'll be the perfect place to relax and do some much-needed soul-searching. A couple of years have passed since they met, but Tyler and Matt are no closer to getting married. They must take a long, hard look at their relationship and decide if they're happy with the way things are, or if they want more—and if they can find the courage to take the next step. A difficult choice is made even harder when two people they thought they'd left behind show up to complicate the issue and turn the whole cruise upside down.

www.dreamspinnerpress.com